Dead Men's Clubs

A Story of Golf, Death, and Redemption

Charlie Ryan

Dead Men's Clubs
A Story of Golf, Death, and Redemption

Copyright © 2012 by Charlie Ryan.

All rights reserved. No part of this book may be used or reproduced by any means, graphic, electronic, or mechanical, including photocopying, recording, taping or by any information storage retrieval system without the written permission of the publisher except in the case of brief quotations embodied in critical articles and reviews.

ISBN: 978-1-4582-0568-1 (e)
ISBN: 978-1-4582-0569-8 (sc)

Library of Congress Control Number: 2012915080

Abbott Press books may be ordered through booksellers or by contacting:

Abbott Press
1663 Liberty Drive
Bloomington, IN 47403
www.abbottpress.com
Phone: 1-866-697-5310

This book is a work of fiction. People, places, events, and situations are the product of the author's imagination. Any resemblance to actual persons, living or dead, or historical events, is purely coincidental.

Because of the dynamic nature of the Internet, any web addresses or links contained in this book may have changed since publication and may no longer be valid. The views expressed in this work are solely those of the author and do not necessarily reflect the views of the publisher, and the publisher hereby disclaims any responsibility for them.

Any people depicted in stock imagery provided by Thinkstock are models, and such images are being used for illustrative purposes only.

Certain stock imagery © Thinkstock.

Printed in the United States of America

Abbott Press rev. date: 10/31/12

This work of fiction is dedicated to all the frustrated golfers who, despite decades of intense effort, suffer with Bad Game to the point of desperation bordering on tears. They are the golfers who wander the fairways, wondering why they play the game; perhaps seeking Divine Intervention, hoping some unknown force will show them the way.

Fore!

Two deceased but very excited golfers looked down on Earth in great anticipation. So many golf courses, so many golfers. The two had assessed thousands of high handicappers over a two-year period. Their intent, their need, was to locate a seriously inept golfer down there. They needed him for the experiment. They had to find him if they were ever again to play the game.

When all the research was completed, there was agreement that a 70-year-old duffer in South Carolina by the name of Munch Malone was their man. Yes, indeed, watching Munch play convinced them he would suit their needs very nicely. They settled back in easy chairs at the Clubhouse, drinks in hand, preparing to watch the action on Terra Firma, through High Definition TV.

One

Munch Malone was pissed off. It was all beginning again. His belief that this would be the day his golf game would finally come together was shot down in flames as he teed off, topping the ball, watching it dribble fifty feet, barely past the ladies' tee.

Munch seethed with anger, resisting the urge to slam the ground with his club or throw the damn thing as far as he could. He knew his golf buddies were watching, waiting for the blowup. Munch's temper and his lousy game were well known.

Barely controlling his emotions, Munch walked back to his golf cart and plunged the driver into the bag. He pulled out his three wood and suddenly felt an intense heat radiating from the club into his right hand, soaring through his arm, knifing into his shoulder. He saw flashes of white and shadowy images danced before him, cavorting across the wide expanse of fairway that flooded his eyes.

Then, Munch felt a pleasant jolt move through his body; immense confidence consumed him as he waggled the three wood. He shook his head to clear his thoughts, stood tall, and walked to his ball. He went through his pre-shot routine and looked down.

The ball was looking back at him, just setting there, daring to be hit. Munch wasted no time; he brought the club back and swung with force, hitting the shit out of that dimpled smile. It was beautiful, about 250 yards. Not bad for a three wood.

Munch grinned broadly as congratulatory shouts came his way. He eased the three wood back into the bag, patted it lightly and clambered into his golf cart, giving a thumbs up to his golfing buddies. This was more like it; maybe it *was* his day, after all.

That hope quickly vanished, however, as Munch hit his third shot, resulting in a banana ball that sliced into the woods, out of bounds. Frustrated, he grimly proceeded toward the green, one bad shot at a time. What had started with excellence ended in agony, with Munch carding a Snowman on number One at Heron Point on Hilton Head Island, South Carolina.

The scenario repeated itself hole after hole and Munch knew he was on his way to another rotten score. At number Eleven he was totally dejected, looking down a fairway that seemed to stretch miles before him. Munch grabbed his driver and prepared for the worst. His golf group stood by intrigued, wondering what would happen this time.

"Steady, slow, keep your head still, straight left arm, take it back low, remember to shift your weight," Munch murmured to himself. The hole was a par five that stretched for 550 yards from the tips. It was beautiful, and the amazing Pete Dye had designed a challenging dogleg left, punctuated with enough sand traps to create a small Sahara around the green.

Munch anticipated the dreaded "outside-in" that always sent his ball skidding to the right and out of bounds. "What the hell," he thought, "balls out." His body stiffened as he began his back swing. He knew he should grip the club lightly, like a feather. Instead, his fist tightened around the driver. The blood vessel in the middle of his forehead bulged, looking as though it might burst at any minute.

"Cock your wrists, pussy to the ball," were additional swing thoughts, along with the realization he could only get the club up to his shoulder, just past a protruding mid-section. "How the hell do they do it?" he thought, reflecting on low handicappers who lazily and effortlessly brought the driver around behind the head, left arm straight, wrists snapping in perfect time, hitting the ball a blazing 300 yards.

Munch's mind wrapped around all the mechanics he needed to perform, clogging his swing with a thousand different thoughts. His downswing was rigid. The head of the club flayed back and forth, connecting with that dull thud Munch hated. The ball veered to the right instead of left and eagerly sought a nearby pond, exiting the fairway just in front of the ladies' tees.

"Son-of-a-bitch! I can't believe it!" he shouted, slamming his club into the ground once, twice, three times.

"Pull out your pecker," Eugene Columbus yelled; the traditional jibe when a golfer fails to hit beyond the red tees. He tugged the zipper to his trousers up and down and pushed his hips back and forth in a humping motion, trying to help Munch through another trauma.

"Asshole," Munch muttered, shrugging his shoulders, managing a thin smile.

Eugene was a golfing enigma to Munch. He was a natural who could play once a year and shoot in the 70's. Munch, who struggled to get to 105 in a round, knew he would never be in any way comparable to the guys in his golf group. But, they and their wives were friends of many years. Hence, Munch was included in the low handicap foursome. Eugene was a 2, Dave Rambo a 5, and John Henry, a 9. Munch's handicap was pathetic, earned by a woeful experience of 30 years of golf.

Munch was 70-years-old and generally pleased with life. People tended to immediately like him; he was social in nature, short, and rotund. He was non-threatening with a ruddy complexion. He had hair on the side and back of his head, but was bald as a cue ball on top. Before retirement he had been a hard working entrepreneur who found success at most anything he really put his mind to.

Munch believed he had succeeded in life because he played fair, worked hard and applied "Critical Mass", i.e., the practice of doing something ten thousand times until perfection is achieved. He was fond of quoting Green Bay quarterback Aaron Rodgers on the subject: "Everyone on the field is talented, but the ones that stick are the ones that put in the time."

One thing did not work that way. One thing produced less when given more. One thing did not respond to his sheer will and determination. That was why that *one thing*—golf—caused Munch Malone to be a mad, mad man. Munch desperately wanted to have Game. He would kill to break 100. He had believed, as he pounded out the hours, that Critical Mass would again give him success. But it was not to be; golf sneered at Critical Mass.

Munch watched his ball skip three times over the pond's surface, threatening a slumbering alligator, and sending Munch into apoplexy. He raised his driver and ran toward the golf cart. Wielding the club like a machete, he swung a wide arc and smashed it into his golf bag. It felt good. Munch wound up again and struck another blow that helped flush out the anger. It felt so damn good!

Eugene shook his head. "Munch," he said to his golf buddies, "is in fine style." The three had seen it all many times before. They loved Munch, but he was a disaster on the course. They had seen him punch his bag; as he continued to do as they watched; throw his clubs; pound the ground; swear after every shot; and become a defeated man at the end of eighteen holes of golf.

Munch's breathing was rapid and his face was drained of all color except red. However, his bag, he noticed upon inspection for any damage, had taken it well. That's why he loved his bag. It was a "Rodney Bag", named for Rodney Dangerfield in the movie

"Caddyshack". Munch was quite aware all the other guys used a grasshopper bag; they were light and functional. The Rodney Bag was heavy, bulky, and took up a lot of cargo space. But, by God, that bag could take a hit. Munch knew he would never give it up.

"Out of bounds," Dave Rambo said, watching Munch inspect the Rodney.

"Dammit, I know it's out of bounds," Munch said, plunging the driver into his bag, retrieving the three wood he had used to success on the previous hole. He walked to the tee box with a determined look, felt a tingle in his arm, teed the ball, took no practice swing, and hit the ball nicely down the middle, 225 yards.

"Beautiful." Dave said, clapping his hands and grinning.

"That felt good, really good, this baby works every time," Munch said, returning his Wild-O three wood to the Rodney bag, smiling broadly.

Eugene teed up. "Poetry in motion," Munch thought, "poetry in motion." Eugene's ball took flight from the tee like an F-14 "Tomcat". It soared skyward, seemed to look out over the course, spotted the dogleg left and veered toward the hole. Eugene's automatic pilot was functioning well.

"Great shot, Eugene!" Dave shouted. "Love it when you cut the corner. Golf shot."

Munch joined in the chorus of congratulatory murmurs, but Eugene's effortless shot caused doubt to immediately replace the surge of confidence he had felt when he grabbed the three wood. He fought back his golf demons as he lamented the fact that while he always hit his three wood well, there was no consistency with other clubs, save his seven iron. He tried to relax and rationalized to himself as he walked toward his ball for his second shot. "I know I have Game; I just hit an incredible shot. But I can't put together two good shots in a row. It can't be all me, *it has to be the clubs*. If I can find the right clubs, I can play this game."

Each year Munch fought his temptation to purchase a new driver when the major manufacturers marketed their latest clubs. The result was always the same; temptation was not to be denied—surely the new club would change his game, and his American Express card took a hit. The result was always the same; the damn driver proved to be no good. The way to remedy that, he reasoned, was to wait twelve months, fight temptation once again, submit to it, and acquire yet another weapon. They loved Munch down at Golf World.

New clubs every year made for quite a sight in the Malone garage as they accumulated and seemed to multiply. They gathered dust, arranged neatly in a row in fifteen golf bags that had been bought over twenty years. The golf club addiction was non-stop, but the bag purchases came to an abrupt end when Munch bought the Rodney five years ago. He took comfort in knowing that at least he had found the right bag.

His thoughts drifted to ads he had seen for the latest Stallard clubs. He lusted for them when he first saw them, convinced they would change his luck; but his Stebbins clubs were just under a year old and he began to once again fight the temptation to which he knew he would eventually succumb. He had been convinced when he bought the Stebbins that *they* would dramatically change his game. They had not.

"Damn clubs are worthless," Munch blurted.

"What?" Eugene said, "What did you say?"

"Aw, shit, my clubs are about as effective as Mark Sanford's security detail," Munch groused as the golf cart rolled down the fairway. "My next shot will probably end up out there somewhere on the Appalachian Trail." Eugene grinned broadly, taking a swig from a lukewarm can of Yeungling. Munch could always make Eugene laugh.

"I'm thinking about new clubs, Bro," Munch said, hopping from the cart, addressing the ball, doubting himself, beginning his backswing. He failed to square the clubface and the ball sliced badly, flying out of bounds thirty yards away. "Shit! Why do I play this freaking game?" Munch shouted, pounding the ground with his five iron, winding up, whipping the club down the fairway.

Eugene shook his head as he followed the airborne club and admonished Munch, "Sorry, but you complain about your clubs, your brand new clubs, every damn year. You paid, what, $400 for that Stebbins driver in your bag? The pros are all using that club. It seems to work pretty well for them, Munch. And then, you pulled that old three wood out of your bag and hit it like a pro. Have you ever, ever, thought it's not the clubs, it's you?"

Munch always rejected any suggestion that his game was not partially a result of inferior clubs. He had a deep inner need to do so. To admit it was all his fault would have caused him to throw his clubs in the pond and walk off the course, never to return. He loved the game too much to do that. He believed that the clubs were somehow not right. That conviction allowed him to hang on, hoping for a better game.

Munch re-teed the ball and used his three wood, hitting a perfect shot. He then selected a hybrid to get him to the green. The shot, his third, was bad, and Munch was in a sand trap ten yards out. He returned to the cart and slammed the Rodney with the club, cursing, his blood pressure mounting.

Eugene, trying to ignore the temper tantrum, drove the cart into the middle of the fairway, extracted an eight iron from his bag, and prepared for his second shot. He exhibited little effort, placing the ball on the green, ten feet from the hole. Chance for a birdie. Munch shook his head and felt like crying. Eugene was down in three while Munch added up eight shots, struggling from the sand to the hole. Dave Rambo carded a par and John Henry bogeyed.

Munch, who never used the "F" word, made an exception for golf. "Another fucking eight," he groused, throwing his club in the Rodney, plopping into the cart, slamming his foot on the dashboard, causing Eugene's Yuengling in the cart's cup holder to splash onto Eugene's trousers, eliciting a baleful stare from Munch's golf buddy.

The day wore on and Munch became a bore to be with. He looked forward to a beer in the clubhouse as the foursome approached the Twelfth hole. It was a par four on Heron Point with water to the left, framed by a waste trap; a dozen or so birds stood like sentinels alongside the pond, watching their compatriots thrash about in the water, taking baths. The hazard ran all the way to the green. Munch ignored his new driver, returning to his used Wild-O three wood.

He sized up the distance to the flag and again felt a warm sensation as he held the club; it seemed alive, filling him with energy. He loved this three wood, he reflected, even though it was reconditioned. It had been an impulse buy months ago as Munch surfed the Internet, searching for insight from various websites dedicated to the most difficult game in the world. His effort that evening found him perusing the Wild-O Golf site where he focused on reconditioned clubs that were offered for half the price of a new weapon. He bought the three wood now in his hands and, whenever he used it, experienced great success.

He gripped the Wild-O with a light touch and swung back with conviction. Gone were the doubts that always clouded his mind when he prepared to hit a golf ball, wondering what would happen. He thought his backswing seemed supple. His spine was a bit more limber. His left arm was horizontal, his shoulder turn was perfection, and his release was to die for. And then came a moment of impact reminiscent of when he was a kid getting hold of a fastball, watching it sail for the fence. And the sound! Such a *lovely* sound as his club connected with the ball.

"Hot damn, Man," John Henry yelled, "You put the wood to that one, Munch!" Munch held the pose, club aloft, pointing toward the target, letting the three wood slip easily through his hands as he watched his ball soar for most of 250 yards, landing just off the green.

The shot was great, the feeling was wonderful. It consumed him; he was somewhere else, looking down on this beautiful course, watching the majestic arc of the ball against the wind as it soared toward the green.

Two

"Sink" Lair and Warren Danson sat nursing their afternoon cocktails, watching Munch and his foursome on a giant High Def TV. The room in which they sat was very, very, large and brilliantly white. The floor was soft, cottony. A bar that shouted "Masculine" was at the far end of the room, featuring liquor and wine from all over the world. At least twenty folks were scattered about the premises. The bartender and wait staff, exquisitely attired in white shirts and trousers, circulated through the room; black ascots for the men, white blouses and skirts for the women. Through the elaborate double doors was a balcony with a view that was heavenly. White clouds stretched toward the horizon as brilliant sunshine cascaded through an extraordinary panorama.

Lair, who boasted a handicap of 2 when he moved upstairs, and Danson, also in single digits with a 3, were seated at the bar, dressed in white slacks and shirts. They were a handsome pair. "We found the right boy, all right," Sink said. "I don't think I've ever seen a more incompetent golfer. If he isn't the worst hacker down there, he's mighty close."

War Danson was not listening to Sink. War was upset, watching his three wood in action on the gigantic wide screen. "Damn! I missed the green! I hate it when I do that," he groused, sipping his gin and tonic.

"Relax, War, you know what they say, 'Dead Men Can't Golf.' Besides, you always were way too much of a perfectionist. Just be glad we got our man," Sink said, smiling, setting his single malt scotch on the bar.

"Bullshit," War snorted, jabbing his thumb at himself. "This dead man is golfing, or at least he is when our buddy down there has my three wood in his hands. I love this 'Channeling' stuff! It's just like being down there. Don't you feel it, Sink? Don't you feel it when your seven iron is in Malone's hands?"

Sink nodded, gazing at the High Def and the green fairway that whisked his mind back to the hues of Scotland. He had been born in the Highlands. His family found their way to the U.S. when Sink was eight years of age. His heart had never left the Glen; he loved the country of his birth, and he loved the Royal and Ancient Game of Golf. The name his parents had bestowed upon him was McCauley Ian Lair, but his golfing prowess as a teen, sinking putt after putt on any course he tackled, quickly earned him the nickname "Sink".

The Scotsman had long ago lost most of the blonde hair that had complemented his angular face and made him so distinctive on the links. He missed his locks, but took great comfort that he no longer needed to apply that messy sunscreen to protect his fair skin from the sun. He also was grateful he had never lost his sense of humor up here, and he continued to loudly express his conservative opinions to one and all. Thank goodness Fox News was broadcast when golf was not televised on the giant Sony screen.

Sink had been CEO of a multi-national landscape company, giving him opportunity to golf the world. He loved the work and his clients loved him. He had wooed them with his easy-going nature and wit, and the endless jokes he would bring to their dealerships. Those traits, and his practice of hosting his many loyal customers at golf's best venues, made it easy to sell his product and build his company.

Sink sighed as he reflected on his current surroundings. He appreciated the fact he could still be social and engaged in the many activities here, but the lack of golf created a void that caused him to grieve. He watched Munch Malone on the giant wide screen before him in a desultory manner, reflecting on the good and bad of the situation. Brooding, he turned and looked at Warren Danson.

Danson had watched Malone's shot with fascination. Pretty neat to not only see it, but feel it, feel his old three wood in his hands — swing that magic stick again! War smiled broadly as he saw Munch's eyes follow his ball straight down the fairway. War, an African American with graying hair and a smile that lit rooms, was 6' 4"; his body naturally athletic, with limber moves and large hands.

He had been elected to Congress from the State of Michigan and served with distinction from the Johnson administration through Ronald Reagan's second term. The political prowess he honed over thirty years made him a household name and his position as chairman of the Appropriations Committee in the House allowed him to spread monetary favors coast to coast. It also provided him ample opportunity to, as he would tell his chief-of-staff, climbing onto some plane provided by a lobbyist friend, "Inspect some lawns—eighteen of them!" Warren Danson played golf to win and had been known as "Man O'War" since he was fourteen, galloping across the courses in Michigan.

War's eyes stayed glued to the Sony, but his body was elsewhere. He had been fascinated to actually hit Munch's shots on holes One and Twelve, fascinated to feel it all! He had played Heron Point when it was the Sea Marsh course. The re-design by Pete Dye was exceptional and the eighteen holes were now of tournament quality. War felt lucky to be down there once again, mastering the South Carolina fairways.

Upon arrival in his current surroundings, War had requested of **The Powers That Be** only one thing—that he could continue to golf. There was sympathy for him, but it was quickly and efficiently explained with great compassion that he would never grip a club here. "Dead Men Can't Golf" became the mantra he heard.

Plenty of space, but no turf, no water and no sand.

Their refusal didn't stop War from trying to find a solution; there had to be a way to bring the game here, he reasoned, and, enlisting Sink Lair in his effort, spent many hours with him over gin and scotch, trying to devise a workable plan. Legions before them had attempted the same thing, and they had made some progress. Their efforts had created golf Clubhouses across the white landscape—Clubhouses with multiple giant screen television sets that allowed the golfers in residence to follow the game. It was a partial solution devised by **The Powers That Be** as they grew tired of being harangued by new arrivals who pounded on their door, demanding they be allowed to play the game.

The fortunate thing for Sink and War had been the technology that blossomed when they checked in. High Definition TV was now king and giant screens were the thing. The technology was always evolving; as each Sony and Samsung technician arrived, their newer expertise was put to use. Collectively they produced larger and larger sets. The ones that now dotted the landscape consumed a massive fifty feet of space, and the reception here was, well, exceptional.

Sink and War had arrived at the Gates at about the same time, in approximately the same manner. They had bonded from the beginning, standing in line, chatting about golf, wading through lengthy admittance interviews, filling out endless forms. Their relationship was cemented by a mutual love of the game and, as they talked, they recognized a shared determination that they, somehow, would once again hit the links.

The Scotsman had died on the seventeenth fairway at Augusta. He was a rock solid Republican who had raised millions for the GOP over the last thirty years. He had enjoyed membership at Augusta for two decades and had adamantly campaigned to eliminate the "Eisenhower Tree" that the former President had so despised. He could not really say whether his advocacy was because he felt the tree was an impediment, or the result of his deep admiration for the historic warrior. Surely Ike was in residence at one of the Clubhouses here.

The Scotsman's last breath had come as he skillfully hit a 170-yard shot on Augusta's Nandina, the Seventeenth hole, with a seven iron. He was proud that he could muster as much out of the club as any pro on the tour. The impact was solid. He had felt the adrenaline rush and was only faintly aware of a sudden jolt.

They say he died a happy man, a phrase used by all golf extremists when the end comes for a buddy on the course. Sink realized the phrase rang true; he had indeed been very happy, feeling the solid connection, watching the ball sail toward the green, falling to his knees, closing his eyes, quietly surrendering to the earth, his seven iron by his side.

"Wild-O" was embossed on the head of the club.

War Danson had his experience on the par four, 5th hole, of the Old White, at The Greenbrier Resort in the beautiful mountains of West Virginia. He loved the "Brier" because the fabled hotel was close to Washington, allowing him to easily slip out of D.C. and head for the lovely mountains. He also favored the resort because of its history with Sam Snead, the longtime pro at the The Greenbrier.

Slammin' Sammy briefly crossed his mind on that final day when War hit his three wood on number Five, the Mounds, eating up most of the 344 yards, landing right of center, the perfect spot to attack the green. The ball soared, finding a home twenty yards from the cup. The three wood was a truly formidable weapon.

On that particular day, War had seldom felt so alive. He watched the ball land, felt a sudden sensation, clutched his chest, and dropped to the ground. He lay prone as his fingers slowly released the club he had held in his hands. A bluebird chirped in the background and a streak of white shot across a crystal blue sky. The afternoon sun reflected boldly off the Wild-O logo on the head of the three wood.

Munch shook his head to clear his thinking. It had happened

again; his shot *had* been different, he thought, just like the last swing with the three wood. It had felt as though the club was not in his hands. "I think I'm getting the hang of this. I'm actually learning to hold this baby as though it really is a feather!" he thought, cupping his hands, he shouted at Eugene, "I'm back, baby, I'm back!"

Munch kissed the head on the Wild-O and deftly rammed the club into the Rodney. There was no way Munch could have known his three wood had belonged to Warren Danson, and his seven iron to Sink Lair. Munch finished the round, alternating between banging the Rodney, cursing, and occasionally getting off a spectacular shot, confined to the three wood and the seven iron. Those shots brought him back.

"You know Munch," Eugene said, nursing his second Guinness in the clubhouse, "you hit some really fine shots out there today."

"That three wood on Eleven was awesome, Munch," Dave said, wiping his mustache free of foam from his Yuengling.

"Not to mention the approach on Eighteen," John Henry said, prodding Munch's shoulder—"You 'da man'!" John was not prone to praise, but he and the rest of the foursome always tried to help Munch overcome his depression at the end of a round.

Munch grinned, finishing his Ultra, checking his watch.

"Thanks, guys. Pretty good day. I've gotta' hit the road if I'm gonna' get home in time for dinner," he said.

Goodbyes all around and Munch tossed the Rodney in his Escalade, slamming the cargo door. He climbed in the driver's seat, hit the ignition, pulled a Montecristo out of his glove compartment, pushed buttons to lower the windows, and lit up. Hopefully, Melinda, his wife, would never notice the cigar's odor if all the windows were open.

Sucking on his cigar, Munch's thoughts returned to the

Wild-O's. The used Wild-O's were really good, so why not buy a *new* set of Wild-O irons? New Wild-O's would surely be superior to the used clubs.

The practical side of his brain began to cipher. It certainly would be *cheaper* to buy more used Wild-O clubs, rather than invest in new ones. If the two used Wild-O's resting in the Rodney were that good, why not try a few more used, rather than new clubs; would he hit every used Wild-O with the same confidence?

"I wonder who owned the clubs?" he asked himself, drawing on his cigar. "Why would anyone give them up? They work like magic." He glanced at the used Wild-O's in his rearview mirror. They seemed to glow in the Rodney bag, reaching out to him, signaling that *they* were the answer to improving his miserable game. They had an aura about them; it was as though they had a mind and game of their own.

Munch knew the only reason he hesitated to add more used Wild-O's was the thought in the back of his mind that some poor fellow had died and the little woman had picked up some coin by selling his clubs to the Wild-O reconditioning boys.

"Shit," Munch said out loud, glancing once again at the clubs that seemed to emit a shimmering glow, "They're 'Dead Men's Clubs', I just know it."

Three

Man O'War motioned to the bar for a second gin and tonic and sat back in delight as Sheila began to mix another round. War really appreciated Sheila; tall, brunette, magnificent chest, legs that were perfection. She purred like a kitten when she was nearby. Her body was like a Lucky Strike...so round, so firm, so fully packed. War was smitten, he had to admit, with the way Sheila would pause momentarily while serving or retrieving a drink. She just bent over, putting both of those magnificent headlights in front of him, pausing there for a moment, glancing up at him, batting those huge eyelashes.

"What a lovely woman," he mused. "She's so appreciative of a gentleman's needs. If I weren't so damn old..."

"Another, Congressman?" she said from somewhere above her Mount Rushmore's.

"No, two of those," he said, looking deep into the cleavage, "are about all I can absorb at the moment." War smiled broadly, continuing to gaze at the perfectly shaped breasts that were a little too close to be fully in focus.

"Oh, Congressman Danson, you are the funniest man," Sheila laughed, taking the empty glass and her bosom off the table, turning and walking away, giving both War and Sink the full view of a beautiful little bottom. War sighed and flashed back to several celebrations with equipment such as Sheila's.

"What are you grinning about, you old fart," Sink asked, seeing War take in the poetry in motion.

"I may be dead, but I'm not that dead," War said as Sheila drifted behind the white bar.

"War, get your mind off pussy and tell me—what are we gonna' do for Munch?" Sink asked, gazing at the High Def and watching the Escalade proceed along Plantation Drive, one of the main Sea Pines thoroughfares.

"Well, if we care about the boy at all, we need to get some more of our clubs in his hands," War replied.

"My bet is he's going back for more, but I think we need to make certain he does just that," Sink said, punching numbers on his iPhone. "I'm gonna' do some homework."

As Sink keyed in the numbers, his screen displayed the Wild-O Golf website. He scrolled down to the "reconditioned" bar and went to the page listing the clubs he once owned. He and War had prepared for a moment such as this. When they realized there was no actual golf available in this land of milk and honey, they began scheming to fulfill, in some way, their desperate need for the game.

They had petitioned **The Powers That Be** and received, after one hell of a fight, special dispensation to initiate "Contagion"—a phenomenon that had come to Sink's attention through media; Sink had read an article while perusing golf web sites that gave him hope and inspiration.

"Wow, this is the answer!" he had said, perusing the article in Science Now by reporter Helen Fields. She had reported that research at the University of Virginia, inspired by a passage in the 1953 book "Zen in the Art of Archery", had produced extraordinary results.

Sink had quickly informed War of his discovery, printing out the report, placing it on the bar in front of the Congressman.

"Look at this!" Sink said, excitement in his voice. War reluctantly set down his gin and tonic and began to read. Field's story referenced author Eric Herrigel's book on archery wherein he recounted his failed attempt to achieve competency on the shooting range. Doing poorly, he handed the bow to his instructor who subsequently used it to perfection, returning the bow to Herrigel. The author said he then shot better; "It was as if the bow let itself be drawn differently, more willingly, more understandingly."

"Yeah, so?" War had said, looking quizzically at Sink.

"Okay, here's the good part. The researchers at UVA decided to test this theory using a golf paradigm in order to quantify the experiment. They recruited undergraduate students and separated them into two groups."

"Uh huh, and your point is?"

"Just hold your horses, and your gin, you're gonna' love this!"

"I'm holding, but getting bored by the second."

"So, it says in the article that both groups were given identical putters. Group One was told each individual would putt with a club that had been owned by Ben Curtis—you know Curtis, dynamite with the putter."

"Yeah?"

"Well, it wasn't really Ben's putter. Point is, though, the control group thought it was."

"Okay—"

"The other group was told the same club was simply a very expensive putter. So, they did this experiment, War, and, guess what? Out of ten putts, students who were told the putter had been used by Curtis sank, on average, one and one half more balls."

"Really?"

"Yep, called it 'Contagion'—placebo effect. The students using the club they thought Ben had used were apparently thinking about Curtis' expert putting and they put a lot more balls in the cup."

"Interesting—"

"And, check this out, this newspaper article says a cultural psychologist thinks that confidence like this could come from a belief in this 'Contagion'. Near as I can figure, 'Contagion' is the belief that an object somehow absorbs the qualities of its previous owner."

"So, the students were 'Channeling' Ben? This 'Contagion' thing really works?"

"Yep, seems so, and I think it'll work even better with our Mr. Malone if we get some help from **The Powers That Be**."

Sink and War seized upon "Contagion" and began petitioning **The Powers That Be**, urging them to allow implementation of such a process with a living golfer, possessing him as he played. War and Sink would swing the guy's clubs—the living golfer would simply be the vessel through which they would play; "Contagion" would gradually cause him to believe that someone else had used the clubs to perfection and that he now possessed the same prowess.

It was a sweet deal, really. **The Powers That Be** liked the idea and said if "Contagion" worked, they might extend it to all the golfers up here. The test run was granted primarily because **The Powers That Be** had grown weary of the aggressiveness the two old golfers had displayed when they insisted on golf relief. "These guys are worse than the lawyers we have to deal with," groused one of the **Powers** as he plowed through the petition.

Finally, the prototype was agreed upon: Sink and War would be allowed to select a subject who had yet to arrive at their Gates and Channel the game through him. **The Powers That Be** cautioned there could be no surprises or embarrassment from the experiment. And, just for fun, they had instructed War and Sink they were to select a serious duffer through which to play.

Munch Malone fit the bill of duffer perfectly. He had purchased two used Wild-O Clubs. As fortune would have it, the three wood that always delivered for Munch had belonged to Warren Danson, and his seven iron had been Sink Lair's. The stage, therefore, had been set for them. All they needed to do was to persuade Munch to buy more clubs—a full set of used Wild-O's—clubs that had all belonged to the Scotsman and Man O' War.

The first step was relatively easy. They needed a geek who could hack into the Wild-O system to maneuver Munch to buy the remainder of their clubs. And just outside the door and down a lovely white street about three blocks from the Clubhouse were enough geeks to float an Airbus.

After only a few inquires of the high tech crowd, the name of "Snarf" Adams emerged as being eminently qualified for the task of finding Sink's and War's clubs. Their sticks had been inventoried with Wild-O Golf after the golfers' wives had cleaned their respective garages of bags, balls, irons and drivers and sold them to Wild-O. Snarf Adams would simply have to make certain the clubs were sequestered and tagged for any inquiry from Munch Malone.

The Snarf was a Chicago boy. His hair hung to his shoulders, and even stern warnings from the authorities were not enough to persuade him to wash his strands more often than once a month. His Lincolnesque face sported a matted mustache in the Pancho Villa fashion that challenged his greasy hair. His fingernails were stained from a three-pack-a-day Marlboro habit.

Snarf banged the door to the Galaxy Espresso open with gusto. He loved Galaxy Espresso and the rush he got from a double shot. Galaxy Espresso was all white with green accessories; white uniforms, white mugs, floors that were a cushy, cottony white, lovely baristas with short, white skirts—no coffee stains to be found anywhere. Snarf grabbed his drink and his favorite additional white accessory, a bowl of vanilla ice cream, and sauntered over to Sink and War. They immediately got down to business.

"We need a man who can hack into any computer system. The guy we need has to possess writing skills, excellent anticipatory talent, and, well, a desire to do something that will help his fellow man. Two out of three isn't bad, and that's why we have selected you to help us guide an unsuspecting golfer to a website where he will buy clubs you have selected for him," Sink advised, slapping Snarf on the back in a congratulatory manner.

"Uh, I don't know, man, I just don't know", Snarf said, as Sink and War further explained the gig.

"What? What is it that you don't know—precisely?" War demanded, leaning forward, peering intently into Snarf's puffy and bloodshot eyes.

"Well, I mean, you know. Look, dude, no disrespect, but look around you. Bad situation, huh? Money don't mean nothin' here and, well, sex would be great but you have to get approval from **The Powers That Be** for that and, you know, dude, they ain't never gonna' give old Snarf that kinda' leeway. Old Snarf got admittance here by the skin of his teeth. You should have seen my rap sheet. How I got in I don't know, but somebody musta' had a weak moment, man. **The Powers That Be** know all about old Snarf, and you can bet your sweet ass they won't give me nothin' but coffee and ice cream for any extracurricular good works. Shit, I'm from Chicago, man."

"So what are you saying, dammit?" War demanded, pounding the table, causing his latte to skitter perilously toward the edge of a gleaming white surface.

"Dude," Snarf said in a long breath between stained teeth, ending in a smile emanating from beneath the Pancho Villa, "what, exactly, is in it for me?"

Silence enveloped the scene as War watched Snarf devour his ice cream. A thin smile began to emerge on his lips and he leaned forward across the table, his face hovering close to Snarf's nose.

"So—you say they'll let you have ice cream?" War asked, looking at the half-filled bowl in front of Snarf.

"Yeah, love it. Nasty habit of mine, can't get 'dat old cocaine up here," Snarf said.

"Snarf, have you ever been to Santa Cruz?" War asked.

"Can't say as I have, man."

'Interesting little ice cream parlor there, Snarf."

"Yeah, so?"

"Seems you can order all kinds of flavors—Banannabis Foster, Straw Man Cheesecake, TRIP-le Chocolate Brownie—good stuff! Near as I can tell each half pint of the product contains about an eighth of high-grade material that equals about, oh, eight joints. Marijuana ice cream has arrived in Santa Cruz—and we can see that it becomes available behind the counter here at Galaxy Espresso. That is, if you're interested..."

Snarf lifted his head, holding a dip of vanilla in front of his mouth, squinting at War, suddenly realizing what the quid pro quo was.

"Done, man!" he said, bolting upright in his solid white chair, slamming the table, high-fiving Man O' War.

Snarf was engaged and Munch was in play. The Snarf would find the task juvenile. Wild-O Golf would be totally unaware when he struck.

Four

Melinda heard the garage door grind open. She hoped Munch would not be in a foul mood as she braced for the unknown. Munch's mood post-golf was seldom good. She secretly wished he would give up the game as bad for his health.

The door from the garage to the kitchen opened and Munch bounded into the room in his stocking feet. "What's for dinner, Mel!" he exuded.

"Hey, babe, salmon; it's fresh catch from Haislip's Fish Market."

"Sweet," Munch replied, carrying his shoes, hopping along as he removed his soiled golf socks, throwing them in a pile of clothes in the laundry room adjoining the kitchen.

"How was your game today," she asked, leaning forward to kiss him as he walked barefoot through the kitchen, afraid of what she might hear.

"Tell you what, I didn't score very well, but I had some fantastic shots and I came off the tee with that used Wild-O three wood like a champ," Munch gushed, reaching for her. "I really enjoyed it!"

"Thank goodness for that," Melinda thought, giving him another kiss and a hug.

"You! You are a very sexy, girl! I say we grill the salmon, have a drink and then do the Viagra thing!" Munch teased, grabbing her bottom.

She could not help but laugh. He was a good guy and she loved him dearly. She knew he felt the same. The other loves in their lives were their kids, grandkids, travel, Melinda's needlepoint, Munch's golf, and their Maltese, Amalfi.

Melinda offered yet another kiss and said, in as husky a voice as she could manage, "Viagra in the morning, big boy, in the morning. By the time you get a shower and a gin and tonic, it'll be time for beddy-bye."

Munch grinned, patted Melinda's bottom, and said, "I got to get me some of that!"

His next stop was his bar where he grabbed a bottle of gin, poured a double shot with tonic over ice and mixed his après golf reward. Then Munch was off to his study where he fired up his Mac, going directly to the Wild-O website as Amalfi sat on his lap, straining to lick Munch's face.

"Wild-O, Wild-O," Munch thought, tapping the computer keys, pondering whether to open his wallet. The Wild-O site popped up before him and he immediately went to the used and reconditioned clubs page. Once there, several irons caught Munch's eye. He moved his cursor and began to read.

Snarf was at his station, prepared. His sticky fingers moved rapidly across the keyboard. A few swift strokes and he smiled as Munch's computer screen morphed from the irons Munch had been viewing to Sink Lair's three and five irons and his pitching wedge. Snarf smacked his lips and swiped at his mustache, digging his spoon deep into a bowl of Straw Man. His mood was sky high. "Who knew freakin' ice cream could be so good! Eat your heart out, Blue Bunny!"

"What the hell?" Munch exclaimed, as the screen flashed, dispensing with the clubs he had been viewing, replacing them with other used clubs Wild-O offered for sale. Munch keyed the return arrow to "go back," but the screen would not respond.

Five

"You know, Snarf, you went a bit far with the reference to Munch's golf bag," Sink frowned, addressing a large Caesar salad topped with blackened chicken breast. He poured a glass of La Source and Summum Chardonnay, pointing a fork at Snarf.

"Hey, I was gonna' call it a Rodney bag, but I restrained myself," Snarf snickered, smacking his lips and swallowing a large scoop of Banannabis Foster.

"This is serious stuff, Snarf, cut the crap and make sure we keep this guy on the hook now that he's bought some of my irons," Sink instructed, as War entered the room.

War shot a glance at Sink and said, "Munch has your irons?"

"Yep, he has my pitchin wedge and my three and five irons," Sink replied, "Just got 'em through some good work by our man here—good work that almost got out of hand," Sink added with a resultant frown as he gazed with disapproval at Snarf. "He also has that seven iron of mine and your three wood that he got earlier. Way I see it; he needs your driver because you always had ten yards on me. You hit the woods better than I do, but Munch needs my irons."

Man of War raised his eyebrows and frowned at the Scotsman.

"Don't get your tighty whities in an uproar, you know what I'm talkin' about, I'm just sayin'! I've got the better short game, always did!" Sink said, raising a hand in the air and shaking his finger at Man O'War.

"Okay," War replied, "You're a Walter Hagen with the short

irons." He plopped into a chair between Sink and Snarf and summoned Sheila who gave a nod in return, pushing her breasts higher in her white uniform that plunged deeply between her most coveted assets.

"Way I see it, he gets my four, six, seven, eight and nine irons," War said.

Sink gave back an incredulous look. "I don't think so, man, like I said, and you just confirmed, I was always much better than you around the greens. He gets my eight and nine and your four and six irons."

"Bullshit!" War said as Sheila delivered once more, leaning across the table with a Hendrick's.

"Boys, boys!" she teased, glancing from Sink to War, rubbing her thigh against War's shoulder.

"By God, I'm not dead," War thought, feeling his "Johnson" twinge.

"Okay, Sheila baby, what do we do—share and share alike?" Sink asked, picking up on the thigh rub.

"Welllll," Sheila said through perfectly formed lips that looked like a red heart with frosting on it, "I'm for sharing if you boys are!" And she walked away, hips moving from California to Connecticut.

"Shit man, you boys are gonna' have to get permission from **The Powers That Be** if you wanna shag that!" Snarf said, watching the tide roll. "You better see who has the blue pill franchise up here!"

"Snarf, does the word 'reprobate' mean anything to you?" War said, shaking his head.

"The major problem we seem to have is that the Snarf Man here thinks his sense of humor is a bigger deal than our mission to fully club Munch," Sink said, pointing to the Wild-O web site on Snarf's computer.

War read Snarf's entry on the web site. He frowned and turned to Sink. "OK, Munch gets your seven, eight and nine irons, and my four, five and six irons. He gets my driver and seven wood—and I get to putt."

Sink's turn to frown.

"No. I definitely putt."

"Boys! Boys!" Sheila repeated from somewhere down the bar.

"Okay," War shrugged, "You can putt. Now, let's kick some ass."

"Right on! Lovely ass," Snarf said, stroking his Pancho Villa mustache, leering toward Sheila.

"How about it, Snarf, get with the program, can you do this? Can you get our boy Munch to buy our clubs? Can you also restrain yourself as you do it? No more ad-libbing?" War asked.

"Shit yes, buddy. I can come up with some stuff that'll keep this guy sniffing for clubs like a Snarf," he said, running his fingers through his long, greasy hair.

"Snarf? There's a definition for Snarf?" Sink asked, arching an eyebrow.

"Snarf. It's probably in Webster's, man. A Snarf is a guy that goes around smellin' girl's bicycle seats. You can look it up!" Snarf smirked.

"Snarf, aptly named—how disgusting," War grimaced.

"Snarf, remember, our plan was approved by **The Powers That Be** after they conferred with the **Highest Authority**. If I were you, I wouldn't want to piss them off and blow this assignment. The ice cream flows only as long as Munch believes and produces. So far, so good. But, as they say in Chicago, shit happens."

Meantime, Munch's "used" three and five irons and his wedge were sensational. He wielded the sand wedge like he was Phil Mickelson. Munch was the talk of the club. How did he do it? What pro was giving him lessons? Shame he couldn't come off the tee with the big club, had to use the three wood. The driver was still a problem; but his iron game was, indeed, sensational, even though he used only his three, five and seven irons.

"Munch," Eugene Columbus said, watching Munch's drive shank into the trees at Harbour Town, the world-class Sea Pines Plantation golf course that hosted the PGA Heritage tournament, "you should use that three wood off the tee or get the pro to work with you on your driver."

Munch shook his head. "I've used pros from here to hell and back—I don't get any better. I'm workin it out on my own."

"Oh, you are?" the Congressman smiled to himself, glancing around the Clubhouse, waiting for his gin and tonic, and Sheila, not necessarily in that order.

Eugene drove his ball a customary 250 yards, letting the club glide smoothly through his hands as he admired his effort. "There's the ticket, Munch, my boy, just let your God-given talent take over."

"Exactly," Sink said, watching Munch's contorted face.

"Think about it, Munch," Dave Rambo said, punching his drive just off the fairway and to the right of one of Harbour Town's magnificent water hazards.

"Think about it?" Munch parroted.

"Yes, you moron, think about it!" Sink shouted, pounding the table, causing Sheila to bounce her headlights as she carried a scotch to the normally placid Mr. Lair. "Sheila, always to my rescue," Sink breathed heavily, savoring the curve of her blouse. For her part, Sheila leaned forward and delivered the goods. Sink could not help himself; he glanced at the partially bare chest and certainly thought about it.

"Yeah, think about it. What is different?" Eugene repeated Dave's message as Munch walked toward him.

Munch looked at the Rodney and resisted the urge to pull his club back and slam the bejesus out of it. He controlled himself and put his club in the bag.

Eugene pulled a flask from his cart and a seven iron from his bag. "Dave's right, Munch, what are you doing differently when you grab the three wood or hit that seven iron?"

Munch looked at the Stallard driver in his Rodney. Big time club. He had bought it two months ago when the new drivers came out. Golf World said it was the best. Didn't work worth a damn for him. Nowadays he seldom took it out of the Rodney. But the used Wild-O three wood? Sweet!

"What *was* different, why did I hit those used clubs so well?" mused Munch, giving up his ball search, taking a penalty drop.

"*Think about it, dammit!*" Sink shouted once again as War approached the table, signaling Shelia with a wave of his arm and a sweep of an imaginary golf club.

"*Think about what?*" War asked, easing into a very white chair.

"Damn boy's too stupid to know the Wild-O's are the difference," Sink snorted.

Munch grabbed his five iron. "Maybe it *is* the clubs," he said under his breath.

He addressed the ball, felt the surge, and delivered a blast that cut the fairway in half with the ball sailing 175 yards.

"Damn, that felt good," Sink said with a smile.

"Yeah." shouted John Henry, "you 'da man', Munch."

Munch smiled. So—maybe it *was* something about the clubs. He *had* felt something; it was as though the swing was completely out of his hands, it required no effort at all. Munch grinned and looked at the club. "My God, I'm playing better than I ever have. Only thing I have to do is use these friggin' 'Dead Men's Clubs,'" he thought, with mixed emotions. Melinda would not be pleased, but FedEx would soon reappear on their doorstep.

"*Get Snarf,*" Sink barked, leaning forward with a huge smile. War reached for his phone and sent a text message on the brilliantly white instrument.

The Snarf was digging into a bowl of TRIPle Chocolate Brownie and was busy hacking into a juicy Internet magazine site. **The Powers That Be** had made porno viewing almost impossible—but as George C. Scott had once said, "If you were good, really, really good—!" Snarf was, indeed, that good. Mainstream porno was tough to access up here, but he had easily been able to find this site. Soft porn was better than no porn at all! Small victory for a man from Chicago with discerning taste.

The magazine offered a video of "Girls of the Vile West". Snarf clicked the play button and found a particular young lady he had greatly admired in previous visits who was about to become a very good friend with the gentleman she was kneeling before. Just as she prepared to become engaged in meaningful work, Snarf was interrupted with incoming text. "Shit, man! Can't a guy get a hard-on here?" Snarf mumbled, reading the message.

"Back to work, Snarf, Munch needs to club himself!" the message read. Snarf put down the ice cream, wiping Chocolate Brownie off his Fu Manchu, wilting with the email message as he fantasized the fun ahead. He readily said goodbye to the Girls of the Vile West and began to move his fingers swiftly over his keyboard. "Let the hacking begin," he grinned, feeling instantly better.

Six

John Short at Wild-O Reconditioned Sales was once Wild-O's National Sales President, but recent times had not favored him. As Tiger Woods' fall impacted golf's fortunes, so had it affected John. His sales numbers were not good. National interest in golf swooned with Tiger. Business decisions were made.

Wild-O decided to give a younger man the chance to turn things around. The company moved John Short to Vice President of the Reconditioned Clubs Division and named Marcus Appleton Interim National Sales President. Appleton would have six months to prove he could boost the numbers.

Short sat in his office and packed his things. At 5', 2", he was known as "Short Sale" John. It was a soubriquet he detested, a name no one referenced to his face. It had not bothered him when he was top of the heap as National Sales President. It *did* bother him now, as employees gossiped in the hallways, saying he had gotten the short end of the stick, no pun intended. Short Sale John was not a happy man.

His replacement, Marcus Appleton, was young, smart, handsome, and cunning. He had burst upon the scene at Wild-O Golf with a marketing degree from Florida State, where he excelled in grades, golf, and women. He joined Wild-O as an assistant to a vice-president in the manufacturing division. The poor bastard taught Marcus all he knew. Soon, Marcus had his mentor's job and the mentor was on the street. Marcus never looked back.

Marcus was tall, had an impressive head of jet-black hair, and a quick smile that hid a deeply ingrained insecurity. His Achilles heel caused him to require everyone who reported to him to profess total allegiance and engage in "LOMT"—Living On Marcus Time. Marcus took pleasure in calling employees day and night, ordering them here and there. He *wanted* them living on Marcus time, jumping anytime he called. Because of this, and his generally arrogant nature, he was widely known throughout the Wild-O Empire as "The Shit".

Upon his promotion, Marcus had issued a directive to all division employees that no one, save his Executive Assistant, Cheryl Woody, could approach or speak with him in common areas at Wild-O Golf because his time was "too valuable" to be spent with lowly employees. The affected wage earners quickly emailed the directive to Wild-O people throughout the world, enhancing, affirming, and forever enshrining Marcus as—"The Shit".

"The Shit's" ego would fill the Astrodome. He craved money and he was willing to step on anyone to get it. Marcus truly did believe that greed was good and lived his life that way. Moments after he ushered John Short out of his corner office and over to Reconditioned, Marcus began a detailed review of Short Sale's national sales figures.

Short Sale's numbers were not good, as Marcus confirmed upon reviewing his predecessor's daily, monthly and annual reports, but, given the state of the economy, and the sport's popularity problem, they weren't *really* that bad. Matter of fact, they were *way* too good, Marcus thought.

Tiger's departure might make it difficult to boost sales numbers in just six months, Marcus feared. If he did not quickly accelerate his bottom line, he reasoned, Wild-O Golf might rethink his promotion and return Short Sale John to National Sales President. Marcus needed time, and more time could be had if John Short were permanently out of the picture.

Making that decision, Marcus' fixation on performance of the Reconditioned Clubs Division became maniacal. He was so obsessed with Short Sale John that the entire division was aware that Short was targeted and would soon be gone.

"Where the hell is Short Sale's stuff," Marcus growled at Cheryl as he came through the office. Cheryl ran closely beside him. Other employees stepped aside and made sure they did not cross the line by speaking to "The Shit", unless they were spoken to.

"I have Reconditioned's daily report right here, sir, just as you have, every hour, requested," Cheryl said with ice dripping from an accent that branded her as Kentucky born and bred. Cheryl could, everyone knew, kick butt.

"Don't be a smartass, Woody," Marcus said, stopping in his tracks, turning around, wagging a finger in Cheryl's face.

Cheryl pointed her finger back, features flushed with anger beneath short black hair atop five feet of sass. "Don't give *me* any of *your* crap," she said. "This stuff is on your desk every morning, and you know it. I get damned tired of 'LOMT' just because 'The Shit' has a bad day."

Marcus looked around the office to see who had heard. He drew very close to Cheryl and said, "Woody, don't do that."

"Don't do what, y'all?" Cheryl said, batting her eyelashes, smiling ever so slightly.

"You know and I know what they call me, but don't, for God's sake, perpetuate it," Marcus hissed in her face.

"Duly noted, boss. I shan't say 'The Shit' in public anymore," Cheryl said with an evil smile.

"I'll hold you to that. Now, gimme' those damn numbers and get me some coffee, pronto," Marcus growled.

Marcus sat in his office consuming the daily sales reports from the Reconditioned Division like a starving man. He was concerned. He knew Short Sale was damn good at any job given him and he was painfully worried that used clubs sales might outperform new clubs. He was determined to keep the ratio in line. Even the slightest blip was cause to excite and concern "The Shit". He knew it was a fine line — the top brass at Wild-O were watching him and he had to appear to be applying pressure on Short to increase Reconditioned sales, while making certain Short failed in trying to do so. Once Short's sales numbers were trending downward on a weekly basis, Marcus knew he could then go to the CEO of Wild-O Golf and make the case that Short should be terminated.

Meantime, Munch Malone was again confused. No matter where he went on their website, Wild-O Golf directed him to only certain clubs.

"C'mon, boy, old Snarf ain't got all night," Adams groused as he manipulated the site. "Guess I'll have to get creative," he grinned, knowing Sink and War would not be pleased. A pop up flashed on Munch's screen. "If you have seen dramatic improvement with Wild-O Reconditioned, consider the possibilities if more clubs were added to your golf bag!"

"Huh?" Munch thought.

"Wild-O Reconditioned enjoys taking golfers to new heights. If you are a current customer, here is the chance to add three additional weapons to your arsenal. Wild-O Golf is now offering a set of three clubs at the astounding low price of…"

"Damn," Snarf said, "what the hell do golf clubs sell for? Gotta' make it a bargain. Lemme' see, a good cigar these days costs ten dollars, so a reconditioned golf club should be a good buy for, say, $10.95."

"Astounding low price of $10. 95 per club or $25 for a set of three."

"Pass that up, asshole," Snarf said to himself, and added, "Wild-O Golf is confident your game will improve dramatically as our clubs are added to your bag. Don't delay, play better today."

"Pretty freakin' great writin', Snarf my man," he complimented himself.

"Wow," Munch said aloud. "Why not? Three used Wild-O's for $25. Not even Melinda can object to this," he thought, tapping the keys, entering his credit card information, moving quickly to checkout.

"Got him," Snarf grinned as Munch selected three irons—numbers four, six and eight. He pushed a button and the clubs flashed on Munch's screen. They would be forwarded by FedEx and be there on two day delivery. "What the hell," Snarf thought, and typed in that Wild-O would not charge for the "rush" order.

Seven

Saturday morning at the Club. Munch greeted Eugene at the driving range. Eugene was hitting his big stick as Munch pulled his five iron out of his bag.

"Mornin', Munch," yelled Eugene, slamming his driver, watching the path of his ball through the last of the early morning fog that glistened off the grass.

"Hey, big guy," grinned Munch. "Glorious morning, great day for golf."

"You bet your sweet ass," Eugene yelled back.

Munch went through his workout routine, loosening up his body. He stretched and bent, leaned and tried to touch his toes. He had not accomplished that, he reflected, in quite a while.

Munch lowered his right shoulder, told himself to keep his head still and down, to rotate his left arm, cock his wrists, rotate his right arm, and hit the hell out of the ball. He came through smoothly and watched the ball after impact, seeing it rise dramatically in the air, flying 193 yards downrange.

Eugene stopped and looked at Munch. "Great hit old shoe, what club was that?"

"Five iron," Munch said.

"You're kidding me," Eugene said, a smile wrinkling across his face.

"No, no, I've been hitting 'em pretty good lately," Munch said, returning the grin.

"Betcha' can't do that again," Eugene teased.

Munch did do it again. And again, and again. Eugene stopped his practice and watched in amazement. He let out a slow whistle and said, "Let's see how that plays out on the course."

John Henry and Dave Rambo pulled up in a shared cart. "Let's go men, tee time," shouted Rambo.

"Hey, guys, we got ourselves a different Munch man here," Eugene said as he and Munch climbed in their cart and the foursome headed for the tee.

"Uh huh, you got 'dat right," Sink Lair said, laughing out loud from his place at the bar. Sink loved hitting that five iron. "Damn, it felt good." The bar was always a good place to be because Sheila's breasts were very apparent as she leaned forward over the white counter to deliver his morning Mimosa. "Life is good here," Sink thought to himself, realizing how ironic the thought was. His gaze drifted back and forth from the titties to the tee as he tried to concentrate on the giant screen behind the bar. It was a great set. Actually, he thought, make that two great sets.

Reluctantly, he swiveled from her Rushmore's, concentrating on the High Def before him. That Samsung guy that had checked in last week had tweaked the system up here and the reception was better than ever. Sink also liked the way he had outlined the screen in all white. Nice contrast to the picture. More in keeping with the surroundings, too.

"Munch, my man, you are knockin' it out of the park. Outdrivin' your buds by 50 yards when you use my clubs! I love it," Sink said with glee. The Scotsman flashed back to a lush fairway at Augusta where he had last gripped his Wild-O.

Sink was suddenly conscious of someone sliding onto the stool beside him, but he could not take his eyes from the screen.

"Man, I'm lookin' at some freakin' great hooters," Snarf shouted down the bar in Sheila's direction, digging into a pint of ice cream.

Sheila paid Snarf no attention, but Sink was livid as he turned to the oily hair seated next to him. "Snarf, you are a degenerate. How in the world did they let you in? You are an asshole!" Sink practically shouted, his Celtic features turning bloody red.

"No, man, I'm no asshole, I'm a Snarf, and if she was ridin' her bike I'd be sniffin' her undies," Snarf chortled, reaching behind the bar, snagging a Bud. At that, Sheila did take notice, and walked briskly forward, grabbing the bottle.

"Hey, big boy, you've got to ask for what you want here," Sheila said, feigning a smile.

"Oh, boy, oh, boy, don't tempt me," Snarf giggled.

By the end of the round Munch's buddies were amazed, flabbergasted and delighted. Munch had shot an 85, his best ever. Drinks were hoisted in the clubhouse and Munch, who just weeks ago believed he would never break 100, was strangely subdued.

"You were a 'Phenom' today," Dave Rambo grinned at Munch over a Manhattan, his favorite drink and a tribute to Munch's achievement. Eugene weighed in with a slap on the back and a question as to whether Munch thought he could continue to "shoot 'em like you shot 'em today?"

"That's also my question," Munch frowned. "I don't really know what's changed and if the change will stick." He stared through the clubhouse window to number Eighteen at Ocean Pines Country Club. The Eighteenth hole was the number two handicap; Munch always thought it was the toughest hole on the course. It had a spectacular approach to the green with marsh on the left that jutted into the landing area for approach shots. Few did well on the club's "Signature Hole" and a par was coveted.

Munch smiled to himself. On this day, he had birdied number Eighteen.

"So, Munch has his doubts does he? War asked, muttering to himself, turning to Snarf. "Snarf, you're moving too slowly. We need Munch outfitted with the complete set of clubs as soon as possible. He needs, let's see now, my driver, and my five and seven woods," Sink said, jotting down numbers on his napkin.

"And my nine iron, fifty-two degree wedge, and putter," War said.

"He needs them now and he needs to have his confidence built," Sink said, finishing off his Mimosa.

War weighed in: "Give him a full treatment. Tell him he needs to compete for the club championship in April."

"How can I do that?" Snarf asked. "I mean, man, he ain't gonna' believe that Wild-O used clubs is kissin' his ass every time he fires up the site—and he ain't gonna' fuckin' believe that some voice out of nowhere knows that he belongs to a country club, let alone wants him in the freakin' championship!"

War looked at Snarf. "Well, which is it?" he asked.

"Which is what, man?" Snarf replied.

"Is it fuckin' or freakin'? You, my hungry stoner, seem to use both words."

"Uh, I guess 'freakin' would be more politically correct, but, you know man, one should avoid unneeded repetition," Snarf said.

"Snarf, have you ever had a conversation without obscene words?" War challenged.

"Don't think so man. I work at it, I really do," Snarf said, with utmost sincerity.

"Forget he mentioned it, Snarf, just get Munch into a Wild-O chat room and convince him to get the driver, woods and irons. Tell him to go out and play some freakin' competitive golf," Sink bellowed in delight, slapping Snarf on the back.

Snarf relaxed. A chatroom was possible, and he was back in good graces. Sheila even smiled over her shoulder at him, bending over the beer cooler, giving him a shot of her posterior that Hugh Hefner surely would consider for the cover of Playboy.

Eight

Munch sat in his study. He was worried and perplexed. How was it possible to come so far in such a short time? He thought he knew the answer, recalling the feel of the used clubs. Somebody else had swung them. He knew it. Everything worked when he used his "Dead Men's Clubs"; his wedge proved bunker play was not a problem, and the three wood was the answer to his struggle off the tee. Yet, he still needed to have a big stick if he expected to continue to play at the level he had achieved in his latest round. Even at that, an 85? Holy cow.

He was startled out of his reverie as his computer pinged, displaying the Wild-O website, causing Amalfi, slumbering on his lap, to jump up, barking.

"Malf, how in the world did that happen?" he asked the dog, assessing the computer screen.

The site flashed in the upper right hand corner—*"Chatroom open for Mr. M. Malone. Log in now, please."*

Munch, fascinated, complied.

"Hello, Malone here," he wrote.

"Hi, you're Munch Malone, aren't you?" Snarf answered.

Munch moved the keys. "Yes, Munch Malone—who are you?"

"Special Wild-O reconditioned clubs rep. My job is to check on our buyers and see if we can assist them in any way after they buy our

clubs." Snarf wrote, hands flying across the keys between mouthfuls of ice cream.

"Much appreciated," Munch wrote, "but my clubs are working nicely, thanks. Matter of fact, I'm playing the best golf of my life since I bought some of your clubs."

"Oh, good, good, good. So, I assume you're coming off the tee nicely," Snarf smirked as he typed.

"Well, to tell the truth, I could do better off the tee," Munch admitted.

"Oh? Let me see here…Oh, well, you are still using your old driver, I see," Snarf replied, closing the net.

"Well, not really using it now, but it's not exactly old, I bought a new Stallard driver last year and the rest of my clubs can't be more than two years old," Munch retorted.

"The rest of your clubs?"

"Yeah, my clubs aren't that old, with the exception of the Wild-O's I bought, I mean, no way of telling how old the Dea—uh, the used clubs are."

"So, you still haven't completed a full set of our reconditioned clubs?"

"Well, no, still need a few, I guess."

"Let me ask you a question, Mr. Malone," came the reply.

"Sure. Shoot," Munch wrote.

Snarf could not resist. "Do ya' play better with the 'old' clubs or with the used Wild-O's, 'Peckerhead'?"

Snarf sat back in his chair. "OmiGod, what have I done," he thought. He eyed the ice cream with reproach. The damn stuff was too good. "I'm too freakin' wasted," he said. "I can't believe I just wrote 'Peckerhead'. I'm gonna' be drawn and quartered by **The Powers That Be.**"

"I thought you were assisting me, not calling me names," Munch shot back.

Dead Men's Clubs

The screen was silent for exactly 45 seconds as perspiration formed on Snarf's forehead, ran down his cheek, through his beard, finally dripping into his bowl of Pralines & Grass. He imagined **The Powers That Be** sitting on his shoulder—his throat went dry as he pictured Sink and War enraged. There would be hell to pay—literally—if he did not handle this right.

"Yes—'Peckerhead'. That's a fond nickname we give everyone who continues to play with inferior clubs when he knows full well our reconditioned clubs have improved his game. Mr. Malone, we consider you one of our best customers and we affectionately have referred to you as 'Peckerhead' each time you have placed piecemeal orders.

"Last time, when you purchased three of our clubs, we said to ourselves, 'You know, we may be able to finally drop the 'Peckerhead' and call him Munch—he seems to be ready to buy the driver, five wood, seven wood, nine iron, 52 degree wedge, and putter that would allow him to complete a full set of reconditioned Wild-O's.' And I would urge you to do that, sir," Snarf wrote, sitting back, hands in mid-air above the computer, fearing they would be singed if he touched the keys. His underarms produced saddlebacks of sweat as he waited.

Silence.

Snarf felt a slight panic. He realized it was not his best work. "Peckerhead" was too pejorative–too in your face. He should have apologized. He had screwed up. Were the hinges to the gates of Hell really that hot? What the devil would he do? For that matter, what would the **Devil** do? "I'm a mess," he thought, as he saw a reply begin to appear.

"Well, I'll say this; I've called myself some names worse than that on just about every round I've played. And the clubs do seem to make a difference," Munch wrote.

Yes! Thank you Jesus! Snarf shouted aloud, pounding the desk, causing Pralines to splatter.

"One thing," Munch wrote.

"Yes?" Snarf typed.

"Are these clubs people traded in for new Wild-O's, or—are they 'Dead Men's Clubs'?" Munch asked.

"Shit, how did he know?" Snarf said to himself. He had to think of a reply that Munch would find reasonable.

"If you mean by the term 'Dead Men's Clubs,' the dearly departed, there is absolutely no way for us to know if the golfers who owned our reconditioned clubs are living or deceased. We are certain, however, that the clubs speak for themselves—superbly engineered and better than new," Snarf composed.

"Well. I agree, doesn't make much difference where they come from, just where they make the ball go," Munch gushed.

"Thanks for liking our clubs, Mr. Malone. Wild-O Golf is prepared to send you, as a three-month trial offer, the seven aforementioned items at the quoted $10.95 per club price. If you don't care for these clubs after three months' play, you may return them at no charge," Snarf wrote, lobbing one over the net.

"Well, thanks. That would be great. Even a 'Peckerhead' can't beat that!" Munch replied.

Snarf had almost forgotten his big order: Build confidence—go for the club championship!

"We'll send the clubs right out. With the full set we find our customers often improve their game to a new level. Many compete for their club championships. Some have gone on to win state open competitions and a select few have participated in the USGA Senior Men's Amateur Golf Championship. We here at Wild-O Golf believe you are one of those rapidly improving customers who can go all the way," Snarf ventured through the ether.

"No kidding, wow," Munch thought to himself. His fingers

moved across the keyboard, "Well, thanks. My game *is* better. I shot an 85 yesterday. The only thing I'm concerned about is whether I can possibly keep that up," Munch confessed.

"Oh, Mr. Malone, with these additional clubs, we believe there is absolutely no question that you will continue to see steady progress. Good luck from all of us at Wild-O Golf."

End of the chat. Snarf was exhausted. Time for another bowl of Pralines & Grass and a nice porno flick.

Nine

"Yes?" Short Sale John said, looking up from his desk.

"Sir," said Janie Germaine, Short Sale's assistant of 15 years, "there is some rather strange activity on our website."

"Yes?"

"Seems a Mr. Munch Malone is in our system and is getting clubs on a three-month trial basis."

"We don't do that," Short Sale said, returning to the documents on his desk.

"Somehow we did, sir," Janie said.

"Is he a regular customer?"

"Yes. Seems he is buying with regularity. And, somehow, the latest clubs we sold him, on approval, were $10.95. He bought a set of three clubs earlier for $25 and no charge for two day delivery."

"Bullshit, we don't sell clubs for less than our cost, and we don't provide free freaking shipping."

"Yes, sir. But it seems we did this time. A SNAFU in the system, I expect," Janie replied.

"Well, fix it," Short Sale said, returning to yesterday's sales numbers.

"Sir, that will take some time—I mean to find out how we made the mistake."

Short Sale looked at Janie and realized she might be just a tad smarter than he and the rest of the Wild-O executive team. She had stuck with him through thick and thin and was invaluable. She held herself erect and fancied black horn-rimmed glasses. She was gorgeous. Long blonde hair, breasts that were just right, and legs up to here and beyond, with the short skirts to prove it. She stood a staggering six feet.

"Okay, Janie, what do you suggest?"

"I think we forget about the price. Let him have the clubs he bought in his last two orders at the discounted prices and let the 'three month trial' offer stand until we find how we screwed up. Meantime, we'll watch the system, target Malone's name, and ring a bell when we again notice any activity by him—just to see if it's our fault or if he has a system of his own," Janie said, adjusting her glasses.

"Okay, do it," Short Sale grunted, returning to the numbers that were to be sent to "The Shit".

Munch's clubs arrived.

The wife was not pleased.

"For God's sake, Munch," she snorted, opening the front door, spotting a FedEx package from Wild-O Golf.

"More clubs?"

"Not a big deal, honey," Munch assured her, hauling the package down the hall toward the garage. "This completes my set—no more to buy! And these are on approval. I can keep 'em three months and send them back if they don't improve my game."

"Munch, you said you'd be happy if you ever broke a hundred, and you just shot an 85," Melinda protested, with arms folded, a frown upon her face.

"I know, I know, but the guy at Wild-O Golf said a full set could take me all the way to the top." Munch exclaimed, stopping to tear the package open.

"To the top?" Melinda questioned, leaning back against the doorframe to the garage, raising her eyebrows.

"Uh, yeah," Munch said, his face turning slightly crimson.

"What is—the top?" she asked.

"Well, you know, the top," he replied.

"The top?"

"Club champion," Munch muttered in a barely audible voice.

"Whaaaat?" she said, cupping her ear and leaning forward.

"Well, you know, this Wild-O guy said I could become Club champion, maybe even win the state open and get into the U.S Senior Men's Amateur Championship," Munch said, pulling the driver out of the FedEx box, followed by the fairway woods, dragging them into the garage.

"Munch, babe," Melinda retorted, following close behind the new shipment of clubs, "the guy is a salesman. He just wants to sell you clubs. Do you *really* need more clubs?" Melinda said, dramatically pointing toward the garage wall, where nine golf bags were neatly lined up, each bulging with hardware.

"Well, those are *not* Wild-O reconditioned clubs," Munch retorted, stomping his foot on the concrete floor for effect.

Silence.

"Ya' know, Mel, every great golfer has his own brand of clubs. A guy has to have a brand," Munch exclaimed, swinging the driver.

"Yes," she responded, turning, walking out of the garage, "Nike for Tiger, MacGregor for the Shark, and 'Used and Abused' for Munch Malone."

"Well—thanks for that vote of confidence, Mel," Munch said to the walls of the garage as he absentmindedly swung the driver. "Damn, that feels good."

Munch loved Melinda with all his heart, but she just had to

understand; golf was his passion. He brooded. He hated to have any dispute with her. His mind drifted to almost thirty years ago when he had first met Melinda. He realized now that it was true, timing is everything. He had boarded a US Airways flight out of Washington D.C., back in the days when he traveled in the first class section. He immediately opened his briefcase, scanning documents in preparation for a meeting in New York. He was engrossed in his reading and grunted when the flight attendant asked him to please fasten his seat belt for takeoff, asking him if she could stow his briefcase overhead.

"Sure," Munch said, glancing up, staring straight into the eyes of a beautiful woman whose cascading dark hair flowed off her shoulders. Their eyes met, and Munch was gone. Throughout the flight he could not take his eyes off her, twisting and turning in his seat as she worked the first class section of the airplane. He caught her name on the US Airways badge she wore. "Melinda," he said to himself, and attempted conversation as she freshened his coffee.

"How long have you been flying?"

"Just over three years."

"Where are you from, originally?"

She brushed the hair back from her eyes, flashing a smile, "Well, from someplace you've never heard of, a map dot."

"That would be—?"

She finished pouring the coffee and smiled again. "That would be No Trees, Texas."

"No Trees, up in the Panhandle."

"Yes! I can't believe it! Are you from Texas?"

"Nope, but I've been all through that area with oil and natural gas clients. Not much there, but they sure have some big football stadiums."

"You've got that right, football is a way of life in No Trees," she laughed.

"Bet you were a cheerleader or majorette, or the beauty queen."

"Majorette—and beauty queen," she grinned.

Melinda returned with coffee several times and Munch began to feel as though he were going to float off the plane when they landed; coffee or love? On the last refill, he made his move.

"My name is Malone, Munch Malone," he said, handing her a business card.

"Your name is Munch?" Melinda laughed.

"Yeah, well, my mother named me 'Henderson', but that went by the wayside in grade school. I was always munching on potato chips, and the other kids nicknamed me 'Munch'. The name stuck."

"How funny, Munch!"

"Are you based in D.C.?" Munch asked, trying to change the subject.

"Yes, based in D.C., a long way from Texas," she said, taking his card.

"I live in Arlington; I have a business there, how about you?"

"I share a place with two other stews in Alexandria."

"I don't want to be presumptive or out of line, but could I call you some time?"

Melinda glanced at Munch's left hand. No ring.

"Well, I guess any guy who's been to No Trees, Texas can't be all that bad," she teased.

"Great! Are you home tomorrow, or working?"

"I have three days before I fly again," she said, writing her telephone number on Munch's card and handing it back to him, once more flashing that incredible smile beneath the thickest, most luxurious hair he had ever seen.

The months that followed were filled with dinners at Café Milano in Georgetown and Landini Brothers on King Street in Alexandria, a cruise on the Potomac, long evening walks, and weekend excursions.

Six months to the day after they met, they journeyed to Virginia and The Inn at Little Washington, where they were married.

Two years later the first child arrived, a son. A daughter appeared the following year. Melinda quit flying when she became pregnant with their first child and joined Munch as a consultant in his burgeoning travel business. It was a great marriage. Twenty-five years later, they sold their company and moved to Hilton Head Island, South Carolina.

"She'll come around," Munch said to himself, still fondling the Wild-O in his hands.

"Okay. Our boy has the full set!" Sink grinned as he slid into the white booth. He rubbed his hands together and said to War, "Time to get started!"

Sheila needed no instructions. She readied the gin and single malt, adding an additional half-ounce to each glass because the old boys looked as though they were in a good mood. "What the hell," she thought, pulling her top down another inch or two. "They do look fine," she thought, admiring her breasts, "and they should be out there." She hesitated only slightly—it was okay. These boys had already had their heart attacks.

Sheila leaned low and delivered. War and Sink smiled collectively, realizing this was indeed a special day. The cleavage was, as that bald guy who filled the big screen during basketball season would say, "Huge, baby, huge!"

"He needs to start winning tournaments," War said, returning to the business at hand. "I say we start the process. He can easily win the club honors, then move on to something regional and break into a big one. He can do it now."

"We should really wait a year, let him build up to it," Sink cautioned, half heartedly trying to dissuade War. Truth to tell, however, Sink also could not bear to wait that long.

"**The Powers That Be** could change their minds at any time," War said, closing the deal.

"Okay. We'll go for it. Club championship, then, regional competition. He'll qualify for the USGA Senior Amateur Championship if we have any luck at all. Remember, War? You and I almost made it, you finished fourth one year and I finished third the following year," Sink said.

"I've heard that tale too many times, what's your point?" War said, irritated that Sink had a better finish and would never let War forget it.

"Point is, we'll win it this time. We can't miss with a team with a combination of your long balls and my short game. Malone can't miss, long as he has our clubs. Always wanted to win the big one, Sink smiled, slapping War on the back. "Life is good today, Long Balls," he said.

Sheila smiled at the reference and the "Johnson" twanged again.

Ten

Munch was the talk of the Club. He enthusiastically entered the Club Championship competition and had no fear. His confidence had gone from near zero to high on the Richter scale. Munch could not wait to hit the ball. It was his first thought every day.

"Another day of golf?" Melinda smiled at him over morning coffee and the newspaper, her "mad" long ago forgotten.

"Got that right, babe—first round of the Club Championship," he chortled, dishing oats out of his bowl.

She was happy for him, but concerned all the same. "Munch, you know how golf is, it comes and goes," she cautioned.

"Hey, I know that, honey," he beamed, "but I just feel so confident now and, you know, everybody says it's a mind game. Whoever said the most important distance in golf is the space between your ears was right," Munch said, wolfing down a piece of toast. He swallowed the rest of his coffee and said, "See you around five, babe," and bolted for the door.

Dave Rambo was on the range watching Munch hit. Damndest thing he'd ever seen. Munch looked like a pro.

"Pretty amazing, isn't it?" Eugene Columbus said, sauntering up to Dave.

"I'd say it's more a miracle than amazing," Dave said, his mustache curling into a smile.

Ball after ball, straight down the line.

"How's John Henry?" Eugene asked.

"Just tolerable. I think he has a hard time knowing that Munch beats him every day now," Dave said.

"Well, shit, he does that to me too, and everybody else out here. He's going to take this tournament, no doubt about it. No one can believe it," Eugene said, laughing out loud.

Munch gazed from the first tee down the fairway from the tips—398 yards, dogleg right.

He then glanced at something that had never before occurred in Club history—he had drawn a gallery of Club members, thanks to a note at the end of this morning's column by a sports writer for the *Island Packet*, Hilton Head's daily newspaper. Sports scribe Matt Moss had written, "Ocean Pines Country Club golfers are astounded by member Munch Malone's torrid advance. The meteoric rise has placed Malone in the low-handicap flight in the Club Championship that begins today. This columnist is not certain, but is quick to say that the incredible advance may be a record anywhere in the country. Club members who know Malone say he uses only reconditioned clubs and Wild-O is his brand. If Malone does well in the championship competition, Wild-O Golf may well see Island golfers scurrying for their reconditioned clubs."

"Munch, you 'da man'," shouted a local standing by the tee box at number One.

Munch felt his stomach muscles tighten. He glanced nervously at the crowd of almost 100 men and women, avid golfers at Ocean Pines. He bounced up and down on the balls of his feet. Fleeting thoughts of topping the ball crossed his mind.

"No, no, Munch my lad, no willies this round," War Danson said, watching the giant screen before him. He closed his eyes and felt the Wild-O driver in Munch's grasp.

Serenity flowed through Munch as he sensed the club coming

alive in his hands. He drew back his weapon, cocked his wrists, and executed a perfect swing, cutting the corner over the large live oak 250 yards away. When the white sphere finally rolled to a stop it was ninety yards from the green.

There was silence from the stunned crowd, followed by loud cheers, whistles and a repeated chorus of "You 'da Man!" Munch had just hit a 308-yard drive.

"Holy shit," Dave Rambo said as he stood on the tee before positioning his ball for his drive. "Let's call this thing off right now."

Rambo, Eugene, and John Henry took their time and studied the approach. Each had respectable shots that reached normal landing areas. They were in the hunt, but they knew Munch was playing way above his head.

Munch felt good but nervous. He wanted to light a cigar as he pranced toward what would be just his second shot, but thought better of it as he realized all eyes were on him. He turned to check out who was watching him and saw Matt Moss running toward him.

"Hey, Mr. Malone! Matt Moss from the *Island Packet*, got a second?"

Munch glanced sideways as he heard the name. "Hey yourself, Matt, read your column this morning."

"Whaddya' think?"

"Well, I appreciate it and all, but, frankly, that really puts the pressure on, you know what I mean? And, please, call me Munch."

Okay Munch," Moss grinned broadly, "what's the secret?"

"What secret?" Munch said, squinting at Moss.

"The secret to your success. Nobody does what you've done overnight."

"Wasn't overnight, I've played for over thirty years."

"Yeah, but you never played like this. And it all happened so fast. Who's the pro? Who's the golf instructor?"

"Don't have one."

So, you must have a gimmick, a secret—you've found the Holy Grail?" Moss grinned.

Munch blushed and said, "Biggest thing that has happened to me is the clubs."

"Yeah, everybody at the club says you hit only used Wild-O's."

"Not used—reconditioned—'Dead Men's Clubs'. Now, 'scuse me, Matt, I gotta' concentrate."

Munch walked away as Moss whistled to himself and hurriedly scribbled "Dead Men's Clubs" in his reporter's notebook. Munch stepped to his ball after watching his partners hit their second shots. Rambo to the right, Eugene in the rough, John Henry in the middle of the fairway.

Munch addressed his ball with his wedge. Wild-O. Ninety yards out.

The energy flowed. The ball was struck. It sailed skyward and rolled left of the pin to the back of the green, veering right, and dropping neatly into the hole.

Eagle.

Matt Moss's jaw dropped. John Henry stared in disbelief, "That's one lucky old fart," he said, shaking his head. Eugene Columbus applauded loudly. Dave Rambo grinned broadly, stroking his mustache. The gallery roared.

Moss underlined the words "Dead Men's Clubs" in his reporter's notebook.

"*Uh, oh,*" Sink said, *downing his scotch, watching Moss repeat the underline several times.*

Eleven

Matt Moss slammed the door to his Honda and rushed into the *Packet* newsroom. He went directly to his desk, sat down at his cluttered desk and punched the keys on his computer.

Google responded and Matt searched the Wild-O Golf website. He found the reconditioned clubs page and began his hunt. No contact names were listed. He dialed the number shown on the site and, after talking with a sales rep, a secretary and an assistant, was finally directed to Janie Germaine, Senior Executive Assistant to Mr. John Short, Vice President, Wild-O Golf Reconditioned Clubs.

Short Sale John was in a foul mood. Not only had he been demoted to head Reconditioned Sales, those sales were down and "The Shit", Marcus Appleton, was on his ass daily, threatening to fire him if his numbers did not improve.

His phone rang. Janie Germaine said, "Mr. Short, there is a sports reporter on the line from the Hilton Head *Island Packet*. It's a newspaper down there, Mr. Short. The reporter's name is Matt Moss, and he says he would like to interview you for a story he's working on."

"Janie, I am not in the mood for a quiz by a sports reporter from fly-over country."

"Sorry, sir, but he says you will like the story. He sounds legit. I advise you to take the call."

"What the hell, at least its not another blast from "The Shit." Put him through."

"Mr. Short?" Moss began.

"Yeah, John Short. Look, I'm busy here, whaddya' want?"

"I thought Wild-O Golf might be interested in a guy named Munch Malone."

"Why's that?"

"Well, he's burning up the fairways at a club championship down here in South Carolina."

"So? Big deal."

"Yeah, well, maybe bigger than you think."

"Look pal, I'm busy here and I don't have time to chat about some amateur golf tournament. Goodbye."

Short Sale slammed the phone into its cradle. He looked out the window at the city of New York and sighed to himself as he put fingers to his temples.

"God, what am I doing?" he thought. "I'm a nice guy. I normally deal with people very well, but I just treated a reporter like crap. Am I losing it? Old Short Sale, the schmuck, with 'The Shit' on his ass. What am I gonna' do to put some juice behind these lousy sales numbers?"

The phone rang again.

"Yeah?"

"Sorry, Mr. Short. Mr. Moss again. He says you really need to speak with him. Shall I say you just stepped out?" Janie said.

"No, no, I'll talk with him, can't piss off a member of the Fourth Estate and I just did—I think," Short Sale said, taking the call.

"Mr. Short, Matt Moss again," the reporter said, gazing at his reflection in the window and thinking to himself, "My God, I'm practically bald. I've got to get some of that 'grow hair' stuff."

"Sorry, Matt, just call me John. I do apologize—I don't

normally go off like that but have you heard that song, "You've Had a Bad Day?"

Matt chuckled, running his fingers across his scalp. "Hey John, we all have them. But maybe I can make your day a little better. I'm doing a story about this Munch Malone because the guy says he has a unique reason for his sudden success."

"Yeah, what might that be?"

"Well, he says he went from a 33 to a 3 handicap because he uses Wild-O reconditioned clubs."

"Huh?"

"Yeah, the guy has a bag full of your used clubs and he touts them as the reason he can play scratch golf. Any comment?"

"Well, uh, I dunno. Are you sure he's using our clubs?"

"Yes. Checked them out in the bag and they were Wild-O's all right. But, of course, he could have gotten Wild-O's anywhere. Could you verify if he really bought them from you, and if they're used, and call me back? I wanna' do the story, regardless, but if they really are *used* Wild-O's, it'll be a neat twist that might get some national play—couldn't hurt Wild-O sales."

Short Sale suddenly felt a glimmer of enthusiasm as his mind considered the possibilities.

"Right, Matt. I'll get right on it and call you back ASAP."

"Thanks John. I really need to know if they are verifiably used, because Malone refers to them as 'Dead Men's Clubs'."

Short Sale's smile faded as Matt hung up the phone. "Shit and double shit. 'Dead Men's Clubs'. Now *there's* a marketing slogan."

"Janie!" Short Sale bellowed.

Janie pounced through the door, notepad in hand. Short Sale briefed her on the call and asked if she had ever heard of Munch Malone.

"Verified, sir," Janie said, adjusting her horn rimmed glasses and brushing back her blonde hair. "Mr. Malone is the—"

"Janie?"

"Yes, Mr. Short?"

"Must you always address everyone as 'Mr.'? You've been with me for, what, 15 years? And you still call me 'Mr.' Just call me John, for God's sake."

"Yes, Mr. Short," Janie responded, and continued, "Mr. Malone is indeed in our database."

Short Sale sighed as Janie, all six feet of her, went on.

"Mr. Malone, you may recall, Mr. Short, was tagged a short time ago—uh, I mean a little while ago—by our system as buying reconditioned clubs on a trial basis, something we do not allow. As you recall, however, sir, you decided to let Mr. Malone keep clubs he bought from us at a discount and to extend his three-month trial period for the clubs—until we determined if Wild-O Golf had erred, or if Mr. Malone is hacking our system—sir," Janie said, removing her classes and lowering her notepad.

"I did?"

"Yes, sir. I urged you to take the reporter's call because I recognized Mr. Malone's name," Janie said.

"The name does ring a bell. How many clubs has the guy bought?"

"Fourteen so far," sir.

"A full set?"

"Yes sir. No duplications, a full set."

"Really? Must like 'em."

"There's something else, sir."

"Yeah?"

The clubs he purchased."

"Yeah, yeah?"

"Well, our records show the clubs were acquired by Wild-O Golf from two ladies—widows."

"So?"

"Most unusual, sir," said Janie, shoving her glasses back over her hair, shaking her head, golden strands tossing back as she did so. "We don't know how Mr. Malone did it, but he apparently searched our database and selected particular clubs acquired from a Mary Lu Lair and Kathryn Danson, both widows. I Googled them. It took some time, but I found some interesting things about their husbands."

"Such as?"

"Well, Mr. Danson was a Congressman from Michigan. Actually, he was a long-time chairman of the House Appropriations Committee."

"You know, that rings a second bell, Warren Danson from Michigan. Helluva' a golfer, too."

"Exactly, low handicapper, good enough for the tour when he was young, so they say. And Mrs. Lair was married to a gentleman by the name of Sink Lair; he had one of the largest heavy equipment companies in the country, and—get this, he was a scratch. And here's the kicker, both men played in the USGA Senior Amateur Championship and did very, very well. 'Helluva golfer,' as you say—that applied to both of them."

"Wait a minute, are you saying that this guy Malone knew which clubs he wanted—he went for the clubs Danson's and Lair's widows sold us—he knew these two guys, Danson and Lair, were balls out golfers?"

"It appears so, sir."

"Whoa, wait a minute, this guy is scamming us."

"Well, impossible to say. He's a good customer and he *might* want the clubs he bought because they belonged to good golfers, but how could he know? It's also possible someone else is hacking us, pretending to be Mr. Malone."

"Okay, let's think about this," Short Sale said, motioning for Janie to take a seat, sinking back in his office chair, swiveling to take in the Big Apple on a rainy day. He perched his fingers as a tent and touched his chin.

"This guy Malone, or an imposter who pretends to be Malone, is a hacker. The hacker is selecting Wild-O Reconditioned and Malone goes from a 33 to a 3. The hacker selects clubs bought from Mrs. Danson and Mrs. Lair, whose husbands were both excellent golfers. With these clubs Malone is on his way to winning his Club's championship. He attracts attention from a reporter. The reporter wants a quote from me, from Wild-O Golf. The reporter thinks this will go national. And the reporter is hung up on 'Dead Men's Clubs'. Where is this going, Janie?"

Warren Danson and Sink Lair were wondering much the same thing as they prepared to report to *The Powers That Be*. Sink shook his head and said, "The reporter, I just don't like it."

"What's not to like?" Lair asked, reading through his notes.

"Well, the reporter is no dummy. Munch's reference to 'Dead Men's Clubs' sounds like a headline to me. If the newspaper goes with that, *The Powers That Be* are not gonna' like that one damn bit," War worried.

"I think you're right, and Wild-O Golf isn't going to like it one bit either," Sink said.

"I'm not so sure about that. There may be a different reaction at Wild-O; every duffer in the world will identify with Munch, if he wins, and gets good media play," War said.

"Did you say 'If' he wins'?" Sink asked, smiling.

Twelve

The Powers That Be sat at a white conference table, awaiting Sink Lair and Warren Danson. The Council had approved the experiment when Sink and War had first made the request, but they did so with caution. The green light to proceed was given only after receiving a nod of approval from **The Highest Authority**. It came with the warning there should be no surprises or embarrassment from the endeavor.

Brawley Rollins, as Chairman, had called the Council meeting as soon as he read Matt Moss' story. He was concerned **The Highest Authority** would not be pleased that the "experiment" had resulted in a newspaper story referencing "Dead Men's Clubs".

The Council, comprised of five individuals, sat in silence as they waited for Sink and War to appear. Brawley took the time to reflect on the golfing interests of his Council members; as a teenager, he himself was an avid golfer. He could have been a contender but he gave up the game when he went off to college, chasing every skirt on campus. He was a hell raiser, still fondly remembered and revered at his drinking fraternity. Brawley eventually found Jesus, straightened up, and built a large and highly successful accounting firm in Atlanta.

Brawley looked down the table at Sid Belch. Sid was a disgruntled lawyer from Connecticut who had never held a club in his hands and tended to distrust golfers. As far as Belch was concerned, he would have wasted his valuable billing time of $450 an hour if he had chased a little white ball. It made no damn sense to Sid. He had told Brawley a man could bill a minimum six hours in the time it took to pack golf clubs in the car, drive to the course, play eighteen holes, drink two beers, drive home and unload the clubs. It was "Balderdash," Sid had said.

Balancing Sid Belch's mistrust of golf and the golfing world was a council member who had been an exceptional player. Big Bill McElfee had been magnificent in his day. He had been a corporate manager with one of the large chemical companies in the Ohio Valley. Slight of build, he could out slam the big boys by 30 yards every time. The name "Big Bill" simply saluted his prowess. Big Bill had been in favor of the idea posited by Sink Lair and War Danson from the beginning.

Rounding out the council were two characters that had been very colorful before they got here. One was a Hispanic boxer named "Retro Elvis" who had fought as "The King in the Ring." Retro's real name was Cole Bissett. He had completed 24 fights and had come close to a welterweight title because of a strong right hook. Bissett, adept at utilizing powerful public relations, invented the name "Retro Elvis" to capture media attention. Retro did not even think about golf—there were no golfers in the Jungle Room.

The last, but not least, council member, was the only female of the group, Betty Bonanza. She too used a pseudonym, legally acquired at age 21, because she hated her real name, "Theodopolous". Betty loved skydiving and was a professional instructor in the art for fifteen years before she quit the fly game, opening "Bonanza's Bar" in Marathon, in the Florida Keys. Regarding golf, Betty said she could jump either way.

"Don't know if we've got a problem or not," Brawley began, briefing the Council members on Matt Moss' story. "Could be a one-time thing, could be the beginning of a media avalanche. Either way, we assured **The Highest Authority** there'd be no surprises, no embarrassment. So, I thought we ought to call these fellas' in and get their take on this media thing," Brawley advised.

The Council nodded in agreement as Sink and War arrived, just outside the spectacular building that housed the offices of **The Powers That Be**. The Scotsman and Man O'War looked up at the massive white wooden doors that loomed above them. War reached out with both hands, lifting the giant knockers. He held them aloft and turned to Sink.

"Remind you of anyone we know?" he said, smiling, banging the knockers against the hardwood.

"All I want to know is why they called us here," Sink replied, shaking his head with a worried look.

The large white double doors opened slowly and they walked into a hallway leading to an enormous conference room.

The five council members sat at the end of a magnificent and ridiculously large table that was somehow dwarfed by the Dutch Masters paintings hanging on the walls and a vaulted ceiling that depicted the generations of men and women who had visited here.

"Wow, a combination of The Sistine Chapel and 'Network'," War whispered.

Sink shot a sideways glance at War and said under his breath, "Let's hope they're not mad as hell."

"Well, c'mon, c'mon down heah'," Brawley said, waiving a burly fist from the head of the table.

Sink stepped forward and began the march to the far end of the room.

"Morning Sirs and Madam," he began, flashing his best smile.

War strode behind him, observing Sink had assumed command.

Betty Bonanza smiled at the two and said, "I hear you boys have gone public."

Retro Elvis shifted in his seat.

War cleared his throat. Time to make his presence known. "No Ma'am, we have gotten some attention with this whole thing, but most folks think we are actually doing *The Lord's* work."

The Powers That Be were stunned into silence. No one was ever so direct, or so presumptuous to mention **The Highest Authority**, when appearing before **The Powers That Be**. Sink was in shock. War had just pied the type, as the old journalists up here were prone to say.

Sink rushed to undo the damage. "Uh, what Mr. Danson means is that we wish to assist you in solving the problem; creating a way for the millions of dedicated golfers here to again play the 'Royal and Ancient' sport."

Brawley sat in silence as the Council members turned their gaze from Sink to the Chairman, waiting for his response to Sink's refinement of War's affront.

"We approved your little experiment with the proviso that we did not want anything untoward to occur," Brawley said, pushing a button on the conference table that caused a High Def wide screen to lower from the ceiling. It displayed a picture of Matt Moss. "This here sports reporter is on to you boys. We're concerned that you've gone public," Brawley said, turning toward Sink and War. "Moss says you got this fella' Malone workin' hard down there, so I guess you've established a pretty good connection with all this 'Channeling'—that there 'Contagion' thing."

Sink breathed a sigh of relief that the Chairman seemed to be pleased with the success to date, even though he might be pissed with the publicity. Sink prepared to address the question when he was interrupted.

"Yes, Mr. Chairman, he is in play and we are confident the publicity will not hurt us," a voice from behind Sink said. Sink turned and saw War continuing his outburst, brushing past Lair, addressing the council.

Dead Men's Clubs

"Munch Malone is in sync with us. We have been able to 'Channel' him and we are gripping it and ripping it with expert 'Contagion'. Media contact was bound to occur with such phenomenal success. Not a problem," War beamed.

Sid Belch slowly raised his head where he had been engrossed in billing $450 an hour, reading through a stack of bank foreclosure appeals. "Say what?" he said. "How can media exposure help? This thing could get out of control and our involvement could become known. I don't like that at all. Not at all!" he bellowed, pounding the table with a hammy fist.

Sink shoved War to the side and said, "We have indeed been successful with our 'Contagion' and 'Channeling'. And I agree with the Congressman that the media coverage will not adversely affect the experiment or 'out' the involvement of the Council. Media exposure will certainly increase if our man Malone continues to win golf tournaments. But we are convinced the media will never expect your involvement."

"Where am I going with this?" Sink worried, thinking on his feet. He continued, with perspiration oozing down his back.

"We have been extremely successful in manipulating our chosen golfer through a Mr. Adams, a quite accomplished computer technician up here. He has done much of this by accessing the golf clubs Congressman Danson and I were using at the time of our arrival here. The clubs were reconditioned by Wild-O Golf and were for sale on the Wild-O website.

"Mr. Adams, through his technical expertise, made certain that only Mr. Malone could buy our golfing equipment and he has enabled us to control those, uh, 'Dead Men's Clubs' with which Mr. Malone is playing. It's working well; Mr. Malone has been buying our clubs for some time now and presently has a complete set of my, and the Congressman's, clubs," Sink said, ending with a wide smile.

"Waste of time," Belch muttered, returning to his documents.

"Mr. Lair," Big Bill McElfee began.

"Yes sir," Lair responded, turning to face "Big Bill." Lair had heard of Big Bill, and his history as a gifted amateur golfer, but had never met him. Now that McElfee was a member of **The Powers That Be**, he was seldom out in public. Sink could not believe how small Big Bill was. He knew they called him "Big Bill" because he could drive the ball more than 300 yards; it was incredible that one with such slight stature could tear the cover off a golf ball.

McElfee peered over the table top, revealing only his face and hands, which rested to the side of each of his ears. He smiled and got right to the point.

"As you may know, I was very much in favor of this experiment. Truth to tell, I would just love to get a club in my hands again. I'm pleased you have been able to, uh, 'Channel', your way into Malone's mind, and his body, but the media thing also bothers me a little. Can you assure us that we won't pick up the New York Times some morning and see a story about your involvement with Mr. Malone's game?" McElfee asked.

"Yes sir, we understand that 'Channeling' is hard to explain, but it's happening. Mr. Adams has apparently used the club grips as a conductor that transmits to a modem that sends to a server up here that streams to War and me when we watch Munch on High Def TV," Sink said, wondering if he was in any way close to what Snarf was actually doing.

"As to the likelihood of any reporter down there accepting a premise that heavenly powers are helping Malone, well, given the cynicism of the media, we don't think that'll ever happen," Sink said.

Belch again lifted his head. "Balderdash!"

Brawley leaned back in his chair, smiling sideways at Belch, wondering why he put up with the pompous ass. "Who's 'Channeling' better—playin' the better golf—you or Congressman Danson?" he asked, again addressing Lair.

"Actually, Mr. Chairman, I believe we're pretty even," Sink replied, "though Congressman Danson might disagree with me." War nodded in agreement.

"So, man," Retro Elvis said. "Far out, you just sit there watchin' TV and you feel it, huh?"

"Yes, that's right. Sort of like entering the ring in our own jump suit," War replied.

Sink rolled his eyes.

Bonanza Betty picked up the slack. "Mr. Lair, Mr. Danson. I'm told that your Mr. Adams is, how shall I say, unorthodox?"

"Thin ice," Sink thought, and replied, "Yes, that is true. He is certainly a 'techie' and gives little thought to his appearance. He has some strange ways, but he did qualify to be here and is, I believe, a good person."

Sid Belch's enormous head tilted forward. "I hear the boy's smokin' weed."

"No, sir. I can assure the Council Mr. Adams is not 'smoking' marijuana," Sink replied, fingers crossed behind his back.

"So, you boys have got this in hand, no surprises, right? You can handle the media thing?" Brawley asked.

"Most definitely sir," Sink answered.

"If we decide to let you proceed, what's next?" Brawley queried.

"Well, sir," War said, "Mr. Lair and I are entered in Mr. Malone's Club championship now. We hope to then advance to local and regional competition and, if successful, compete in the USGA Men's Senior Amateur Open."

"My, my," Big Bill grinned, "you fellows think a lot of yourselves."

"With all modesty Mr. McElfee, "we believe that a combination of Mr. Danson's game and mine will take us to great heights—or rather, take Mr. Malone there," Sink said.

"And then, would the experiment be over?" Brawley asked.

"Yes sir. We would present our final report then. We believe it will fully convince the Council that 'Contagion' is an excellent way to respond to the millions of requests to play golf while in residence here. Our work, and your willingness to let us continue, also will fulfill the dreams of the hackers down there like Mr. Malone," Sink replied.

"Council, may they proceed?" Brawley questioned, looking around the table.

Retro Elvis cracked his knuckles, adjusted his sunglasses, and said, "I'm in."

Belch grumped but did not protest. Betty Bonanza said, "I'm with Retro. I'll be interested to see how this plays out."

Big Bill gave a thumbs up.

"Awright boys, you may proceed. Just be sure—no surprises," Brawley said, banging his gavel, "Adjourned!"

Sink and War breathed deeply as they left the room, walking briskly through the courtyard and along a wide and glistening white path, eventually leading them to the street that would take them back to the Club.

"Stretched it a bit on Snarf and that weed question, didn't you?" War grinned as they strode over cobblestones of many centuries.

"Nope. Snarf does not smoke marijuana. He eats it," Sink replied, and the two old fellows jumped in the air as they did a high five.

Thirteen

Munch rolled over in bed and felt for Melinda. He located a warm and supple surface and rubbed up and down, his eyes closed

"Ummm—nice," he said. No response. Munch smiled, gently increasing his massage, opening his eyes as he did so.

Amalfi, their Maltese, was on his back, enjoying the tummy rub.

"Oh, sorry Malf," I thought I had hold of Mommy," Munch said, scanning the bed for his wife.

"Honey!" he shouted—"Babe, where are you?"

"In the kitchen, sweetie," came the distant reply. "Eggs and bacon, toast, grits—a real man's breakfast for my man," Melinda yelled, placing bacon slices on the griddle.

Munch looked at the Maltese in his bed and said, "Game day, Malf." He grabbed his bathrobe and headed for the kitchen, Amalfi following, tail wagging.

"Better hurry, Mr. Malone, the gallery awaits you," Melinda said, directing Munch's attention to the *Island Packet* as he planted a kiss on her cheek.

Munch rubbed his eyes and reached for his glasses. Matt Moss' column was on the front page of the sports section under a headline that said "All Eyes On Malone."

"What the?" Munch said, sitting down at the breakfast room table while Melinda shoved a coffee cup in his hand.

"Read all about it babe, you're the talk of the Island," she said.

Munch read with fascination and trepidation.

"All eyes are on Munch Malone in the Ocean Pines Country Club Championship on Hilton Head Island. Malone is the Ocean Pines golfer who has done something unheard of in the lowcountry. The remarkable progress of the 70-year-old-golfer has drawn a substantial gallery as word has spread that Malone may be a phenomenon that flies in the face of reason. He shot a seven under par 65 yesterday at Ocean Pines. He says he owes his newly found prowess to used Wild-O golf clubs; he refers to them as his 'Dead Men's Clubs'."

Question is, can he keep it up, or was it just one of those incredible days that an amateur experiences once in a lifetime? That's what the crowd will want to know today when Malone's foursome tees it up at 1:00 this afternoon."

Munch stood on the first tee box. He could hardly get his glove on. He fumbled with a new sleeve of golf balls, hoping he would not have to take a leak anywhere on the course. He estimated 500 people had turned out, incredible for a championship that normally drew only Club members. He glanced about, nervously shifting his gaze from the course to the crowd.

"My God, I don't know if I can do this," he murmured to himself, swinging his driver back and forth, attempting to loosen up.

"Sure you can," War smiled, imagining the driver in his hand, "Channeling" his thoughts to Munch. "Posture, eye on the ball, easy backswing and horizontal left arm over the shoulder—let it rip!" he said, in great anticipation.

Munch's swing found the driver's sweet spot and the ping that followed launched the ball, drawing it 250 yards, landing in the middle of the fairway.

The crowd burst into applause and Munch again heard the sound of "You da man!" ringing in his ear. Munch grinned and looked at Eugene, with whom he was paired.

"Very nice, very nice," Eugene said with a twinkle in his eye. Eugene then proceeded to match Munch's drive, to equal applause.

War was seated in the clubhouse with Sink and several spectators, golfers all, who had become aware of the experiment and wanted a first-hand look at the play.

Eugene selected a seven iron for his second shot. It landed short, to the left of the green. Munch pulled a nine iron from his bag.

"You sure? Nine iron? Pin's way back. Looks like 170 yards to me, Munch," Eugene warned.

"I know, man, but I just feel like I can do it," Munch said.

Sink took control. He closed his eyes, saw the green and swung. "Contagion".

The ball landed two feet from the hole.

Applause, shouts and high fives.

Munch finished with a birdie.

And so it went. War with the driver. Sink with the short game. These guys were good. They reveled in the competition and the congratulatory crowd that rushed Munch when he won the Club Championship going away.

"The big guys on the tour might take some lessons from a short little guy down in Hilton Head, South Carolina," wrote Matt Moss in a guest piece for *USA Today*. "Munch Malone, a local golfer at Hilton Head's Ocean Pines Country Club, set records in winning the club championship, lowering his handicap to a 1, causing speculation he may want to consider qualifying for the USGA Senior Men's Amateur Championship in the fall.

"Malone was a 33 handicap two months ago and has jaws dropping with his play. He has in his bag only used Wild-O golf clubs, calling them 'Dead Men's Clubs' because of his belief that the used Wild-O clubs he prefers were once owned by golfers who have checked out.

"This reporter has verified with the Wild-O Reconditioned Clubs Division that Malone is using its restored clubs. I can only tell you it is an incredible sight to see him wield the 'Dead Men's Clubs'. Malone is phenomenal at 70-years-of-age."

Fourteen

"Mr. Short," Janie said, "have you seen *USA Today*—today?" Short Sale John was in the middle of preparing his quarterly report for "The Shit".

"No, and I have not read the *Wall Street Journal*, or *People*, or the frigging *New Yorker*," Short Sale snorted, looking up over his glasses, grunting, reaching for his fourth cup of coffee that day.

"Well, no need to be short with me—I mean—uh, sarcastic, Mr. Short," Janie said, adjusting her glasses and turning slightly crimson.

"Sorry, Janie, sorry, 'The Shit' is on my ass, that's all," Short Sale said with a shrug.

"Oh, no problem, Mr. Short. It's just, well, you may want to read this," and she placed the *USA Today* on his desk, turned, and left the office.

Short Sale glanced at the newspaper with little interest and then read the words "Dead Men's Clubs" followed by the name "Munch Malone".

"Son-of-a-bitch!" he said, consuming the article. "Oh, my God, this is something. This is the guy that's been scamming us."

Short Sale punched the intercom, "Janie, back in here!" he screamed.

Janie, standing outside the door, strode into the office.

"Janie, this is the guy. He's the guy that's been scamming

us. What's he up to? He's callin' our clubs 'Dead Men's Clubs'. I mean, it's publicity and all that—but, is this good or terribly bad?" Short Sale stammered.

Janie adjusted her glasses.

"Well, Mr. Short, I have researched Mr. Malone and he appears to be, how do you say it…a 'stand up' guy. He seems to have been directed, somehow, to buy the clubs, and the offers of low price and trial periods seem to have been made by Wild-O Golf—or at least that's what the paper trail revealed as we reviewed emails and chat rooms."

"Why, in God's name, are our people doing that?" Short Sale demanded.

"Don't know. Seems like it just, well, just happens. Everybody in tech says they can't understand who is chatting with and directing Mr. Malone to various pages on our site. It's very mysterious," Janie answered.

"Never mind—we're in *USA Today* with friggin' 'Dead Men's Clubs', good or bad?' Short Sale asked.

"Well"—her glasses were adjusted and the six feet shifted from one long leg to the other—"it could, actually, be quite good. If Mr. Malone were to enter and be a contender in, say, the USGA Senior Men's Amateur, he could capture the imagination of a majority of golfers out there, those over 55, who would see him as having the answer to a better game," Janie smiled.

Short Sale got up from behind his desk, walked to the sales chart on the wall, and slammed his right fist into the palm of his left hand. "By God, I think you're right. This could be one friggin' big shot in the arm for Reconditioned Sales."

One floor above Short Sale's office Marcus Appleton put down his copy of *USA Today*. "Good, or bad?" also was his question, as his phone rang.

"Appleton, what's this story in *USA Today*? It says some guy is calling our reconditioned clubs 'Dead Men's Clubs'. What the hell is that all about?" D.E. Wildoe, CEO of Wild-O Golf snorted.

"OmiGod, my worst nightmare, Wildoe himself. This thing is not only bad, it's off the scale," Marcus thought. "Yes sir, I'm on it. The guy is using our reconditioned clubs all right, and apparently doing pretty well with them," he said.

"Yeah, but we can't have the guy calling them 'Dead Men's Clubs', can we? We'll sue his ass."

"Got that right sir, I'll get John Short in here and tell him to put a stop to it."

"I sure hope so, Marcus. I wanted you as President of National Sales because I thought you could market the hell out of us. Now I'm reading in friggin' national media that we are the distributors of 'Dead Men's Clubs'. My God, I thought I had a star in you, but this crap—I dunno'…"

"Sir, you'll see no more of this, I promise."

"All right then, handle it! And keep me posted," Wildoe instructed, cradling the phone.

"Cheryl!" Marcus shouted at his executive assistant.

"Yes sir!" Cheryl shouted back, walking into "The Shit's" office.

"Get Short Sale in here and get him in here now! I don't care if he is in the can, get him in here and get him in here now!"

"Let me get this straight, can or no can, you want him in here now!" Cheryl shouted.

"Yes, dammit, now!" "The Shit" screamed, his face turning crimson as the blood vessels in his neck swelled until they looked as though they would explode. "I just had a call from the freakin' CEO and I want Short Sale in here now!"

"Now!" Cheryl screamed.

"Now! Now! Now! " Marcus screamed back.

Up and down the halls at Wild-O Golf the heads were turning as "Now!" echoed through the corridors.

One employee turned to the next and said, in a whisper, "Now."

The recipient of the whisper responded with a "Now."

Soon "Now!" was being shouted by every employee around the floor, loud enough that D.E. Wildoe, seated in the penthouse, wondered what the hell was happening on the floor below.

Cheryl heard the shouts outside Marcus' suite and smiled.

Marcus walked to his office door, opened it, and shouted, "All of you need a big steaming cup of 'Shut the fuck up!' " His face flushed and one large vessel in the middle of his forehead bulged as he walked back into his office, bent down, coming to within an inch of Cheryl's upturned face. His eyes narrowed and the vessel seemed to expand even more as he hissed, "Now!"

Cheryl winked at him, smiled, and said "Yassuh, you want him in here now. Yes suh. Right away, suh." She saluted him, backing out the door, slamming it hard behind her, turning around.

The halls were filled with employees from throughout the executive offices. Several hundred concerned workers were crammed together, consternation on their faces, all looking at her. Silence for a moment, then Elizabeth Lauren, Vice President of Accounting, gave Cheryl a sympathetic smile and said, in a small voice "Now. Now."

One after another the men and women who had been bruised by "The Shit" picked up the cry, their voices growing louder by the minute, until, in unison, they began shouting, as loudly as possible, "Now! Now! Now!"

Within the hour John Short walked into Marcus Appleton's office, knocking on the doorframe as he did so. "I understand you wanted to see me, uh, *now*, Marcus?" he said.

"Damn right, what's this all about?" Marcus said, throwing the *USA Today* on the desk in front of Short Sale.

"Oh, yeah, I saw that. We know about this guy. We've been tracking him."

"You *know* about him, and you let him call our clubs 'Dead Men's Clubs'?" Marcus spat across the desk.

"Well, yes, we know about him, but we can't control what he says—we just know he somehow seems to have manipulated our website to buy only certain clubs," Short Sale said.

"Let me get this straight, Short Sale, you know someone is manipulating our site and you have done—what?"

John Short tugged at his shirt collar and looked away, gathered his courage, and looked back at "The Shit", wondering if he should return a soubriquet. "First, I don't appreciate being called 'Short Sale'; second, we're still trying to figure out how someone is hacking in; third, Malone's getting some great play out of the clubs; and, fourth, it could be some excellent publicity for us."

"Bullshit, bullshit, bullshit. I have just been reamed by our CEO who thinks; guess what, that 'Dead Men's Clubs' may not be the best brand we could have!" Marcus shouted, slamming his fist on his desk.

"Uh, yes, I heard that, I mean, we know that's not good, but we, uh, perhaps could ask Mr. Malone to not say that anymore—I mean, in reference to our clubs," Short Sale said.

"Fuckin' A, Short Sale! You tell that bastard that he stops calling them that or we will sue his ass from here to Bum Fuck Egypt and back!"

"Okay, Marcus, I'll make contact with Malone and apprise him of your position, but I don't know that it'll do any good."

"No, no, you don't 'apprise' him, you tell the son-of-a-bitch to stop immediately or we'll tear his throat out!" "The Shit" retorted.

Fifteen

Short Sale's plane touched down at the small Hilton Head Island airport at 10:45 in the morning. Janie had a car waiting for him. He tossed his briefcase in the rented Ford, threw his suit jacket in the back seat and climbed behind the wheel. It was hot and he was appreciative the air conditioning had been running long enough to cool his apprehension.

He pulled out of the parking lot, marveling that there was little traffic. Within minutes he was on Highway 278 toward Sea Pines Plantation. The Island was incredibly beautiful this morning; to his left Short Sale caught sight of a Great Blue Heron's wings as the majestic bird glided across a fairway of one of the Island's many golf courses, coming to rest beside a pond bordering a pristine green.

"Wow, picture book," Short Sale thought, contemplating his meeting with Munch Malone, scheduled for 11:30 at Ocean Pines Country Club. He drove through the roundabout at Sea Pines Circle on the south end of the Island and turned into the Visitors Center. He stopped at the drive-through window and was given a guest pass by a charming brunette who welcomed him to the "Plantation."

He proceeded to the Sea Pines gate and was waived through by an animated guard with the name "George" emblazoned on his uniform. George's right hand pointed one finger at the guest pass displayed on the car's dash, and did a little dance with his other fingers, ending with an arm sweep toward Greenwood Drive. In his rear view mirror Munch caught sight of George petting a Golden Retriever leaning out the car window, snatching a treat from George's outstretched hand.

Just inside the gate and to the right was Ocean Pines Country Club. Short Sale drove for just under a mile, passing immaculate homes. He turned right, into the Country Club property. Parking his car near the entrance to the Club, he walked across an impressive marble Ocean Pines logo embedded in the driveway and pulled open double doors where he was greeted by a smiling receptionist.

"Hi, I'm John Short, I'm having lunch with Mr. Malone," he said, approaching the desk.

"Welcome to Ocean Pines Country Club, Mr. Short. Mr. Malone is in the Pub waiting for you," the receptionist said with a smile. She motioned toward the far end of the club, next to the pro shop, where Malone was waiting.

Short Sale walked past a wall with a long line of wooden plaques featuring gold embossed names, listing club golf and tennis champions. Ocean Pines Country Club was extraordinarily beautiful with a breathtaking view of the Eighteenth green; it was framed by sea marsh and blue sky. The scene washed over Short as he walked into the Pub.

Short saw a paunchy fellow seated at a table, nursing a Michelob Ultra. The little guy looked up, saw Short Sale, pushed back his chair, got to his feet, extended his hand and said "Hi, Munch Malone, you must be John Short."

"Great to meet you, Mr. Malone," Short responded, thinking, "This guy is almost a scratch handicap? My God, he's shorter than I am."

Munch grinned, sensing Short's thoughts. "Ok, not what you

expected, huh? Call me 'Munch' and I'll call you John," Munch said.

"Wonderful," Short Sale said, smiling, immediately liking the guy, relaxing for the first time in days. He pulled up a chair and set his briefcase on the floor. Lunch was ordered as Munch regaled Short Sale with stories about Hilton Head, Ocean Pines Country Club, and the quality of life on Island.

"Munch, we're very proud that you are using Wild-O reconditioned clubs in this extraordinary run you're having," Short Sale said as "She-Crab" soup was placed before him. He adjusted a napkin, dipping a spoon into the soup. "Damn. That's delicious," he said.

From somewhere above the steaming bowl, he heard Munch say, "I'm flattered that you guys even know I'm a customer."

"Well, we were curious about you when you seemed to commandeer our website, selecting the very clubs you wanted, and then we were even more intrigued when that *USA Today* story came out," Short explained, wiping soup from his chin.

"I didn't 'commandeer' anything. Your chat room guy directed me to all my clubs."

"Really?"

"Yeah, it was like he knew me. Incredible what you're doing with the technology."

"Uh, huh."

"I tell you, John, when I hit those clubs it's like I'm someone else. I can't believe it! 'Dead Men's Clubs' are the best I've ever had!"

"Actually, Munch, you've just mentioned the real reason I'm here."

"What's that?" Munch asked, reaching for the pork sliders that appeared before him.

"Well, we would appreciate it if you would quit calling them

'Dead Men's Clubs,'" Short Sale said, smiling, preparing to make his pitch.

"Because—?" Munch queried.

"Bad for business. No one is going to buy our clubs if they think they're playing with 'Dead Men's Clubs,'" Short Sale said.

"Well, pardon my French, but, shit, why would that be so? I love these clubs, 'Dead Men' or not. I'm also thinking that any golfer out there would be glad to latch on to a 'Dead Man's Club' if they played like the clubs in my bag," Munch said. "You know, John," he continued, looking around the room, leaning in toward Short, whispering, "There's a theory, actually more than a theory. They did research at the University of Virginia that 'Contagion' may be at work here."

"Contagion?" Short said, his eyebrows lifting.

"Yeah, they quantified it with a study. If someone *thinks* he's playing with clubs once used by good golfers, he plays better."

"How do you know who owned your clubs?" Short asked.

"Well. I don't," Munch said, leaning back in his chair, "but *something* happens when I grip 'em, and I always get the feeling they were used by some guy who was one helluva' golfer."

Sink and War smiled proudly. They were starting to really like this guy.

"Right, right, could be, I guess; you know, the mind does amazing things."

'It's more than that, John. The clubs have some special power; I'm convinced of it. Don't think I'm crazy, I just know I can't play like this, gotta' be the clubs! Maybe this could happen to anyone if they were to get hold of Wild-O 'Dead Men's Clubs.'"

"I doubt it, Munch. I don't think just anyone can play like you, with or without our clubs," Short Sale said, hoping to please, wondering if Munch were, indeed, a little wacky, casting an eye at the dessert menu.

"Well, thanks for the compliment, but I sucked at the game before I bought those used Wild-O's. I'm convinced the clubs have given me Game, John. I don't wanna' hurt your business, but I'm damn sure I'll not be told what I can or cannot call my clubs by a company with which I have spent good money. You should be thanking me, not tryin' to tell me what I should or should not say about my golf game, golf clubs, or any other 'daggone thing,'" Munch protested, leaning back in his chair, crossing his arms over his chest.

"Agreed, agreed. We would not think of such a thing. I'm simply here to say we're concerned when we hear you say 'Dead Men's Clubs', and I flew down here to ask you, with all due respect and admiration, if you could simply refer to the clubs as 'Wild-O's', or 'Reconditioned Wild-O's'. Actually, I would prefer you'd say 'Reconditioned Wild-O's,' "Short Sale said, nervously glancing about the room, averting his eyes from Munch's glare.

"Tell you what, if you're *asking* me to do that, I'll do my best. If you're *telling* me, the answer's no, not on your life," Munch said.

"Asking, Mr. Malone, asking, by all means," Short Sale said, extending his hand across the table to Munch, salivating over the chocolate mousse that was placed before him.

Sixteen

The United States Senior Men's Amateur Golf Championship is a national tournament for amateur golf competitors at least 50 years of age. Sectional qualifying is required, with fifty-one sites around the country hosting the play. Those making the cut begin their quest for the Championship with 36 holes of stroke play; the top 64 competitors then advance to the match play portion of the tournament. Golfers must have a USGA handicap index of 7.4 or lower to enter. Six days of play are required to narrow the field to the final match play day.

At the insistence of his golf buddies, discussion with the Ocean Pines Club professionals, and the friendly guy in the Wild-O chat room, who always kept in touch, Munch began the process of qualifying. He had discussed it with Melinda, who encouraged him to "Go for it, babe."

With the assistance of the Club, Munch completed the process and crossed his fingers. He put the envelope containing the form in his pocket and drove to the Hilton Head Post Office on Palmetto Bay Road, mailing his application form.

"Look at that. He's got a Ronald Reagan stamp on that baby!" War yelled.

"Ronald Reagan?" Sink said, eyebrows lifting.

"Yeah, yeah, Reagan has his own stamp now, courtesy of the US Postal Service. I use Reagan stamps all the time," War replied.

"I thought you were a Yellow Dog Democrat."

"Yeah, but I loved Ronnie. Cut me a break, dammit."

"You're sending letters—from here?"

"Yeah, habit I guess. I'm not sure if anyone's getting them, but think of the surprise. Here's a letter from old War. My God, he died years ago."

Word from the USGA came back in ten days. Munch tore open the envelope as Melinda watched. He slowly perused it, smiled, held back tears, reached for his wife, and gave her a hug and kiss. He gave the letter to her and she began to read.

"Yes!" Munch shouted, doing a high five, dancing around in the kitchen, shouting, "I'm in!"

"Yes, by golly, you are, Munch. I can't believe it. This is amazing." Melinda said, shaking her head, laughing. "Hey babe," he responded, we're going to Music City!"

Sectional qualifying for Munch was at Belle Mead Country Club in Nashville. Munch and Melinda stayed at the Opryland Hotel, visited Tootsie's and made the pilgrimage to the "Grand Ole Opry". Munch loved the "Opry" and he loved the course. He qualified with what appeared to be an effortless round on the 6,732 yards of Bermuda grass. He finished six under with a 66 on the par 72 course, catching the eyes of Nashville media who had noted Matt Moss's story about "Dead Men's Clubs".

The Nashville Tennessean was impressed, topping the sports section with Malone's achievement: "Belle Mead's USGA Senior Men's Amateur got a look at South Carolina's Munch Malone this week. At 70-years-of-age, he's the oldest golfer ever to seek the amateur Championship. He's not only in a very select group; he's rather unorthodox in his choice of clubs. Malone plays with Wild-O reconditioned clubs, referring to them as his 'Dead Men's Clubs'. Some say he believes in 'Contagion', a theory that an object, in this case, golf clubs, somehow absorbs the qualities of its previous, now deceased, owner. Judging from Malone's performance at Belle Mead, the golfers who owned his clubs were quite good indeed."

As their plane touched down at Hilton Head, Munch's elation post Belle Mead turned to apprehension. The USGA Senior Men's Amateur Championship tournament would begin in three weeks at the famed Greenbrier Resort in White Sulphur Springs, West Virginia. The next twenty-one days would be the longest of his life as he ventured to and from rounds at the Club, worrying he might embarrass himself or South Carolina if he performed badly. "My God," he thought, "I may be in way over my head."

The stress grew, day by day.

"Mel!" Munch yelled, packing his suitcase in their bedroom. "Where's that Tiger Woods shirt I bought over at Palmetto Bluff?"

"Got it right here, babe," she said, exiting the laundry room where the dryer was pounding out golf shirts, shorts and socks. You'll need at least four shirts and I'd take six pairs of slacks. You'll need a blue blazer for evenings and any official function. And don't forget to pick out the socks and underwear you want."

"Okay, okay, nervous as a cat," Munch said. Amalfi barked. "Sorry, Malf," Munch said, leaning over to rub Amalfi under the chin. "I love my little guy, yes I do, such a good little guy, my baby! Will the little man cheer for his daddy today?" Munch chortled as Melinda leaned against the counter, taking in the scene, rolling her eyes.

"Amalfi gets all the attention, USGA man, how about the little woman, maybe she could calm you down with a little *action?*" she teased, moving next to him, rubbing his back. Munch grinned broadly, embracing her. "Where's my Viagra? Let's get it on, luscious," he said, grabbing for her, burying his head in her throat, wondering where his iPod was—thinking he needed to dial up some Marvin Gaye, obediently following as Melinda led him to their bedroom.

Seventeen

Day One of the USGA Senior Men's Amateur Championship. The Old White Course at The Greenbrier was simply stunning this sunny and cloudless September day. Munch Malone was in a field of 156 amateurs, all ready to climb the mountain. Bobby Jones was in the mind of each player who awoke that morning. Could this be done?

Munch stood on the putting green striking ball after ball, watching them go into the cup. He had drawn a small crowd.

"Hey, Munch, how are the 'Dead Men's Clubs'?" Matt Moss asked, approaching from the rear.

"Ah, Mr. Moss, I see you have broadened your coverage to the fabulous Greenbrier," Munch replied.

"Pretty exciting, huh, gorgeous setting, Munch," Moss said, spreading both hands and looking around at The Greenbrier's expanse of green lawns and Old South. "Magnolias and sweet tea. Quite a place for 'Dead Men's Clubs', don'tcha' think?"

"Yep, I love these Wild-O's and I feel good today, Matt," Munch answered, being careful not to parrot Moss's club reference.

"I saw the Tennessee newspapers," Moss responded.

"Whaddya' mean?"

"C'mon, you know what they said! I'm pretty confident you read your own clippings."

"Not really," Munch fibbed.

"OK, have it your way, Munch," Moss laughed. "They said some folks believe you put a lot of credence into that UVA study; that your clubs were owned by some pretty good golfers and you're now playing like them."

"Look, Matt, I don't know what causes me to play like this and I don't care. All I know is, I play damn well with these clubs."

"That's an understatement. So, you don't discount the 'Contagion' theory; somebody up there is 'Channeling' to you?"

"At this point, Matt, I don't discount anything."

"Okay. Go get 'em, Munch, make the old geezers out there proud," Moss said, fist bumping Munch.

"I am sure as hell gonna' try," Munch assured him, gently fondling a three wood in his hands.

Munch did make the senior set proud, thanks to some exquisite 'Channeling' from above. Both War and Sink hit the ball as well as they ever had. All quarreling about who was the best golfer disappeared as they delighted in Munch's performance that electrified the crowd. Munch was sensational as he blew by the field, winning in a manner that caused the gallery to roar and the media to extol his play.

Melinda held her breath until the very last putt of the day and raced across the Eighteenth green to embrace Munch. "I love you, babe!" she shouted above the din, throwing her arms around Munch's neck. He gave her a kiss as he held the Wild-O putter aloft. "Pretty freakin' amazing, Mel, this is one hell of a ride," he said.

Moss filed with the *Associated Press*. He had been requested to do so after his initial *USA Today* article generated a significant number of emails, texts and inquiries from other media outlets. "Dead Men's Clubs" were unique and the sweet smell of something different was in the air.

"South Carolina's Munch Malone, a 70-year-old golf phenomenon, fired a five under par 67 at the storied Greenbrier Old White Course in West Virginia today. Malone displayed a sizzling driver and accuracy around the greens that could not be matched by the other amateurs here who harbor the dream of winning the United States Senior Men's Amateur Golf Championship.

"That dream could become reality for Malone, one of the oldest golfers to compete at this level. The gallery was stunned and delighted with his play. He hit the fairway on every drive and consistently drove the ball ten to twenty yards longer than his closest competitors.

"Malone's amazing display occurred as he played with reconditioned clubs by Wild-O Golf. Malone says his game actually took off once he began wielding the used clubs. He has dubbed them 'Dead Men's Clubs', because he believes golfers who are now deceased once owned them. He has referenced a University of Virginia study that quantified golfers who believed they were playing with golf clubs once used by experts vastly improved their game; the effect was dubbed 'Contagion'. 'Dead Men's Clubs?' If they are, Malone has made them come alive here at The Greenbrier."

The *Associated Press* article ran on sports pages throughout the country. "Golf Contagion At The Greenbrier!" screamed the *Miami Herald*. The *Chicago Tribune* featured a picture of Malone at the top of its sports section: "South Carolina Golfer Seeks Amateur Title With 'Dead Men's Clubs'."

"Well, really, I'm not sure I like being referred to as a 'Dead Man,' War laughed, sipping his morning Mimosa, reading the headlines on various newspaper websites.

"Well, you are dead," Sink said.

"A detail I prefer to overlook," War said, winking down the bar at Sheila.

"Tell you what, War, why don't you see if this 'Channeling' works both ways—get Munch to send you some of his Viagra," Sink said, doing his own wink at Sheila as she moved beyond earshot, wiping and polishing the exquisite bar at which they sat.

The same morning, at precisely 5 a.m., D.E. Wildoe slipped quietly out of bed and began his early morning routine. He ambled to the bathroom to take a leak, grabbed his bathrobe and slippers, and descended the flight of stairs that served the rear portion of his mansion. He opened a cabinet door, retrieved his favorite coffee mug, placed it under the pour spout of his automatic coffee maker, and inserted the individual brew cup in place. He pressed the brew button and turned to make his trek toward the morning newspaper that had been tossed on his driveway at 4 a.m.

Wildoe ambled down the winding pavement, stooped and picked up his *New York Times*. He read the headlines above the fold, walking past brilliant mums that lined the path back to the house. He strode into his kitchen, picking up a cup of steaming hot coffee, turning the paper over to read the headlines beneath the fold.

Mrs. Wildoe, sleeping in the enormous master suite above the kitchen, was abruptly awakened by a scream, followed by a stream of obscenities. She rushed down the staircase and into the kitchen to find Wildoe angrily pushing buttons on the house phone, as he brushed frantically at his coffee-soiled bathrobe. He winced as he displayed red fingers that had been burned as his coffee cup tilted back when he read "Dead Men's Clubs Deadly At Senior Amateur Championship."

"What happened, dear?" Mrs. Wildoe exclaimed.

"Freakin' disaster, that's what!" Wildoe screamed at her.

Within minutes Marcus Appleton was wide awake, his cell phone blasting D.E. Wildoe's obscenities in his ear. The scene was repeated moments later as the same obscenities were directed at John Short who was awakened from his morning slumber by a frantic Marcus Appleton.

Cheryl Woody was the next Wild-O employee to be rousted from her bed and she, in turn, woke Janie Germaine. Together they coordinated an emergency meeting of all parties at Wild-O headquarters later that morning in an attempt to create some order out of the chaos.

War and Sink sat in the Clubhouse, eyes glued to the giant High Def screen, entranced. They had invited the Snarf to join them to watch the proceedings, in case his technical expertise was needed.

Brawley Rollins also had gathered **The Powers That Be** *after reading the morning papers and sending a text to Sink Lair—a reminder that* **TPTB** *did not want any shit hitting the fan.*

Melinda picked up the hotel phone on its first ring.

"Hello?"

"Hi, Mrs. Malone, John Short here, I hope I'm not calling too early, but is Mr. Malone there?" Short Sale began, loosening his tie.

"Yes, he went to bed late last night, as you might imagine, but he's up—hold on."

"Babe, John Short," Melinda said, handing the phone to Munch.

"Hey, John, Munch here."

"Munch! Good to hear your voice. Congratulations on making history down there at The Greenbrier."

"Uh, thanks, John—thanks for the clubs!"

"You know, Munch, you promised me."

"Promised you what?"

"That you wouldn't call them 'Dead Men's Clubs'!" Short Sale screamed into the phone.

"Whoa, buddy, whoa, I never, ever, called them 'Dead Men's Clubs'."

"Says so right here in *USA Today*," Short Sale said, trying to control himself.

"Read it carefully, John, those are the reporter's words, not mine. I did *not* use the phrase—Matt Moss did, and I can't control what a reporter says, now can I?" Munch retorted.

Short Sale scanned the article. Munch was right. There was no quote, just the reporter's reference.

"Sorry, sorry, Munch. You're right, my bad. It's a little tense here. Every time you're in the paper and 'Dead Men's Clubs' are mentioned, I am getting shellacked by my bosses. I just met with my CEO and the President of National Sales—the position I used to have—and, guess what, Munch, they think the *Associated Press* worldwide plastering of 'Wild-O Dead Men's Clubs' is bad marketing for us. Nobody, but NOBODY, will want to buy Wild-O clubs if they think they're playing with 'Dead Men's Clubs'," Short Sale said, desperation in his voice.

Munch remained calm in spite of himself. He sighed heavily and said, "John, like I said before, if I, Munch Malone, desperate golfer, picked up a *USA Today* and read that some duffer went to a 1 handicap, I'd be beating down your doors, looking for 'Contagion'."

"Really? The 'Contagion' thing?"

"Really."

"Really," said Sink. Snarf nodded. War smiled.

Brawley clapped aloud. Retro Elvis cracked his knuckles.

"I dunno'—'Contagion'. I kinda' like that, but I dunno' if I can sell it to my bosses, they're on my ass like flies on horseshit," Short Sale said.

"Well, run it up the flagpole, you may want me to start shouting 'Contagion' wherever I end up on this crazy ride," Munch retorted.

"Okay, okay—market research may be the answer—thanks Munch—back with you soon," Short Sale sighed, and rang off.

Eighteen

"Janie! Call Regency Research in Cincinnati. Get Rex Reynolds in here as soon as you can. Tell Rex emergency, emergency, emergency! I need some ammo for my personal "Shit", Mr. Marcus Appleton," Munch sputtered.

Reynolds, Chairman and CEO of Regency Research, lost no time responding to his old friend and Gold Star client, John Short. Reynolds was in the air that afternoon, winging his way to New York and Wild-O Golf as day two of the USGA Senior Men's Amateur Championship was well underway at The Greenbrier

"Interesting assignment," Reynolds thought, mentally reviewing his conversation with Janie Germaine. Regency Research had worked many years with John Short when he was head of National Sales at Wild-O Golf, but no assignments were forthcoming from Marcus Appleton when Marcus took over.

Word had it that Marcus had hired an uber-expensive firm in Paris to do his market research because Mr. Appleton wanted not just marketing information, but to be regularly feted in stays at 5-star hotels around the world, dinners at the Four Seasons in San Francisco and lunches at Barbuto when he was forced to stay at headquarters in New York. "No wonder they called him 'The Shit'," Reynolds thought, looking out into white clouds that seemed somehow alive.

"Is this guy any good?" War said to Snarf as Reynolds' face

appeared side-by-side with the Amateur Championship on the giant High Def screen.

"Damn right he's good," Snarf said, "marketing research guru for a whole list of Fortune 10 companies, he's got a great track record."

Over in the conference room of *The Powers That Be*, Retro Elvis viewed Reynolds' image and said to his cohorts, "Handsome fella', looks a lot like Elvis, the way he holds his lip when he's concentratin'."

"How fast? How fast can you get a sample?" Short Sale asked, the clock on his desk passing 4:30 in the afternoon, his flat screen featuring Munch Malone on number Sixteen at the Old White.

"I'll start this evening. We'll do it with a 600 sample, overall margin of error of four percentage points, and I'll get you a report on every increment of 100 'completes' with cross tabs by handicap and demographics. We'll also run the data with the appropriate statistical tests of significance," Reynolds replied, nursing a Diet Coke.

"Sample from…?"

"We're using a purchased list from the two leading golf magazines, best listing of golfers over 50—high handicap group with money to buy as many clubs as they want. From the purchased list, we've selected a random sample representative of all subscribers in the U.S. We'll monitor the profiles of respondents by USGA data of golfers over age 50 and statistically weight the findings, if necessary, to be as close to a rep sample of all golfers in this age cohort as possible."

"Good, good. So—can you get me at least 100 completed interviews by early evening?"

Reynolds smiled and said, "I'll do my best to get it by 9 tonight. What will you do with a hundred? That's not enough of a sample to legitimately call this thing."

"I know, but it'll buy me some time with 'The Shit' and the CEO—I hope."

National media loved the story. Munch Malone was a great name and "Dead Men's Clubs" was an angle too juicy to ignore. *WSAV-TV* in Savannah transmitted file video footage of the earlier Sea Pines Country Club Championship win, and Sunday afternoon Munch was all over *ESPN*, just as Reynolds' phone bank began to call senior golfers who subscribed to the two biggest golf magazines.

"If you think your golf game has died on you, take a look at this guy who hails from South Carolina," *ESPN* anchor Jan Houston began. "He's 70-years-old and he has his eyes set on winning the USGA Senior Men's Amateur Championship.

Malone says he wins with used clubs from Wild-O Golf. He says he started collecting them, one by one, earlier this year, and he claims his play got better every time he bought another club from the used racks. He calls them, are you ready? 'Dead Men's Clubs'. Whatcha' think, guys, can we get some of those clubs?" Laughter all around on the *ESPN* set.

As media reported the story every hour on the hour, Rex Reynolds' canvassers were hard at work: "Overall, what is your opinion of used or reconditioned clubs sold by golf club manufacturers?" asked the Regency Research caller.

"Well, from what I read and see on TV, some old guy is using them and winning, so I guess they're fine."

"Based on what you have seen, read or heard, how likely is it that you would buy reconditioned clubs? Is it extremely likely, very likely, somewhat likely, not very likely, or not likely at all"

"That'd be extremely likely. Damn right, if I could play like that."

"Have you heard, seen, or read anything about the theory of 'Contagion'?"

"No, what's that?"

The 'Contagion' theory was explained in call after call. The response was overwhelming: "I'd like to try that," was the gist of the growing replies.

And so it went through the day and evening, fueled by media interest that was building by the hour. Munch completed day two of the tournament with yet another stellar performance, finishing well ahead of his competition.

The call came at 9:30 p.m., just after Reynolds had delivered 100 completed calls to John Short's office.

"Mr. Short," Janie said, interrupting Short Sale and Reynolds who were huddled over a spreadsheet. "Sorry to say," Janie said, adjusting her glasses, "but Cheryl Shout says Mr. Appleton wants you in his office, pronto."

"'The Shit' is burnin' the midnight oil, huh?" Short Sale chortled. "I'll just bet he wants me there, I'll just bet," Short Sale said, allowing himself a tight little smile. "Rex, how does it look—be candid, please."

"Looking good; it's media, pure and simple," Reynolds replied, pointing to the *Golf Channel* broadcast where Munch Malone's play at number Eighteen was being reviewed. We completed one hundred interviews with a high cooperation rate. The respondents were very aware of the media coverage of Malone and eager to talk."

"Are these results trending?"

"Well, ordinarily I'd hedge my bet on that, but this thing is all over *The Golf Channel* and *ESPN* just picked it up. I'd say it would trend very, very well. You've got a 90% favorable rating and an incredible purchase intent score, and it could go higher. Compelling story—old guy, duffer, shows up the younger guys, appeals to America's baby boomers. 'Dead Men's Clubs', 'Contagion'—great stuff."

"Yeah baby—Rex, you 'da man,'" Short Sale beamed, bumping fists with Reynolds, hurrying out the door, his tie askew. He was back a moment later. "Forgot my jacket," he said, grabbing his blazer, once again bouncing out of the room.

"OK, this could be fine," Sink said, watching Short Sale rush to Marcus Appleton's office. "No way we're gonna' avoid lots of media, but, by God, it's got to be good for Wild-O Golf, if only Wild-O and **The Powers That Be** could see that!"

Short Sale walked into Appleton's office, waving his research results.

Appleton looked up from where he was sitting watching *ESPN* show yet another re-play of Munch Malone's day. He jerked out of his chair and came charging before Short could get a word out.

"Goddammit! I told you to clean up this mess and you've gone and stirred more shit!" 'The Shit' said.

"Marcus, calm down, look at these numbers."

"Screw the numbers, this guy will take us down if we don't stop him," Marcus said, his hissing sound reverberating in the room.

"Marcus, listen to me. I've got research here from Regency out of Cincinnati—we've been calling all evening and the response to Malone is overwhelmingly positive—the golfers out there are gonna' make a run on our reconditioned clubs. I think my sales are going to shoot right through the roof."

This was not what "The Shit" wanted to hear.

"Bullshit, what's the margin of error? And why didn't you use my research firm in Paris?"

"I've always used Regency. They're the best," Short Sale said.

"So you say—gimme' that!" "The Shit" shouted, grabbing the file in Short's hand.

Appleton smiled as he read the synopsis, "Sorry, Short, old buddy, but you've got only one hundred assholes here and that's not a valid sample. While you fiddle, Wild-O Golf burns, old buddy," Marcus said, throwing the document to the floor, cynicism dripping from his voice.

"Uh, well, don't think so, Marcus, Rex Reynolds is confident these numbers will not only hold, but trend upward. If that turns out to be the case, we have a great marketing opportunity at hand," Short Sale said.

"Call him off," Marcus grunted.

"What?"

"Call it off, stop the phone calls, I'm not spending Wild-O's money on this shit. This is ridiculous and I'm not gonna' be responsible for a wild ass goose chase called 'Dead Men's Clubs'!" Marcus said.

"I won't do that," Short Sale countered, shaking his head. "This is the right thing to do—this is an opportunity—"

"Call it off or pack your bags." Marcus said.

"You'll fire me? Are you serious?" Short Sale laughed, incredulous.

"If you're not out of here in 30 seconds, axing your research firm, I'll fire your ass so fast you'll think you're in a time warp. Not only that, I'll see that you never work in golf again. I'll keep you on a breadline that not even a congressional bailout can end!" Marcus screamed.

"OK, Marcus, I'm going. You can stop *me*, but you can't stop Malone. If he wins, you'll rue this day," Short Sale warned, turning, walking away, furious with "The Shit".

Nineteen

The first round of the USGA Senior Men's Amateur Championship had drawn incredible interest. The field had been narrowed to the low 64 scorers and a 70-year-old guy was in media crosshairs. He had a winning way and unique angle, but he was raw meat to be eaten, digested, and spit out. The tournament organizers made sure Munch Malone was a featured player, putting him front and center at the post-match press conference that ordinarily saw a relatively small number of journalists in attendance. This year was different. *ESPN* decided to broadcast the news conference live. *The Golf Channel, NBC, The New York Times,* and *The Wall Street Journal,* were present. There was a buzz in the air.

"Mr. Malone!" *The Golf Channel's* Chad Ray signaled, raising his hand for recognition.

"Munch, please," Munch smiled, feeling the perspiration under his arms begin to slide down his torso. "Steady," Munch thought, "Try to handle this like Bubba did."

"Munch," Ray said with a grin, cameras clicking throughout the room, "You're a pretty incredible story. Hard to believe you could do what you've done, particularly at your age. What's the secret to your success?"

"This oughta' be good!" War said, slapping his thigh and laughing out loud.

Marcus Appleton was glued to the Sony.

In the corner office, the CEO of Wild-O Golf felt his pulse beginning to race.

Short Sale John and Janie Germaine sat in Wild-O Golf's Reconditioned Sales conference room, recording every word from *The Golf Channel*.

The Powers That Be *also were assembled. Brawley Rollins' large fist held a cigar as he took a liberty while watching this enormously interesting experiment begin to take on a much larger scope than he had imagined. He tried not to show it, but he was a little nervous. He was certain that the* **Highest Authority** *now knew of the experiment and was bound to be holding judgment as the whole thing unfolded.*

"Well, first of all, let me say that I never, in my entire life, believed I'd be answering questions from Chad Ray," Munch said.

"You'll find I'm gonna' ask a lot more if you keep hitting those clubs the way you did today!" Ray laughed.

"Well, I really don't know how I've turned my game around. I keep coming back to the clubs I use. I've tried them all, but Wild-O's are the ones that work for me. Without 'em, I just don't play well," Munch said, trying to be as straightforward as possible.

"You're an amateur, any deals with Wild-O Golf? Are they paying you in any way for an endorsement such as that?" asked *The New York Times*.

"Certainly not, I haven't received anything from Wild-O but invoices for my clubs," Munch replied.

Some laughter in the room.

"Munch'" *The Wall Street Journal* chimed in, "You have become the poster boy, or poster 'Senior' for all the old guys out there who think their game can improve, even at their age. What do they have to do, buy Wild-O's?"

"Gee, I 'dunno what will work for somebody else. I just tried a lot of clubs and I spent so much money my wife got on me so I bought used Wild-O's after that—and they worked better than anything else," Munch replied. He looked at Melinda, who smiled.

From the back of the room NBC's man on the scene stood up, "Munch, you've been quoted as calling the used clubs 'Dead Men's Clubs', tell us about that."

Appleton, sitting in his office, knocking back Red Bulls, froze. D.E. Wildoe, standing at the windows in his penthouse office, looking out over Manhattan, snorted and turned his attention to the television. Short Sale and Janie, working the numbers in Short's office, sat motionless and waited for yet another blast of 'Dead Men's Clubs' to hit the airwaves.

Brawley drew a long pull on his Macanudo. Sink grinned, War laughed, blowing Sheila a kiss as she walked by. The Snarf had a frown on his face.

Munch hesitated. How could he steer away from mentioning 'Dead Men's Clubs'? He had promised John Short he would not go there.

"Well, they are reconditioned clubs, after all. I don't know who used them, coulda' been some of the guys who aren't here now, or could be that the clubs are from golfers that just gave up the game, or traded them in for new Wild-O's," Munch said, relieved that he had not uttered the phrase.

"Golf's a mind game, as we all know; are the 'Dead Men's Clubs' a psychological thing? You think you can hit them better, like a champ, and you do?" NBC asked.

"Uh, first of all, I think we should, out of respect, refer to them as 'used' or 'reconditioned' clubs, not, uh—you know. And, you could have a point, I do think—no, no, I *know* that I think more positively with the clubs in my hand. Mind game, it certainly is—just like Harvey Penick says, 'It's all between your ears,' " Munch said.

"Munch, let's follow up on this 'Contagion' thing," *Sports Illustrated* said. "You've been quoted as saying you don't reject the UVA research that said people play better when they think they've got a club in their hands a pro used, and you've indicated you're benefitting from 'Contagion'."

"Yes, well?"

"Do you honestly believe that's why you play better? Do you believe the deceased who once owned these clubs, if indeed they are deceased, are 'Channeling' to you? Are you playing the great golf we are witnessing, or are they?"

"I, uh, all I know is I started playing well when I got these clubs—and I know it sounds crazy, but I do have to confess that it feels like someone else is hitting them when I play."

A chorus of questions erupted in the room as the attending USGA official stepped in to end the news conference, promising more was to come as the Championship continued.

ESPN ended the live feed with a promise to follow Munch Malone and his "Dead Men's Clubs". *The Golf Channel* said pretty much the same thing and the newspaper dailies headlined "Dead Men Playing Golf" above the fold on the sports page. *The Wall Street Journal* Saturday sports page devoted a full page to Munch Malone, "Contagion", and "Dead Men's Clubs".

Back in New York, John Short called Cincinnati and told Rex Reynolds he had to stop polling. Rex knew Short had been given the order from Marcus Appleton, "The Shit", and felt for John, who had always been an ardent supporter of his firm. Bearing the cost himself, and unknown to Short Sale, Reynolds not only continued the polling, he intensified it: "Depth of emotion; affinity for Wild-O clubs; affinity for Malone; belief that the clubs would improve play; belief that the clubs were 'Dead Men's Clubs'; belief in 'Contagion'; would you buy these clubs?" All these questions were being asked of senior golfers without Short's knowledge. Reynolds felt driven to continue the tracking, and he would wait and see where and how his information could best be used.

Marcus, "The Shit", checked the daily sales numbers. The report was positive, but not for Marcus. Reconditioned sales were astonishing, while new clubs sales were stagnant. "Dammit! this is not good," he thought. Ever insecure, Marcus worried the CEO would think Short Sale John had a winner in Munch Malone, if the sales trend continued.

"This is absolutely not gonna' happen," Marcus said aloud. He pressed his intercom button and said to his weary assistant, "Woody! Get in here!"

Twenty

Munch Malone finished stroke play as the tournament Medalist. The field was cut to 64 players. His performance on the par 70, 6,652 yard, 72.1 rated Old White was brilliant. He hit every fairway and every green. He carded three birdies and conducted a clinic on the short game. Munch was again the talk of the tournament.

"Proud of the boy! Proud of us!" War said as he and Sink raised their drinks in celebration. Sheila brought some fine little snacks to the table and made sure to hover and press leg flesh. The old boys were very, very happy.

"I cannot believe that I'm playin' The Greenbrier," War gushed. I love the Old White! It's been there since 1914—older than I am. Had my final round there!"

"Yeah, so I've heard," Sink responded with a grin. War had told him countless times about the final shot at The Greenbrier with the Wild-O. It was damned exciting to see the old Congressman slapping his knee in excitement.

At 7:30 the next morning, Short Sale paced in his office. Today would be big, he knew, with three days of storybook performances by Munch Malone—with "Dead Men's Clubs".

"Boy, oh boy, oh boy, this is incredible. If Malone wins, this thing could bring me back and squash 'The Shit'," he said aloud, rubbing his hands together, looking at the huge color photo of

Munch Malone on the front page of *USA Today*. The headline screamed "Munch Channels Dead Men's Clubs At Greenbrier!"

Janie delivered a latte and from under her arm, dropped *The New York Times* on Short's desk beside *USA Today*, turned, and left the room. *The Times*, the great gray lady, had a sports story on the front page, *above* the fold. The headline said "Stunning Senior Smokes Senior Amateur With Dead Men's Clubs." Short felt a sudden rush and said, "Holy shit. I hope I can market this. We should have never stopped polling. I need to know what the numbers are."

The Golf Channel was on in the background as *Morning Drive* debated the chances of a 70-year-old with "Dead Men's Clubs" to be even credible against "Seniors" in their fifties. Janie was back, placing a stack of messages on Short's desk. Calls were coming in from media outlets across the country.

"Janie, get PR on this, tell 'em we've got a freaking meteor on our hands."

"Will do, sir," Janie said, adjusting her glasses. The phone rang before she could leave the room.

"Short, Marcus here. Mr. Wildoe and I want you up here at high noon in the CEO's office. You've got a real problem, buddy, this 'Dead Men's Clubs' thing you've started is a fuckin' disaster!" Short heard the phone slam before he could comment.

Short Sale dropped into his office chair and leaned forward on the desk, placing his head in his hands. He looked up at Janie and said, "Get Reynolds, tell him it's an emergency. Maybe he can get me some updated numbers that'll impress the CEO and save my ass. He could start calling again and get me a few more hours," Short said, looking at his watch. "If anyone has any ideas, it'll be Rex. Maybe he can pull a rabbit out of the hat." Short said.

Janie called Reynolds on his cell and got his voice mail. She left a message and then placed a call to Regency Research offices where the receptionist said the boss was celebrating his 30th anniversary with his wife, a beautiful redhead. She and Rex were spending the week in New York at the New York Royal Arms Hotel.

"Outstanding!" Janie said, not believing her good luck. She phoned the Royal Arms and asked for the Reynolds' room. The phone produced an automated message that said the Reynolds' were not in their hotel suite. Janie hung up and called Lily Caroline, a college sorority sister who was National Vice President of Marketing for the Royal Arms Hotels.

After exchanging pleasantries, Lily put Janie on hold to see if she could locate Mr. and Mrs. Reynolds. Minutes passed and Lily was back on the phone with Janie. She informed her that the Royal Arms Concierge in New York had made lunch reservations for the Reynolds at a French restaurant in Manhattan called "Le Chateau". Janie thanked Lily, promised to join her soon for a shopping spree, and rang off.

Janie phoned "Le Chateau" and found a rather haughty Maître d' who said "Sorry, Madame, but ze Reynolds are in ze dining room and cannot be disturbed."

"Oh, you speak French?" Janie asked sarcastically, frustrated by the snobby attitude she had encountered.

"Oui, Madame," the Maître d' answered, shaking his head in disbelief.

Janie hissed into the phone, "Well, my French is a little rusty, but I'll give it a try." She stood up at her desk and shouted into the phone, "This is bull-sheet! Get Mr. Reynolds now or I will come down there and stick ze Eiffel Tower so far up your ass—"

The phone went dead.

Janie counted to three, adjusted her glasses, took a deep breath, and called again.

The Maître d' again answered.

"I'm so sorry, my French and my manners are a little off these days...I'm with Wild-O Golf in New York." Janie said, and took a shot in the dark, asking, "Are you a golfer?"

"Oui, Madame, it is not only ze bloody English that play ze sport!"

Janie smiled and said, "If I were to forward to you, at no charge, a full set of our golf clubs, would zat get Mr. Reynolds to ze phone?"

"It is amazing, Madame, how ze French has improved!" her target replied.

Janie chatted up the Maître d', obtaining his email and mailing addresses. She then suggested he go find Reynolds and get him to the phone.

"After that, get on our website and select your clubs," she purred.

"Consider it done, Madame!" the Maître d' responded.

Janie sat back and waited, listening to elevator music as her conquest hurried to find Reynolds. Her wait was a short one.

"Hello? This is Rex Reynolds."

"Rex, Janie Germaine. Sorry to do this to you, on your anniversary, and all that, but Mr. Short asked me to see if you could be interrupted for just a moment for an emergency phone call from him. Again, he is very sorry..."

"Not a problem, Janie, I'm always available to John Short," Reynolds said.

"Good man," thought Janie." She thanked him and put him on hold.

"Rex," Short Sale said. "Thanks for taking the call."

"John," Reynolds said, "you can call me anytime." Rex listened to Short Sale as a smiling Maître-d' busied himself at a computer, perusing the Wild-O Golf site.

"Rex, I know it's probably too late, but, could we start polling again—immediately? I'm on the carpet in the CEO's office today at noon and I'm gonna' get shellacked again because they think I'm destroying the brand—freaking 'Dead Men's Clubs'," Short Sale said, rolling his eyes and breaking the pencil he was holding in half.

"Not too late, John," Reynolds said.

"Meeting's at noon. Janie says you're here in New York, which is fortuitous, but, I realize you can't do much—" Short lamented, as Reynolds interrupted.

"You're right, couldn't get many interviews completed—couldn't even get them started."

Short slumped at his desk.

"But, it does give me time to get back to the hotel, get my computer, and catch a cab to your office," Reynolds said.

"What are you talking about?"

Reynolds looked around to see if anyone was paying attention to his conversation. The Maître d' was oblivious. Rex turned his back to the restaurant entrance and said softly into the phone, "John, I've been in the field sampling consumer sentiment on this every day since Marcus ordered you to quit interviewing. I just couldn't bring myself to stop.

"We're in the field polling as we speak, and the tracking is incredible. You should see the numbers. Outta' sight. They love Munch, they love the clubs and they think Wild-O Golf hung the moon. When you combine this data with the social media tracking we have in place, the buzz about this product is incredible." Reynolds said. "I'll come over there and roll these numbers out for the CEO at noon. He'll go ape shit. Dynamite stuff."

Short Sale could not believe what he was hearing. "I knew it! 'Dead Men's Clubs' could be a marketing phenomenon! Thank you, Jesus," he said, shouting at Reynolds, "I love 'ya, baby. Get a cab—see if you can get here by 11:45, time for a quick review. You 'da man', baby!" Short Sale screamed, slamming the phone down, screaming a "Yahoo!" that could be heard on the floor above.

Reynolds smiled as he ended the call. One problem solved. Now, a much bigger problem. How to tell Mrs. Reynolds that she would need to lunch alone, on their anniversary, while he scurried to a business meeting. That would take some real finesse —- and an afternoon at the Royal Arms Spa.

Twenty One

Reynolds entered John Short's office at 11:45. Short was obviously nervous as Janie reviewed a number of favorable articles from wire service reports and summarized them as supportive to Munch Malone and his amazing "Dead Men's Clubs". Sale and Reynolds briefly discussed strategy and then walked out of the office and down the corridor where Short hit the elevator button for the 56th floor.

They walked into the CEO suite at exactly 12:00 noon. They waited twenty-five minutes in the reception area. Rex walked around the room, looking at large autographed pictures of Arnie, Jack, Tiger, and the Shark. In the middle of the room was a ten-foot high sculpture. It was a Wild-O golf club with the head encrusted in diamonds. The inscription at the bottom of the base upon which the club was resting read, "The Jewel Of The Golf World."

The receptionist opened the large double doors to the CEO's office at 12:25. D. E. Wildoe was sitting behind a desk that looked like an aircraft carrier. He was drumming his fingers while reading the *Wall Street Journal's* take on Munch. Marcus was on the other side of the large expanse of carpet, putting golf balls toward a pewter tray with a golf flag attached. He looked up when Short entered.

"Who's your friend?" Marcus asked, striding across the room, club in hand.

"This is Rex Reynolds, my pollster," Short answered.

"No, no, no, you don't, John," Marcus said, pointing the putter at Short.

"Mr. Wildoe," Short Sale said, ignoring Marcus. "I think you'll want to see what the public thinks about Munch Malone and, more important, what they think about Wild-O Golf," Short said, holding up a sheaf of papers in his hand.

Wildoe looked at Reynolds and then at Marcus, and again at Reynolds. "Couldn't hurt," he said. He motioned Rex to a conference table that fronted on a large picture window framing sunlight that reflected off the Hudson. Wildoe motioned for everyone to sit and said, "Let's see what you've got." Marcus threw up his hands in frustration and moved toward a chair. Reynolds sat across from the CEO, opened a well-worn briefcase, and began passing out a thick report to all parties.

Rex began, "I've been tracking this for some time now. In my twenty-five years in this business, I've never seen numbers like these. Right now— as of our tracking calls last night—Malone himself has a 90 percent favorability rating. Wild-O Golf has an 85 percent confidence level with those polled, and Wild-O reconditioned clubs a whopping 96 purchase intent score."

A cheer went up from the gallery pictured on the flat screen as the Golf Channel reported Munch Malone had just finished the first round of match play for the day, 1-up. The CEO sat straight up in his chair, watching the TV and then returning to the numbers. "Reynolds, how sure are you? What's the credibility here?" Wildoe asked, leaning forward in his seat, sensing opportunity as Munch Malone waved at the crowd.

"We've employed two methodologies to validate our findings. In addition, the overall margin of error is +/- four percentage points at the 95% confidence interval and 2.5 percentage points for the purchase intent questions. It's a 600 baseline representative sample of golfers over 50 and we re-contacted 300 of that baseline in every track. Statistically, it's as strong as anything we've ever done," Reynolds said.

"And here's the really fantastic news. When asked if they would buy Wild-O used clubs, even though they have been referred to as 'Dead Men's Clubs', 85% said they would be extremely likely to purchase, and another 10% said they would be very likely to buy. That's a 95% top two-box score for purchase intent. No product or concept we have ever tested has had a purchase intent score this high, and we've tested the viability of new products for everything from mouthwash to the iPhone. This is more than a winner—it's the closest I've ever seen to a sure bet." Reynolds concluded.

Wildoe's eyebrows went skyward. "Are sales up?" he asked Short.

"The latest overnights show the same trend—the numbers are definitely up, exponentially, yes sir," Short answered.

"That doesn't mean *anything*, we see spikes all the time. Happened every week before Tiger crashed and burned," Marcus scoffed. "We can sit here and blather on and on about this, but does anybody in this room think that it does Wild-O Golf any good to have every Tom, Dick and Harry calling us the 'Dead Men's Clubs' company? Talk about trashing a brand!" Marcus scoffed.

"I've seen your new club sales, Marcus, and they are definitely *not* up! But, you may be right. Hard for me to believe this could be good for us. Even if senior golfers are buying our used clubs, the overall brand could suffer. Malone could be a flash in the pan, and we're stuck with a black mark that nobody will forget," Wildoe said. "On the other hand, it's hard to deny the polling," he finished.

"Exactly, sir," Short Sale countered. "Malone has our clubs

and he's in one of the biggest tournaments of the year. The media loves to ram home the fact that he plays with Wild-O 'Dead Men's Clubs', even though Malone has stopped calling them that. They love to think they can buy one of our clubs and maybe feel 'Contagion'. You heard Rex—this is a sure bet. This ball will roll and we need to manage this and get as much out of it for Wild-O Golf as we can," Short said, with as much determination as he could possibly muster.

"Good point, John" Wildoe said, quickly switching his gaze to Appleton. "Marcus, I think John is on target with this—let's figure out a way to minimize any downside and maximize the hell out of the high side. Any immediate thoughts, boys?" he asked, looking at the three men sitting at the table.

"Yes sir," Reynolds answered. "We need to continue the tracking through Munch's run and determine during, and at the end of his 15 minutes of fame, what fallout—or opportunity—we have."

"It'd be a helluva' sight better if we rang Legal and asked them to go after a restraining order that would stop the media from saying 'Dead Men's Clubs'," Marcus complained, hunkering down in his chair.

"Don't be a dumbass, Marcus," Wildoe frowned, "you can't sue the media, they'd make us a laughingstock. Reynolds—pretty impressive! Keep polling, and, Marcus, get PR on this right away!" Wildoe ordered.

"We've already asked PR to put a plan together, sir," Short said.

"Good, glad somebody here realizes we've got to manage this thing," the CEO said, shooting a sideways glance at Appleton, who spread his arms wide in exasperation and looked at the ceiling.

"John, keep me apprised on the tracking, and I want you and

Marcus to let me know where sales are going. This *could* be a goldmine rather than a disaster." He pointed a finger at Appleton and then at Short, "This meeting is over. Right now I don't know who I should promote or fire, but I sure as hell will know when this tournament ends."

And the end *was* nearing. That afternoon Munch Malone completed his second round of match play for the day, 2-up. Tomorrow would be the third and final round of match play, leading to the Quarterfinals.

Twenty Two

"Call this number," Marcus instructed Cheryl, barging into her office, "ask for Mr. Frong's assistant."

"Frong"?" Cheryl said.

"Right, he's in Las Vegas. Tell his assistant I have to talk with Mr. Frong and find out when the call can be arranged."

"Who is Mr. Frong?"

"Just call the number, dammit, tell him I need to talk with him and I'm available anytime."

"Yas suh!" Cheryl saluted.

Marcus had met Jimmy Frong in Las Vegas on a trip five years ago, in a most interesting way. He was scouting the Majestic Hotel, just outside the Strip, determining if Wild-O Golf's annual meeting could be held there. Great hotel, excellent golf course and spectacular pool, given the beauties that lounged beside it.

Marcus was sitting there, poolside, just soaking up rays, when along came Tiffany.

She was a dark-haired beauty with points way up high. It was impossible for Marcus to resist temptation as Tiffany sat on the chaise beside him and let one strap of her bikini top slip. "Sorry," she had said, adjusting her halter with a smile that meant she was not at all sorry. She had him from the quick glance of pink on an ample white breast, and he immediately turned on the charm.

The 600 count sheets in one of the finest suites at the Majestic were soon wrapped around them. Marcus could not get enough. He *had* to have it. They met each day at noon, ate lunch poolside, and then adjourned to Marcus' suite for "dessert".

Marcus humped merrily away for most of the week, not realizing Tiffany was the wife of a very jealous and extremely dangerous man. Tiffany's hubby was Jimmy Frong. He was born and raised in Brooklyn, but he was half-Asian, half-Hawaiian, and looked like "Mr. T" from the old television series. He was 5'-8", weighing close to 300 pounds, with an enormous bald head, eyebrows that shifted upward, giving him an evil look; all atop too many gold necklaces and bracelets to count. He had "Klingon" ears and a thick mustache that spread down around his mouth, completing a large Fu Manchu. His eyes were dark; his stare was wicked, with intent to terrify.

He was Vice President of Security at the Majestic, one of the hallowed positions at a hotel with big time gambling. The Tiffany and Marcus liaison that took place every day in suite 2012 could not long escape Jimmy Frong's most trusted lieutenant, Rooster Rittenhouse.

Frong was an avid golfer who muscled the ball with gorilla-like arms; his fireplug of a body never turned as he struck the ball. Frong was on hole Four, a par five at the Majestic's championship course, when a customized hotel golf cart driven by Rooster Rittenhouse pulled up to the tee box. Rooster waved frantically to his boss as his short legs rested on raised accelerator and brake pedals that accommodated his dwarf-like status. Frong, playing with two hotel guests and the Majestic's Marketing Director, Harry Lee, strode to the cart. It was 1:30 in the afternoon, scorching under the desert sun.

"Trouble?" he asked. Rooster shifted in the cart, leaned in close to his boss, and whispered that there was a security tape Frong would want to see.

"Can't it wait?" I gotta' great round goin' here," Frong growled.

"Don't think you'll want to put this off, boss. It's, uh, something you need to see—right now," Rooster said.

Frong knew Rooster would not interrupt him for something trivial. He made his apologies to the group and jumped into the cart. Rooster quickly covered the half-mile to the Majestic's Security Offices, escorting Frong to a conference room where he slipped a disc into a computer attached to a 72" monitor. Bodies filled the screen.

Frong watched the video over and over again. It featured his wife Tiffany, wildly thrashing about in bed with Marcus Appleton. Rooster provided background; Appleton was an executive at Wild-O Golf, a golf club manufacturer, and he was scouting the hotel for its next Annual Meeting. He had been shagging Tiffany for days. They made little secret of it, causing a suspicious Rooster to install a hidden video camera in the hotel suite that proved to be a fireworks display for a "Black Light".

Frong's anger grew as he watched the Olympic endeavors. Frong knew his wife had slipped off her rings before, but this was an affront he could not ignore. This was a major slap in the face –at his hotel! In front of his security people! This called for actions that would be *Vegas style*. Mr. Appleton and Mrs. Frong needed a lesson.

Twenty-four hours later, Marcus was poised over Tiffany's naked body with an impressive erection. He smiled down at her and nestled in between her legs. "Give it to me, give it to me!" Tiffany moaned, writhing on the sheets and grabbing Mr. Appleton's manhood. She spread her hips wide as Marcus prepared to thrust. He froze when he felt something cold and sharp at the back of his neck. The fabled four-hour Viagra erection had no chance.

Tiffany screamed as she saw her husband's face appear above and behind Marcus' head. Both Marcus and Frong were looking directly into her eyes. Marcus with sheer terror, Frong with a ghastly grin.

"Afternoon, kids," Frong said. "Mr. Appleton—'da wife and me—seems we have a reason 'ta communicate."

Marcus felt himself being bodily lifted out of bed by two hefty security men from Frong's crew. They carried him to the suite's balcony; tossed him outside, onto an expansive tiled floor, closed the double doors, and left him naked 20 floors up. It was 1:30 in the afternoon. Below, the pool was crowded and people walked to and fro through the beautiful gardens of the hotel. Were they looking up?

Tiffany sat upright on the bed, clutching the sheets to her throat.

"Sweetheart, my little sweetheart" Frong said, sitting on her bed, we gotta' problem here."

"Jimmy, darling, I can explain—"

"Oldest cliché in 'da books, hon', I got it all on tape, no need 'ta explain," Frong smiled.

"What, what are you going to do?" she stammered.

"Well, babe, you and I are gonna' have a come 'ta Jesus moment. Youse are gonna' tell me you won't do 'dis again. If youse do—" he said, pulling the sheets from her, grabbing a breast, placing the point of his knife to her nipple, "we'll cut 'dese 'liddle beauties off, one by one. Shame, 'dere are only two, and 'den, we move on 'ta—"and he placed the knife at her neck.

Tiffany got the point. Frong would not have to repeat the process.

As for Marcus, that was another story.

Marcus cowered in the corner of the balcony, covering himself with his hands. "Can't jump, too high," he thought. "Shit, who's the 'Beast'? Husband? She's married? I gotta' get out of here! This guy is gonna' kill me for sure," he thought, listening for, but not hearing, any additional screams from Tiffany.

The balcony doors flew open, the goons grabbed him again, and carried him into the living room of the suite.

Frong sat on the large sectional sofa, his massive body testing the springs, Tiffany cowering in the corner, sobbing. Frong ignored her, grinning at Marcus.

"As youse perhaps have deduced, Mr. Appleton, I am 'duh cuckolded husband. 'Cuckolded'—such a nasty 'woid, Mr. Appleton! Do youse know the origin of 'duh 'woid? It's all about 'duh Cuckoo 'boid. 'Duh 'boid lays its eggs in another 'boids nest and 'den flies away." Frong shot a glance at Tiffany, and then focused on Marcus. "Youse is a Cuckoo 'boid, Mr. Appleton, but youse ain't got no wings, can't fly away. You had youse chance, out 'dere on 'duh balcony. Such tough shit, Mr. Appleton! Now, since we are engagin' in erudite 'tings here, let's try a scientific experiment, Mr. Appleton."

Pointing his knife at Marcus' cock, Frong asked, "What's 'da amount of time required 'ta cause an inflated object to deflate when 'dat object is inches away from full penetration by 'dis extremely sharp instrument here? "

Marcus stood, mute, nude, hands functioning as a fig leaf, afraid to speak.

"Well! I 'tink we know 'da answer," Frong grinned, further brandishing his Bowie knife, a long blade made famous by Jim Bowie, who used it to dissect and disembowel wildlife and, here and there, frontiersmen and Native Americans with whom Bowie often had disputes.

Marcus began to stammer as Frong ran his fingers over the blade. The goons stood to either side of Appleton, chuckling as they watched.

"I, I didn't know she was married," Marcus began.

"Did 'ja ask, Mr. Appleton?"

"Uh, never, never occurred to me—I mean, she came on to me, Marcus protested, gesturing toward Tiffany, black mascara streaming down her face.

"Let's cut to 'da chase, so to speak, Mr. Appleton," Frong said, rising from the sofa with his knife extended.

Marcus was hoisted off the floor by the two goons and held aloft. Frong approached, and Marcus felt Frong's hot breath on his chest, the knife on his testicles. Marcus prayed he would not live up to his nickname and shit himself.

"Youse are a guest of 'da Majestic, Mr. Appleton, which is why I call you 'Mr. Appleton' and not the spineless piece a dung youse are. Here's 'da plan. Youse are 'ta cancel 'da rest of your stay and leave 'da hotel and 'da city 'dis afternoon. Youse are 'ta have no more contact with my wife and youse will never, ever, again visit our fair city. If youse do, I will know," Frong said, gently moving his knife sideways, further withering Marcus' lower regions.

The goons dropped him and "Mr. Appleton" fell to the floor.

"Frong looked down with disgust and said, "Now get 'da hell out of Vegas before I do somethin' 'dat would make old Jim Bowie proud!"

Frong's goons grabbed a partly clad Tiffany and followed Jimmy from the suite, slamming the door on the way out.

Marcus headed for the bathroom.

Twenty Three

His tail between his legs, humiliated by Jimmy Frong, Marcus slouched back to Wild-O headquarters in New York. He tried to forget about the unfortunate turn of events in Sin City, except when he was tempted to go to Vegas, saw a knife flashed in some movie he might be watching, or bedded some young thing. As months passed, he regularly sat in his office hours on end, day after day, pondering Frong. Would Frong come after him? Was he safe? Probably so. Frong had, indeed, made his point.

Nevertheless, Marcus felt compelled to research Frong's history. The results were interesting and frightening. Ten years as a cop in Honolulu where Frong had a reputation for bashing heads and asking questions later, as he destroyed a major drug cartel. Five years as a detective in San Francisco where he was referred to as a latter day "Dirty Harry" Callahan. Then, five years at the Majestic. One story in the Las Vegas papers detailed Frong's ironclad security formula and his "take-no-prisoners" attitude when the well being of the Majestic's guests was threatened. He was regarded in Vegas as one tough son-of-a-bitch.

Marcus' fascination with Frong became an addiction, causing him to Google the "Beast" with regularity. Late one Wednesday evening, after Appleton had annihilated two employees who had disagreed with him on some minor marketing point, "The Shit" again surfed the Internet, looking for additional insight into Jimmy Frong. Something caught his eye.

Frong was a golfer. He was good enough that Harry Lee, the legendary Majestic Marketing Vice President, asked him regularly to golf with the Fortune 500 companies and national associations that booked the big money into the Majestic Hotel. Frong was a seven handicap. He was addicted to golf, further Google searches revealed.

Marcus turned, reached under the credenza, pulled out a fifth of Johnny Walker Black and a crystal snifter with "Wild-O" embossed on it. He poured two fingers of JWB and pondered Frong's golf addiction. It couldn't hurt to try to get on a better side of this maniac from Honolulu, Marcus reasoned. Would Frong get pissed if the man that had cuckolded him were to send gifts? Normally, yes, he thought, but he was confident Tiffany had been around the block many times, and he, Marcus, was just another notch on her faulty chastity belt.

Making a decision, he put Cheryl Woody in action. Cheryl placed calls, did the research, and then, did her magic, making suggestions regarding perks to be sent Mr. Frong's way. The following week, Frong's office received a huge package from Wild-O Golf, courtesy of Marcus Appleton; forty boxes of golf balls engraved in gold with Frong's monogram; twelve dozen FootJoy gloves; hundreds of assorted golf items; free magazine subscriptions to every golfing periodical imaginable; new Wild-O irons and the most recent Wild-O titanium driver.

Similar shipments were made several times each year. Cheryl regularly updated the stream of goodies, highlighted by the annual issuance of Wild-O golf's new driver. Tickets to Broadway plays also were sent, as were box seats to Major League ball games. To Marcus' knowledge, Frong used none of the tidbits—but the golfing items were not returned. This went on for almost two years, with no word of acknowledgement from Frong.

The long silence was broken in November of the second year

with a note: "Stop sending me all this shit. Send only the new clubs each year. Vegas is now open to you, the little woman has flown the coop." The note was signed, "Frong".

Most men would have considered the case closed, no need to fear Frong any longer. But because of his insecurity, and a need to believe that he could make Frong respect him, Marcus made it a point to convince Wild-O executives to schedule their Annual Worldwide Meeting each year at the Majestic, making certain the Majestic's management knew Wild-O was there because of Appleton's great admiration of Jimmy Frong.

The annual stream of Wild-O money to the hotel did indeed cause Majestic corporate to take notice. Recognizing that Jimmy Frong's connection with Wild-O Golf produced impressive bookings, he was amply rewarded by his employers.

Frong was not one to forgive and forget, but Marcus's determination to regularly rain money on the hotel was making Frong a wealthy man. Frong was impressed, and he reciprocated, absolving Marcus of all past sins, insisting "Mr. Appleton" once again enjoy Vegas and the Majestic. He pulled Marcus aside at the end of a round of golf with Harry Lee one hot summer day and said, "If anybody ever tries 'ta mess with youse, let me know, my boys can take care of it." It was a high compliment for Frong to deliver to one who had once landed in his nest. Marcus' ego failed to recognize Jimmy had erased his error and was offering respect, going out of his way to do so. "The Shit" simply shrugged his shoulders and said "Thanks," rolling his eyes when Frong turned away. "Why would he ever need one of Jimmy's goons?" he thought, recalling the knife to his testicles.

Twenty Four

Three years after Frong's offer of help—if it were ever needed—Marcus had changed his mind. His conviction that he would never need assistance from Jimmy vanished with the looming threat of fallout from "Dead Men's Clubs".

Marcus sat in his office with the same snifter he had used three years ago, renewing his Johnny Walker Black. He waited for a 10:30 p.m. conference call that Cheryl had arranged. As he did so, he began to doubt Frong would come through with the promise he had made. Marcus had continued booking the Majestic, and he knew Cheryl made sure to send Wild-O's newest driver each year, but was it really enough?

Was the "Beast" really over Marcus' indiscretion? Would Jimmy Frong come through for him? Frong was totally weird. He was always coiled, always ready to strike. Maybe it was just the memory of that Bowie knife to the nuts, or the fact that Jimmy was correct about the amazing ability of one's cock to shrink when faced with—"

The phone rang.

"Marcus here." he said, picking up the phone.

"Yeah, Jimmy here, how's it hangin'?"

"Smart ass," thought Marcus, and tried to answer with a smile in his voice. "Things are good on the East Coast, how's Sin City?"

"Same 'ole, same 'ole," what's up—I'm busy here," Jimmy said as Marcus imagined him looking at his watch, cleaning his nails with the Bowie knife.

"You told me a few years ago that I could call you if anyone screwed with me."

"Yeah? Offer still stands. Whaddya' need?"

"Well, there's this situation here at the Company," Marcus began, and explained his need in detail.

Frong was a man of few words. "Rooster will call youse," he said, hanging up. Marcus counted the words Frong had uttered. What were they, how many? Maybe—less than 25 words?

The phone rang within minutes.

"Yes?" Marcus said.

"Hey, Marcus, Rooster here. Jimmy told me to call youse. I can be in New York tomorrow morning. I'll take the Red Eye. Meet me at JFK at 8:30, I'm flyin' Jet Blue. Your little problem sounds like fun," Rooster said, and hung up.

Marcus cradled the phone and muttered to himself, "Fun, huh? Like hell. This is war."

Marcus entered the JFK terminal at 8:15 Wednesday morning, about the time Munch Malone teed off at The Greenbrier. He caught a portion of a CNN piece on one of the flat screens that dotted the terminal and recognized Malone's face. The old fart was everywhere, but where was this Rooster? Rooster had not been in the hotel suite on that ill-fated trip to Vegas, so how was he going to recognize him?

Marcus needn't have worried. Walking off the plane and into the terminal, Rooster looked like he was right out of central casting. A baldhead and rumpled white suit accented his five feet of height. His tie askew, a full day's beard growing rapidly, he looked around, his bloodshot eyes barely visible under bushy black brows, and headed directly for Marcus.

Dead Men's Clubs

"Let's get the fuck outa' here and find me a beer, I hate these freakin' red eyes," he said.

"I figured that was you, but how did you know it was me?" Marcus asked, looking down at Rooster with surprise.

"Your face, dickhead, the shocked look on you face! Never seen a dwarf before?"

"You, you're not a dwarf."

"You are correct, sir, one gene shy of a dwarf. Get your ass in gear, shithead," Rooster said, walking toward the sign that said "Baggage Claim". The Rooster—and he looked like a Rooster, Marcus thought—had just one bag. It was small and apparently contained very limited and well-worn clothing, judging from the soiled tie that jutted out of the soft bag's zipper track.

Marcus asked the cabbie to take them downtown to the Waldorf where he could leave Rooster's bags, and then to a bar Marcus knew would be open. Rooster fell asleep as soon as he settled into the back seat, snoring loudly and farting. Marcus rolled down the window on his side of the cab, even though it was already a hot and sticky New York morning.

Rooster awoke the moment the cab stopped at the Waldorf.

"Ok, ok, Waldorf, I like it!" he said, reaching into his vest pocket, pulling out a cigar and lighting it. "Where's the bar?"

"Five minutes away," Marcus said, handing off the luggage, tipping the bellman and re-entering the cab.

"Titty bar?" Rooster asked.

"Nope, just a bar," Marcus answered.

"Shame, I like titty bars," Rooster said with a big draw on his cigar that emitted a smell more foul than his farts.

"Billy Jean's," Marcus said to the cabbie.

Five minutes later the cabbie pulled in front of Billy Jean's, a 24-hour bar Marcus favored because of the Louisiana gal who always catered to Marcus' need to be recognized as a New York player. Billy Jean grew up in Plaquemine Parrish and played piano like Marcia Ball. Marcus loved the joint.

They sat at a table in the corner. Rooster's legs dangled from the chair in which he was sitting. The place was empty this early in the day except for the bartender and one guy at the bar checking his phone messages.

"See that guy?" Rooster said, pointing to the man at the bar.

"Yeah?"

"Loser."

"How do you know that?" Marcus asked.

"How do I know what?"

Marcus shrugged, "That he's a loser."

"Cheap suit, heels worn down, in a bar at this time of the morning. Huge freakin' loser," Rooster laughed.

"Well, *we're* here, aren't we?" Marcus said with a baleful stare at the ill kempt little man in the soiled shirt and scruffy suit that sat before him. Marcus was also certain that, if he could look under the table, he would see battered shoes that had never seen a shine.

"No, no!" Rooster said with a surprised look on his face. "We are here on 'bidness! All the difference in the world. Jimmy told me this assignment was of the highest importance and I do my best thinkin' in surroundings like this."

"So, Jimmy really wants to help me?"

"Listen pal, if Jimmy Frong has the Rooster catchin' a red eye with two hours' notice, you can bet your sweet ass he wants to offer no small amount of assistance," Rooster said, unaware of the irony.

A Heineken was placed in front of Rooster, a latte for Marcus.

Rooster took a long drag, calling after the waitress, "Keep 'em comin', baby!" He turned to Marcus and said, "What's 'da story?"

Marcus talked non-stop for thirty minutes. Rooster drank three beers during the discourse, giving Marcus pause for concern, but the little guy exhibited expressions that indicated his mind was working toward solving a problem.

"So, let me be sure I understand 'dis," Rooster said. "You want me to do some serious bodily damage to 'dis guy?"

"For God's sake, no!" Marcus protested, almost tossing his latte. "I just want you to get those friggin' clubs away from him; they've got to be the reason for his success because he couldn't hit the side of a barn before he got his hands on those clubs. For some reason, they make him a friggin' Jack Nicklaus. If Malone does well in the Championship, sales of our reconditioned clubs will probably shoot through the roof, and I'm gonna' lose my job to the asshole that runs the reconditioned clubs unit. Even if he loses, I still get pissed on because the Wild-O brand will have 'Dead Men's Clubs' written all over it; but at least I'll still be runnin' the show. You need to get those clubs!"

"Easy, pal, I'll just break into his house, steal the clubs and toss 'em in the nearest river," Rooster laughed, burping loudly.

"No, no, no, no!" Marcus said. "It's got to be subtle!"

"Subtle? Uh, what the fuck is that?"

"You have to make the clubs disappear in a manner that seems plausible."

"Plausible....?"

"In a way that seems quite logical—Malone loses them in air transit; he forgets they're in the trunk of the cab he's in; the hotel he's staying in misplaces them—shit, I don't know—-he accidentally melts them down with acid! This is your department, Rooster! Come up with something."

Rooster peered at Marcus over his third Heineken. "Subtle, huh? I got it. Let's get outa' here, I need some real food," Rooster said, sliding the bill to Marcus.

Twenty Five

Munch finished his third round of match play 2-up, qualifying for the Quarterfinals, and he and Melinda wanted to celebrate. They clearly savored the celebrity status at The Greenbrier where Munch's face was prominently featured in the pages of the national newspapers in the hotel gift shop, his face oozing from flat screen television sets throughout the massive hostelry. It had been that way since he and Melinda had arrived at The Greenbrier, along with his clubs, packed in a green cylindrical tube with "Munch Malone, Hilton Head Island, SC" emblazoned on it.

Munch was, as ever, overly protective of his Wild-O's. He did not completely believe they were the sole reason for his success, but why tempt fate? So, this evening, as he had done each day after play, Munch shouldered his bag and personally carried it back to his room, stashing the clubs in the closet, where he was sure they would be safe, pausing momentarily to take in the view from the room's expansive balcony.

Melinda and Munch showered and changed for dinner. They walked from their room to the elevator, waited for the doors to open, revealing a couple that moved to one side as they entered. The woman was lovely and flashed a wide smile. The gentleman was huge and grinned broadly, recognizing Munch.

"Hey, Munch Malone! We're gonna' be seeing a lot of each other, buddy."

Munch was uncertain at first, but quickly recognized Nick Carman, a former Senior Amateur champion.

"Nick Carman. Nice to see you. Great play today! You're right—we will be getting to know one another the next few days." Munch gestured toward his lady and said, "My wife Melinda," making introductions to Jed and his wife Lauren.

Carman took Melinda's hand with a light touch and stepped back, making an imaginary golf swing. He winked at Melinda and said, "Understand you're husband's using some pretty special clubs."

"Yeah, yeah, everybody knows about that," Munch grinned in reply as Melinda rolled her eyes. Munch liked Carman. Big Teddy Bear.

The elevator descended to the lobby and the door opened as Nick said, "Would you like to join us for dinner, guys? Lauren and I are headed for In-Fusion and then the tables at the Casino.

"Capital idea," Munch beamed, feeling just fine, looking at Melinda, who was nodding in agreement as she and Lauren bonded.

The four walked through the large lobby in the world famous resort and headed down the staircase that led to the lower level of exclusive shops, Café Carleton and Draper's Café. They descended yet another flight of steps to the exquisite Casino, past a twenty-foot tall white open oyster shell fountain spewing frothy water through which a rainbow of lights cascaded. They ambled through the Casino, passing craps tables and slot machines that created a cacophony of sound, and into In-Fusion, one of the many restaurants within the enormous Greenbrier complex. As they approached the restaurant they were unaware of a short figure in a rumpled suit who sat in the Twelve Oaks bar, nursing a Bloody Mary, following their every move. Rooster Rittenhouse, fresh from a US Airways flight from New York to D.C., and a rental car drive from there to White Sulphur Springs, West Virginia, pulled his cell phone from his pocket and texted Marcus Appleton. His eyes were bloodshot, his beard bragged of three days with no attention.

Marcus' phone pinged.

Rooster walked out of the bar and to the red elevator that serviced the Casino. He pushed the button and wrote with his thumbs, "I'm moving in on the clubs in a very, very, subtle way. I'll get back to you."

The elevator doors closed.

Marcus checked his text and texted Rooster back as the elevator in which Rooster was riding continued its rise. He exited and then took the stairs to the magnificent main lobby. His phone was pinging with Marcus' reply to his message.

"Glad 2 hear you r on the case, do all u can 2 get them quickly! Need 2 shut this down!" Marcus typed, finishing the text.

Rooster read the message as he punched the button beside a second elevator that rested between Dorothy Draper wallpaper boasting giant rhododendrons. He replied, typing, "Got it under control here, moving in! On top of it! U talkin 2 the Rooster here!"

"Yeah," Marcus sighed, texting, "you da man—now get the clubs, dammit!"

Rooster arrived on the second floor in the main wing of the hotel just as a young, good looking kid with a mop of blonde hair came down the hall from the Conference Center.

"Hey, Blondie', Rooster said, "Mr. Malone in 5193 needs some help. He needs to move his golf clubs downstairs for storage."

"Says who?" the bellhop replied, "I worked with him the day he checked in. He told me to make sure the clubs stayed in his room. Who are you, anyway? And my name isn't Blondie, its Blake!" the bellhop retorted.

"Easy, easy, Blondie, no disrespect. I'm Mr. Malone's brother-in-law, he asked me to find a bellhop to move his clubs to the bag check room, and here you are. Turns out his bride doesn't want to share her closet with a golf bag. Wimmen! Can't live 'wit 'em and can't live 'witout 'em," Rooster said, pulling a $100 bill out of his pocket, waving it at the bellhop.

"Bring it on!" the bellhop said, reaching for the $100 bill, running a hand through his long sun-bleached hair, retrieving the master room key he carried in his pocket. He unlocked the door to 5193 and moved to the closet, grabbing the golf clubs, returning to the hallway. He placed the Rodney bag on the luggage cart, turned and studied the short, strange-looking little man who stood beaming before him.

"Mr. Malone will need a baggage chit to get the clubs out of storage," the bellhop said

"Just leave it at the front desk, Blondie, I mean Blake—tell 'em Mr. Malone's brother-in-law will stop by for it," Rooster said, slapping the bellhop on the back. Rooster practically danced toward the elevator. He turned and said, "Pretty freakin' subtle, huh, Blondie?"

"Whatever," Blake replied, shrugging his shoulders.

Rooster sang to himself in the elevator and exited a few minutes later in the lower lobby of the hotel. He walked to the front desk where he drew the desk clerk's attention and said "I'm expecting my brother-in-law's golf clubs to be sent down here for storage in your baggage area. When they arrive would you please ring my cell. I need to get something out of the bag for him," Rooster explained, handing the desk clerk a card with his cell number—and a $100 bill.

"So, you are Mr. Malone's brother-in-law?" the desk clerk asked, ignoring the hundred.

"Yeah, 'Munch', 'Mr. Malone', is my brother-in-law, room 5193," Rooster answered.

"All right sir, I'll ring you when the bag arrives," the clerk said, looking over his half glasses at the little man in the rumpled suit.

"So," Rooster said, feeling what he considered to be a condescending stare. A moment of silence ensued as the two men studied one another.

Rooster thumbed the $100 bill on the counter, looked away, and then back. "Want the hundred?" he asked, squinting at the clerk's half glasses.

"No need for that, sir," the desk clerk answered, a thin smile on his lips, turning to study his computer screen.

"Excuse me, my good man," Rooster said in his cheeriest mood, standing on tippy toes in front of the desk.

"Yes?" the clerk said, again glancing down at the little fellow.

"Is it at all *plausible* that I may have offended you in some way?"

"No sir, good day, sir," the desk clerk said, looking back at his computer screen.

"Tell 'ya what, bud, this is too freakin' subtle for me. Here's four more Ben Franklins, make sure you call me when the bag gets down here!"

The desk clerk looked up, saw the five $100 bills, and quickly palmed them.

"It's my pleasure, sir," he said, looking down at the strange little man who was smiling broadly, holding aloft his middle finger.

Twenty Six

Rooster danced once again to the far end of the lobby where he flopped into a wing chair and pulled out his phone. "Got my mojo workin," he texted Marcus. "Bag on way downstairs—will call u when job done." He jumped from the chair and headed down the massive white marble staircase to the Café Carleton, pushing a diminutive, silver-haired grandmother and her Jack Russell dog aside as he did so.

"Asshole," the senior citizen shouted, grabbing for a brass handrail that was polished to a high, golden sheen.

Rooster paid her no mind as he bounded past her and down the stairs. He came to a skidding stop on brilliant black and white marble floors. Hearing her rant, he turned and saw Grandma hanging onto the handrail, clutching her dog to her chest. He stared up at her, flashed a smile, and shot his middle finger once more.

"Damn!" Sink said, watching the action on High Def. "What a nasty little fellow! Why's this freak trying to rip off Munch's clubs?"

He reached for his iPhone and texted Snarf. "At Galaxy Espresso, Snarf—Emergency! Drop whatever you're doing, get here now!" Sink wrote, thumbs flying.

Snarf ran his hair through his greasy locks as he heard the ping. He glanced at his iPhone and saw the text.

"Shit," he exclaimed, slamming his laptop closed, ending his Google search for women who could suck a tennis ball through a garden hose. "These old geezers think they own the Snarf!" he said to himself, kicking back from the desk. He scratched his balls, and headed out the door.

Sink summoned War who arrived at Galaxy Espresso, also looking irritated as he walked through the door. Snarf's anger quickly evaporated as he eyed the barista with the mini-skirt who was leaning over Sink's table serving a Frappuccino.

"You woke me out of a nap, this better be good," War groused, ordering a double espresso.

"Munch's clubs are in danger of being stolen," Sink said.

"The beat goes on! I love it!" Snarf said, sitting upright.

"What are you talking about?" War asked.

"Some weird looking little guy just conned the desk clerk at The Greenbrier into believing the 'Dead Men's Club's' are his," Sink frowned.

"Is this random or is somebody making a play for the clubs? Why would someone want Munch's clubs?" War asked.

"Dude," Snarf replied, "the guy believes in' Contagion'! He's tuned into the news media! He thinks he'll play the way Munch does if he has his clubs."

"May be, but I'll bet my bottom dollar this guy's not a golfer, he's practically a dwarf," Sink said.

"Hey, man, I'm just sayin'—those clubs are gonna' be hot property—everybody will want 'em. What's the scam, man, am I needed here? I mean, I'm good suckin' this coffee as long as Bunny Barista is bending over, but, whattya' want from me?" Snarf asked, feeling the urge for some Vanilla Bean.

"I want you to hack into that phone the little man is using and see if you can find out what's going on," Sink answered.

"Mary Jane Vanilla is runnin' low, man," Snarf advised.

"Just ask the barista, it's behind the counter. Better get it home before it melts," Sink scowled.

Twenty Seven

Rooster sat in the check-in lobby, strategically seated behind a column near the hall leading to The Greenbrier Shops. From there he could keep an eye on the baggage storage room. He busied himself with a Heineken from Café Carleton and a *Playboy* he had purchased in the hotel's newsstand. He peeked around the sides of the magazine as he watched the elevator. Thirty-five minutes had passed when the doors to the lift opened and Blondie emerged with Munch's clubs on his cart. The kid left his cargo at the door of the baggage room and walked away, heading toward the front desk.

"Shit, grab 'em now!" Rooster said to himself.

He threw the magazine down and advanced toward the cart.

As he started to reach for the clubs, thinking how easy this was, a voice behind him said, "Excuse me," and Munch Malone, en-route with Melinda and the Carmans to the Casino, stepped in front of Rooster, lifting the travel bag containing his clubs from the baggage cart.

"No problem," Rooster said, frowning and backing away. He walked past Nick Carman and moved swiftly behind one of the four large columns that graced the hotel lobby.

"What the hell are my clubs doing here?" Munch asked Melinda.

"I don't know, dear, it's not my day to watch them," Melinda replied, chatting with Lauren, looking down the hall toward the ladies' shoe store in the corridor of boutiques just off the lobby area.

The bellhop returned from the reception desk with the baggage room key in his hand.

"Mr. Malone! Good timing. Your bag claim check is at the desk. I thought your brother-in-law was gonna' pick it up," the good-looking blonde kid said with an engaging smile.

"My brother-in-law? My brother-in-law is in Tucson," Munch said.

"Nope, he's here in the hotel. He asked me to move your clubs down here for storage." The kid leaned close to Munch, grinning, and whispered in his ear so Melinda could not hear, "He said Mrs. Malone didn't want your clubs in her closet, too many shoes. I guess she asked your brother-in-law to get the clubs moved."

"Pardon me, young man, but my brother-in-law is *not* here, my wife did *not* ask for the clubs to be moved, and I sure as hell am *not* leaving them down here for some imposter to steal," Munch protested, grabbing the Rodney bag and his clubs.

The Snarf easily hacked into Rooster's phone and retrieved the texts between Rooster and Marcus. It quickly became clear that the little man who was obsessed with Munch's clubs worked for a fellow by the name of Marcus Appleton who was employed by Wild-O Golf. The Snarf ran the Google searches and discovered Appleton was National Sales President for Wild-O Golf. Further Google searches on the dwarf named Rooster yielded few results.

Snarf texted Sink: " 'Marcus' is marcus appleton, pres, nat sales, wild-o golf—he wants 2 steal munch's clubs 2 stop media's continuing reference 2 them as dead men's clubs—little man is called rooster, works for appleton who thinks malone's success with dead men's clubs will damage wild-o image. Says once he gets malone's clubs he'll make sure malone will never again b able 2 buy a wild-o reconditioned club. Could not find diddly squat on rooster."

Sink sat in the Clubhouse with War, nursing a scotch, monitoring Munch and Melinda as they returned Munch's clubs to their room, double checking the lock, retracing their steps to the lobby. He re-read Snarf's message that contained the exchange between Marcus and Rooster and relayed the content to War.

"If this guy gets our clubs, were 'SOL'," Sink said.

"Well, we're up here and he's down there, so, I agree. We're SOL," War responded.

"Let's think about it," Sink said, again reading Snarf's text, searching for ideas. He came to a conclusion and turned to War.

"We have High Def as long as Munch and the clubs are together. This guy may have done us a favor. Our boy Munch won't let those clubs out of his sight now, I'll bet. That at least will let us monitor any shenanigans that Appleton and his nasty little man try," Sink said, staring at Munch and Melinda as they hurried from their hotel room to rejoin the Carmans at the Casino.

"Yep, we can just sit here and watch this guy—what did Snarf says his name is—Rooster? We can watch him try time and again to get Munch's clubs and we can't do a damn thing about it," War said.

"I'm just saying—we need to think about this. Who's got skin in the game? Who can help us down there?" Sink said, drumming his fingers on the table.

"Well, let's see, Appleton, the Rooster guy, Wild-O Golf, the used Wild-O clubs division. This guy John Short who is the Vice President of Reconditioned—"

"That's it, there's an opening. We'll get Snarf to hack into Short's phone and advise Short of any plans Appleton has and get him to derail the train," Sink said.

"I 'dunno, Short may be as interested in getting 'Dead Men's Clubs' out of the media spotlight as Appleton is," War suggested.

"You could be right, but let's think about it," Sink said. The evening wore on and more liquor was consumed. The two old golfers perked up when the High Def came to life, featuring Munch and Melinda returning to their room.

Basking in thoughts of a splendid evening they had spent with the Carmans, and with the 'Dead Men's Clubs' safely in their closet, the Malones brushed their teeth, flossed, took their vitamin pills and statins. Munch waived a Viagra pill in front of Melinda, smiling. She nodded affirmatively and they switched off the light and crawled under the fluffy, white down comforter.

Munch nuzzled on Melinda's ear until he was fully erect and rolled over to put his balls in play, when he was startled by a loud "ping" from somewhere in the room.

"What the hell is that?" he thought to himself, twisting around, his eyes immediately going to the smoke alarm on the ceiling of the overhanging roof of the room's balcony. Amalfi rolled over at the foot of the bed, refusing to be awakened.

"What's wrong, babe?" Melinda asked.

"Damn smoke alarm, battery must be dead. The damn thing pings every ten seconds," Munch replied, throwing back the covers.

"What are you doing?" Melinda asked, suddenly wide-awake.

"Munch hoisted himself out of bed and shuffled toward the noise, his bare behind exposed, his erection leading the way. "I'm gonna' get the battery out of the damn thing," he said.

"Call the front desk, Munch, "let them do it," Melinda countered.

"Naw, I can reach it."

"Don't be ridiculous, Munch, the ceiling is at least 12 feet high, and the smoke alarm is way out there—you can't reach it!"

"I think I can, if…" Munch said, looking around for something to stand on. He pulled an ottoman to the front of the balcony, stood on it, and stretched his short frame out over the ledge.

"Munch, stop it, you'll kill yourself."

"Naw, I can reach it," Munch assured his wife, moving from the ottoman to a perch on the ledge of the balcony railing.

"Munch! Stop! I'm calling downstairs!"

"If I can just reach the overhang and balance myself…" he said, reaching out, grabbing the roofline, securing a hold on the roof ledge. He balanced himself there and stretched his body forward with one hand grasping the ledge, the other reaching for the smoke alarm that continued to ping with regularity. His erection grew larger.

He slipped. And then regained his balance.

"Munch! You're going to fall!" Melinda screamed.

Munch, stretched to the hilt, looked back at Melinda and grinned. "Naw," he said, "I got it!" and made the mistake of looking down. He was almost horizontal as he peered into the blackness, five stories from the ground. The uplighting on the hotel seared through the dark in myriad streams and Munch immediately became disoriented. His feet slipped from the balcony ledge and Melinda screamed bloody murder.

Munch felt his body swing forward as he held tightly to the roof ledge, his bare buttocks and impressive and engorged appendage swinging wildly in the breeze.

"Call 911!" he screamed, "Call 911!"

Munch held on for dear life. The smoke alarm, just inches from him, continued to ping, ignoring Munch's plight. Melinda leaned from the balcony, shouting words of encouragement—and critique. "Hang on, Munch, I'll get help! Why won't you listen to me! You are *such* an ass!" Amalfi, now fully engaged, barked with excitement.

The door to the hotel room began to vibrate as three Greenbrier employees banged on it. Melinda rushed to give them access, wondering how they knew of the predicament. She didn't ponder the question too long, pointing toward the balcony as the three men rushed forward. Hotel lights blazed to life and the corridor outside the Malone room started to fill with guests in their pajamas.

Munch began to perspire heavily as he felt his grip loosening. A searchlight from below zeroed in on him and he suddenly realized he was naked. "Oh, fine," he thought, "I hoped I'd be remembered at The Greenbrier, but, for God's sake, not like this!"

"Hold on sir, we've got you!" a voice said from below.

Munch looked down and saw a platform rising toward him. The portable platform lift used for washing upper floor windows had, somehow, suddenly appeared and it rose alongside the now illuminated hotel front, coming to a halt as Munch's bare feet touched the platform floor and his erection vanished. Munch grabbed the side of the steel savior with one hand to prevent himself from collapsing while doing fig leaf with the other hand as he looked down. Cheers went up from below where a small crowd of onlookers had gathered.

The platform edged to the balcony of the Malone's room and The Greenbrier employees hoisted Munch to safety. Munch looked back, realizing the crowd was now being mooned. A dog was barking madly and it wasn't Amalfi. Munch looked down and saw some old dame with a dog straining on its leash. Was it a Jack Russell? As the crack of his behind slipped over the ledge and out of sight he heard the old lady shout "I've got $5,000 on you in Vegas to win this tournament, Malone, get your ass in gear or I'll kick it back to South Carolina!"

"Glad to know Munch can still get it up, but that was close, very close," Sink said, laughing, pressing the "*off*" button, dousing the High Def.

"Yep, glad we were tuned in," War grinned, "Nice—the way you roused that desk clerk and got that rig under Munch, so quick and all that."

"Yeah—well, you heard what the old gal said," Sink chortled, hoisting his scotch, "We've got our money riding on the boy and we need to cover his ass, not to mention his erection!"

Twenty Eight

John Short and Rex Reynolds had been working the phones for days. As far as Short was concerned, D.E. Wildoe had given him the green light to take down Marcus Appleton. He also knew Appleton had come to the same conclusion and would be out to "deep-six" reconditioned sales and one John short with it. This was serious business and Short Sale's career was at stake.

Voice mail from Short to Reynolds: "Step up the research in any way you deem advisable. We're in a contest now with Appleton. He'll do anything he can to sabotage Malone and the Reconditioned Clubs Division. I want to know what the golfing public thinks about Malone, 'Dead Men's Clubs', 'Contagion', and every other positive or negative impression you find. You have approval to move without regard to budget constraints. Thanks for all you've done to date, now, let's step it up. Thanks, Rex."

Snarf hacked in and read texts and listened to voice mail on each of the three phones belonging to Rooster, Appleton, and John Short. He whistled softly to himself, reached for a Bud, and headed for the Clubhouse where he brought Sink up to date as the Scotsman sat back in his chair, assessing the information.

Sink nodded his head approvingly and turned to War. "Okay, thanks to the Snarf's good work, we know Appleton and Rooster are intent on stealing the clubs, which would bring an abrupt halt to any chance Munch has to win the Tournament. We know John Short is equally intent on Malone succeeding and that he knows Appleton's plan. So, we have an ally in Short. We also need some logical way to let Malone know when trouble's afoot."

Snarf ran his fingers through his greasy locks and said, "Well, the Wild-O chat guy can text Malone's phone."

"Good idea, that makes sense," Sink said.

"I can get it started with some simple stuff about how proud Wild-O is, yada', yada', yada'," Snarf said.

"Sheila!" War shouted, "Bring Snarf some ice cream!"

Munch and Melinda awoke to a splendid morning in the mountains and a sensational day for golf. The antics of the night were discussed and what was an embarrassing near-death experience quickly became a funny story to tell and then forgotten, as spectators streamed onto The Greenbrier grounds. Helicopters came and went, ferrying coal and oil and gas executives who were being given VIP treatment from the suppliers of continuous mining machinery and manufacturers of pipe to move natural gas. Ten thousand people would line the course this day.

Munch was visibly nervous, and his arms were sore from hanging on for dear life the night before. He started shanking balls on the driving range, waiting for the Quarterfinals to begin. He waved to Carman, to his right. Nick was casually and easily talking with the gallery. He seemed to have no stage fright.

"God" Munch thought, 'I've got to relax and concentrate."

From the range he moved to the putting green, waiting for his tee time. As he approached the green he was accosted by autograph seekers, a new and strange experience.

"Dead Men's Clubs!" yelled a fan, and the rush was on. Middle-aged and senior golfers who wanted to shake his hand surrounded Munch. Encouragement and best wishes were tossed at him like confetti. He shook hands for twenty minutes and felt the soreness in his arms begin to relax. He stroked putts for half an hour, and headed for the first tee.

Munch knew that his opponent, Nick Carman, had *won* the Senior Amateur two years earlier. Nick was 59 years old, eleven years younger than Munch. He was a really big guy; six feet, six inches tall, with a rosy complexion. Media loved him. He was gregarious and the press had taken to calling him "The Big Teddy Bear." Munch and Melinda had enjoyed their evening with Carman and his wife Lauren, and even Munch could not help but like him.

The distinguished announcer at the first tee, Dean Elliot, dressed in plaid pantaloons and a Tam O'Shanter cap, bellowed; "Now playing, from White Bear Lake, Minnesota, Nick Carman!"

Melinda caught Munch's gaze as she stood just outside the ropes. She gave him a bright smile and a thumbs-up. He spotted his golf buddies, Eugene Columbus and Dave Rambo, who had taken a few days off just to come and, as they had put it, "watch history." Munch shook his head and grinned at the absurdity of it all—that *he* should be playing in the Senior Amateur! His buddy John Henry, he knew, could not attend. John had several surgeries that day, but the flat screen in his OR was tuned all day to *The Golf Channel*. It was a testament to his friendship with Munch, because *The Food Network* was normally on in the doctor's office and OR.

Munch stood on the tee, waiting for Nick to tee off. He removed his cap and wiped his forehead clean of the beads of perspiration that were beginning to form. He winked at Dave and Eugene as they looked his way, thumbs up, grinning ear to ear. He was not aware that Snarf was trying to text him. His phone was in his bag beneath his rain gear.

The Snarf swore to himself and left a text informing Sink and Lair that Munch was not answering. "The dude ain't even aware he has a phone with him—we need a new approach," he wrote.

"Gotta' settle down when I get up to the tee, gotta' breathe deeply, gotta' waggle the club, gotta' stay in the zone, gotta' whistle softly, gotta' get oily like Snead used to do," Munch chanted to himself, looking again at the gallery and once more losing all concentration. To make matters worse, he had a new caddy whose reputation intimidated the hell out of Munch from the moment they had met.

Pumpkin Jones was older than most of the bag boys on the course and was well known in golf circles. He had made a living at the game since he was in his twenties; and was a sensation in the 70's, qualifying for the PGA Tour with ease. Munch had followed his short career.

"Munch, ready to bruise the ball?" a voice asked. Munch turned and looked into Jones' face. He felt a tinge of embarrassment, realizing his nervousness was showing. "Right, bruise the ball!" Munch stammered.

Jones looked like a golfer. He was 6'2", sun-wrinkled and perpetually tan from hours on the course. His dark brown hair was peppered with gray and tied into a ponytail that hung halfway down his back. The craggy features said he had been around a while, along with a certain gait that labeled him as an athlete. Those were the positives. The negatives were his bloodshot, squinty eyes and a certain nervous tremor that appeared when too much alcohol had been consumed the night before, giving rise to the realization that Pumpkin's game was yesterday's news.

Pumpkin had been a vicious contender in his time, but now he was known only as a ruthless caddy. He had experienced some bad years on the tour and had come to detest the game he once loved and the people who played it. His reputation attracted golfers who wanted a caddy who would do anything to help them win. Pumpkin willingly aided them if they wished to cheat and he was well paid for it.

His downfall toward the life he now lived had been his lifestyle. Three failed marriages, one bankruptcy, and a heavy dependency on cigarettes and bourbon. Pumpkin had lasted just one year on the Big Tour, where he thought he had a future; now, those hopes dashed, he lived hand to mouth.

Snarf emitted a strange giggle, watching Munch on the first tee, nervously chatting with Jones, glancing toward Carman who was ready to tee off. "That boy's shakier than a banana in a blender. Shame he can't get my text!"

"I'm afraid you're right," Sink said, looking at War. "War—Munch has that driver of yours in his hands. Settle him down."

Nick, the big Minnesotan, began his backswing on number one, known simply as *First*—449 yards of fairway, a par four. Munch watched, nervously massaging his driver, starting to withdraw it from the Rodney, stopping in mid-draw, watching Carman's ball take off like a bullet, easily carrying over a deep bunker shielding the right side of the green. It was a beautiful drive.

"My God, he *can* bruise the ball! That's got to be a 275-yard drive! First this damn caddy, then a shot from a cannon! That's all the intimidation I need," Munch thought.

Munch's alarm began to fade as he re-gripped his driver and fully yanked it from the Rodney bag. How different it was when he touched these clubs! It was happening again. Confidence began to ooze through his body. He looked at the driver, and felt 'Contagion'—he was someone else, intensity mounting as he fondled the club. He gently massaged the shaft and kissed the big head.

"God, I wish he wouldn't do that! I feel like I've been violated!" War said, recoiling back into the big easy chair in which he was sitting.

Dead Men's Clubs

"He loves you, man!" Snarf said with a snort, slapping War's forearm with force, knocking it off the bar.

"Dammit, Snarf, don't ever do that! I've got a golf match to play here and I don't need a broken arm!"

"Easy, War, just 'Channel', just 'Channel'—concentrate," Sink said.

"Now playing at the first tee, Munch Malone from Hilton Head Island, South Carolina!" Dean Elliott bellowed once more.

Munch stepped authoritatively to the tee. He glanced up at the big clock that ticked away just over the tee. The Greenbrier logo, spelled out through innovative landscaping just to the left of the fairway, was hard to ignore. Beautiful. A view worthy of the gods.

Munch felt the rush. 'Contagion' was flowing.

"That's the guy with the 'Dead Men's Clubs'," someone against the ropes whispered, loud enough for Munch to hear. Munch hesitated and stepped back from the tee, swinging the driver in practice.

"Quiet, quiet please!" shouted the marshal to the crowd, glaring at the offender who had caused Munch to step back.

The spectator's voice was saying exactly what Chad Ray was relating to *The Golf Channel* audience as the cameras closed in on Munch's face and panned down to his driver.

"Malone has caused quite a sensation here with the clubs he's using. They are, he says, Wild-O Golf used, or, reconditioned, clubs—he refers to them as 'Dead Men's Clubs' because he thinks they were once owned by golfers who are among the dearly departed. There are those who think Malone may be getting some help from above!" Ray said with a chuckle.

D.E. Wildoe grunted with displeasure, lifted one cheek of his ass and farted with emphasis as he viewed the broadcast on the big screen in the CEO's office in New York.

"And my understanding, Chad, is that Wild-O reconditioned sales *are* being affected—in a positive way. Golfers are buying them, hoping for what they are calling 'Contagion'—a little extra help from former players, the same result Malone says he's getting," Ray's fellow broadcaster, Cheryl Anne Roane, said.

"So I've heard. Have you placed your order yet, Cheryl?" Ray needled.

Wildoe grunted again, reaching for the single malt he had poured in anticipation of the broadcast.

Munch cleared his head and addressed the ball.

War closed his eyes and concentrated.

Standing just under the ropes was Rooster. He held his phone next to his chest and surreptitiously texted Marcus. "No chance 2 grab clubs on course. Could try 2 bribe caddy–guy has a rep for fast buck–pumpkin jones, big loser–how much can I offer?"

Munch felt the surge of power as he turned his hips and brought his arms to a full rotation, receiving a blast of 'Contagion'. The golf ball imitated that shot of Eugene's he had so admired. It soared left of center, seeming to put its hand to its forehead, studying the fairway. It landed with a clear view of the green, settling in nicely 144 yards from the green.

The crowd burst into applause.

"Nice shot, I love it!" Pumpkin said, taking the driver from Munch, ramming it in the Rodney, walking down the fairway beside his golfer.

"What's in your bag? This thing's heavier than a concrete truck," Pumpkin asked, bending under the weight of the Rodney.

"It's mostly the weight of the bag itself; I like a good sturdy bag, Pumpkin," Munch answered, feeling like a pro with a caddy on the bag, starting to relax with Jones, warming to him.

"Well, 'ya got one, that's for damn sure," Pumpkin said, moving the Rodney from one shoulder to the other.

Sink admired Munch's shot and fist bumped War. "Nicely done, my man," he said. "Good shot, great 'Channeling'!"

"Sheila! Let's have a round! MacCallan's and Hendrick's for the old fart golfers and ice cream for the soon to be stoned hacker!" Snarf shouted across the room, watching Sheila approach.

"Just thought I'd check to make sure bad boy here has your approval," Sheila said to War, looking disapprovingly at Snarf.

"Yes! He's the horse we're riding today!" War said. Sheila winked and walked away.

Snarf's eyes followed Sheila and he could not contain himself. "And what a beautiful filly she is! I'd sure like to saddle up on that!" he leered, licking his chops.

"I think you'll have to stand behind War, old boy," Sink said, smiling broadly, watching War watch Sheila with great appreciation.

Twenty Nine

The day and the Quarterfinal wore on. John Short half walked, half ran, through the throng that was moving around the course. He had wanted to meet with Malone prior to the round, but his flight had been delayed in Charlotte, North Carolina and he would not have an opportunity to see Munch until later in the day. He had asked Reynolds to establish a work center in one of the cottages on the course, in order to give him instant feedback on the tracking numbers. Sales were picking up and he was convinced today's *Golf Channel* coverage, if Munch did well, would provide another boost.

Marcus Appleton's chartered Learjet touched down at the Lewisburg, West Virginia airport that served The Greenbrier. The waiting dark green limousine whisked him down Interstate 64 for the short drive to the hotel. Marcus had not been to the "Brier" before, and he was duly impressed as the limo entered the grounds that had hosted numerous Presidents and heads of state. He knew that, under the limo's wheels, existed a gambling casino and the "Bunker" that once served as an emergency headquarters for the United States Congress in Cold War days.

"Where to begin?" he wondered, as Del, the Greenbrier's veteran Front Door Lead, welcomed him and took charge of his luggage. Marcus was behind schedule and Rooster's text flashed on his iPhone screen while Del gave Marcus a lay of the land at the historic hotel. As Del rattled on, Marcus' mind was elsewhere.

Rooster's message was clear—the little man thought he could bribe the caddy to steal Munch's clubs. Outstanding. Only the caddy had ready access to the Rodney bag. Marcus reached for his iPhone and began to text.

"Offer 5K. Caddy must replace clubs–all clubs. Bogus clubs 2 arrive later today via fedex. Get them 2 caddy and tell him 2 replace half clubs tomorrow, half before final round. We'll find out if the damn clubs make a difference."

Rooster read the text and thought to himself, "Pretty freakin' subtle!"

The front nine seemed to sweep by. Munch and Nick finished Ten and Eleven, and arrived at the Twelfth hole, known as *Long*, a design concept that mimicked number Fourteen on the Old Course, St. Andrews, Scotland. Munch assessed his situation. He had hit a 200 yard drive on the par five, a 568 yard hole, a cross bunker, leaving him 368 yards to the pin. Now he had to negotiate the "Hell" bunkers and the creek that crossed the fairway from right to left. Not easy.

"What are you gonna' do, War," Sink said, *calmly sipping his scotch, enjoying the moment, moving his gaze from the high def to Man O'War.*

"I'm gonna' make "Hell" disappear and ignore the creek. I'll use a six iron and drop the ball on the false front," War said, shifting in his seat, zeroing in on the Rodney bag.

"Do that, and Sheila will wet her pants for you," Sink smiled.

Munch told Pumpkin to pull the six iron.

"Whatcha' gonna do, man?" Pumpkin asked.

"Put it on the false front," Munch said.

"Forget it. Don't you know that front rejects just about every shot that lands there?" Pumpkin asked, incredulously.

"Yep, gimme' the six iron."

"Your funeral, man, go for it," Pumpkin said, puffing on a cigarette. He handed Munch the club.

"I wish you wouldn't do that," Munch said, looking at the cigarette.

"Tough shit, man, I'm here to caddy for you, not to change my lifestyle."

Sink took a practice swing, looked down range and shifted his left foot back just a bit. He hesitated, rocked back and forth on his feet, imagined the shot, and began his backswing.

Munch hit the shot.

"Damn, man, that's pretty incredible," Carman said to his caddy in astonishment as the ball landed on the false front, reversed its spin, and stopped cold. The gallery exploded with applause.

"Let's take another look at that! This has to be the shot of the day! That shot was classic!" Chad Ray said as the replay filled the screen.

Nick Carman walked over and slapped Munch on the back, nearly knocking him down, "Just about the greatest freakin' shot I've ever seen, Munch! I think I'll get me some of those 'Dead Men's Clubs'," he winked.

Munch walked the fairway as though he were walking on clouds.

Sink then took control from War. His pitch and putt were classic. He was down in four—birdie!

The gallery was ecstatic.

Sink jumped to his feet and pounded the air, yelling, "Yeah, baby! 'Contagion' is Rage'n!" He bowed from the waist, addressing the giant High Def that was focused on the fans in wild applause as the Golf Channel panned the fairway. "Thank 'yew, thank 'yew very much," he said, in his best Elvis imitation.

Dead Men's Clubs

"You're a piece of work!" Pumpkin said to Munch as they walked down the fairway.

"Thanks, sometimes I think the clubs are swingin' by themselves," Munch said.

"So, they *really are* 'Dead Men's Clubs' and somebody up there is swingin' em for 'ya?" Pumpkin asked, shifting Munch's Rodney from one shoulder to the other.

"Don't know I'd go that far, but my game sure has changed with these clubs," Munch said. "You know, Pumpkin, I remember when you were on the tour. You were damned good. I liked you a lot."

"Yeah, well, that was then and this is now," Pumpkin said with a shrug. "My past and a hundred bucks will get me laid."

"Just my luck, a real jackass for an Eighteen hole walk that's the biggest of my life," Munch thought, realizing his earlier assessment of Pumpkin was off target.

Munch finished the Quarterfinal round 2-up. He was "The Man" and the media intensified its focus. He was whisked away to a news conference when play ended. He left his Rodney and clubs with his caddy, instructing him that the bag was not to go out of his sight. Pumpkin shouldered the Rodney, walked to the Media Center, stood at the rear of the room, and watched his golfer field questions.

"Munch, pretty impressive today; how's it feel to be leading here when, less than a year ago, you were virtually unknown?" asked *NBC*.

"Well, pretty incredible. Like I said before, I never thought I'd be taking a question from guys like you," Munch answered. The reporters in the room laughed in unison.

"Munch," *CBS* asked, speaking of 'impressive', we understand you were sort of 'hanging out' at the hotel last night."

"Huh?" Munch replied, confused.

"We're told you had a smoke alarm problem."

"Oh, that! Yeah, pretty embarrassing. Impressive? Well, all I know is I stood out like a sore thumb," Munch grinned, looking at the zipper on his trousers.

Laughter all around.

"So, not all your clubs are dead, huh?" *The Golf Channel* asked.

More laughter from the reporters.

Thirty

A frown crossed the face of Marcus Appleton as he stepped out of the shower, grabbed a towel and watched Munch fielding questions. He texted Rooster. "Can't let this go on. Where r u and what r u doing to get hands on clubs?"

Rooster was watching the post round quiz, standing just behind Pumpkin Jones. He placed a hand on the six iron. No one was looking.

Pumpkin shifted his weight and Rooster quickly released the club.

The questions ended and Munch was shaking hands. Pumpkin exchanged congratulatory fist bumps with those passing where he and Rooster stood.

Rooster leaned around the caddy and said, "Scuse me, pretty remarkable out there today. I got a proposition for 'ya that I'd like to have a little time to discuss. If we could meet in the Twelve Oaks bar at the hotel, in an hour or so, I could make it worth your time."

Pumpkin turned, saw no one, wondering from where the voice had come.

"Well?" said the voice, and Pumpkin looked down.

There, below him, looking up with a quizzical stare, was a strange little man in a rumpled suit.

"Make it worth my time?" Pumpkin asked, repeating Rooster.

"Yeah, $5,000 worth."

Pumpkin did not hesitate. He pulled a cigarette from his third pack of Marlboros for the day, nodded at Rooster, and said, "See you in an hour."

"Mojo workin–caddy 2 meet me in 1 hour–will offer 5k 4 xchange of clubs–do u have the bogus clubs?" Rooster texted Marcus.

"In my hotel room, ready when u need them," Marcus texted back.

"Pretty freakin' subtle, huh?" wrote Rooster.

"Just get the damn clubs," Marcus responded.

Rooster shrugged, brushed at the soiled sleeve of his white jacket and headed for the hotel. He walked to the staircase leading to the Casino, trundled down two flights, walked past thundering slots and up the two steps leading to Twelve Oaks Bar. He signaled the barkeep as he walked past dark wood that featured a massive bronze sculpture of horse and rider that dominated the bar. He settled into a chair in the rear of the room and waited for the caddy. Within thirty minutes Pumpkin descended the staircase, adjusted his eyes to the vibrant Dorothy Draper colors, and focused on the strange little man who waved to him from deep within Twelve Oaks.

"So, what's this all about?" Pumpkin asked, taking a seat across from Rooster.

"Hey, it's all about a big payday for 'ya, pal!" Rooster grinned, his face just above table level, legs dangling in mid-air.

"Payday for what?" Pumpkin asked, motioning to the bartender for a Heineken to match Rooster's.

"First, this conversation is off the record, Okay?"

"Whatever."

"Okay, I'll take that as a 'yes,'" Rooster said. "I have a client who very much would like to have the pleasure of owning those golf clubs your golfer Munch Malone is using."

"I'm not sure he'll want to sell 'em after that round today, but, in any case, he won't be able to part with 'em 'till he finishes the tournament."

Rooster took a long draught from the Heineken. "Subtle, subtle," he reminded himself.

"Actually, Pumpkin—may I call you Pumpkin? My client will need the clubs *before* tee time tomorrow."

"Are you freakin' crazy? Malone can't give up his clubs, he'd be disqualified. Besides, he's paranoid about them, says he almost lost them in the hotel," Pumpkin said.

"Screw subtle," thought Rooster. This was getting way too complex.

"Yeah, I almost had 'em in the lobby, but timing is everything." he said.

"You're trying to steal Malone's clubs?"

"Yeah, that's the long and short of it. You've got access to the clubs; I've got duplicate clubs to replace the ones you lift. If you can pull it off without him seein' 'ya, he'll never know the clubs are gone. If Malone loses, you, my fine fellow, will pocket $5,000," Rooster beamed.

"Why does your client want the clubs?" Pumpkin asked, lighting a cigarette.

The waitress was on Pumpkin like a fly on honey. "You can't smoke in here, sir."

"Lady, what does it look like I'm doing—get outta' here," Pumpkin said.

"I'll call the manager!"

"Call whoever you like, sweetheart," Pumpkin retorted, exhaling a torrent of smoke.

Rooster shifted in his chair and tried to get his elbows on

the chair arms, without success. "Uh, my client, okay? He's a collector; he wants to have these rather remarkable clubs in his collection."

"Why? They're used clubs, everybody knows that. Malone even calls them 'Dead Men's Clubs'."

"Correct, correct," Rooster said, searching for rationale. "You see, my client knew the, uh, dearly departed who owned these clubs and he just *has* to have them for, oh, sentimental reasons!" Rooster said, making it up as he spoke.

"Well, tell him to make Malone a legitimate offer when the tournament's over. I'm sure he'll sell them at some price. I might kick a ball or two on the course, make a few bets, but I'll be damned if I'm gonna' lower myself to stealing golf clubs," Pumpkin said, draining his Heineken and rising to leave before the manager arrived.

Rooster tried to reach across the table to stop Pumpkin but ended up flailing his arms at the caddy. "No, no, don't go! Time is of the essence to my client!"

"And to me. Thanks for the beer, but I'm outta' here," Pumpkin said, turning to leave.

"Ten thousand! He'll pay ten thousand," Rooster said in a voice high enough for Pumpkin to hear but not loud enough for the golfers sitting at the bar to discern.

Pumpkin's mind flashed to a host of harassing phone calls to his home, threatening him to make good on thousands of dollars in debts. He looked back at Rooster. The strange little man looked almost pathetic.

Pumpkin sat down, folded his hands before him, sighed heavily, studied the table, and said without looking up, "Twenty-five thousand."

"Are you freaking crazy!" Rooster said, his voice rising.

Several patrons at the bar looked across the room to the table where the conversation was taking place.

"No, I'm thinking you're the crazy one," Pumpkin said quietly, shuffling his feet as though to leave.

"Okay, okay, twenty five, what the hell," Rooster said.

"Half now, half when I hand you the clubs. Cash," Pumpkin said.

"You're not very subtle, are you?" Rooster asked.

"What?" Pumpkin said.

"Never mind, cash it is," Rooster replied. "I'll get it to you in the morning."

Thirty One

Rooster sat in his cottage and gauged his approach. Subtle, subtle. He texted Marcus: "Caddy in play–knows he has 2 get clubs b 4 tee time 2morrow–will need bogus clubs 2 night." He then threw what he knew would be a bombshell— "1 other thing, caddy demands 25K in cash, half now, half when clubs delivered."

Marcus answered the text with anger. "U r crazy if u think I'll pay 25K–what's your cut? I won't stand 2 be blackmailed by a bald headed 5 foot dwarf in a spaghetti suit!"

Rooster read the text and chuckled. He waited five minutes, smiling, flipping channels on the TV. He then replied. "Let me digest this and think about what u just said, ok?" he texted. He got up, walked to the mini bar by the door, opened it, grabbed a Heineken, searched for a bottle opener, popped the cap, and took a long swig. He then began to text.

"Ok, game over. That's caddy's price. If u think this dwarf's on the take u better be ready 2 answer 2 jimmy frong…he knows the rooster don't take what he's not entitled 2—I got 2 much respect 4 jimmy's unique enforcement of the rules 2 take side money… have a good day, on my way 2 vegas in my spaghetti suit…I'm sure Jimmy will b calling u!"

Rooster grinned, waiting for the response. It came quickly.

"Sorry, lost my temper 4 a moment–u r correct. 25K it is, in cash–can't get that kind of money 2 night–can have it wired in a.m. and have it in your hands by noon. Greatest respect 4 jimmy," Marcus wrote.

"Ok, was just packin bags. Will unpack & talk with caddy," Rooster texted, chuckling.

Marcus felt his sphincter loosen.

"Damn," he thought, "The $5,000 was going to come out of Wild-O petty cash as incidental expenses, but I can't stretch it to $25,000." He shrugged, "In for a dime, in for a lousy $25,000." He picked up the phone to call his broker with an order to sell some stock and wire him the money. He reached again for Johnny Walker, looking out on The Greenbrier's wide expanse of perfectly manicured lawn.

The Snarf read the texts and smacked his lips. He assessed the ice cream in his bowl. Strawberries and Mary Jane, interesting combination.

"So," thought Snarf, "I gotta' admire 'ole Pumpkin. Man reminds me of myself. "Ya gotta' take the cookies when they're passed!" He shoved his empty bowl aside; checked his beard to see if it needed a trim but decided against it; slammed the door behind him; and headed for the Clubhouse.

Snarf hailed Sink and Lair and ogled Sheila as he sat at the bar and opened his laptop. He accessed the text messages from his iPhone and settled back with a Bud. Sink and War listened with concern as he read the texts.

When he had finished, War said, "It seems to me we need to have the Wild-O Golf chat man warn Munch."

"Yep, but old Munch ain't answering his phone texts and he's not likely to go on the freakin' Internet. And even if he did, how do we fashion the warning?" Snarf asked.

"He's right, Munch can't simply get a message that his caddy is a thief and Vegas is in on the heist. I mean, Rooster's right—we've got to be more subtle than that," Sink said.

"May I offer a suggestion, fellas'?" Snarf asked, slurping his Bud, wiping his beard with the back of his hand.

"Please," Sink said.

"Well, we could simply text the tournament officials that Wild-O reconditioned has gotten an anonymous phone call that someone has plans to steal Munch's clubs and his caddy may be involved," Snarf suggested.

"Won't work," War said. "We can't get the USGA involved. That would cause the shit to hit the fan and outing the caddy might jeopardize Munch's qualification for the tournament."

"How about this," Snarf chimed in. We let the caddy know we're onto him. An anonymous email to Pumpkin that threatens to spill the beans if he tries to lift the clubs?"

"I rather like that idea," Sink said. "We could just text him that the jig is up. Steal the clubs and you'll go to jail."

Sheila joined in from behind the booth in which the trio was sitting, "Better yet. Why not go after Appleton? He's the key. No money for the caddy, no clubs for Rooster."

They turned in unison, three faces just inches away from Sheila's marvelous assets, which were resting on the upper edge of the padded booth.

"Why, Sheila, I didn't know you were back there," Sink smiled in appreciation.

"Yeah, didn't know you were stayin' abreast of the game here," Snarf chortled.

"My, my, Sheila, you are a delight. I think you've got something there, my dear," War said, reaching out and patting her hand while Snarf did his best to get his nose closer to the cleavage.

John Short sat in Rex Reynolds' Greenbrier cottage on Paradise Row and reviewed the poll tracking.

"Unbelievable," he said, shaking his head in amazement.

"It *is* unbelievable, never seen anything quite like it. Of course, we've never seen anything like a guy playing with 'Dead Men's Clubs'," Reynolds said.

Short continued to shake his head. "So, they like Malone, they like Wild-O Golf, they believe in our reconditioned clubs, want to buy 'em, and they love the fact that they're called 'Dead Men's Clubs'. In-freaking-credible," Short Sale said.

"Yep, you've got a marketing machine in Mr. Malone, John," Reynolds said, smiling. "Congratulations."

Short opened his computer and began checking the sales numbers. Before he could finish, his cell rang.

"John, D.E. here," said the Wild-O CEO.

"Yes sir, Mr. Wildoe!" Short said.

"Call me D.E."

"Yes sir, D.E.!"

"Have you seen your numbers?" Wildoe asked.

"Just logging on now, Mr.—"

"D.E., call me D.E."

"Just logging on, D.E. I'm down here in West Virginia at the tournament, just got in and—"

"Good! That's good, stay down there, and stay close to the action. Your numbers are through the roof, John. We are sold out on the orders we've taken so far. My God, they love 'Dead Men's Clubs'. Tell that Reynolds boy he was right on the money. Tell him he's gonna' be workin' for Wild-O Golf."

"Yes—-D.E.," Short said.

"Take care of Malone, he needs to win this thing. If he comes through down there, I see big things for you, John! Just make sure he comes through for us. If he doesn't, I don't want that 'Dead Men's' thing hanging around my neck."

Just like that, D.E. was gone.

"OK?" Reynolds said, looking at Short Sale, who stood holding the phone.

"Yeah, yeah, he's in a great mood. Clubs are flying off the shelf."

"Great," Reynolds said.

"Yeah, he says you're gonna' be workin' for him."

"Double great," Reynolds said.

"Yeah, all I have to do is make sure Munch wins. If he doesn't, I'm outta' here, I guess," Short said with a shrug.

Thirty Two

Pumpkin lay on his bed in his room on the second floor of The Greenbrier two-story cottage that was reserved for caddies. "Pretty cool," he thought. He was sleeping here for free and he had never seen caddy quarters like these. Plush furniture, fireplaces, and flat screen television sets. He eyed the fully stocked wet bar just across the room, doing his best to ignore the free booze inside.

Pumpkin placed his arms behind his neck, cradled his head and smiled to himself. He closed his eyes and began to consider his situation. Twenty-five thousand would get him back on top again, if he could just stay away from the booze and the women. Regardless, that amount of money, tax free, would give him a good ride, even if he blew it all in a few short months, as he feared he would.

A knock on the door caused him to jump with a start, ending his reverie.

Opening his eyes, he yelled, "Yeah? Who's there?"

"It's me, Rooster!"

Pumpkin rolled out of bed and unlocked the door. He looked down at the strange little man standing in front of him. He was clutching a golf bag that was equal to his height.

"Dwarf," Pumpkin thought, "One gene removed."

"Lemme' in, I got the bogus clubs for 'ya."

Pumpkin backed away from the door and Rooster rushed into the room. He began emptying the clubs from the bag.

"We can't replace his bag, Munch would know if it's different—but he'll never pick up on the bogus clubs," Rooster said. The little man's face was covered with perspiration and his suit jacket was even more wrinkled than Pumpkin had remembered.

"How am I supposed to make the switch? Hide the clubs in my underwear?" Pumpkin grumbled.

"Must be twenty-five thousand ways to make the switch, man," Rooster grinned up at him, wiping his forehead with the sleeve of his coat as a sand wedge clanged to the floor.

"Speaking of which," Pumpkin said, "Where's the money?"

"My client is wiring it tonight. Why don't we have breakfast in the morning and I'll give it to 'ya with your bacon and eggs," Rooster said.

"Who's your client, little man?" Pumpkin asked.

"No, no, I can't divulge that information. Like I said, it's a fella' who has a personal interest in the 'Dead Men's Clubs'."

"Eight o'clock. Draper's," Pumpkin said. "My guy tees off at 1:15."

"See 'ya then, sweet dreams," Rooster said, grinning, reaching for the doorknob, dancing out of the room, slamming the door behind him.

Pumpkin climbed back into bed. "If I can find a way to exchange the clubs, it might work," he thought. "Malone is an amateur. He might not know the clubs have been replaced. It's not like he's been married to them for forty years and knows every mark on them. He won't know the difference. I just need to get at them when he's not looking."

Having convinced himself for the moment, Pumpkin rolled over and fell immediately into dreams of wine, women and song.

Dead Men's Clubs

The call came at 6:43 the next morning.

"Yes?" Sink said.

"Sink, Brawley Rollins here," the Chairman of **The Powers That Be** said.

"Yes, Mr. Chairman," Sink replied, sitting up in bed, glancing at the clock, rubbing his eyes, reaching for his trifocals.

"Hear your boy is doin' well."

"Yes, Mr. Chairman. Today is a big day."

"**The Powers That Be** met again last night," Brawley said.

"Yes—and?" Sink said, immediately concerned.

"We hear tell there's some chicanery afoot."

'Well, we're dealing with a very complex situation—"

"Yep, know all about it. **The Powers That Be** have lots of sources, 'ya know. Just wanted to tell you we got your back if 'ya need help. We like Malone and the good feelings he's generated down there amongst all those golfers who usually are a pissed-off lot," Brawley intoned.

"Yes, Mr. Chairman, much appreciated. We're hoping for the best. We just want to make sure you and your cohorts are satisfied with our progress."

"So far, so far—course we don't want any negative ruckus outa' this; be sure to keep an eye on that media thing. We're enjoyin' the tournament up here, hopin' your boy's gonna' win. Good luck!"

Brawley was gone. Sink sat in his underwear on the side of the bed, looking at the phone in his hand. "Amazing," he thought, "**The Powers That Be** are glued to this thing."

Rooster texted Pumpkin at 8 a.m. as the caddy was crawling out of bed.

"25 thousand being wired by client this morning. Can't get first payment 2 u until later in day. What's tee time again?" Rooster asked.

"Like I said last night, 1:15," Pumpkin texted in return.

"Doubt money here by then. Can u just grab the clubs?

"No cash, no switch," Pumpkin replied, "tell your client."

"Ok, ok, but if u on course, how do I get money to u?" Rooster wrote.

"Must be 25 thousand ways," Pumpkin replied.

Rooster had to grin and thought, "Pretty subtle, this guy."

"I'll get back 2 u," Rooster texted, pocketing his phone.

Snarf reported in to Sink and War that Marcus was waiting for the bribe money and Pumpkin had the bogus clubs in his possession.

"How's he gonna' make the switch?" War asked.

"Well, Rooster's correct—Pumpkin probably is looking at twenty-five thousand ways," Sink replied.

"He'll need 'Divine Intervention' to pull that off," War said.

Sink flashed back to Brawley's call, thinking "Divine Intervention" might not be a problem at all.

Thirty Three

Dawn broke bright and early on the day of the Semifinal. It began as a beautiful morning in the mountains, but the forecast again warned some rain showers were possible during the day. Munch rolled out of bed, yawned, and nudged Melinda. "Wanna' order room service and have breakfast in the room? I don't tee off until 1:15," he said.

Melinda turned to him, revealing a bare breast, and said, "Great idea, we can just relax."

"Uh, do you think Viagra would slow me down today?" he asked, taking in the view

"I'll phone for breakfast. You take the pill," she grinned, reaching for the phone.

"But, will it slow me down?"

"What?"

"Viagra."

"I don't think so, never has," she assured him, smiling. "But look, honey, we can wait until the tournament is over."

Munch took one more look at the bare breast and said, "No, no," reaching across the bed, grabbing the bottle of little blue bills. Life is good.

They lay in bed for an hour or so after making love. The talk ranged from golf to family to golf. The kids and grandkids would soon arrive at The Greenbrier to watch Munch play. He and Melinda couldn't wait to see them.

After eating breakfast in their room and checking *The Golf Channel* every fifteen minutes, Munch left the hotel and meandered down the long path to the clubhouse. He did his time on the driving range and rolled as many putts as he thought were required to prepare him to play.

This was the Semifinal. This was the big time.

"It's been an interesting tournament thus far, with Munch Malone and Nick Carman battling it out. Radar shows we may get a rain delay, and judging from that dark cloud bank approaching from the west, there can be little doubt Malone and Big Nick will have to cool their respective heels in the Clubhouse until this thing passes," Chad Ray said to his *Golf Channel* audience.

The heavens burst open and the rain poured at precisely 2:45 p.m. The warning horn blew and Munch and Pumpkin sought safety in the golf bunker under the clubhouse. As they hurried to the tunnel leading to the locker room, Pumpkin looked up and saw the strange little man standing in the downpour, motioning to him. Pumpkin glanced sideways to see if Munch had noticed. No way; he was concentrating on play to come. Pumpkin focused again on the little man. Was the little dude really dancing?

Rooster rocked back and forth with his thumbs up. He mouthed, "Got the cash!" as rain ran down his torso. Pumpkin nodded, feeling a surge of energy as he envisioned $25,000 in cash, no taxes. "What would it look like? Would it be in a suitcase? Would it be in $100 bills, all neatly arranged in $1,000 stacks? That would mean twenty-five stacks, so the suitcase would not be that big. Briefcase, maybe. Would they put it in a paper bag? It would be less noticeable that way. Or, maybe in a golf shoe bag—better yet!"

"I'll watch the clubs," Pumpkin said as he and Munch started down the tunnel. "You oughta' watch the replays in the player's lounge—you can take lessons from yourself," Pumpkin grinned.

"Maybe he's not such a shit after all," Munch thought, turning to Pumpkin, saying, "Hey man, seriously, I really need you to be my guide out there. This is all new to me, and I need all the help I can get. My apologies if we got off to a bad start. I really appreciate your help, and I need it," Munch said.

"You got it, man," Pumpkin replied, bumping fists with Munch. He did a thumbs up and walked away, thinking to himself, "Schmuck, loser. Not a bandit's bone in his body. Easy game."

Pumpkin headed immediately for the caddy's locker room and made small talk with the other bag jockeys, waiting for them to clear out. When he was finally alone he grabbed several towels from the locker room shower, walked outside and down the path to the caddy cottage, entered the unit and took the stairs to the second floor. He turned right and walked down the hall to his room, slipping the key into the lock and entering. Once inside the room he wrapped seven of the bogus clubs—a five iron, three wood, pitching wedge and six iron in one towel, and a seven wood, eight iron and putter in another. He would have to make a second trip for the remaining clubs if he were to have any hope of pulling off the switch without being noticed. Too many clubs at one time could attract attention.

Pumpkin left his room and walked down the hall, clubs in hand, covered by the towels. Two caddies came toward him, engaged in animated conversation. One looked at Pumpkin and said, "You got 'da man' out there, Pumpkin!"

"Yeah, screw it, doin' our best," Pumpkin said, hurrying by.

"Same old Pumpkin, a real douche bag," the caddy said to his companion, as Pumpkin entered the stairwell.

Pumpkin descended the stairs and walked outside, dodging

raindrops as best he could. He headed back up the path to the locker room and did a quick inspection as he pushed through the door. The room was empty. He walked to Munch's bag, took one more look around, and pulled the three wood from the bag, holding it up, inspecting it.

"Strange," he thought, this club does feel different." He felt an immediate urge to walk to the course and hit with the club. A rippling sensation shot up his forearm, creating a sting and pulsing effect that caused his bicep to bulge.

"Dammit" get your thieving hands off my club!" War said, watching the High Def, his anger growing, 'Channeling' intensifying ten times over. "Careful with the blood pressure, Congressman, old Pumpkin looks like Popeye! He might explode!" Snarf laughed, egging him on.

"Easy, easy, Congressman," Sheila said, rubbing his shoulders with a gentle massage, failing to calm him as War's blood pressure and 'Johnson' responded, rising up a few more degrees as he felt Sheila against his back.

Pumpkin dropped the three wood to the floor, trying to shake off the strange, stinging feeling that continued to radiate up and down his arm. He cleared his head, pulling six more clubs out of the bag—the five, six, and eight irons, the seven wood, pitching wedge and putter. Each club transmitted power, assurance, and consistency. Shaking his head and trying to calm himself, Pumpkin picked up the three wood from the floor and replaced the clubs he was about to steal with the seven bogus clubs. He quickly wrapped the "Dead Men's Clubs" in both towels, covering them as he prepared to return to his room. Saddlebags of sweat emerged under his armpits.

"Hey, Pumpkin, can Munch keep it going?" said a voice behind him.

"What the shit?" Pumpkin said, startled, jerking around to face Warren Danson.

"Who the hell are you?" Pumpkin asked, holding the covered clubs to his side.

"Warren Danson, used to play a little golf here. Can you help your boy? Can he win it?" the tall, dapper African American asked.

"Yeah, he's just one big freakin' ray of sunshine," Pumpkin said.

Danson extended his hand, exhibiting a smile as big as Michigan. "Honored to meet you, Pumpkin. Can I buy you a drink or a cup of coffee?" he beamed.

"Can't do it right now, Warren. Never know when the 'all clear' will sound. Know what I mean? Maybe later, huh?"

"Sure, sure, I understand. Thanks for all you're doing for Munch. We love the guy. He's the best. If you knew how frustrated he's been with golf all his life, and to see him now, well, it's a miracle, I'll tell 'ya!" Man O'War said. "You sure I can't buy you a drink?"

"I don't drink on the job, but I make up for it later. If I see you in the bar, you're on," Pumpkin said.

"Great! I'll be around all evening. Hope to see you; I'll be looking forward to it. I bet you have some pretty amazing stories to tell!" the Congressman said.

"Yeah, you might say that," Pumpkin replied.

Pumpkin's visitor seemed to stare straight through him.

"This is mighty important, son, and a lot of people are watching you. If I were you, I'd be mindful out there to take real good care of Malone. If you don't, Pumpkin, there'll be hell to pay, I can promise you that," Danson warned.

Pumpkin laughed with derision, looked down at the Rodney bag, and said, "Don't threaten me,"—only to see as he looked up that the tall African American gentleman was gone. Too fast, too weird; how did the old guy disappear? What he said; it unnerved

Pumpkin. Was there more working here than he thought? Tension racked him and a cold sweat broke on his forehead.

Pumpkin walked out of the locker room and slouched against the wall, avoiding what was left of the rain. He felt as though all energy had been drained from his body. "How in the hell can I carry this off?" he thought, bracing for the effort of retracing his steps back to his room, covering the remaining bogus clubs in a towel, heading back to the locker room, maybe encountering another dickhead Munch friend, and switching the remaining clubs.

His dilemma was solved as the horn blared, signaling the all clear. "Shit," Pumpkin thought, "no time for the second switch."

"You did what?" Sink said.

"Absolutely, went down there."

"You are crazy, man, your ass will be sent packing if **The Powers That Be** find out about your little gambit."

"Had to do it. Wanted the doofus to know somebody is taking notes. Now he knows."

Sink continued to condemn War with his eyes, but heard himself say, "Have a drink. It's on me."

Pumpkin texted Rooster, his hand shaking: "Replaced 7 of 14 clubs during rain delay–all clear just sounded–back 2 course–won't get chance again–I got seven clubs, but I still got no cash from u–what u want me 2 do?"

Rooster read the text and, in turn, texted the information to Marcus. Marcus tapped instructions: "Tell P to just make sure M uses as many of the bogus clubs as necessary 2 lose match–if M flames out promise him bonus of another 5K."

Munch came out strong after the rain delay and was 1-up at the 5th hole, called the *Mounds*, with a twenty-foot putt for birdie. His tee shot on number Six, *Lookout*, was extraordinary for a conceded birdie to give him a two-hole advantage.

The trouble began when Munch unknowingly accepted from Pumpkin a bogus club at number Seven, *Plateau*, and gave a hole back with a three-putt bogey. His head moved like a penguin as he tried to control his clubs. "My God, I'm back to the same old shit! Everything's moving but my bowels!" he said to himself, trying to control his emotions.

Viagra crossed his mind.

"Uh, oh," the *Golf Channel's* Jennifer Allison cautioned her television audience, "that shot didn't work for Malone. He's obviously tense."

"Yes!" Marcus, shouted, jumping from the sofa and splashing Johnny Walker Black around the room.

"Munch may need more than 'Dead Men's Clubs' if he wants to get back into a rhythm," Jennifer intoned to Chad Ray.

"Son-of-a-bitch, don't say freaking 'Dead Men's Clubs'!" Marcus shouted at the TV.

At number Ten, *Principal's Nose*, Munch was back in control and used his "Dead Man's Club" to great advantage, taking the next three holes, going 4-up.

Munch was ecstatic. Eight holes left and he was 4-up. In the fairway on Eleven, *Meadow*, Munch hit his drive well, cutting the corner over the sand on the long hole, leaving a clear shot at the green. He asked for his three iron.

"Why not try the five iron?" Pumpkin asked, lifting another bogus club from the bag.

"You think so, Pumpkin? I dunno', distance-wise, it's a three iron for me," Munch replied.

Pumpkin handed the five iron to Munch and assured him, "Trust me here, you had a great tee shot, it's a shorter distance to the green than coming up on the right, and you're hitting the five iron like a champ, use the five iron."

"Bastard!" War muttered as he watched the High Def.

Munch took the five iron, hesitated, and swung. He shanked the ball and it flew to the right, coming to rest in the rough, just inches from the out of bounds marker.

"Oh, oh, do we have a blow up here?" Ray asked.

"Yeah, baby!" Marcus yelled.

"Rush Limbaugh shot, Munch," Pumpkin laughed, "way to the right, but still in bounds."

"Very freaking funny!" Munch said, glaring at Pumpkin. The caddy sighed, lifted his arms sideways and said, "Shit happens. That's golf."

Munch demanded the eight iron and Pumpkin readily agreed. "Gotcha' by the shorthairs," he thought.

Munch had been shaken and tried to remain calm. It wasn't happening. Viagra? He stopped and gave the club back to his caddy.

"What's wrong?" Pumpkin asked, refusing to take the club.

"Changed my mind, I'm gonna' grip down on the seven iron."

"Bullshit, that's a fool's game."

"Just give me the seven iron, dammit."

"Okay, baby, your funeral," Pumpkin said, handing over the club.

"If I didn't know better, I'd say Malone is arguing with his caddy," Allison whispered to the television audience. "Once again, a sign of someone who has not experienced this kind of tension. Always take the caddy's advice; he's been here before."

Munch felt calm return with the seven iron in his hands. "Contagion" filled his body as he gripped down on the club and executed a perfect swing, coming to a stop ten feet from the cup. He executed his follow-up well, making a two-foot putt to go 1-up.

"Good job, Munch, let's work together on the club selection, man. I mean, I know this course and I can help you, if you'll just let me," Pumpkin said, trying to leverage his chances of redirecting Munch to the bogus clubs in his bag.

"Fine by me, Pumpkin, I need all the help I can get," Munch said, wondering if Pumpkin was schizoid.

Pumpkin's phone pinged with a text as he walked the fairway with Munch.

"Better turn that thing off, Pumpkin," Munch said to his caddy. I need your help out here."

Pumpkin scowled at Munch and said, "Like I said, Munch, I ain't out here to change my lifestyle."

"Fine, Pumpkin," Munch said, "up yours."

Pumpkin ignored Munch, pulling his phone from his pocket, glanced at the incoming texts, stopping in his tracks. He stood still, reading the text from Rooster as Munch headed on toward the tee.

"Client says direct M 2 bad clubs—M loses, $5 K added to $25K—$12,500 cash now in your room—under bed," Rooster had texted.

"How the hell did he get in my room?" Pumpkin asked himself. But then again, a simple lock would be no problem for Rooster.

"K," Pumpkin replied to the text, smiling.

Pumpkin was thrilled with the figures, and dismayed with the fact that he was still taking Rooster's word that half the cash had been delivered.

The Semifinal match ended with Munch and Nick Carman among the eight golfers who survived.

"Well, it was quite a day here with Big Nick Carman and Munch Malone getting all the attention. Tomorrow could be a classic day; the 'Teddy Bear,' Big Nick Carman, was sensational out there today while Malone had a strange afternoon. He often appeared volatile and clearly was arguing with his caddy," Ray noted.

"Please join me, Cheryl Ann Roane and Jennifer Allison tomorrow for the final round of the USGA Senior Amateur from the Old White Course in beautiful White Sulphur Springs, West Virginia. It's sure to be a great day!" Chad Ray said, signing off.

Thirty Four

Rooster and Marcus were to meet in The Greenbrier Casino that evening. The gaming palace located just under the lower lobby of the hotel was hopping with registered guests as Rooster walked down a staircase that seemed to have been transplanted from "Tara". Indeed, The Greenbrier marketing slogan said "Where Monte Carlo Meets Gone With The Wind".

Rooster practically preened as he walked onto the Casino floor, drawing stares from the clientele in the immediate area. The Casino required a jacket, and Rooster complied, barely. His rumpled and soiled white suit was a bit off the mark for what The Greenbrier dress code had in mind.

Rooster found a seat at one of the Blackjack tables, his feet dangling in mid-air from the high chair he occupied. He was sizing up the cocktail waitress as she flowed from one guest to another, serving drinks. Rooster found himself checking her legs and laying his hands on whatever part of her body came closest as she completed her rounds.

"I see you're hard at work," Marcus said sarcastically, sitting down beside Rooster, signaling for liquid refreshment, placing a bet at the same time.

"Yeah. This freakin' place is great. One hundred thousand square feet, 320 slots, 37 table games. Not bad!" Rooster said.

"Never been in a casino?" Marcus asked, one eyebrow lifting.

"Yeah, well, this place ain't Las Vegas, but it's got real class. 'Ya' feel like 'ya gotta' have a *tuxedo* on down here with this bunch. Friggin' *high* class man! I got to get Jimmy here 'ta see this. Harry Lee could market the shit outta' this joint!" Rooster exclaimed.

"Where are we with our little project while you sit here wasting my time and spending my money?"

"Marcus, my man, our boy has made the switch and he's 'k' with the deal!" Rooster said, grinning, as the dealer swept cards from the table, preparing to deal from the shoe.

"That's good, that's some progress. This thing has to work. You follow Pumpkin on the course, make sure he delivers. I'll stay in my cottage and monitor the TV coverage. Keep texting me," Marcus instructed, watching his chips being swept away by the dealer.

Rooster played on, eventually doubling down as Marcus watched, amused. Rooster glanced at Marcus and said, "I can't wait to see if those bogus clubs make any difference! If they don't, you're shit outta' luck, Marcus!" he laughed.

"Just keep the texts coming," Marcus demanded, throwing back his drink, tossing a $100 bill on the table as he rose to leave. "Lose that and then get out of here. You've got a busy day tomorrow." Two hours later, the $100 gone, and another $5,000 erased from his liberal expense account, Rooster called it a night.

Snarf opened the laptop and War and Sink studied the latest texts.

"So," War frowned, "Pumpkin's stolen seven of our clubs. God help us."

"Exactly. We need to visit **The Powers That Be**," Sink responded, reaching for his cell phone. A few moments later he reached the Chairman who graciously agreed to see Sink and War at 10 p.m., indicating the call was fortuitous; The **Powers That Be** also needed to talk about some things.

The walk was long between the Clubhouse and the enormous structure that housed **The Powers That Be**. The two old golfers ambled along as stars twinkled about them.

"This has gotten pretty complicated, War. They said they had some things they wanted to talk about?"

"Yep."

"Such as?"

"Don't know."

"Tell me something, War. Would you start down this road again?" Sink asked, shoving a hand in his pockets to retrieve a pack of bubble gum. He slowly unwrapped it as War watched.

"Bubble gum? When in the hell did you start chewing gum? Shameful habit!" War teased.

"Just like baseball, man. They're always chewin' and spittin'. No tobacco, just bubble gum. They do it to relieve stress. And I'm definitely stressed," Sink replied, popping two wads of gum in his mouth.

War motioned toward a park bench and the two sat down, clouds at their feet. War leaned back on the bench and stretched his legs. He looked up and said, "Nice close view of the Milky Way, don't you think? How peaceful. You should just lighten up Sink. If we weren't doing this, what else would we be doing? This is fun! Let's enjoy it no matter where it goes!" War laughed, slapping Sink on the knee.

"I know you're right, I just want this thing to work. I wanna' keep playing golf," Sink complained, blowing a large pink bubble.

"That thing's gonna burst. Don't jinx us—" War groused, as the bubble gum splattered against Sinks's face.

There was a moment of silence, and then, they both broke into hysterical laughter that went on for several minutes.

"I needed that!" Sink guffawed, tears running down his face.

"Oh, my, my sides hurt! C'mon, let's go, we don't wanna' be late. Give me some of that stuff," War demanded, hoisting himself off the park bench, grabbing some bubble gum from Sink's outstretched hand. As they walked to the Clubhouse, chewing gum and blowing bubbles, they continued to glance at one another, breaking time and again into gales of laughter.

Sink rang the knockers on the big door, blew another bubble, placing his hands around it as though he were fondling a breast, putting War on the ground.

Admission was granted, and the tone turned serious as they were escorted to the big conference room by a prim little woman who uttered not a word. Sensing the proper decorum, neither Sink nor War spoke as they removed their bubble gum, wrapped and pocketed it.

Thirty minutes ticked by on the antique clock in the hallway. Steps were heard in the vestibule leading to the conference room and voices ricocheted against the walls.

"What's this all about, Brawley?" Sid Belch's voice boomed, "It's time for all honest souls to be in bed!"

"Dunno' what they want, just got a request from those golfin' fellas. Somethin' about needin' the Lord's help. Works for me, we have some questions, too."

"I'm losin' $450 an hour doin' this, I hope you know," snorted Belch.

"You should try retirement, Sid," Retro Elvis sang out, walking through the door. "Folks ask me if I get tired of doin' nothing, and I tell 'em, yeah, but a man can't quit just 'cause he's tired."

"Very funny, very funny," Belch replied, looking with obvious distaste at the King in The Ring.

The three rounded a corner and entered the conference room where Sink and War waited.

"How y'all doin'?" Brawley smiled, ambling toward them, hand extended. He wore a tie that was not really tied, just sort of looped over at the neck. Brawley, Sink thought, looked as though he was rolling along on hidden roller skates.

"We are doing fine, sir. Just a little bump in the road about which we need to seek your counsel and advice," Sink answered, grabbing Brawley's beefy hand, pumping it with gusto. War did the same and the two turned to Belch, who ignored them and walked toward his seat at the table.

Retro Elvis adjusted his glasses, gave them a "V" for Victory sign and instructed, "Just tell it like it is, boys," and curled his lip.

Bonanza Betty and Big Bill McElfee joined the group, engaged in animated conversation.

"I don't care what you say, Bill, the Sox are gonna' to do it this year. Those damn Yankees can't depend on Jeter anymore and they're never going to be the same," Betty said.

"Nonsense, my dear, the Yankees have the greatest franchise ever and Jeter will be merely a footnote in their storied history," Big Bill replied.

"Let's get to it!" Sid Belch roared from his seat at the table.

Brawley, looking amused, plopped into the Chairman's executive seat at the head of the long mahogany surface, while motioning for Sink and Lair to sit across from the other four council members.

"What's up, fellows?" Brawley asked, " It's late and we all wanna' be in bed."

"Well, sir, it's a bit complex," Sink answered.

"That's all right, as Retro over there put it, just tell it like it is," Brawley smiled.

"Yes sir, how can I explain? We, uh, need more leverage down there," Sink began.

The Powers That Be listened attentively as Sink explained the course of events that had caused him and War to seek the meeting. He ended his monologue with War's quote, "We seek 'Divine Intervention'."

"Hmmm," Brawley said, looking intently at Sink, then switching, glancing at War. "Understand you, Congressman Danson, sorta' took it on yourself to visit, uh, down there. Lookin' for 'Divine Intervention' in, maybe, the wrong place?"

"Sorry about that, sir lost my mind for just a moment. But, glad I did it, the caddy isn't all bad, he could be converted, I sensed that, standing there, face-to-face. Glad I did it. My bad. My apologies."

Brawley sat there, no expression, and nodded his head in understanding.

"But," War said, "We still need 'Divine Intervention'."

"Well, what's that mean? What do you want? I'm a busy man and I'm sure my fellow council members also have better things to do!" Sid Belch barked in a loud voice.

"The help we need," Sink said, standing and glancing around the room, "is approval by this body to allow War and me, and our technical expert, Mr. Snarf Adams, to broaden our 'Channeling' in the course of the prototype in which we are engaged."

"Yo, break it down for me, man," the King in the Ring said—this time with no lip curl.

"We currently 'Channel' Munch when he is in the vicinity of his clubs. We also can see, through High Def, the immediate area in which the clubs are located, allowing us to monitor the Old White Course. Fact is, lotsa' times the picture's pretty limited. In the past, as an example, the only thing we saw was a view of Mr. Malone's garage, which, incidentally, he keeps quite clean," Sink said.

"Sink—get to the point—you're drifting here," War admonished.

Brawley shook his head affirmatively and Sink cleared his throat, trying to get to the point. "Why am I so damned nervous," he thought, feeling perspiration begin to form.

"Uh, we have used the technical transparency expertise of our associate, Mr. Snarf Adams, to review phone text messages to really understand what is happening down there. Those messages have made it clear we need to counter the corrupt efforts of Marcus Appleton and Rooster Rittenhouse if we are to have any chance of preventing them from doing harm to Mr. Malone's heroic effort," Sink said, wondering if he sounded deranged.

"You mean, 'Your' heroic effort, don't you?" Big Bill McElfee asked.

"Damn right, sir!" War responded, leaning forward over the table.

Sink froze. "Damn, I cannot control the man, he thought. How can he have the discipline to consistently hit a driver 300 yards when he can't behave in front of **The Powers That Be?**"

Brawley just smiled. "Glad 'ta see that you're fully invested in this, Congressman Danson."

"What we need," Sink said, finally arriving at the crux of the matter, "is to be able to 'Channel' Mr. Adams' information to an operative down there who can assist us."

"Well, well," Brawley intoned, seems great minds work together. We've talked with our law firm and they're concerned we've got some problems here."

Thirty Five

"Problems? What problems?" Sink asked.

"The law firm thinks we might be 'aiding and abetting' in illegal activity, a felony, to be exact," Brawley answered, frowning.

Sid Belch lifted his eyes from the documents he was reviewing, interrupting Sink as he forged ahead with his arguments to the council. Challenging Sink, he said, "You've called Mr. Adams' activity 'technical transparency'? That's a euphemism for 'hacking', isn't it?"

"Well, I wouldn't exactly say that, but—"

"That's what got Rupert Murdoch in hot water, isn't it?" Brawley asked.

"With all due respect, sir, this is different."

"How so," asked McElfee, his hands tented before him, elbows resting on the table.

"Here we know there are two very nasty guys—Appleton and Rittenhouse. Here we know that these two individuals are themselves committing a crime. Here we know that a noble effort will die if we do not intercede," Sink argued.

"Yes, but, speaking of criminal activity, you would not have known any of this if you had not first hacked into the Wild-O system and then into Mr. Rittenhouse's phone," Betty Bonanza countered.

"Yes, but we knew a corrupt initiative was afoot," Sink replied.

"How did you know that?" Betty asked.

"You will recall, we can 'Channel' and observe through High Def the area where the clubs are located. We saw Rooster–Mr. Rittenhouse–

attempting to steal the clubs in the lobby of The Greenbrier Hotel. That's when we went proactive with Mr. Adams," Sink explained.

"That's when you started to hack?" Belch asked.

"That's when we decided to stop that little bastard!" War shouted, springing from his seat.

"War! Remember where you are!" Sink warned, enraged by the outburst.

Brawley banged his gavel. "Boys, boys!" he said. "Let's be civil here! Mr. Danson, you are testing the limits!"

War offered an abject apology and sat down.

"So," Betty Bonanza continued, as the tension in the room began to clear. "You want us to give you permission to 'Channel' to this person down there who will act in your behalf to blunt the actions of these fellows Appleton and Rittenhouse?"

"Yes, and we need to see all the action at the USGA Senior Men's Amateur Championship at The Greenbrier in which Mr. Malone is playing," Sink responded.

War's phone twanged and he pulled it from his pocket. AP Mobile's alert was on the phone's screen reporting "Malone and Carman to play for USGA Men's Amateur Championship."

War leaped forward, "News alert from AP! Our boy Malone just finished the Semifinal—he's playing for the Championship tomorrow!"

Sink fist bumped War and turned with a smile to the Council. "So, now it's apparent we have an historic opportunity that we cannot afford to miss. Please, we need full 'Contagion'. We need to see the whole course, not just the area where the clubs are."

"Well, I have to say, this is pretty good news," Brawley said, looking at his Council, "and, I have to fess up. I called Mr. Lair here a day or so ago and told him I liked what I saw happening. They've encountered no problems with the media coverage, even as it has increased dramatically, and Munch Malone seems like a decent guy. I told Mr. Lair that we had his back in this effort." He looked at the Council members and added, "Hope I didn't do anything that would upset y'all."

Silence.

"Now," he continued, "I understand the position of the legal eagles—they're always tellin' us 'don't do that,' cause that's what they're paid to do. But, let's face it, we simply wanna' do what's right, not what some arcane legal opinion tells us to do. I, for one, see no problem giving these boys a full picture of what's going on down there. We'll just give all the Clubhouses up here a direct feed from the Golf Channel, every televised shot and camera-ready shot. Their boy Malone won't be able to go to the bathroom without them seein' him. By the way," Brawley said, turning to Sink, spreading a large grin across his face, placing his hands across his stomach," to whom do you wish to 'Channel' in this little fiasco?"

Sink could not believe his luck—the Chairman had made up his mind and would deliver the Council members! And they would have full view of the whole experience! Yes!

"On a roll here, on a roll," Sink thought, and said "We would like to communicate with a gentleman by the name of Rex Reynolds.

"Who is he?" Bonanza asked.

Sink breathed deeply and began: "He is a practitioner of public opinion research and works for Mr. John Short, Vice President of Wild-O Reconditioned Clubs Division, who has Munch Malone's best interests at heart. Reynolds is 'tracking' daily public opinion about Munch. Our Mr. Adams will connect with Reynolds to apprise him of the nefarious plans Appleton and Rittenhouse have to scuttle Malone's effort. Reynolds can then pass that information to John Short who will then take action to thwart Reynolds and Rittenhouse."

Finishing the spiel, Sink muttered to himself, "God, I need a scotch."

"Balderdash!" Belch grunted, "Mr. Chairman, with all due respect, I think they've overstepped their bounds. This is a case without merit. These boys are asking us to partner in illicit activity and I ain't buyin' it!"

The room again fell silent. Sink and War realized they might, at the last minute, lose their bid to establish golf 'Channeling', bringing the game to millions of golfers up here, and satisfaction to the struggling hackers on the courses down there.

"Mistuh' Chairman," said a voice that rang with rockabilly familiarity.

Sink turned to see the King in the Ring taking off his sunglasses, shooting the sleeves of his jumpsuit, revealing wide, baby blue cuffs.

"Retro?" Brawley said.

The lip curled ever so slightly. "Way I look at it, these fellows are tryin' to do the right thing. This here Rooster is a gangster. The Appleton guy is obviously white-collar crap, and they're riggin' the match. Now, I saw a lot of this stuff where I came from. Y'all know I spent a number of years in the boxing ring. The bastards —sorry Mr. Chairman—that rig the fight game are the worst slime. I left that game and went to wrestling, where everybody, by God—uh, sorry again—knew the matches were fixed. At least that was honest. I, for one, won't sit idly by and watch these bas—uh, vermin—have their way."

Again, silence.

The stillness was broken by Big Bill McElfee who leaned forward, looked at Brawley, and said, "Mr. Chairman, I applaud your leadership and I endorse Retro's comments. Call the vote!"

The tally was four to one, Sid Belch being the obvious objection. **The Powers That Be** decided that Reynolds could be communicated with via Snarf Adams' technical avenues, provided Snarf confined the process to the USGA Senior Men's Amateur currently underway. Permission also was granted for access to the phones belonging to Marcus Appleton and Rooster Rittenhouse. That, too, was to end when the Championship came to a close. And every scene caught by Golf Channel cameras, whether broadcast or not, would be sent to the High Def upstairs. The whole enchilada!

Thirty Six

Snarf, Sink and War met for lunch at the Club. Champagne was ordered to celebrate their successful visit with **The Powers That Be**. They chose a table near the giant High Def where they focused on the Championship at The Greenbrier.

"I'll have the black and blue salad. Have to watch my weight, even up here," Sink complained,

"Never was a problem for me," War said. "I can eat anything I want and never gain a pound. I'll have the Pasta Primavera. How about you, Snarf?"

"Gimme' a Bud Light and ice cream. Maybe a little crème de menthe over the ice cream," Snarf replied, tinkering with his laptop he had placed on the table. "Where's the heavenly chest?"

"If you're referring to Sheila, she's working the evening shift," War frowned.

"Tell me something, War," Snarf asked.

"Yes?" War responded, accepting his glass of bubbly from Sibelius, his second favorite waiter, his eyes still glued to the TV.

"Do you really think you stand a chance of shagging Sheila? I mean, I'm just sayin'—you're at least twice her age—or, you were at the time..."

"Dammit, Snarf, I firmly believe that if we can get a golf prototype okayed by **The Powers That Be** it shouldn't be out of the question to get a Viagra study approved up here. And when it happens, I'll be, as they say 'ready!' " he argued, a steely gleam in his eye.

"Snarf, he may be dead, but, as he's said repeatedly, he's not that dead," Sink grinned, ramming a fork into the Black and Blue. "Course, way he's eating, he may eventually weigh five hundred pounds, and 'ole slim here can do the shaggin'!"

"Let's get down to business. Back to The Greenbrier," War said, gesturing at the High Def. "Question is, how do we pass information to Reynolds?" War asked Snarf, ignoring Sink

"Well, let's see, Reynolds is asking, oh, about 200 people every day what they think of Munch. We just 'Channel' one of those people and let the caller know what's up," Snarf suggested.

"No, won't do. We can't control that. A caller may not pick up on the message or think he or she is going crazy. We have to firmly control the 'Channeling', manage it, and Reynolds has to believe it," Sink countered.

"Okay, let's back up. **The Powers That Be** have given us permission to hack into Reynolds' email or texting, and send him instructions, correct?"

"Yeah, but who's the stuff supposed to be coming from, Snarf? What will he believe?" Sink asked.

Snarf went silent, waiting for his Bud Light.

War asked, "No need to say who they are coming from, we simply access the texts passing between Marcus and Rooster and send them on to Reynolds. You could rig something up so Reynolds thinks there is some glitch that results in his receiving their text messages."

"Shit yes, man! I'll make Reynolds think there's a glitch of some type in, I dunno', maybe the server at The Greenbrier, and the damn texts start showing up on his phone and his laptop. Reynolds will say he ain't never seen anything like that before, but he'll take the bait once he sees Munch's name," Snarf replied, resisting the urge to burp.

"Perfect! Let's give it a try. Congrats to War for innovative tinkering—Congress could use you. And let's have some more champagne, Sibelius," Sink said, pointing to his glass.

Snarf finished his meal. Feeling slightly woozy and sky high, he said his goodbyes, returning to his pad where he went to work. It was going to be more difficult than he had let on. Damn ice cream was making him manic again, he thought, trying to comfort himself, wondering if the hair of the dog would help.

Could he make it happen? Could he actually send the texts between Rooster and Marcus to Reynolds' laptop and phone? Snarf went to his fridge and snagged a pint of ice cream. It took only two spoon fulls to convince him he could make it happen. First, he had to hack into Reynolds' system. He began by using a combination of different passwords. He knew 200 trillion possible passwords of at least eight characters, both upper and lower case, were confined to the ten digits on a telephone keyboard. He was confident that Reynolds used a four-digit PIN, as did most users, and those four digits carried 10,000 variables. Each letter boosted the number. Snarf tried "POLL," "ASKS," and "PUSH" with no success.

The evening wore on and Snarf's patience grew thin. He went to Regency Research's website and re-read the firm's branding statement. He then reviewed Rex Reynolds' "Message from the Chairman" and tried to decipher the mind of a man immersed in the business of providing a tool to achieve strategic thinking for competitive advantage. Snarf thought about it as he focused on Reynolds' photo. It was a determined gaze. The snarf's fingers began to move. He looked at what he had entered: "SOAR."

Bingo. Snarf was in.

Thirty Seven

Rex Reynolds loved a big breakfast. The morning of the final round of the Senior Amateur he arose early at his Greenbrier cottage, ordered room service and went outside on the porch, breathing in the fresh mountain air. Breakfast arrived via a small bus, and the accompanying waiter smiled and chatted as he set fine china and flatware on a wicker table.

Reynolds signed the check and bid the friendly waiter adieu as his thoughts drifted to his five kids and his wife at home in Cincinnati. They loved to create kitchen magic every Saturday morning. Today the magic before him came from a Greenbrier chef, and it was his alone.

He heaped orange marmalade atop a buttered biscuit and began to devour his bacon and eggs. He opened his laptop to view the overnight tracking and bit into his second biscuit. He reached for a linen napkin and wiped marmalade from his mustache. Only then did he see the message.

The laptop screen read, "You have incoming texts. Do you wish to access or delete?"

"Texts? I don't get texts on my laptop," Reynolds thought, sensing a scam. He started to press "delete" until he saw the name "Munch Malone."

He immediately moved his cursor to "access."

He read each text exchanged between Rooster and Marcus,

starting with Rooster's foiled attempt to access Munch's clubs in The Greenbrier lobby.

"My God," he thought, "John has to see this." Russ grabbed for his napkin and got up from the table. He pulled his phone from the pocket of his robe, dialed John Short at his cottage and said, "Meet me at Draper's, now."

"For what?" John asked.

"For something that you're going to want to see—big time," Reynolds said, signing off.

"Oh my God," Short Sale exclaimed, reading the texts as Reynolds scrolled through the messages. "Marcus is totally corrupt. I've got to go to the CEO with this," he said.

"John, let's think about this before we pull the trigger," Rex responded. "We have these texts, but I'm not sure where they're coming from, or why. The message said something about the server going awry, but I've never seen anything like this—texts from cell phones being shot out in an anonymous fashion. And, come to think about it, are they anonymous, or is someone deliberately sending them to me?"

"Are you saying they're bogus?" Short Sale asked.

"Don't know—but they sure are suspicious, and intriguing," Reynolds answered.

"Rex, listen, we do know from the texts that this Rooster is no more than five feet tall, bald, has a rumpled suit—we have a perfect description. If we locate Rooster among the spectators, we confirm the texts are legit," Short Sale said.

"Good idea, but easier said than done. There are about twenty thousand people out there, final day of the Championship," Reynolds responded.

"Yeah, but there's only one dwarf on the course, or so I would assume," Short Sale countered, reaching for his phone.

"Janie," he said, as she answered the call.

"Fairly easily, sir," Janie replied, answering Short's question of how one could find Rooster among the crowds on the course. She sat down, in her hotel room, half dressed in panties and bra, placed one leg over the other, adjusted her glasses, and continued.

"We know he'll be following Malone. We ask The Greenbrier to program its surveillance cameras to focus on that twosome wherever possible and we'll ask the marshals to alert us if they see a dw–, or, extremely short person in the crowd."

"And why would The Greenbrier do that for us? What's our story?

"We tell The Greenbrier we need the video for our management team to assess using the hotel and Old White for the Wild-O International Convention in two years; they'll know we can pack 1500 people in here, fill the place," Janie assured him.

"Right," he said, "that could work. Remember, though, Janie, time is of the essence here. We've got to find this guy, if there is such a guy out there, damn quick."

The final round of The USGA Senior Men's Amateur Championship, an historic day at The Greenbrier, found Munch Malone up early, after another restless night. He could not decide if he should eat breakfast, fearing he might not retain it. He turned on the TV, going from channel to channel, trying to concentrate on something, failing. His stomach this morning felt like a bowl of Jell-O. Munch wondered what his nervous indigestion would do next—Ferris wheel? Vesuvius?

On the floor above his and Melinda's room Big Nick Carman read the newspapers. Kicked back in an easy chair, he wolfed down a huge omelet, drank his fresh-squeezed orange juice, and took congratulatory calls from friends. He guffawed at the jibes his buddies gave him via text and emails, and surfed the net for exotic vacation sites he could book following the Championship. Big Nick was loose and totally at ease, farting at will.

The two men could not have been more different on this morning as they met on the tee at *First*, just to the left of the huge green clock that towered over the assembled crowd. The word "Greenbrier" was emblazoned at the top of the fifteen feet of metal hour and minute hands ticking toward—what? History? Or a collapse by the little guy from South Carolina?

Munch tried to clear his head, vaguely realizing he was shaking hands with Nick, each of them wishing the other well as *The Golf Channel* recorded the exchange. Big Nick pounded Munch on the back, shouting his admiration for the phenomenon from South Carolina. Munch smiled nervously, his stomach retching back and forth.

Nick was first off the tee, blasting a 275-yard drive, left of center, leaving a clear view of the entire green. Munch stepped to the tee, swung, and came in from the right, where he would have to carry over a deep bunker guarding the right side of the green. It was complicated and Munch finished his walk to the ball by selecting the wrong club; he found the bunker, and then swore silently as he watched Nick Carman finish the hole with aplomb.

Number One saw Nick 1-up, but number Two, *Hog's Back*, squared the match, with Munch placing a tee shot over Howard's Creek right of center, near the pot bunker. Perfect. From there he had an ideal angle to attack the pin placement. On *Hog's Back* Munch was "The Man".

Carman bogeyed on number three and Munch was 1-up, paring the hole. Carman bounced back on four, known as *Racetrack* for its straight run. He began to take control as he approached *Racetrack* with two straight shots while Munch deviated to one side, finding a cross bunker of his own.

Consistency problems returned for Munch, and Carman won the hole. Square at the end of four.

At number Five, the *Mounds*, Munch assessed Carman's strategy as Big Nick placed a moderate shot right of center—smart play. Carman won the hole and was again 1-up. Number six saw Carman maintain his lead, going 2-up.

The tournament twisted again as Munch's drives began to hit fairways with accuracy; his putting was steady as he progressed. He won number Seven, Six and Nine, going 1-up. And then, Munch fell apart on Ten, *Principal's Nose*. Here he went left off the tee and found sloping greens running away from the line of play. Big Nick assessed the hole accurately and Munch began to feel that nagging doubt about his game. Square once more at the end of ten.

As the afternoon wore on and anticipation mounted as to who would win the Championship, the gallery following Munch and Nick grew exponentially, making it increasingly difficult for Rooster to see the action unless he was on a knoll looking over the crowd, or if he could force his way to the front of the ropes. He had been delighted to see Malone miscue on Ten and his fragile approach here at Eleven, the *Meadow*, where he had blown up the day before. Carman was in good form and neatly found the green, then putted with accuracy. Munch was clearly nervous. His putter wiggled like a snake as he tried to control himself. He drew back the shaft. The club and his stroke moved rapidly forward. The ball ran ten feet beyond the hole.

"Yes!" Marcus shouted, pounding the coffee table.

Munch took a deep breath and walked to the ball. "Steady, steady," he said to himself in a low voice. He felt the "Contagion", but the yips were all over him. He could not settle down. He knew he was going to miss the putt. He carefully placed the putter in front of the ball, took the club back just inches, and stroked for a second time. The ball ran to the cup, appeared to go in, and then lipped out.

"Yeah, baby! All lip and no hole!" Marcus shouted, leaping from the couch.

"Uh oh, Munch missed it," Chad Ray said as the gallery murmured, watching the ball circle the hole.

Munch swore silently to himself, walked to the ball, and tapped it in, finishing Eleven. Big Nick was again 1-up.

"Whoa," Ray intoned. "Mr. Momentum may have shifted to the big guy from Minnesota."

"Shit," Sink said. "Breakin' my heart. Can't believe I screwed that up. Lousy putting."

War's eyebrows went way up. The Scotsman never missed a putt like that. He placed a hand on Sink's shoulder and said, "Just hang in there, Sink, lots of golf to play. Not all your fault, Munch is gyrating like a juice blender." War returned his gaze to the High Def, muttering, "Munch, buddy, calm down—don't listen to the caddy, and believe in yourself, man."

Munch's swing on number Twelve, *Long*, was delivered with as much force as he could muster; his stroke carried the ball to left of center of the fairway, a safe shot, but now he would have to get by the "Hell" bunkers and creek crossing the fairway from right to left.

Big Nick took the riskier bet and slammed his drive toward the cross bunker, placing the ball perfectly, creating a shorter route to the green.

Fate smiled on both men, as their second shots were worthy of any PGA pro. The third Carman shot was even more spectacular, finding the green. Munch misjudged his longer shot, and came up short, twenty yards out. "Pitch and a putt," Nick yelled at Munch, "you're on a roll."

"Was Nick trying to rattle him?" Munch thought. His stomach answered; it was indeed on a roll.

At the green on number Twelve, the gallery following Malone and Carman was dense. Rooster tore through the spectators. He shoved aside an old woman who was sitting in a lawn chair near the edge of the green, plowing his way to the ropes, creating a stir amongst the spectators.

"Hey, asshole, watch who you're shovin'!" yelled the grandmother, looking up at Rooster standing at the ropes.

"Up yours, lady," he retorted, looking down and sneering at her.

"Quiet!" the marshal hissed, overhearing the foul words, shooting a warning glance at Rooster. "Good Lord, a dwarf with a sewer mouth!" the marshal thought.

Rooster grinned at the marshal and silently mouthed "Fuckya'," almost causing the glaring official to drop the paddle he was holding aloft, signaling for silence. The marshal deepened his frown and decided to collar the dwarf and call security after Carman and Malone had putted out. There was no place for such goons on a golf course, particularly this one.

Munch pulled his 52-degree wedge from the bag, only to feel Pumpkin's hand on his shoulder. "Wrong club, man," Pumpkin said.

"Uh, Pumpkin, I hit this 52 degree wedge like a champ. I always use it when I just need to chip on," Munch responded.

"The 52's a tough club. Trust me, anything but the 52."

Munch hesitated. Pumpkin was, without a doubt, nuts. "Nope, thanks Pumpkin, but I know the 52 works for me," Munch said, walking away with the club.

Rooster, close enough to read the conversation between Munch and Pumpkin, shielded his phone from the marshal's sight and texted Marcus, "Pumpkin tryin', but munch may b on 2 him."

Marcus jumped from the sofa as soon as he read the text and his thumbs began to fly. "Tell Pumpkin he better do more than try or he'll find himself in the east river."

"K–soon as I can get 2 him," Rooster replied as Munch hit the 52 degree wedge onto the green. The argument with Pumpkin had further unnerved Munch and the ball hit the green's false front, rolling well down an incline, coming to a rest in the high grass that would be below Munch's feet upon address. The rough was deep. It would grab the club, no doubt, making it difficult to follow through with the swing.

"*Uh, oh,*" *War said, ordering a gin and tonic, glancing at Sink with question marks in his eyes.*

"*It'll be okay, just watch,*" *Sink countered.*

Munch looked at the green and saw undulations that looked like an outline of Penelope Cruz's body.

"Munch is on tender hooks here. Carman has the momentum. Let's see what the 'Dead Men's Clubs' can do," Ray whispered into the microphone.

Munch stayed with the club. He loved this 52-degree wedge, but it was a club that had always given Sink the willies.

The Scotsman closed his eyes and shifted his weight to his left foot. This did not feel good. "Contagion" was difficult with the 52.

Munch hit the ball on the hosel, scattering the shot into a bunker.

"*Shit, I knew it. Screwed it up!*" *Sink howled, pounding his fist on the bar.*

Another roar erupted from the green as Carman won the hole, going 2-up, his ball pinging in with a ten foot putt that gracefully navigated Penelope, ending Munch's agony.

Sink sat back in his chair, wondering how he could have performed so poorly.

"Not to worry, Sink. Still lots to play, old shoe!" War shouted in encouragement, astounded that Sink was blowing the match. He had never seen the Scotsman so down. Not good. Not good at all, if they were to win this thing.

Upstairs at *The Powers That Be* Brawley Rollins sat watching the High Def, pen poised over a legal pad. He accessed his computer, logging on to "allyouneedtoknowaboutgolf.com" where he searched for "Secrets of The 52 Degree Wedge—Scoring with The Flop Shot."

Brawley glanced at *The Golf Channel* and the happy Minnesotan pictured there. Big Nick Carman seemed coiled and ready to strike again.

The marshal had waited until Carman and Malone had completed the hole, and then he turned, looking for the vile little man with the trash mouth. He was gone, nowhere in sight. The gallery moved on and, five minutes later, a young man from John Short's staff pulled to the green in a golf cart. He introduced himself to the marshal as a Wild-O Golf employee and asked if he had seen, during the day, an unusual looking little man about five feet tall with a bald head—probably wearing a wrinkled suit.

"I sure have, the creep was just here—right over there," the marshal answered, pointing at the ropes on the left side of the green. He dropped the 'F' bomb on me."

"Are you sure? Short guy? Bald head? Dirty white suit?" the young man asked.

"Listen, kid, he was the first and only dwarf I've seen out here today. Yeah, I'm damned sure," the marshal assured him.

"Thanks! Big help!" the young man responded, texting Janie. "Just missed him–he's on the course with the gallery following malone & carman—thousands out here—impossible to find him."

Janie adjusted her glasses and texted back. "Understand—we r on it!"

Thirty Eight

"They saw him!" *Snarf shouted, reading the texts.*

"Mr. Short! The little man was spotted on number Twelve—he's following Malone and Munch is on his way to Thirteen!" Janie yelled, running into Short's cottage, bursting into the sunroom where Short Sale and Reynolds sat, reviewing numbers.

"Let's go," Short Sale exclaimed, dropping a handful of papers and heading for the door.

Short Sale, Reynolds, and Janie climbed aboard the double-seated golf cart parked outside the cottage. Short Sale put the cart in motion and accelerated to top speed. Janie sat in back, behind Short Sale and Reynolds. The crowds around the course made progress difficult and they moved at a snail's pace.

Short Sale finally pulled the cart to a stop 100 yards from the green where Carman was hitting his second shot on Thirteen. The ball was nearly perfect, landing seven feet beyond the flag, but staying above the cup, avoiding a precipitous drop as the green stretched beyond the hole.

Munch was in the fairway, laying two on the par four. He was 180 yards out. This would be a four iron for him. He asked for the club.

"I think you can get there with a six iron," Pumpkin said, offering the bogus club. "See that dip just below the hole? You don't want Carman's problem. Use the six iron and roll the ball onto the green," Pumpkin said.

"Looks like Malone's caddy, Pumpkin Jones, wants him to use another club—Munch has his hand on, what? I think it's the six iron," Jennifer Allison commented as *The Golf Channel* camera zoomed in on the discussion.

"Get the little bastard in line!" Marcus shouted in his cottage. He picked up an ashtray off the coffee table and threw it at the television. The flat screen cracked into a thousand pieces and went black.

"Shit!" he screamed, and immediately scrambled toward the front door, grabbing his phone, heading for the golf course. He texted Rooster as he walked briskly down a flower-laden path toward the gallery–"TV reception went blank–on my way 2 join u. Looks like the bastard caddy is screwin up, can't control malone!"

Rooster stood in the midst of the crowd, catching only glimpses of Pumpkin, jumping up and down, trying to see over the gallery that loomed above him. He read Marcus' text and replied: "I heard dat–tryin 2 see caddy—I gotta' find a ladder!"

John Short, Rex Reynolds and Janie Germaine spread out, looking for Rooster, texting one another as they searched. As they swept back and forth they did not see the strange little man hurrying toward Thirteen. But he was clearly visible to the audience upstairs.

"Well, looks like the whole gang is here," War laughed, "*a freaking yard sale!*"

"Let's inform Mr. Reynolds where our boy is, Snarf," Sink instructed, *settling in for a long afternoon with the High Def.*

The picture from White Sulphur Springs was spectacular. The trio sitting in the Clubhouse upstairs was treated to every scene from The Golf Channel, as cameras panned around the stunning course, looking for a shot the director might broadcast. Almost as good as being there.

Munch hesitated, not knowing whether to hit the six or four iron. "I can't figure it out, one minute I hit the ball like a champ, next minute I'm friggin' Munch Malone, the world's worst golfer—again," Munch groused to Pumpkin, looking skyward, seeking Contagion. Nick Carman strode briskly by, laughing, chatting it up with his caddy, waving at the fans.

"Munch, get your mind on the game, dude. 'Ya gotta' listen to me if you wanna' win this," Pumpkin warned.

"Okay, Pumpkin. You make the call," Munch said, shaking his head, coming down to earth, wondering why he was listening to this asshole.

Pumpkin slapped Munch on the back, turned, and saw the strange little man standing just off the green. He had a grin on his face and was waiving a fistful of greenbacks. Pumpkin assumed the dwarf was totally crazy.

Munch made a decision, doing a '360', disagreeing once more with his caddy. He demanded the four iron. Pumpkin decided not to make a scene, handing Munch his club of choice, Munch felt the power, the confidence, as he seized the club. He hit a great shot.

He wondered again about the vagaries in his performance. "Why am I able to ace it with one club and scrub it with another?" he kept asking himself. "If somebody up there is hitting these clubs, why is he so freakin' inconsistent. For that matter, have I gone insane—clear off the deep end? I'm blaming a ghost, or something, for my poor play. It's freaking mind-bending. And there's old Nick, totally at ease. And here I go, decision time again. God help me!"

Pumpkin handed Munch the pitching wedge for his approach

to the green. He looked at the club and at Pumpkin for a long thirty seconds, and took the club.

He took several practice swings and finally addressed the ball and swung. To his horror and dismay, he topped the ball. Angry, he walked to the ball, swung again, and once more topped it. He felt like he was going to burst into tears.

He asked Pumpkin for the 52-degree wedge.

"No, man, stay with the pitching wedge," Pumpkin retorted.

"Are you absolutely crazy? I can't *hit* the pitching wedge, obviously! I just made myself look like a fool with it. Not once, but twice. Now gimme' the 52 degree, dammit!" Munch demanded, with teeth firmly clenched.

"Whoa, man! Here's the freaking 52," Pumpkin growled, throwing the club at Munch's feet.

Sink readied himself. "Can't mess it up this time. Need to trust the club." He concentrated, not his favorite weapon, but he was going to make this work.

Brawley addressed his notes on the 52-degree wedge. He 'Channeled' directly to Sink, rather than Munch. "Open stance, hands ahead of ball, descending blow—you are now the Master of the 52 degree wedge."

Sink took a practice swing and suddenly felt confident he could fully swing the wedge. "This," he thought, "is more like it!"

Munch bent over, picked up the club, walked to the ball, swung without a practice swing, watched the ball arc upward and out, hit the green, roll in backspin, and finally come to rest one inch from the hole.

Brawley smiled and closed his notebook and sighed, "Just like the old days, felt damned good—I'm back. I may have to consider a return to the links if this 'Contagion' thing works so well. I will definitely have to stay tuned."

"Well, with that finish by Malone, Carman drops back to 1-up. Malone may have won the hole, but he lost control, arguing with his caddy who was so upset he threw a club at Munch's feet," Chad Ray told his TV audience.

"Yep, Malone needs to get control of himself," Jennifer Allison whispered into her microphone, "Carman has the momentum and, even though Pumpkin Jones is doing everything he can to calm Malone down, the 70-year-old amateur seems to have gone ballistic with the veteran pro on the bag. No wonder Jones threw the club to the ground," she said, tossing it back to Ray, who broke for a series of commercials.

"There, that felt better," Munch thought, walking off the green after tapping his short putt into the hole.

"Thanks for all the help, Pumpkin," Munch uttered, sarcasm coating his voice, "I guess I'll go with the 52 from here on in and keep the pitching wedge in the bag."

"C'mon man, sheer luck back there, you've gotta' trust me on the clubs, Munch," Pumpkin replied, holstering the putter.

"The guy is absolutely nuts." Munch thought.

Thirty Nine

Reynolds, Short, and Janie pushed through the crowds, guiding their golf cart carefully through the congestion, searching for Rooster.

"What do we do when we find him?" Reynolds asked Short.

"I don't know, just keep him under surveillance for now, I guess," Short replied.

'Janie adjusted her glasses, "Sir, if I may suggest—"

"Yeah, yeah?" Short queried.

"Sir," she said, "I propose I pose as a data collector for the USGA. I will attach myself to this Rooster fellow and see what I can find out."

"What good will that do?" Short asked.

Reynolds answered Short's question. "It's a good idea. Janie can get a read on how crazy this guy is. That alone would be helpful. I've got a clipboard and standard questionnaire forms," he said, reaching into his briefcase at his feet. "Make up the questions, of course. Text us what you find out, he'll think its all part of the interview routine."

"Okay, but be careful, this guy could be wacko, he's a hired Vegas gun," Short cautioned as Janie stepped from the cart and moved into the crowd, quickly realizing she had a problem. It was as though she were searching for the proverbial needle in a haystack—a very small needle.

"He's practically a dwarf, they say, so he has to be near the green in order to see the play, or he's got a vantage point of some kind," she thought to herself, eyes darting back and forth, surveying the crowd without luck, impossible to find a dwarf in this crowd.

Brawley Rollins was glued to the action. He had come to like this young woman with the black horn-rimmed glasses. Mighty good looking, and she could use some help, he thought. Unlike Janie, Brawley had no trouble locating Rooster. Once he pinpointed the strange little man, his gaze returned to Janie's rather delightful facial features; and then he could not help himself; he looked down at a pair of exquisite legs. He chastised himself and quickly returned to the comely face. He concentrated on her, perhaps a tad long for a man in his position, and then he moved his eyes to Rooster as the little man watched from a nearby knoll that gave him a view of the green. As Brawley's eyes moved, so did Janie's, in perfect 'Channeling' synch.

"Got him," she said aloud and began plowing through the crowd.

Brawley smiled and reached for the fifth of Old Weller's whiskey on his desk. He loved the stuff, hard to find up here, but he had a contact in Kentucky who kept him supplied. It was so smooth on special days such as this one. He tipped the bottle, filled his glass, and stared at the High Def.

Janie hurried toward the strange figure that stood near the green. He was trying to attract Munch Malone's caddy, waving wads of money as discreetly as he could. Nevertheless, several onlookers were obviously wondering who the weird dude was. Janie moved as fast as she could, elbowing her way, saying softly, "USGA Research, USGA Research." Finally, she sauntered up to Rooster and adjusted her glasses.

"Excuse me, sir," she whispered, leaning down to the little man.

"Yeah?" Rooster said, continuing to gaze at the caddy.

"USGA Research, sir, we're conducting on-course interviews to gauge spectator interest in golf in the wake of Tiger Woods' performance in the last year. We'd like to get some insight from you," Janie again whispered.

Rooster caught a whiff of Chanel, looked up and was instantly engaged. His mind left the caddy and a grin filled his face, "Hey, babe, where 'ja get them legs?"

Janie could not help but laugh. How strange. Instant attraction. She felt herself blush.

"Well, if you'll buy me a beer at the Michelob tent," she answered, jerking her thumb toward one of the several VIP tents situated along the course, "I'll be glad to tell you." She gave him her best smile, adjusting her glasses, feeling warmth begin to move through her body.

"Uh, can't do it now, sweetie" Rooster replied, glancing back and forth from the caddy to Janie, just as the crowd cheered another Malone approach shot.

"How about after the match you and me get together and really get into that research thing?" he asked, again flashing his best smile.

"Nope, that won't work," she replied, leaning closer to him, giving him an ample view of her cleavage. "It's now or never," she smiled, wondering why she was so aggressive.

Rooster's knees went a little weak as he looked up and down at the best looking woman he had ever seen.

"What the hell," he thought, "time enough to grab a couple a beers, swing by the cottage, climb those legs and get back to work."

"Let's go," Rooster responded, escorting her off the course, his hand placed strategically behind, and just below, the small of her back.

Marcus, unaware that Janie had lassoed his agent, frantically searched for Rooster. He texted, but received no response. "Where is the little bastard?" he thought to himself. "Incompetent caddy, worthless dwarf," he fumed under his breath.

A golf cart carrying two men pulled beside Marcus as he hurried down the fairway, his perspiration growing as his tension mounted.

"Marcus!" shouted D.E. Wildoe, exiting the cart that had "Wild-O Golf" emblazoned across the front.

Marcus looked to his left and saw the CEO walking toward him.

"Perfect storm," he thought. "No caddy, no dwarf, and the freakin' CEO."

"Mr. Wildoe" I didn't know you were planning to be here."

"John Short gave me a call and said I should come down," Wildoe barked.

"Well, judging from Munch Malone's play today, I'd say Short gave you a bum steer," Marcus responded.

"Maybe," the CEO replied, "but he's certainly correct about one thing—if Malone wins, expect sales to go sky high. Have you seen Rex Reynolds' numbers? Incredible. Short smelled out this opportunity and, so far, he's on a roll. Better than I can say for you, Appleton."

Marcus bit his lip, "Well, we'll just have to see what the golf gods have in mind, sir."

"Damn straight, where's Short?"

"No idea, sir. I'm going to follow Malone. Perhaps you should have your driver take you to the clubhouse where you can relax and get out of the sun—grab a martini, sir."

"You've got my cell number, Appleton; call me the minute you spot Short," Wildoe grumbled, retreating to his golf cart, chauffeured by an attractive blonde. Marcus watched as the cart drove off.

Wildoe abandoned Marcus' clubhouse suggestion the moment he saw the Michelob tent off to his right. He turned to the driver, Liz Shandon, Vice President of his Wild-O Golf Education Program, and said, "Let me off here, Liz, I'll be closer here if Appleton finds Short."

"Yes sir," Shandon replied, stopping the cart, bidding goodbye to the CEO, winging the vehicle around, heading for the clubhouse.

D.E. entered the tent and walked to the bar, passing a table where an extremely good-looking, tall blonde with black horn-rimmed glasses and a very short skirt sat, sipping a Michelob, apparently doing an interview. He thought he had seen her before, or maybe it was just that she was so damned attractive. Odd that the tall drink of water was sitting with one of the shortest, ugliest little men he had ever seen.

Wildoe ordered one of the fancy Ultras in the ice-cold aluminum container from the Rotary Club geezer who was volunteering as a bartender. D.E. took a long drink and walked back past the odd couple. He could not help but notice that the blonde seemed absolutely captivated by the little guy, who was sitting as close to her as possible, answering her questions and gesticulating madly. Wildoe sat down behind a life-size poster of an Ultra bottle, in order not to be seen by the couple, but near enough to see and hear their conversation.

"USGA Research is interested in the fan base. What's your reason for attending this tournament Mr.—?" the blonde asked, smiling at the little guy.

"I'm here as a consultant," Rooster answered, figuring it would not hurt to tell her he was a "professional." "The name is Rooster"

"Rooster? Odd name. Rooster who?"

"Last name's not important, just call me Rooster."

"Okay, Rooster. What kind of consultant?" Janie asked.

"Well, I have a client who is interested in these 'Dead Men's Clubs' that Munch Malone uses," Rooster answered, quaffing his beer."

Wildoe inched a little closer and listened carefully, his ear just behind the Ultra sign that bifurcated the seating area in the tent.

"How so?" Janie asked, reaching for her Michelob.

"Tell 'ya what, I'm staying at that cottage just off the green up there, why don't we slip over there and I'll answer just about any question you have, darlin'," Rooster said, flashing what he believed to be a winning smile.

"I'll bet you would," thought Wildoe, grinning in spite of himself. He noticed the blonde did not seem offended. Instead, she reached out and patted the little fellow's hand. "I'll think about that, Rooster, but right now I'm working, and if you can't answer any more questions I'll need to get back on the course. But I truly have enjoyed meeting you." Wildoe thought she seemed to mean it.

Their heads turned in unison as the gallery roared. Munch Malone had just hit another green in regulation.

Marcus Appleton hustled past the Michelob tent when something caught his eye. Was he seeing things? The shithead of a dwarf was having a beer with some babe! "Son of a bitch!" Marcus thought, "I can't believe this! My career is in jeopardy and the little vermin is on a pussy hunt!"

Marcus stormed into the tent and accosted Rooster, grabbing him by both lapels and jerking him off his feet. "What are you doing here, you sawed-off runt? You're supposed to be following Malone and those friggin' clubs! I didn't hire you to sit around sucking beer with some golf course trailer trash!" he fumed.

Wildoe, hidden by the large Ultra sign, could hardly believe his eyes. His President of National Sales was accosting the dwarf!

"Hey, back off, Marcus," Rooster yelled, dangling above the floor. "Get your hands off me and try to respect the fact that there is a lady here!"

"That's no lady – that's golf course trailer trash!" Marcus repeated, glaring at Janie and turning back to Rooster. "Get your ass out there and tell that caddy he'd better grab Malone's clubs and crush him or he'll end up in tomorrow's Waste Management reports," Marcus seethed at Rooster through clenched teeth.

"Let me down, you shit!" Rooster demanded, dancing in mid-air, his feet flailing about, his face turning crimson.

Marcus did not see the half-full Michelob bottle descending rapidly toward his head. It hit him just above the hairline with force; his hands went limp, and he saw stars as he dumped Rooster on the floor. Janie dropped the bottle in her hand and knelt to attend to Rooster, who was covered with beer. The bartender had turned just in time to see Janie wielding the Michelob. He grabbed his cell phone, calling Security.

"Are you okay, little buddy?" Janie cooed to Rooster as she rubbed his arms and helped him sit up. "Why am I so attracted to this little guy?" she thought to herself, with alarm.

Rooster smiled at Janie and patted her cheek. "Thanks, doll," he said, slowly getting to his feet. Standing over Marcus, Rooster poked his finger at the dazed face that looked up at him.

"You're the asshole, big man! You didn't hire me and I don't work for you, you ungrateful bastard. I work for Jimmy Frong, and I'll bet your sad ass that Jimmy will be flyin' here from Vegas as soon as he hears from me. You're out of your friggin' mind!" Rooster yelled.

Marcus' head slowly cleared as he nursed his scalp where the bottled had struck. He thought of Jimmy Frong's knife at his balls and began to backpedal. "Oh, my God, I am so sorry, Rooster. I went totally berserk for a minute there. My bad. I've been under incredible pressure lately and I just went off," Marcus pleaded as he struggled, but failed, to get up.

Security bolted into the tent and a small group of onlookers gathered. The bartender told it as he saw it; the blonde had wielded a beer bottle, assaulting the guy who was sitting on the floor, nursing a rapidly growing knot on his forehead.

The security detail, two off-duty county policemen moonlighting at the tournament, hurried over to Marcus and helped him up.

The older officer, fighting a beer belly that strained the buttons on his shirt, asked "Is that so, sir? Did this lady assault you with a beer bottle?"

"No, no, officer, we just got excited watching the tournament on the flat screen over there and I lost my balance, fell off my chair, hit my head, that's all." Marcus replied.

"Is that blood in your hair?" the younger officer asked.

Marcus put his hand on top of his head and felt something wet. He looked at his hand and saw the blood.

"Oh, my. Guess I ought to see about that."

"Sir, do you wish to press charges?" the older officer asked, looking at Janie, picking up the blood covered Michelob bottle.

"Goodness no, it's just like I said, officer, I fell off my chair."

The older security cop shrugged and pulled up his sagging trousers. His partner warned all three offenders that rowdiness, drunkenness, and disorderly conduct would not be permitted, and if security was summoned again that they would all be subject to arrest and battery charges.

Janie and Rooster left the tent, slipping out as Marcus assured the security detail there would be no further disturbance. The two cut across the fairway. Rooster put his nose to his sleeve, glancing sideways at Janie. "Geez, I smell like a brewery. Let's go to my cottage so I can change clothes," he said. Janie, to Rooster's surprise and delight, readily agreed.

D.E. Wildoe, sitting out of sight behind the Ultra poster, was stunned. He had just witnessed his President of National Sales in a bizarre scenario; he mentally reviewed the entire scene, wondering what he should do next. He waited until Rooster, Janie, and Appleton were gone, ordered another Ultra, and considered his options.

Wildoe was a man who had gained prominence in business by always thinking things through. He again replayed the remarkable events he had just witnessed, trying to analyze what they would mean for his baby, Wild-O Golf.

"This is incredible," he thought, "Marcus is obviously trying to stop Malone from winning. He's paid the caddy to steal Malone's clubs? Why? He has a contact named Jimmy Frong in Las Vegas. Is this a mob connection? How could I have misread Marcus this badly? I know they call him 'The Shit', but I can't believe he's got mob connections. My God. This is awful. Is Marcus bribing the caddy through this guy Rooster to make sure Malone loses?"

Wildoe reached for his phone and called John Short. He left a voice message. "I want a meeting ASAP with you and all of our people who are here with you—Marcus Appleton is through at Wild-O Golf and we may need to help Malone finish this thing."

Wildoe pocketed his phone, paid for the beers, walked out of the tent and called for Liz and his chauffeured cart. He glanced at *The Golf Channel* cameras carrying the tournament to the world. The brand, the Wild-O brand he had worked so hard to build, had to be protected. "Where," he wondered, "was the odd couple—the dwarf and the incredible leggy blonde?"

Forty

Rooster fumbled for the key to his cottage as Janie massaged his shoulders where Marcus had held him aloft. "Subtle, subtle," he thought to himself. Janie looked down at Rooster's baldhead and thought, "My God, why *am* I so attracted to him? This doesn't make any sense, there must be something that's turning me on like this—I can just sense it."

Rooster pushed the door aside and the two fell through the opening, clutching at one another. Rooster grabbed for her blouse and she ripped his shirt off. She was quite tall and Rooster came up short as he reached as high as he could, just missing a hold on her blouse. Janie took control, pulling the blouse off, unsnapping her bra, pushing her panties to the ground.

Rooster's eyes bulged as he fell backwards onto the floor, frantically tugging at his trousers while looking at the marvelously naked woman. Janie, breathing heavily, pulled off his pants as she stood over him, legs spread wide. Rooster was in monstrous heat. His erection grew, causing him to struggle to pull off his jockey shorts. Janie reached down, grabbed the underwear, and gave a yank, freeing the contents.

She gasped. No wonder she felt such an attraction; Rooster was hung like a horse!

She threw Rooster's shorts in the air and jumped on his erection, all six feet of her consuming him. The fact she was taller than Rooster did, indeed make a difference. He *was* a little short—his head was nestled and compressed between her breasts. It was wonderful! He thrust forward, leaned back, opened his mouth and loudly yodeled, "Cock a Doodle Doo!"

"Yeah, baby!" Snarf said, watching the action on his laptop, rubbing his hands together, "This is better than a Chicago gang bang. Finally! Some real porn! Go, Rooster, go!" he yelled.

War was leaning over Snarf's shoulder. Try as he might not to stare, it was just too bizarre not to look. After what seemed like too much time for even a Congressman to study the events, War slapped Snarf on the back and set a dish of ice cream at his elbow. "Tell Janie to keep him occupied," he said, walking off.

Rooster rolled over, squinted at Janie and grinned. "That was unbelievable, babe—I'd like to stay here and do it again, but I got a job to do." He reached for his pants.

"So, level with me, Rooster," Janie said, beginning to dress, "What's the job? Are you sabotaging Malone?"

"Well, you heard Marcus; he wants me to keep Malone from winning. Apparently 'The Shit' thinks if Malone wins, he loses his job. Marcus contacted my boss, Jimmy Frong, out in Vegas, and Jimmy sent me here to grab the 'Dead Men's Clubs'. Marcus thinks the clubs are the reason Munch wins. And from what I've seen out there, he's right," Rooster said.

"Why would you want to help Marcus out, after what he did to you?" Janie asked, searching for her skirt and glasses.

"Got nothing to do with Marcus. Until my boss man Jimmy calls me off, I'm on it," Rooster said.

Janie nodded in understanding and finished dressing. Her phone pinged; a text from John Short. The CEO was calling a meeting at John Short's cottage. She and Rooster ran to the golf course where intensity was mounting as the Championship wore on.

Munch Malone was unaware of their mad dash. All he knew

was, he was on a different level, and it was rattling him. Big Nick Carman never stopped charging. On Fourteen, *Narrows*, Carman, using his driver as though it were a finely tuned instrument, swung easily, flying the ball 260 yards, over the right side cross bunker.

"Damn," Munch said to Pumpkin, "The guy never lets up."

"This is big time golf buddy, just when you think you 'da man', you ain't—you're nobody," Pumpkin spat, looking directly at Munch as he said the last two words.

"He's friggin' crazy," Munch thought, grabbing his big stick. He walked up to the tee, gauging the direction, waggling the club, feeling the renewed sense of power and assurance. Odd, some of these clubs made him feel like he was Phil Mickelson. He swung and felt the sweet spot. His ball took off like a rocket, flying straight down the *Narrows*, middle of fairway, eighty-four yards out, in front of Nick's drive. "Take that," he thought, glancing at Pumpkin, who seemed unimpressed.

Carman was equally nonplused. He walked away, chatting with his caddy, asking for a club as he ambled to his ball. Big Nick was enormous. Munch thought he would have given the gargantuan President Taft, a golf junkie, a run for his money.

Carman took his nine iron, hesitated for only seconds, executed perfectly, landing the ball on the small elevated green.

"Beautiful. You'll have a hard time takin' this one," Pumpkin grinned, his gaze moving from the course to Munch.

"Thanks for the vote of confidence asshole. Gimme' the pitching wedge," Munch demanded.

Pumpkin eagerly handed over the bogus club. "Sorry about that, Munch. Go get 'em, boy," Pumpkin taunted, seeing Rooster and a blonde hurrying toward the hole. "Damn, a looker with the dwarf," he thought.

Munch visualized his shot and took a practice swing. "Again, this club does not feel right," he thought. "Am I getting tired? Am I up to this?" He told himself to settle down. He visualized the shot, and swung.

The club descended, striking the ground with a thud and the ball skittered thirty feet, rolling to a stop that presented a problem. A large tree limb bent low across the edge of the fairway. Munch's next shot would have to go over or under the limb, or, he would need to play it safe.

This time Munch asked for the 52-degree wedge and safely pitched the ball into the center of the fairway. He slammed the club back in the Rodney, ignoring Pumpkin's effort to perform the task. Munch then kicked the bag, swore, and lashed out again, his face reddening.

"Oh, wow," Chad Ray whispered to *The Golf Channel* audience. "I was told Malone used to have a temper on the course and that's the first sign we've seen that the man with 'Dead Men's Clubs' might be showing such tantrums again."

"Just a chip and putt," Munch muttered, and asked once more for the 52-degree wedge. Pumpkin shook his head and immediately engaged Munch in conversation. "I know you want the 52 and that's ordinarily exactly what you would need," Pumpkin advised, "but not this time, use the pitching wedge."

"Why in the hell would I do that? I can't hit that friggin' club," Munch protested.

"Believe in yourself, Malone! The pitching wedge will work this time. The 52-degree is tricky, everybody knows that! " Pumpkin insisted.

"Well, the bag boy's right about that," Sink said, a worried look on his face as he addressed the High Def. But, bullshit! I am the Master of the 52 degree wedge."

Munch looked at the distance between him and the green and reluctantly took the pitching wedge.

"Damn," Sink frowned.

Munch addressed the ball. A bogus club was in his hands.

"Like my cupcake of a caddy says, I need to believe in myself," Munch thought, sarcasm oozing as he struck the ball. The shot was beautiful, on the green, inches from the cup. Munch had performed on his own.

"Damn," Munch grinned.

"Shit," Pumpkin muttered.

"Yes!" Sink exclaimed, "even a blind squirrel can find an acorn every once in a while."

Carman shook his head, a big grin on his face, and went about the business of judging the direction of the grass on the green. He stood over his putt, rolled the ball, and was down in three, finishing the hole 2-up.

Rooster and Janie were watching with interest. "Oh, oh, Munch has his work cut out for him now," Rooster said, he's down two and Pumpkin won't let up."

"Pumpkin's trying to talk Munch into using only certain clubs?" she asked.

"Yeah, Pumpkin was able to get some bogus clubs in the bag and he's tryin' to convince Malone to use them, but if Malone can hit like that with the bogus club..." Rooster trailed off.

Janie's phone vibrated. "Hurry, meeting, my cottage, 10 minutes—absolutely imperative u b there," John Short texted.

"K," she texted back.

"Rooster, got to go, duty calls."

"Okay, babe, but when the match is over, let's play 'Cock a Doodle Doo' again as soon as possible," he leered, squeezing her buttocks. She patted his head and walked away.

Forty One

"Nice job with the pitching wedge, Munch. Now will you believe me when I tell you which club to hit?" Pumpkin asked.

"Okay, okay. Thanks for helping me come back." Munch said, without conviction. He felt a renewed confidence as he began the walk down the fairway, with storm clouds gathering in the distant mountains.

"You know," Pumpkin yelled at Munch's back, "it was still sheer freakin' luck!"

"Schizoid," Munch muttered, without looking back.

Number Fifteen, *Eden*, was just ahead. Both tee shots stayed beneath the cup on the par three, avoiding the deep "Strath" pot bunker in front of the green and the awesome "Hill" bunker on the left. Both Munch and Nick parred the hole with Nick staying 2-up.

As the action at Fifteen concluded, John Short texted D.E. Wildoe that he had, at Wildoe's direction, set up a meeting with all Wild-O personnel on the course, summoning them to his cottage on The Greenbrier's Paradise Row. Wildoe read the text and headed for the elevator. He moved rapidly through the hotel, exiting at the front entrance between large columns framing the massive white structure. He looked around, spotted a green uniform and recognized Russell, the bellman.

Raising his hand, Waldo shouted, "Limo to Paradise!"

"Only at the Greenbrier, sir, only at the Greenbrier," the experienced and expert bellman smiled, signaling for a limousine to transport Wildoe to Paradise Row.

The dark green Lincoln Town Car moved slowly through the luxurious grounds surrounding the hotel, stopping in front of Cottage number seven.

The CEO strode through the door of the cottage without knocking, looking around approvingly at the plush interior. He was anxious to begin. "Let's get started," he said to John Short and Rex Reynolds as they looked up from the statistics they were reviewing on the coffee table in the cottage's spacious living room.

"Got to wait for Janie, she's been on the course and may know something," Short said.

"Janie who?" D.E. asked, appearing agitated.

"My Senior Executive Assistant. Haven't you seen her around?" Short asked, "She's pretty hard to miss."

Reynolds smiled in the affirmative.

"Nope, don't think so," the CEO frowned, as the door to the cottage opened and Janie walked in.

Short knew something was wrong as soon as he saw his boss' reaction when Janie entered the room.

"You're Janie?" Wildoe asked, staring at her.

"Yes, I am, Mr. Wildoe," she replied, adjusting her glasses, staring intently, no hint of being intimidated.

"John," Wildoe said, turning to Short, "you've got a problem here. Your Senior Executive Assistant," he snorted, "is a turncoat."

"What do you mean, turncoat?" Short demanded.

Wildoe turned and looked accusingly at Janie. "I just happened to be in one of the Michelob tents an hour or so ago. Your little Janie here was throwing beer bottles and cozying up to this Rooster guy who's trying to screw with Malone and his clubs," Wildoe replied.

"What the hell is he talking about, Janie?" Short asked.

"I can explain, Mr. Wildoe," Janie said, adjusting her glasses and her skirt as she sat down. "Am I too messed up here?" she thought, checking for any evidence of Rooster's leftovers on her clothing.

Janie explained the charade; posing as a USGA Research interviewer she had convinced Rooster to confide in her. Marcus' subsequent attack on Rooster had filled in all the blanks, giving her a full picture of Appleton's plan to destroy Munch Malone's game.

"The ploy worked, but not in a way I had envisioned," she said. "I thought I'd get him to the tent and ask Rooster some questions and find out why he was stalking Mr. Malone. I never dreamed Mr. Appleton would accost Rooster and spill the beans," she said.

"So, Marcus' tirade confirms that the texts being sent to me from the undisclosed party are accurate?" Reynolds asked.

"Wow, you hit Marcus with a beer bottle?" Short beamed.

"She sure as hell did. She also seemed to take a shine to Rooster," Wildoe said.

Janie hesitated and turned toward Short Sale. "It's funny, Mr. Short, I do like the guy. I totally did not expect that, but I really do like him. I think he's simply following orders from this Jimmy Frong in Las Vegas. Rooster's not an evil guy, I just know it," she pleaded.

"I can't believe Marcus has gone totally berserk like this," Wildoe interrupted, "the bastard obviously doesn't give a shit about Wild-O Golf. All he wants is you out, John, and any benefit we might get from Malone scuttled, just to save his hide. He's through, right now, and you, John, are *back in the saddle again*."

Hearing the phrase, Janie turned crimson, adjusted her glasses and straightened her skirt. No one noticed but the CEO.

Reynolds cautioned, "If I may suggest, Mr. Wildoe, perhaps we should think very carefully about this."

"Okay, careful it is, what do you have in mind, Rex?" Wildoe said, sitting back in his chair.

"Well, neither Marcus nor Rooster know we're on to them—" Reynolds said, as the CEO interrupted him.

"They don't know, unless—" and Wildoe turned to Janie, "unless you told Rooster, Janie."

"No sir, I absolutely did not. I mean, he's very nice and all and I don't think he'd do this unless he had to and, you know, I think he thinks he has to—I'm just saying—" and she trailed off.

"My God," thought John Short, "I've never seen her so rattled. Could she possibly be sweet on the dwarf?" Short immediately scolded himself, remembering all the "short" barbs he had delivered.

"Listen, if Janie says she said nothing to Rooster, you can take it to the bank. I love my job, but if I'm proven wrong, I'll take a walk, D.E." Short said, glancing from Janie to Wildoe.

"Okay," Wildoe said, raising the palms of both hands toward Short in surrender, "good enough for me, John." D.E. then turned to Rex and said, "Whaddya' have in mind, Reynolds?"

"Well, let's not get too focused on finding Appleton and letting him know he's through," Rex suggested. "We can do that later. Right now, the critical question is, who controls the game?" Reynolds answered his own question, "The guy that selects the clubs, that's who. The caddy is our target. Now, how do we get to him?"

"*Damn right, bring the caddy down. Let Munch play his own game,*" Sink snorted, pounding on the bar.

"The caddy is on the course. We can't call him aside and

whisper in his ear. It's pretty near impossible to make contact or to stop this altogether, unless we go to the tournament officials and tell them what we *think* is going on. We don't know the answers ourselves, so we're not gonna' do that. We're at a stalemate unless we get blessed with divine intervention." Short lamented.

Just then, the heavens opened, lightning flashed and rain again poured on the twenty thousand lining the historic Greenbrier course.

Automated warning systems came into play as loud crashes of thunder rolled in the distance; the horn blew, clearing the course. Jennifer Allison said to her *Golf Channel* viewers, "I have never, ever, in my life, seen anything like that. It's as those someone up there flipped a switch and opened the heavens!"

Brawley Rollins winked at **The Powers That Be** *sitting around the conference table, saying, "That Allison lady has got some insight, doncha' think, folks?"*

The group chortled together as they watched the High Def. Even Sid Belch let go of a little smile as he read through the documents he had brought to the meeting. Retro Elvis stood, did a little bow, and said; "I'll say it for all of us, Mr. Chairman. Thank 'yew, thank 'yew very much."

Forty Two

Wildoe, Reynolds, Short and Janie stood silent and shocked as the wind whipped against the windows of The Greenbrier cottage and hail as big as, yes, golf balls, rattled on the roof.

Watching the *Golf Channel* focus on golfers and caddies scurrying for the clubhouse as the warning horn blared; Short Sale turned to his assembled group and said, "Let's move fast, this may be a weather cell that will swing by in minutes. Janie, let's reverse course, try to find Rooster and tell him who you are, what we know, and that we will bring charges against him, Marcus and Pumpkin unless he plays ball with us."

He turned to Reynolds, "Rex, churn up the interviewing as Munch finishes, we might be able to break some news with the public that will send sales through the roof if he wins. I'm going to follow Malone and Carman to see if there is any way we can get to the caddy—let him know we're aware of what's going on—that we'll put his ass in jail if he continues to mess with Munch."

Short turned with leadership authority toward the CEO. "D.E. stay here and monitor *The Golf Channel* and text us if anything breaks that we need to know. Uh, I mean, if that's okay with you, sir."

Wildoe frowned and said, "Dammit, John, drop the 'sir'. Let's do what Rex says, focus on the caddy — but slap the piss out of Marcus when you find him—and tell him he's fired and you're back as President of National Sales for Wild-O Golf. I like your style, John."

"Yes, sir, I mean, yes, D.E. Let's spread out and stay in touch; text anything new," Short barked, as the Wild-O Bunch headed for the door.

"Alright, alright, this is working out well. If they can bring down the caddy, we'll have clear sailing," Sink said, watching the High Def.

"It ain't over 'til it's over," War said.

"Got that right, man, it ain't over until the dwarf sings," Snarf warned.

At that moment, "The Beast" appeared at the front entrance to The Greenbrier.

The giant fireplug of a man that walked toward the reception desk seemed to fill the expansive lobby. Del, Supervisor of Front Door Operations, looked up from his post across the broad expanse of marble, nudged his buddy at the bell stand, and exclaimed, "Whoeee! That is one mean-lookin' Motha'!"

All heads turned toward Jimmy Frong. The desk clerk was visibly nervous as he confirmed the reservation for the frowning, menacing-looking man that stood before him. Keys were placed in a large paw of a hand as Frong asked the receptionist, "How do I get to 'da crowd followin' Munch Malone?" The clerk raised his hand and Del appeared. Jimmy repeated the question, extending a $100 bill.

Del palmed the bill with an ease that bespoke many such transactions and years of seniority. He moved to the bell stand, made a call and spoke in the voice of a CEO. He then turned to smile at the huge figure before him. "Got him, Mr. Frong. I'll getcha' there! Golf cart's outside, let's go!" Del led Frong to the exit, and said, "Here's my card, anything you need at The Greenbrier, you just call Del!" Jimmy stared intently at Del, making a mental note that he could use Del's leadership back at the Majestic.

Frong had arrived at The Greenbrier thanks to a text from Rooster. Jimmy was in the Majestic's corporate jet the moment he heard his man had been accosted by Marcus Appleton. Appleton, who *owed* Jimmy Frong. Frong did not take such a challenge lightly, or at all. Rooster was family, in effect, and *nobody* screwed with Jimmy Frong's family.

Frong texted Rooster, "At greenbrier–got cart and driver–where r u?"

Rooster responded with enthusiasm, "Jimmy–fantastic–meet me at slammin sammy's–rainin cats and dogs."

Rooster turned to run for Sammy's as Del made arrangements to chauffeur Jimmy to the restaurant near number Eighteen. Rooster ended his phone call just as he bumped into the waist of Janie Germaine.

"Janie, baby," he grinned, his eyes traveling appreciatively up her body.

"Rooster, we have to talk," she said, holding a golf umbrella as rain-soaked spectators flew by, seeking cover.

"Can't now baby, *Jimmy Frong* is here."

"Frong? Where is he?" she asked.

"On his way to Sammy's, gotta' hurry," Rooster replied, reaching up, patting her behind, moving away from the gallery.

Janie ran after him, covering him with the big umbrella.

"Rooster, I'm not who you think I am," Janie shouted, adjusting her glasses, fogged from the rain.

"Don't care who you are, sweetie, you're 'da one for me," Rooster replied, grabbing her hand, giving it a wet smooch.

Janie stopped walking, grabbed Rooster, reached down, and placed a hand on his shoulders, struggling to control the umbrella that was responding to the gusts of wind blowing across the fairway.

"I am not a USGA Research employee. I work for Wild-O Golf. I'm the Senior Executive Assistant to John Short who is Vice President of Wild-O's Reconditioned Clubs Division," Janie said.

Rooster processed that for just about two seconds as his shoes slid in wet grass. "You mean you work for the guy who runs the 'Dead Men's Clubs' Division at Wild-O?"

"Yes, Rooster. I'm so sorry I misled you, but I wanted to pump you for information," Janie apologized, the rain whipping across her face, hiding tears that ran down her cheeks.

"No apology necessary, babe, turns out it was I who pumped you," Rooster smiled, reaching up, wiping her tears away.

"Oh, Rooster, you need to get out of the sack and onto the green, sweetie," she laughed. "You and I need to talk with Jimmy Frong. He needs to know what Marcus said when he jumped on you, and he needs to know who the enemy is," Janie emphasized, patting his wet cheek.

Forty Three

Jimmy Frong met Rooster and Janie as they headed for the restaurant named for the legendary Sam Snead. The three of them walked into Sammy's, wet and shivering. Frong flashed a fifty-dollar bill that put them near the window where they could monitor the rain. The large, menacing looking man took up his entire side of a large booth at which they sat. Rooster and Janie were across from him.

"Boss, I can't believe you're really here!" Rooster exclaimed, fist bumping the big man, leaning forward in the booth, legs dangling in mid-air.

"Rooster! Glad 'ta see 'ya still got a way with the lookers. 'Dis one's fine, fine, fine. How 'ya like his equipment, sweetheart?" Frong leered.

Rooster shook his head, "Boss, this is different. Janie and I have got a serious thing goin' on here," he said.

Frong's expression changed immediately and the menace disappeared from his eyes. "Oh. I am truly sorry, Rooster, I had no idea." He looked at Janie, "My heartfelt apologies, Miss. I did not know that youse and Rooster here was a serious event. Please know of my high regard for 'da Rooster and my equally large respect for any lady with who 'da Rooster considers a serious relationship," Frong said, practically bowing in the booth.

He looked at Rooster once more and asked, "Now, 'da girl is

beautiful, but, Rooster, she's a tad taller 'dan you." He turned to Janie, "Is 'dat a problem for 'ya, Miss?"

"Mr. Frong, thank you. I accept your apology and I can tell you I *am* greatly impressed with Rooster's equipment, and the height differentiation is not at all a problem," Janie smiled.

"Glad 'ta hear it, sweetheart! Sorry—I mean, 'Miss,'" Jimmy beamed.

"Sweetheart is fine, Jimmy. May I call you Jimmy?" Janie asked, brightening the smile.

"I like her, I like her, Rooster! Yeah, sweetheart, it's Jimmy," Frong affirmed.

"Jimmy, I work for Wild-O Golf, same as Marcus Appleton, who hired you."

Frong bristled. "Dat shit didn't hire me, I ain't for hire. Appleton asked for a favor. I *give* favors to people. Appleton said he needed a job done, didn't say what, but said it would take some finesse, a *subtle* approach, so I sent him my best man, 'da Rooster here."

Frong leaned back, took a long drink, finishing his Chimay, a Belgian beer he favored. He set down the bottle, reached across the table and patted Rooster on the shoulder with one hand, motioning for a second Chimay with the other. "Tell her, Rooster, Jimmy Frong ain't for hire."

Janie picked up the slack. "You should have asked Appleton's intentions before granting his favor, Mr. Frong. He's determined to make Munch Malone—"

"The old guy? The guy that's knockin' em dead with 'Dead Men's Clubs'? I gotta' see it," Frong said.

"Yep, the very one. Appleton asked Rooster to steal Malone's clubs so he would lose and Marcus could save his job. It's a long story and I won't bore you with details. Our CEO has already authorized my boss to fire Appleton as soon as we find him out there on the course. Thing is, we need you to allow Rooster to step down from this assignment. Rooster won't do it without your say-so," Janie said.

"What's the skinny, my little man?" Frong asked, turning to Rooster.

"Boss, Appleton is a mess. He's friggin' possessed with Malone and the 'Dead Men's Clubs'. Janie's right, the creep is afraid he'll lose his job to Janie's boss if Munch wins."

Janie nodded and adjusted her glasses. "We have a situation where 70-year-old Munch Malone may create golf history by winning the USGA Senior Men's Amateur Golf Championship. One selfish shit, excuse my language, wants to see Malone's chances crushed simply because he has so little confidence in himself," Janie said.

Frong's golf juices began to churn. "So, this guy Malone really has a chance, even though he's 70? He's really that good?" Frong asked.

"We don't know if he's that good or if his skill is somehow tied to the clubs he's using," Janie replied.

"Freakin' unbelievable, you're talkin' about the 'Dead Men's Clubs', right?" Frong asked.

"My boss, Mr. Short, still has a problem with folks calling them 'Dead Men's Clubs', but he's coming around as our sales numbers increase," Janie responded.

"Listen, sweetheart, he better come around, the entire country's callin' 'em 'Dead Men's Clubs'. That train left the station a long time ago," Frong said.

"I believe you are correct, sir, and we at Wild-O Reconditioned are attempting to manage this—'situation'—as best we can. Strategically, we believe it is best to have a clear-cut opportunity; we want Malone to win, even if the buying public continues to call his Wild-O's 'Dead Men's Clubs'. Our public opinion research shows the public likes Malone, loves the clubs, and, in purchase orders in the last two days, is emailing and calling with one specific request—they ask for 'Dead Men's Clubs'. We sense great opportunity here. If Malone falters and does not perform well, we're 'SOL'—'Dead Men's Clubs' and no winner," Janie explained.

Janie hesitated and then delivered the message she had been instructed to give to Frong. "I don't mean this to offend you, sir, but this is critical to Wild-O Golf. As much as it pains me to say it, D.E. Wildoe, our CEO, has instructed me to tell you that unless you, 'back off,' as he put it, he will seek criminal charges against you and your operatives."

Rooster was looking at her with, what, admiration? Or was he looking at her chest? Either way, Janie was pleased to have finally delivered the message without triggering any violent response from Frong, who quietly finished his second Chimay, burped, and ordered another.

" 'Scuse me, sweetheart," he said, eyes narrowing, "Are you threatening me?"

"Absolutely not, sir. Mr. Wildoe does not know you, and I just met you, but I know enough to understand that you folks are not the problem here, it's Marcus Appleton. And he's still a threat to Munch Malone and Wild-O Golf, if you are behind him," Janie assured Frong.

"Does Appleton know he's been, or will be—soon as you find him—fired?" Frong asked, appearing to step back from the threshold of violence.

"No, he doesn't know that yet. We've got to find him first and time is running out. Munch is on the course and this delay could end any minute—it's already starting to clear up," Janie answered.

"But 'duh key here is 'duh caddy, right? He's got control of 'duh clubs, and Malone 'duzent know half of 'dem are bogus. What's amazing to me is that there must really be somethin' kinda' magic in 'dose clubs. You don't suppose 'da old farts that used to own 'duh clubs are playing for Munch, do 'ya?" Frong asked, smiling, once again, amiable—as amiable as he could be for such a large, threatening hulk of a fellow.

"Whoa, you 'Da Man' Jimmy Frong!" War shouted at the High Def. "Finally, somebody has figured out we are playin' the game," War exclaimed.

"Not so fast, let's not encourage any more of that," Sink cautioned.

"Whaddya' mean?" War asked.

"*The Powers That Be*. Remember, they warned against us exposing our involvement in 'Contagion' and they probably will not take kindly to public utterances down there that somebody up here is roaming fairways," Sink warned.

"Like the man said," Snarf chimed in, "that train left the station a long time ago."

Forty Four

Janie, Rex, Short Sale, D. E. Wildoe, and, now, even Jimmy Frong, were frantically searching for Marcus Appleton to force him to call off Pumpkin Jones. They would apprise Appleton he was fired and that Wild-O Golf would bring legal action against him and Pumpkin on multiple levels, ranging from destruction of the Wild-O Brand, to willful violation of USGA rules, and anything else Wild-O "Legal" could come up with.

But Marcus Appleton and Pumpkin Jones were not to be found. They had simply disappeared into the massive thunderstorm that continued to wreak havoc over The Greenbrier course.

Their disappearing act began as Appleton commandeered one of the golf carts deployed to pick up players and caddies when the downpour started. He searched for Pumpkin and found him trailing thirty yards behind Munch as golfer and caddy headed for the Clubhouse. Marcus cut off Pumpkin as he struggled with the Rodney bag, hustling to escape the rain.

"Get in the cart," Marcus shouted.

"Who's this dude?" Pumpkin thought, but he did not hesitate to accept the offer of a ride as the rain sheared into his face. He strapped Munch's clubs on back of the cart and hopped in.

Appleton floored the accelerator and turned off the fairway, racing through the yard of a $6 million dollar home, veering toward the caddy's cottage.

Dead Men's Clubs

"Where 'ya goin', man?" Pumpkin said, "Clubhouse is the other way."

Marcus kept one hand on the wheel and extended the other to Pumpkin. "I'm the client, Pumpkin!" Marcus shouted through the downpour.

"Client?" Pumpkin shouted back, but with obvious caution.

"Client. As in $25,000 and a $5,000 bonus. I hired Rooster and Rooster hired you—with my *own* money," Marcus yelled over the noise of the cart. "Name's Marcus Appleton, I'm President of National Sales, Wild-O Golf," he said, handing Pumpkin a Wild-O brochure with Appleton's picture on the cover.

Pumpkin glanced at the brochure and stuffed it in his back pocket. "Okay, Appleton, so you're the client. What I wanna' know is why in the hell would the President of National Sales for Wild-O golf want to screw with his own clubs—Wild-O clubs?" he shouted over the torrential downpour.

"Simple," Marcus answered, rain spattering off his forehead, "If Malone wins the Open and 'Dead Men's Clubs' become synonymous with Wild-O clubs, the brand will be screwed and I'll be blamed. If that happens, I'll lose my job. We've gotta' make sure Munch blows up and loses the tournament," Marcus said, careening around a curve on a path lined with flowers that were horizontal in the wind and rain.

"Whatever, man, I'm just here to serve—as long as I get the rest of my money," Pumpkin shouted over the pelting rain as thunder and lightning cascaded around the course.

Marcus pulled up to the caddy cottage and turned to Pumpkin. "The rest of the money's in your room — under the bed. Now go get it and switch the rest of the clubs—Malone could win this damn thing unless we can fill his bag with the bogus clubs."

Pumpkin complied, jumping out of the cart, grabbing the seven legitimate 'Dead Men's Clubs' that remained in the Rodney bag. He ran through the pouring rain to his cottage, climbed the stairs, put the key in the lock and threw the 'Dead Men's Clubs' on the floor. He got down on his hands and knees and checked for money under the bed. By God, it was there, in a Greenbrier shopping bag.

"Damn, I was right, a friggin' shopping bag," Pumpkin grinned. He started to empty his pockets of the cash and put the money he was carrying into the bag, but stopped short. He reversed himself, re-pocketing the cash he had taken out of his pants, stuffing the rest of the cash from under the bed into his trousers. He looked in the mirror.

"Lumpy," he thought, and shrugged. "What the shit, I ain't leavin' the money here for Rooster to steal." He patted himself down as best he could, turned, swept up the rest of the bogus clubs, leaving behind Munch's originals. He headed downstairs where he put the bogus sticks in the Rodney bag.

"Do you think Munch will know the clubs have been switched?" Marcus asked, glancing at them. "They *look* used, but can anyone tell? What if the tour officials are suspicious?"

Pumpkin again inspected the clubs; he himself had trouble telling the difference between the kosher and bogus sticks. But, Appleton was correct, if anyone *even suspected* the clubs were changed, Malone would be disqualified. He'd not only lose the match, but there would be an investigation. Too messy? Too many loose ends? Doubt hovered in the moment.

Pumpkin took one more look at the clubs and made up his mind. "He's an amateur, he'll never know if his clubs are switched," he mumbled.

Marcus was not sure. "I don't know, do you think we should leave the original three wood and putter in the bag?"

"It's your call, man, I'm just the instrument of your aggression," Pumpkin smirked, irritated.

"Let's leave the driver, three wood, the putter, and maybe the five iron," Marcus said, "if he looks at the other clubs and thinks they look different, and then at the 'Dead Men's Clubs' and thinks they're okay, he'll at least second guess himself if he has any suspicions. I want him to lose, but not to know *why* he's losing. You'll just have to keep him away from the four 'Dead Men's Clubs' " Marcus said.

"Whatever," Pumpkin sighed, grabbing the bogus driver, three wood, putter, and five iron, setting off to make the switch one more time. He was gone for less than ten minutes, returning with the four designated "Dead Men's Clubs", tossing them in the bag, sitting down in the cart.

"Whaddya' think? Was that a good decision?" Marcus asked, looking at Pumpkin.

"Is this Groundhog Day? Do I have to climb the freaking stairs again?" Pumpkin asked, throwing up his hands, exasperated.

"Nope. No. Let's go," Marcus said, gunning the cart.

They arrived at The Greenbrier's north entrance where buses unloaded and loaded passengers bound for the Lewisburg airport. There they found Cyrano, a Greenbrier bellman who answered to Del, Supervisor of Front Door Operations.

"Cyrano, we gotta' problem. You look like just the man who can help us!" Marcus said, peeling off two $100 bills from a wad of money in a gold Wild-O money clip.

Cyrano, seeing the hundreds, said "Never seen a problem I can't solve, sir!"

Marcus shoved the bills in Cyrano's jacket pocket and explained he needed to hide his cart and golf clubs, and find a place he and Pumpkin could stay out of sight until play resumed on the course.

Cyrano rubbed the hundreds in his pocket and took command; he jumped in Marcus' cart, driving it into a service area, hit the brake, stepped out, and slammed the storage area door closed, effectively hiding the cart and Munch's clubs. He then hopped in a baggage cart, and yelled "Get in!" Marcus and Pumpkin did as they were instructed, and Cyrano headed down the long driveway alongside the hotel.

He headed west, past the Top Notch and Copeland Hill Cottages and veered off the paved thoroughfare and into the woods. The bellman raced down a hillside and came to a locked gate at the bottom of the mountain, directly under the West Virginia Wing of the hotel. He punched in numbers at the security gate and it swung wide, revealing one hundred yards down the driveway an isolated large green door that seemed to be the entrance to an electrical equipment site. A white sign on the door shouted, "Warning: High Voltage!"

Cyrano entered yet another set of numbers at this checkpoint and pushed the door open, revealing a massive steel blast door that Marcus estimated to be thirty feet high, twenty feet wide and weighing twenty-five tons.

"I'll be a sonofabitch—-this looks like something out of James Bond," Pumpkin muttered.

"Better than that," Cyrano grinned, entering another security code. Immediately, the multi-ton, blast-resistant door began to swing open on its massive hinges. Cyrano got out of the cart and motioned for Marcus and Pumpkin to follow him. "Welcome to Project Greek Island, boys. That's what they called it when President Eisenhower decided to build the Bunker. No tours today, you won't be bothered. Lights are off, but you can use those flashlights over there to find the light switches once I close the doors," he instructed, pointing at a rack of heavy-duty flashlights twenty feet beyond the open portal.

Cyrano hurried back to the cart, waived merrily to Marcus and Pumpkin and said, "I'll be back when the all clear sounds."

He eased the cart backward. Clearing the entrance, he punched in the code and the giant door slowly closed behind him, sealing Marcus and Pumpkin in a cavernous room beneath tons of earth, steel and concrete. Daylight receded as the blast doors hissed upon sealing. Blackness enveloped them, mesmerizing the two. In unison, they switched on the flashlights in their hands. The West Tunnel, inside The Greenbrier Bunker, loomed before them. A shiver ran up Marcus' spine as he peered down the tunnel that seemed to evaporate into the distance.

The Bunker was the underground compound built to house Congress in the 1950's, in case of a nuclear attack during the Cold War. It had been kept secret for decades until the Washington Post broke the story in the early 1990's. Once the bunker was public knowledge, the government gave it to The Greenbrier and the hotel turned the vast underground area into a tourist attraction.

"Damn, they're in the Bunker. Eisenhower built this in the 50's. Damdest thing I ever saw. Ike made sure it was all secret. The Greenbrier built a brand new hotel wing that made the locals and hotel employees think all that construction was hotel expansion. Went right into the side of a mountain. C&O Railroad owned the hotel at that time so Ike hid the cost in military contracts the government had with the railroad," War said, glued to the screen, his excitement growing.

"We all went down there to see where we might be hanging our pajamas. Gave me the cold sweats. We Congressmen had a hole to hide in if the Russians unloaded on us, but there was no provision for our families. Thank God we never had to leave the Hill and go underground," he said.

Sheila listened intently to the Congressman, glued to the High Def and what seemed to be Science Fiction, while Sink Lair summoned Snarf Adams. "Get on your computer, Snarf, and let Rex Reynolds know where Messer's. Jones and Appleton are. Get 'em to the Bunker," Sink instructed.

The Snarf quickly complied with a message that read: "The Greenbrier Bunker is a top tourist attraction at the famous White Sulphur Springs, West Virginia hotel. The Bunker has even caused spectators, players and caddies at the USGA Senior Men's Amateur to leave the fairways and descend to the famous two-story 112,000 square foot hideaway tucked beneath the mountains surrounding this majestic hostelry."

"Bunker...they're in the Bunker!" texted Reynolds to John Short, D.E. Wildoe, and Janie Germaine.

Janie, sitting with Frong and Rooster, read the text and exclaimed, "They've found them. Marcus and Pumpkin are in the Bunker!"

"What's a Bunker?" Frong asked.

"It's under the hotel; it was supposed to be a bomb shelter for Congress during the Cold War. It's a tourist attraction now," Janie answered, adjusting her glasses.

"How do we get down there?" Rooster asked.

"West Virginia Wing, the Exhibit Hall. I learned all about it on a hotel tour I took a couple of days ago. The wing should be practically deserted because of the tournament. If there are no tours today the whole area should be a ghost town. There's an inside-the-hotel entrance to the Bunker, problem is, I don't know how we find it or how we open it, once we locate it," Janie responded.

"I don't think 'dat'll be a problem," Frong smiled, reaching for his phone and dialing a number. "Jimmy spoke a few words, pocketed the phone, and said, "Let's go." Janie texted the group to meet in the West Virginia Wing, downstairs.

They all descended the stairs to the vast Exhibit Hall at about the same time. There to meet them was Del, Supervisor of Front

Door Operations. Jimmy Frong counted off five $100 bills and Del led them to what appeared to be an interior wall of one of the large meeting rooms in the West Virginia Wing. Del accessed a small panel and entered a code. Slowly, the wall began to move, sliding outward in an accordion fashion, revealing the Bunker door. It was considerably smaller than the one at the bottom of the mountain, but it was at least two feet thick. A second code was entered, and the massive steel portal began to open.

Forty Five

Underground and two miles away from where Frong, Janie and Rooster were entering the Bunker in the deserted Exhibit Hall, Marcus and Pumpkin walked through the West Tunnel, training their flashlights on the walls, looking for additional light switches. Pumpkin's flashlight illuminated a large metal wall plate that related the history of the Bunker. Next to the plate was a control panel. Pumpkin hit the buttons marked "Tunnel Interior Lighting," activating the incandescent bulbs for sectors of the underground cavern. He and Marcus walked for what seemed a mile, exiting the tunnel itself, finding a corridor and series of rooms.

They proceeded cautiously along the corridor and came to a blue-tiled decontamination center where Congressmen would have deposited their clothes and personal belongings as they entered the underground fortress. Next were shower facilities where the lawmakers would have washed away any radioactive fallout.

They walked past a room that was obviously used for record keeping in the days before computers. Then, a large dining room, followed by a theatre designed to function as the United States House of Representatives in case of nuclear attack. Four columns helped support the ceiling, and green padded seats, theatre style, were in place for the transplanted butts of Congress. It was spooky.

The outside corridor featured rows of firearms. Marcus and Pumpkin ran their fingers across gun racks housing M-1 "Garand" rifles, oiled and ready for combat. The media center reflected 70's technology and a telephone switchboard with thirty swivel stools upon which operators would perch, plugging in and connecting calls from around the world.

Next came 18 bunk-bed dormitories, and eventually, the medical clinic that once kept current all medicines prescribed for every member of Congress who might be whisked to The Greenbrier, should there be a nuclear threat.

Pumpkin looked at the twenty-foot ceilings and the massive concrete walls. "Weird, man, I sure as hell wouldn't want to be in here very long," he said. "Too bad Cyrano didn't have keys to the Casino. I'd really prefer that to solitary."

"Just pretend it's the 1960's and the 'Rooskies' are about to strike," Appleton said, looking at a locked medicine cabinet full of meds.

"Is this really necessary? This place gives me the freakin' creeps. C'mon, I say we quit this shit and mix in at the hotel," Pumpkin said.

"Too public, my sense is there is a frantic search going on right now to find us. We're gonna' stay here until Cyrano gives us the high sign," Appleton ordered.

"Then what?" Pumpkin asked.

"Then we're gonna' get you back on the course without anyone grabbing you," Marcus replied.

"I don't like this one bit. What if we're arrested?' Pumpkin asked.

"For what? What laws have you broken? None. No need to worry," Marcus said, fiddling with the lock on the medicine cabinet. The lock snapped. "Shit, I broke the lock," he exclaimed, reaching into the cabinet, picking up a prescription bottle. The

High Def clearly showed the label and Marcus read aloud, "Viagra, Congressman Warren Danson, 32 refills." He turned to Pumpkin and exclaimed, "How did this stuff get here? Viagra wasn't around during the Cold War."

"Bastard. He's got my Viagra. Put that back, you son of a bitch!" War shouted, just as Sheila walked through the door, looking at the High Def. "Sumbitch doesn't know the blue pill was developed for Congress long before it was released to the public. FDA sure knew how to lobby."

"Hot damn, Sheila, thirty-two refills," Snarf yelled. "Old War made sure he would always be ready down there in that Bunker—too bad he can't get it up here. Whoa, a double entendre; too bad he can't get it 'up' here. Ha, ha, if he could get it 'up' here, he'd be all over 'ya, babe," Snarf yelled from a booth where the ice cream was freely flowing.

Sheila was impressed. She walked to the bar where War sat and gave him a peck on the cheek. "It's always good to be prepared, Congressman," she said with a smile, walking away, activating her bottom.

"No, no, not dead," War said softly to himself, his trousers rustling under the bar as he followed Sheila's every move.

The Wild-O Bunch rushed to the West Virginia Wing while Pumpkin and Marcus continued their trek. Pumpkin moved to one of the tens of rifle racks and sighted over the padlocked barrels. "I hate to be pushy, Marcus, but how can I be sure I'll get the $5,000 bonus I'm promised if Munch loses?" he asked, shaking his bulging trousers.

"In for $25,000, in for another $5,000—decimal dust," Marcus said, unbuttoning his shirt to reveal a money belt. He loosened it and tossed it to Pumpkin. There's the $5,000. Now you've got it all, including the bonus — I'm sure you'll earn the extra bucks," he said, sarcasm dripping from his lips

Pumpkin smiled for the first time. "Money, money, money—feels good," Pumpkin said, grabbing the belt in mid air. He began to unload the cash, stuffing it in his pants, throwing the money belt aside.

"You look like the Pillsbury Doughboy, man," Marcus said, almost laughing.

Their heads turned as they heard the echo of the interior doors to the Bunker, located deep in the West Virginia Wing, swinging open.

"Is that Cyrano?" Marcus asked, dropping the Viagra bottle, pills spilling across the floor.

"Can't be, judging from the sound…must be Bunker doors inside the hotel!"

"That makes sense."

If they're in the tunnel we may have some company in a few minutes," Pumpkin said.

"What should we do? We're trapped in here." Marcus whispered, his voice cracking.

"Don't know. I'm not the freakin' tour guide," Pumpkin hissed, reaching into his trousers, again checking the money in his pockets. As he withdrew his hand, several bills fell to the floor. Then they heard the faint sound of someone yelling.

"Marcus, Pumpkin—we know you're in here! Let's talk!" John Short shouted into the cavernous labyrinth of rooms, his voice clanging down through the corridor where Appleton and Jones stood, the echoing voice riveting past them, fading into the concrete walls surrounding them.

Marcus motioned silently for Pumpkin to follow him. They eased out of the pharmacy and through the bunker's reading room that had been supplied with new periodicals every week for thirty years—just in case Congress happened by and someone wanted the latest issue of *Time* or *Playboy*.

They continued their exploration, maneuvering around what appeared to be a giant pizza oven. Marcus suddenly realized it must have been designed to dispose of bodies in case a Congressman or staffer died underground. He felt the urge to heave.

"Good place to hide, they won't come back here," Pumpkin whispered, directing Marcus toward and behind the oven. Marcus obliged, stifling his need to hurl, following Pumpkin as he moved forward and hid. The two hunkered down as the Wild-O Bunch approached.

"Are you sure they're in here?" Short Sale asked, his pupils growing smaller as the group moved from flashlights to incandescent lighting.

"My mystery e-mailer has been right on target so far, no reason to doubt him now," Reynolds affirmed, passing the huge oven behind which Pumpkin and Marcus cowered.

"Look at that, disposal of casualties. Makes my skin crawl," D.E. shuddered, pointing out the oven-shaped cylinders.

Several miles passed underfoot and the group eventually came to where Appleton and Jones had entered the underground hideaway.

Marcus and Pumpkin waited until the Wild-O group was just a distant noise and moved swiftly in the other direction, toward the West Virginia Wing where they were certain the Wild-O Bunch had entered the Bunker. Once there, they found their second large metal door of the day. It was tightly closed. They had no way to escape.

"How the hell do we get out of here?" Pumpkin whispered to Marcus. "If Cyrano shows up and blows our cover while we're trapped in here, we're shit out of luck."

Marcus did not answer. He did not need to. There was a loud click as his back pushed against and activated a large red button that protruded from the wall. A section of the sleek metal surface turned 180 degrees and Marcus and Pumpkin were carried with it. They swung from inside the bunker to an outside wall, causing them to lose balance; they fell loudly into The Greenbrier's mammoth Exhibit Center.

The near-by exhibit area's huge fifteen-foot high double doors were open to a thickly carpeted hallway, showcasing a young woman and her boyfriend who were strolling through The Greenbrier's halls. They stopped in their tracks, staring in disbelief, as Marcus and Pumpkin appeared to magically roll through the wall of the meeting room.

"Sweet! The Rolling Stones!" screeched the young lady, who had downed too much beer on the golf course. Her date emitted a high-pitched sound and sang, "You Better Move On!"

"Right, exactly so!" Marcus shouted as he and Pumpkin regained their footing and hurried out of the room, past the teetering couple, running down the corridor, hurrying to their hidden golf cart and Munch's clubs. Marcus looked back down the hall, pointed at Pumpkin and yelled to the twenty-something female just before he turned the corner, "He's Mick Jagger, I'm Keith Richards!"

"Sheeeeit!" screamed the girl's companion. "The Greenbrier has everything."

Forty Six

The Wild-O bunch, still in the Bunker, slowly made their way forward, lighting one section of the complex after another. Fifteen minutes went by as they searched and shouted. Janie walked past gun rack after gun rack, and suddenly spotted something on the floor. She leaned over and picked up a $100 bill, the money belt, and a small vial with the name "Warren Danson" on it.

"Bingo!" she shouted, displaying the cash and money belt, while palming the vial of Viagra. She flashed back to Rooster's impressive equipment, wondering if it could possibly grow any larger. She silently pocketed the little blue pills.

"A one hundred dollar bill and a money belt," she exclaimed, "I'd bet our man Marcus has just delivered the cash to Pumpkin."

Before anyone could respond to Janie's discovery, they heard the massive mountainside door begin to move. The Wild-O bunch ran toward the sound. As the door swung wide, the group scattered, finding places to slip out of sight as the sun shone in.

Cyrano drove his baggage cart through the open portal and shouted—"Hey, guys! The 'all clear' just sounded. We need to get going. Where are you?"

"Hey yourself," Rooster shouted, coming out of the shadows and into the light, "You've got some answering to do!"

As the confrontation took place below ground, Munch walked the rain-drenched course with Nick Carman. As usual,

Carman was in a jolly mood and never stopped talking. He joked and cussed and continued to wave to spectators, shouting back at them as they offered boisterous encouragement. "This guy never shuts up," Munch thought, "How in the hell does he concentrate on his game?"

"Munch, when this is over we need to get together. I've really enjoyed watching you turn the golf world upside down," Big Nick smiled, placing a big bear of a paw alongside Munch's shoulder, roaring a monstrous laugh. "We should go for that Mercedes golf package they'll auction off after the tournament. I bid on it last year, didn't get it, but I'm drivin' the biggest ass Mercedes those Germans make," he chortled.

"Sweet, Nick, let's make it happen," Munch responded, looking around for his crazy caddy, trying to concentrate, thinking Carman certainly needed a big ass automobile, given his rear end, and wondering how the big man could have anything but golf on his mind. "Where is Pumpkin?" Munch thought, searching once more for his errant bag boy.

Munch's caddy and "The Shit" were frantically trying to make it back to the course, racing through the hotel toward its north front, startling onlookers. They pushed the doors open and practically knocked down an elderly woman carrying her Jack Russell.

"Outa' the way, grandma!" Pumpkin growled, kicking the dog, trying to rush by. The Jack Russell would have none of it, responding with its own growl, lunging at Pumpkin, fangs bared, grabbing in his teeth a large chunk of pants and right buttock belonging to the caddy. The incensed dog's chops were firmly clamped on Pumpkin's posterior as the howling caddy raced down the hallway, the dog hanging on with all his might. Marcus trailed after them, frantically grabbing for the dog in an effort to dislodge him from Pumpkin's butt.

Pumpkin ran through a revolving door, catching the tormenting canine in the turning frame, ripping the dog's hold loose, tearing a portion of skin from the caddy's butt. Marcus, in hot pursuit, came to a skidding stop just short of the turning door, banging into the howling dog. He grabbed the Jack Russell's tail, whipping him around and around, finally sliding the screaming little guy down the marble hall like a bowling ball. He watched the dog bounce thirty feet down the corridor, giving the little old lady a "tough shit" look as he followed Pumpkin through the revolving door.

"See-kur-uh-tee! See-kur-uh-tee!" the old woman screamed at the top of her lungs, waving an umbrella and shouting "Assholes!" The Jack Russell, stunned but still spunky, came to a sudden stop, barked madly, and resumed the chase. The calamity echoed up and down the vast Greenbrier hallways, resounding off a sign on the wall that read: "Shhhh, it's sleepy time Down South."

Marcus ripped the door to the service area open and jumped in the cart that awaited the fleeing pair. Pumpkin brought up the rear as he lunged for the cart. "Son of a bitch, that little bastard was vicious!" he cried out, tears in his eyes, his hands rubbing his ass.

Marcus put the pedal to the metal and Pumpkin held on, doing his best to assess the damage to his right cheek. The trouser tear was jagged, some cloth was gone from his jockey shorts, and a portion of his buttock was exposed. The caddy's fingers traced the curve of his butt and then moved on to check the cash stuffed in his pockets, making certain the Jack Russell had not made a withdrawal. Marcus ignored Pumpkin's plight and rapidly drove through the growing gallery on the cart paths, winding his way, frantically looking for Munch Malone.

"There he is!" Pumpkin yelled to Marcus, pointing out Munch in the distance. Pumpkin jumped from the cart before Munch could spot him, shouldered the Rodney bag and began walking toward the tee box.

"Where the hell have you been?" Munch said, walking away from Carman and toward Pumpkin. "I've been looking all over for you. You damn well oughta' know I'll get a two-stroke penalty if we don't tee off on time."

"Munch, don't friggin' lecture me. I've forgotten more about this game than you'll ever know," Pumpkin said, glaring, ejecting a cigarette from a package of Marlboros.

"Still smoking those cancer sticks?" Munch said.

"Like I said, man, I ain't out here to change my lifestyle," Pumpkin sneered, thinking the cash in his pockets might do just that.

"What happened to your pants?" Munch asked.

"Got caught in the revolving door back at the hotel," Pumpkin answered.

"Revolving door?" Munch asked, with a raised eyebrow. "Your ass is hanging out!"

"Story of my life, man," Pumpkin growled, ignoring Munch as they marched toward the tee box.

Number Sixteen, the *Cape*, required a shot over Swan Lake for a short iron approach that would be obstacle free. Nick Carman, 2-up, teed the ball and swung. Beautiful.

"Wow, 305 yards, that's a major swing anywhere in the pro ranks," Cheryl Anne Roane said as *The Golf Channel* audience picked up coverage following the rain delay. Then, she just could not resist adding, "Munch Malone may be dead in the water if those 'Dead Men's Clubs' fail to come to life."

"*Awful, awful! She needs some original writing, that's for damn sure. I've never heard such crap, not even in Congress,*" War snorted.

The Golf Channel switched cameras and focused on Pumpkin

as he handed Munch the driver for his tee shot. The audience watched the two exchange words, out of range of microphones.

"That's a helluva' drive. Let's see what you can do, Munch. "Don't embarrass me by screwing up, " Pumpkin smirked.

Munch stepped toward Pumpkin. Pumpkin was pleased to see he had royally pissed off Munch Malone.

"Not to worry, Pumpkin," Munch said. He held the driver aloft, waving it in circles near Pumpkin's head. The cameraman zoomed in tight on the two, thinking, "This is really weird."

Munch's face was inches from Pumpkin's chin. He continued to hold his club aloft, and then slammed the stick on the ground. The cameraman closed in on Munch's face as he hissed at Pumpkin, "Let the 'Dead Man' hunt!"

"Atta boy, Munch. We'll show em, my man!" War shouted at the High Def, grinning.

"Did he say what I thought he said?" Chad Ray asked. Ray's broadcast colleague, Jennifer Allison was standing by on the Sixteenth tee.

"Jenn, did he say—?" Chad Ray began.

"You got it, Chad, really no need for your question, is there? Great time for that close-up, huh? Anyone watching this telecast clearly read Malone's lips — pretty good twist on a golf line! 'Let the Dead Man hunt' — that is classic," Jennifer exclaimed. "And, Chad, have you noticed the caddy's slacks? Can we get a shot of Pumpkin Jones' backside? Or, maybe we shouldn't. There may be too much skin exposed for a family broadcast," Jennifer chuckled.

"Pissed off. Munch is pissed off, and so am I," War cried, watching the confrontation and the torn pants in the High Def close-up. He prepared to 'Channel' Munch's tee shot, concentrating, 'Contagion' to the club, direction to the green, point of contact. Sheila stood

behind him, squeezed his shoulders, and said, "Put it out there, Congressman!"

Snarf moved over to the bar to see if War really would put it out there.

War's eyes were half closed, he seemed in a trance. His hands gripped the club as Munch settled down and teed his ball. "Contagion"! He "Channeled" all he had into Munch's swing. He was back in the saddle.

Forty Seven

Assessing his approach at Sixteen, Munch rejected the urge to play safe with an angle away from the water, judging correctly that the shot would present a difficult approach over a left greenside bunker. He decided to pursue Carman's ball.

His swing was precise. His body had torque like Tiger, and the result was extraordinary. Munch outdrove Carman by 15 yards. The tale of the tape was a drive of 320 yards on the par four 402-yard hole.

"Ohhh, Congressman Danson, I love it when you do that!" Sheila squirmed.

Snarf noted that War had a hand on Sheila's thigh. He held it gently, just as he would grip a golf club.

Pumpkin was astonished. Munch had been boiling mad, confused, seemed to rush the shot, and yet, he had nailed it. "So much for getting the guy angry — friggin' 'Dead Men's Clubs' are still workin'" Pumpkin thought.

"Well, well, well," Ray said. "This old golf announcer has never seen anything like this. You heard it—'Let the Dead Man Hunt!'—yowzer. The 'Dead Man' definitely had his Wheaties this morning."

"Or maybe he's into ice cream," Snarf said.

"Damn fine shot, War," Sink said, "Now, move over, my turn with the short game."

"Another round, gentlemen?" Sheila asked. They replied in the affirmative and Sheila leaned toward War, whispering in a voice loud enough for all to hear, "Personally, Congressman, I'm glad Mr. Lair is playing the 'short game,' and not you."

War grinned. Snarf laughed out loud. Sink snorted and prepared for 'Contagion'.

The Wild-O bunch rushed toward the fairway as Pumpkin walked toward the landing area.

"We've got to tell Munch he's being screwed by the caddy," Janie said.

"Got it covered," Rooster replied, starting across the fairway.

"Look out there, someone is in the fairway, walking toward Malone," Cheryl Ann Roane said as *The Golf Channel* zeroed in on a short man in a disheveled and very soiled white suit, hurrying toward the golfers on the course.

A marshal rushed toward Rooster, "Sir, you can't be out here!" he shouted, as Rooster ignored him, pressing on.

The gallery paused and switched its attention from golf to the drama on the fairway.

" 'Dead Men's Clubs', Munch, You ain't got all the 'Dead Men's Clubs'!" Rooster shouted, trying to get Munch's attention. Munch turned, but his concentration was on his game, his attention wavering only momentarily, "Looks like the dwarf we saw when Melinda and I checked in the other day," he thought.

Janie and the Wild-O bunch began screaming. "Rooster, Rooster! Get back here!"

The two security cops that had warned Janie and Rooster during the altercation with Marcus in the Michelob tent were rushing toward the scene in their golf cart.

Janie Germaine and John Short decided to act. Janie ran after Rooster and shouted, "Rooster, don't, don't!" Short Sale ran after Janie, screaming, "Rooster, you can't do this!"

The cops stopped their golf cart in Rooster's path, jumped out and pulled their Glocks. Rooster stopped in his tracks, throwing his hands in the air in surrender.

The Golf Channel had never had it so good. *ESPN, CBS, NBC, CNN* and *Fox* picked up the feed.

"Guns drawn at U.S. Senior Men's Amateur Tourney in West Virginia," said the crawl at the bottom of the *MSNBC* picture that appeared on the High Def in the clubhouse in which War and Sink sat.

"Whooooeeeeeee!" *Snarf said, pounding on the bar as he grabbed the remote out of Sink's hand, turning up the volume.* "Partee'! Partee'! Partee'!" *he yelled.*

Jimmy Frong followed Janie and Short Sale, dashing to the center of the fairway in pursuit of Rooster. Frong walked toward the drawn Glocks with his arms spread wide.

"Dis' here is just a misunderstanding. 'Dese people are 'wit me and I can assure youse 'dey won't cause no more trouble," Jimmy said, smiling at the cops, a difficult thing for Jimmy to do.

"Out of the way, sir, or you'll go to jail also," the cop closest to Jimmy warned, swinging his weapon toward the menacing-looking monster approaching him.

"Well, sadly, this screws the pooch," *Sink said, watching the scene unfold.* "**The Powers That** Be are not gonna' stand for this. Talk about media. We've got a media circle jerk on our hands here—the Council is gonna' shit when they see this."

Indeed, Brawley and the Council members were watching the tournament hi-jinks with growing concern.

"We've got to do something, they'll get killed, and it will all be because we authorized this," Betty Bonanza cried. "**The Highest Authority** will not be pleased."

"Let em rock and roll," Retro Elvis grinned.

"I knew this would come to no good," Sid Belch grunted.

"I just love golf!" Big Ed McElfee sighed.

Brawley assumed leadership. "Tell 'ya what, we can fix this with a little 'Channeling'. Any objections?"

"Well, if that's what you think will right the ship—I think we can all follow your lead," Betty answered, challenging the others with a long stare. Retro readily agreed, McElfee smiled a 'yes', and Sid Belch nodded ever so slowly in the affirmative.

The Chairman closed his eyes and appeared to be meditating. He focused on the Glocks, 'Channeling'.

The older cop with a large belly protruding over his belt looked bewildered, slowly lowering his gun. The younger security guard followed suit.

The scene was frozen. No one moved.

"Well?" Frong said.

"Okay, get off the fairway. Don't dare get outta' line in any way or we'll handcuff you and put you away where the sun don't shine," the older officer admonished, wondering why he was not cuffing them.

"And we'll be watchin' you," the second cop added, holstering his Glock.

Munch and Carman watched the unbelievable scene unfold and turned to resume play as Rooster, Janie and Jimmy were escorted from the fairway, joining D.E., Rex and John Short at the ropes keeping spectators at bay. Pumpkin looked at Frong, Short Sale and Rooster, all walking in descending order of height. "Man, looks like a freakin' Randy Newman convention," he smirked.

"My God, how did that happen? They dropped the Glocks, did they just let 'em go?" War asked in amazement. Sink slapped the bar and exclaimed, "**Powers That Be!** We just saw Divine Intervention! They're with us! Holy Cow!"

"Well, looks like Security is going to cut those folks a break.

That was scary," Cheryl Ann Roane remarked on *The Golf Channel*. "They may have gotten a break from Security, but I'll bet the USGA follows up on this. To my knowledge, nothing like that, Glocks and Cops, has ever happened on a golf course, here, or at any course in the United States," Ray replied.

"Guns and Roses," Jennifer Allison added, standing alongside one of the beautiful rose beds lining the Greenbrier course, peering out over a rose she was holding in her hand.

"*Shit, she's as bad as the other broad,*" War complained, shouting at the High Def, "*Get a writer for those people, for God's sake!*"

John Short was mortified as the Golf and Glocks scenario unfolded. "There goes any opportunity to capitalize on 'Dead Men's Clubs'. We're a train wreck with 'Wild-O' written all over the bodies," he lamented. The CEO of Wild-O Golf was thinking exactly the same thing.

Rex Reynolds, watching D.E.'s apprehension grow as the fairway frolic came to an end, said, "There's an upside to this, D.E. Guns on a fairway catapults this tournament way beyond the sports audience. It's now a national, maybe international, news story. We're gonna' be all over the network newscasts tonight, media exposure like that builds audiences and drives sales; we have to see how this is playing with the public."

"Find out fast, Rex," D.E. said, his eyes narrowing.

"Nice going, Mr. Chairman," Ed McElfee beamed, as Brawley's eyes opened.

"Powerful, powerful," Retro Elvis applauded.

"Absolutely inspiring, sir," Betty Bonanza gushed.

Sid Belch grunted.

The Chairman smiled, folded his hands across an ample stomach, and settled in to watch the rest of the match.

Forty Eight

Marcus Appleton observed the melee through binoculars, one hundred yards away atop a knoll. Rooster and Frong, he realized, were no longer in his camp. The good thing was that Pumpkin was now in a bubble out on the course. No one could approach him or Munch Malone and Malone did not know that bogus clubs were in his bag. All Pumpkin had to do was make certain Munch used as many of the replacement clubs as possible, and Munch would lose the tournament.

Sink and War had exactly the same thoughts. "We've got to do something. Munch is down to four of our clubs," War exclaimed as Sheila signed off her shift and slid onto a barstool next to War. She placed her hand on War's leg and said, "Congressman, better alert Reynolds."

"Exactly," said Sink. He turned to Snarf and said, "Let's get some texting to Mr. Reynolds, Snarf."

Snarf's fingers flew.

"Tournament reports from The Greenbrier in West Virginia indicate—"

Here Snarf hesitated and wondered what he should write next.

'Any ideas?" he asked the group around the bar.

Sheila squeezed the Congressman's leg a little farther up, turned to the Snarf and said, "Text this–'Reports from The Greenbrier in West Virginia indicate tension is mounting as Munch Malone seeks to penetrate the voluptuous prize know as the USGA Senior Men's

Amateur Golf Championship.'" Sheila said, running her tongue over her upper lip, squirming.

"Finish it," she said, "by saying 'Only his driver, three wood, five iron and putter are legitimate—he needs more of his original clubs to bring this event to a,"—here Sheila closed her eyes, pressed her bosom against War's arm, emitted a soft moan, and finished with a breathy—"*full and glorious climax!*"

Sheila was moist.

Perspiration formed on War's upper lip.

Sink Lair's underarms had saddlebags.

"Hot damn," Smarf said, writing Sheila's words verbatim.

Rex Reynolds forwarded the text to the Wild-O bunch, messaging, "Don't know how marcus did it–but munch down to four dead men's clubs–driver, 3 wood, 5 iron, putter."

"We're screwed," Rooster said. The security detail won't let us out of their sight and we've got no friggin' way to get to Munch."

"Not only that, we don't know where the rest of the 'Dead Men's Clubs' are," John Short said.

The phone pinged.

Snarf paused, and began texting, saying to himself, "Rooster's right, screw subtle."

"The 'Dead Men's Clubs' are in Pumpkin's room, stupid. Tell Rooster to go get 'em," he wrote.

"Gotcha!" Reynolds said, relaying the message to Rooster and the Wild-O bunch.

Rooster summoned Del and his baggage cart with a quick phone call, and he and Del rushed to Pumpkin's cottage. Del waited in the cart while Rooster climbed the stairs, quickly picking the lock to Pumpkin's room. He saw the "Dead Men's Clubs" strewn on the floor. He scooped them up, ran out of the room without closing the door, descended the steps, felt a funny sensation as he handled them, and jumped in the cart.

While Rooster completed club retrieval, Janie plotted how they could get the "Dead Men's Clubs" into the Rodney bag. She had a plan by the time Rooster and Del topped a nearby knoll.

With determination, Janie walked to the little man, placed her hands atop his shoulders, adjusted her black horn-rimmed glasses, and said, "Rooster, here's the deal. When Munch finishes Sixteen he and the caddy will walk to Seventeen by going down the path and around the stands facing the green. They will then go through the canvas tunnel next to *The Golf Channel* booth and that's where we can get the clubs in Munch's bag. I'll distract Pumpkin and you'll need to be on the ledge that sticks out on the side of *The Golf Channel* broadcast booth, switching clubs."

"On the ledge?"

"Yes, there's a ledge there. You'll be on it with as many of the 'Dead Men's Clubs' as you can manage."

"Tell me this again? I mean, how do I pull that off without Pumpkin knowing?"

"See these?" she said, pulling down her white t-shirt to her waist, exposing her breasts. "I'm betting Pumpkin will take a minute to look at a groupie's titties, regardless of the work at hand."

"Got that right," Snarf said, reaching for his ice cream.

Rooster smiled, drinking in the view. He started to grab at her, but Janie jerked her shirt back to cover her chest. "Later, Rooster, later," she smiled at the little man who made a cooing sound to her. "Cock a doodle doo," he chuckled, collected himself, and asked, "Uh, what about the other people?"

"What other people?"

"Uh, the 20,000 spectators on the course."

"They won't see us. That's a blind spot where they turn the

corner going into the tunnel. I just have to have perfect timing, that's all."

"Yeah, perfect timing and 'Divine Intervention'!" Rooster shrugged.

"That's where we come in," Brawley said, winking at the Powers That Be. Betty Bonanza winked back and the others, save Sid Belch, smiled in approval.

Rooster moved to the Sixteenth green and walked around the broadcast booth. He saw what Janie was talking about. The booth was perched where the pathway for golfers dipped down to easily allow them to pass through a canvas tunnel that was open to pedestrian traffic now, but would be roped off as the golfers and caddies passed through, preventing the gallery from entering.

Perfect.

Once a golfer walked off the green and down into the tunnel, he disappeared from view for about ten seconds. All Rooster had to do was find a way to climb onto that ledge that jutted out just above the golfer's head and he could reach the clubs in the Rodney bag Pumpkin carried.

The golfers and caddies passing below the ledge might see an ordinary person, but Rooster's diminutive size would make him hard to spot. Timing was everything in this endeavor. Rooster had to hoist himself onto the ledge, lie down, grab and replace the clubs, and get the hell out of there as soon as the spectator ropes were lowered. He could not stay on the ledge too long because the perch was precarious at best. But, how many clubs could he manage in such a short time? In the end, Janie and Rooster opted for just two clubs, and they would hope for the best.

After scouting out the area, Rooster saw that he would have to crawl onto the ledge just behind the broadcast booth. Doing so might attract attention, but he doubted it, especially if the players were on the green and attention was focused on the putting. He needed to get in position, but how? "Even Air Jordan would have to punt on this," he thought, mixing a metaphor.

Rooster looked at the structure, noting several areas where the siding was uneven. He stuck the two clubs in his belt, grabbed a board with one hand and reached for the next protruding shingle. He moved up the side of the booth, dragging the clubs. They made a thumping noise. He hesitated, and then tossed the clubs over the side, securing them, as he finally scooted onto the ledge. He was exhausted. He would wait for the golfers.

Janie positioned herself directly beside the broadcast booth where the golfers would start into the tunnel. They could only hope Munch would be last in. Even at that, she would have to wait until Munch and Rooster passed, and then duck under the ropes. A marshal might spot her and follow, but she'd have to take that chance. All the more reason for moving fast. "If only we had a diversion," she thought.

Brawley smiled, "Don't worry about that, dear."

Carman was 2-up as they approached the Sixteenth green. Carman hit a perfect stroke that put him on the green, in position for a birdie on the par four.

Munch insisted upon using the seven iron for his second shot, overruling Pumpkin's choice.

Sink smiled broadly, gripping down on the club. Munch's seven iron was one of his most reliable weapons. The Scotsman lodged the ball just on the green, thirty feet from the cup.

Both Nick and Munch lay two, and each would have a shot at birdie.

"Your go, bucko," War said to Sink, "try not to mess this up."

Sink replied, "I'm gonna' drain this baby."

"In your dreams," War said.

"Hold my scotch and watch this," Sink chortled.

Munch eyed the line and struck the ball.

Sink realized at the last moment he had 'Channeled' just a little too hard. He leaned back, putting on the brakes. The ball rolled steady but fast, hit the back of the cup, went straight in the air, and dropped into the hole.

Birdie.

War did a high five with Snarf and slapped Sink on the back.

The crowd roared and Rooster tensed, knowing the golfers would be on the move, toward him. He had not counted on the slight slope of the ledge, designed to let water roll off. He slipped as he moved closer to the edge, almost losing his balance, juggling the two clubs in his hands. He grabbed the corner of the precipice and finally gained traction. Perspiration soaked his dirty little jacket.

"Wow, Birdie. Let's see if Carman can match it," Chad Ray said in the broadcast booth just a half-inch of wall thickness away from Rooster, who lay prone, again exhausted, clutching the seven and eight iron—"Dead Men's Clubs".

On the green, Nick Carman tugged on his trousers, surveying the bend of the grass. He wasted little time, confidence surging. The crowd quieted and Janie got ready. Carman walked confidently to the ball and struck it.

"Oh, wow, he misread that one," Chad Ray said as Nick's ball ran above the hole, settling in ten feet from the cup. Nick shrugged his shoulders as Munch won the hole. Nick, now 1-up, gave his putter to his caddy and joined the trek to the tunnel where Rooster lay in wait.

For Janie's plan to work, Pumpkin had to be the last of the foursome through the tunnel. Janie froze as she realized Pumpkin was in front of Munch, Carman and his caddy. The ploy was coming unraveled.

Suddenly, and for no apparent reason, the Rodney bag fell

off Pumpkin's shoulder. Pumpkin stopped, gave a "What the...?" look, stooped over and tried to re-sling the bag. The Rodney proved difficult to pick up, seeming to be a good ten pounds heavier than it had been.

Brawley smiled, nodding approvingly as his closed eyelids fluttered.

Pumpkin struggled with the bag, and Munch moved beyond him, as did Carman and his caddy, all three entering the tunnel. Pumpkin finally reloaded the bag on his shoulder and headed for the tunnel. He would have no one in front, and no one behind him, when he entered the opening. For some reason, the plan was back on track.

"Very nicely done, Mr. Chairman," Retro said.

"All in a day's work," Brawley said with a smile, cracking his knuckles.

"Now, let's have a little more fun," the Chairman chuckled, once again closing his eyes.

Thousands watched Munch, Carman and his caddy exit the tunnel as they advanced toward Seventeen, the par five, 554 yard *Oaks*. Pumpkin lagged behind, still struggling with the Rodney bag. The gallery's collective gaze suddenly shifted from the golfers to the heavens as a bolt of lightning flashed, striking a tree just off the fairway, followed by an enormous clap of thunder.

As the lightning singed the air, Janie ducked under the ropes without being seen. She ran into the tunnel and moved rapidly behind Pumpkin, placing a hand on his shoulder. Pumpkin stopped and looked back.

"Hey, Pumpkin, I'm simply mad about you and I've followed you all day just to prove it to you!" Janie smiled, grabbing her tight t-shirt, pulling it to her waist, exposing her breasts.

Rooster almost forgot to make his move when he saw Janie

bare her chest to Pumpkin. He hesitated, concerned that his woman was half-naked in front of the caddy.

"Nice tits, hon, why don't we get together after this round—," Pumpkin beamed, as Janie interrupted him.

"Touch them, please!" Janie implored, leaning forward, shoving her chest out and up so Pumpkin would look down and in. He reached out with his left hand.

"Both of them!" Janie said, lifting both her breasts, backing up just a bit.

Pumpkin grinned again and sat the Rodney bag on the ground. He moved forward, away from the bag, intent on fondling Janie's impressive presentation.

Lightning again flashed on the fairway and thunder rolled. The gallery shrank back as the Chairman's closed eyelids quivered.

With Pumpkin distracted, Rooster leaned down, grabbed a bogus club from the caddy's bag and began making the switch. Janie, with one eye on Rooster, leaned her head back, moaning loudly as Pumpkin massaged her breasts. Rooster stopped the switch process, looking at Janie with a worried eye.

Janie, taking advantage of her height, grabbed Pumpkin's head and shoved it between her breasts with one hand, waiving frantically at Rooster with the other, mouthing the words, "Hurry up!" Rooster got the message, grabbed the eight iron, and completed his task. He grinned at Janie, mouthing "Great tits," giving her a thumbs up.

Seeing Rooster succeed in making the switch of both clubs, Janie grabbed Pumpkin's hair and pushed his head straight back, with force. Pumpkin's eyes bulged and he released his hold on her breasts. Janie pulled her t-shirt up, covering herself, fluttering her eyelashes. She reached out, grabbed Pumpkin's crotch, squeezed it hard enough for Pumpkin's eyes to bulge a bit more and said,

"Ohhh, Pumpkin, meet me in the hotel lobby after the match and we'll put the ball in the hole!"

"You got it, babe," Pumpkin said, laughing out loud, patting her bottom, moving back to the bag, picking up the Rodney. "I love this game!" he said, winking at her, shouldering the Rodney, rushing out of the tunnel.

Janie adjusted her glasses as Pumpkin turned the corner, leaving her alone. Rooster quickly jumped down from his perch and the two ran out of the tunnel just as the ropes blocking spectator access to the area were lowered. Oddly enough, any evidence of lightning was gone, leaving *The Golf Channel* to again speculate on the unbelievably strange weather in the West Virginia mountains.

Forty Nine

Marcus Appleton pulled his iPhone from his pocket and walked to an area where he could make a call. He sensed he might be through at Wild-O Golf, and if that were so, he would get his pound of flesh by upping the game. He could screw John Short and damage the Wild-O brand, all with one phone call.

He dialed *Golf Channel* producer Ryan Andrews, whom Marcus had met three years ago at one of Wild-O Golf's tents at the Memorial in Columbus, Ohio. He and Ryan had hit it off. Andrews had been a star soccer player at Princeton and migrated to golf after college. He had made a major mark in television sports and was a "Big Foot" at the *Golf Channel*.

"Ryan Andrews," the deep voice said.

"Ryan, Marcus Appleton, howya' doin'?" Marcus asked.

"Marcus! Good to hear from you! Things are going great, you?"

"Couldn't be better," Marcus replied.

"What's up? Can't talk long. I'm in the middle of a broadcast, I'm down here in West Virginia at the Senior Amateur Championship, producing this one," Andrews said, tugging his headset to one side to better hear Marcus.

"Thought you might be, I'm also here. Are you interested in 'Dead Men's Clubs'?" Marcus asked.

"You know it, pal! You guys are getting lots of play with Munch Malone, the public loves it," Andrews replied.

"There's a big story about the clubs that no one has uncovered, Ryan," Marcus said.

Andrew's reporting antenna twanged and he took the bait. "What story is that, Marcus, do you know something?" Andrews asked.

"Ever hear of John Short at Wild-O?" Marcus responded.

"Nope, don't think so," Andrews said.

"He's head of our Reconditioned Clubs Division, and he reports to me. He's got skin in this tournament. If Munch Malone wins with equipment everybody calls 'Dead Men's Clubs', Short thinks the Wild-O brand will be trashed," Appleton said.

"Trashed how?" Andrews asked.

"Think about it, 'Dead Men's Clubs', Ryan—Short's convinced no one will buy his used clubs if they think they belonged to 'Dead Men'," Marcus replied. "That's why he bribed the caddy."

"Bribed the caddy? To do what?" Andrews asked, his eyebrows raising, watching the stack of monitors before him.

"To mess with Munch's head so he'll blow up and lose the match."

"Do you have any proof of this?" Andrews asked.

"Just look at Pumpkin's pants."

"Yeah, we've done that. Half his ass is hanging out!"

"Not only that, they bulge a little, wouldn't you say?"

Andrews looked at the monitor that showed Munch and Pumpkin Jones.

"Yeah, they do look funny, why is that?"

"Pumpkin's pockets, all four of them, are full of cash. He's carrying thousands of dollars in bribe money."

"Does this have anything to do with that circle jerk out there a little while ago, where the cops drew their Glocks?"

"Probably, but I don't know. I just thought you'd want some inside information."

"Damn right, but, how do you know about this?"

"I know *everything* that happens at Wild-O—even the bad shit. I found out about this one too late to stop it, but you can tell the nation that John Short is messing with the royal and ancient sport. Gotta' go, 'bye Ryan," Marcus said, ending the call.

Marcus thought to himself, "Okay, it's now John Short's word against mine. Next step is to make it worth Pumpkin's time."

Marcus texted Pumpkin. "Forget 25k and 5k bonus in your pockets–100k in it 4 U now–golf channel knows you've been bribed 2 screw with Malone."

"What's this shit," Pumpkin muttered, reading the text as he walked the fairway. He almost dropped the Rodney bag.

The text continued: "Tell authorities at end of match that *john short* bribed u 2 mess with Munch cause he thinks dmc's will trash wild-o brand–tell them u turned chicken 2 take the cash and u want 2 come clean–toss the money in your pockets on the ground—do it on tv. Do that and 100k will be wired 2 off shore account in your name—*if* u do this."

"Bullshit—how can I trust u 2 do that?" Pumpkin texted back.

"Easy. All I have 2 do is push a button on my phone to transfer 100 big ones 2 u–if I don't pay u then u can out me to authorities—lemme' know–text me back 'yes' and u finally get big golf payday," Marcus frantically tapped out.

Back at *The Golf Channel* broadcast tent, Andrews looked at the phone in his hand and realized Marcus was gone. He looked again at the monitor showing Pumpkin Jones.

"Steve," Andrews said to Steve Goldenblue, his redheaded Director, "give me a shot of Pumpkin Jones and pan up and down on his trousers." "Chad," he said to Chad Ray, "let's have some comment about Pumpkin Jones' pants. His ass is hanging out, we all know, but let's pay some attention to the lumpy look of those pants."

Ray got the message and deftly brought the audience's attention to Pumpkin's trousers. "There are those trousers again," he said, as the camera featured Pumpkin, standing by the Rodney bag. "Munch Malone's caddy, Pumpkin Jones, told someone that he got caught in a revolving door back at the hotel, and the encounter tore a hole in the seat of his pants. He still has most of his trousers, but they're a little tight, dontcha' think? Pumpkin must have really chowed down last night, judging by the bulky look. A bit of a roll at the waistline—looks like my wardrobe," Ray said.

Pumpkin re-read the text from Marcus with growing alarm and elation. His mind whirled. He whistled slowly, "One hundred thousand dollars. I'd have more money than I've ever dreamed of. Can I trust Appleton? Am I gonna' give up a sure $30,000 and live to regret it? Will I face any charges? Damn, my stomach's boiling, I may throw up."

"You okay, man? You're white as a ghost," Munch said.

"I hate that reference," War complained, slamming back his scotch.

'I'm okay, something I ate during the rain delay," Pumpkin assured Munch.

His phone pinged again.

"Time of essence–need 2 know NOW," Marcus texted.

"Huge risk, man–don't want jail time," Pumpkin texted.

"Won't happen–once u turn over money, no harm, no foul," Marcus wrote.

"Says u," Pumpkin responded.

Marcus shrugged. "Shit," he said and texted back. "Ok–any legal problems, I provide attorney 4 u."

"How can I trust that?"

"Again, u can out me."
"Money to be wired—in my name—now?
"Yes, now."
"Bank? Where?"
"Off shore. Bahamas."

Pumpkin took a deep breath and made a decision. "Prove it," he texted.

Marcus pulled up Safari on his iPhone, accessed the "Off Shore" site, entered his pass code and instructed his personal banker to place $100,000 of his reserves into an account for a Pumpkin Jones. The banker asked a number of questions and then texted to Pumpkin's phone the transaction and a code that would allow Pumpkin to access the money at any of the bank's branches. Pumpkin broke into a wide grin reading the banker's text as his bulging pants rustled along the fairway.

Ryan Andrews was immersed in what he sensed was a major story unlike any *The Golf Channel* had heretofore covered. "Stay with Malone and the caddy, see if they are cordial or are in each other's face," Andrews said to Goldenblue. The Director relayed to Chad Ray that the Producer wanted him to give some focus to the apparent tension between the golfer and his caddy, something unheard of in Championship play.

Number Seventeen—616 yards from the tips. Carman would be first off the tee, 1-up. Big Nick conferred with his caddy and decided to go right center of Howard's Creek. If his shot was on target, the hole would become a short par five. Success was written all over the shot and Nick was well placed to score with conviction on the *Oaks*.

Munch could not help but admire Carman's drive as he assessed his approach. Taking no chances, he decided to play safe to the left. His second shot would have to wend its way through three strategically placed bunkers that guarded the undulating green.

"Three wood," he said to his caddy, "I'm gonna' go to the left."

"Yes!" Sink Lair exclaimed, eager to grip and rip with his old and faithful weapon.

"You don't want to do that, Munch," Pumpkin frowned.

"Like hell," Munch said, "That's the shot, I know it."

"I heard 'dat," War shouted.

"Yeah, baby," Sink joined in.

Pumpkin, practically salivating with the thought of huge money in his bank account if he could make Munch lose the tournament, assumed his most humble stance. "Listen, Munch, I may have given you some shit, but I really want you to win," he lied. "Three wood's too much. The three iron is what you need. That'll set you up to avoid those bunkers."

Munch hesitated.

Pumpkin went for the kill.

"I'm thinkin' you're 'Channeling' Slammin' Sammy with these 'Dead Men's Clubs', when Sammy went left, he used the three iron, set him up perfectly for the second shot," Pumpkin said, fabricating the story from thin air, handing the club to Munch.

Munch took it.

"Son-of-a-bitch," Sink muttered, eyes on the High Def.

Janie, Rooster, D.E. Wildoe, and John Short were all gathered around the green at Seventeen.

"What's he doing?" Janie asked.

Short Sale, looking through binoculars, said, "Damn, looks like Pumpkin's talking him out of his club choice."

The Golf Channel's Chad Ray said, "More conflict; it appears Malone's caddy disagrees with the club choice by Malone. He's gotten Munch to use another club. What can you tell us, Jennifer?"

Ray asked Jennifer Allison who was covering the action at the Seventeenth tee.

"Chad, Malone wants to challenge the bunkers to the left and he asked for his three wood. I believe, from what I can gather, that Pumpkin Jones insists he club down to—I think, a three iron. This is taking some time—wait a minute, Malone is following his caddy's suggestion—he'll hit the three iron" Allison informed Ray and the audience.

"Damn, can't get my hands on my club. This is ridiculous," Sink said.

Munch gripped the bogus club. It felt heavy in his hands. "Slow, slow, slow, and stay down on it," he thought. He swung the club. The ball sliced hard to the left and careened into deep woods, out-of-bounds.

"Oh, wow. This is pretty ugly, he'll be hitting three when he re-loads," Allison said as Ryan Andrews called for a split screen that showed on one side the ball finding the forest, and on the other side, Pumpkin Jones' bulky and torn pants.

Brawley made a decision. He closed his eyes once more and concentrated.

Munch simmered for just a moment, trying desperately to control himself, then losing it. He turned to run to the Rodney to slug the bag. He stopped short when he glanced at the nearby electronic leader board. He stood and read the message that began to crawl across the screen.

"Munch. Your clubs have been messed with. The only 'Dead Men's Clubs' in your bag are the driver, three wood, five, seven, and eight irons, and putter. Use only those six clubs and you will win. DO NOT TRUST YOUR CADDY."

Munch dropped the club and rubbed his eyes. Big Nick Carman walked up behind him, slapped Munch on the shoulder, and said, "Hey, its golf, Munch. Take it easy, bad shots just happen sometimes."

Munch jerked crazily around to Nick and shouted "Look at the leader board, Nick, can you believe this?"

Carman looked at the board. It said "Malone OB on 17."

"Yeah, everyone knows you're OB. Don't let it bother you, Munch. Just tee it up and go again," Carman grinned

"But, look, look at what it says!" Munch exclaimed, pointing again at the board, where the screen was blank to everyone.

Everyone but Munch.

"You're the only guy getting this message, Munch. No one else sees it. Divine Intervention, my friend. Now, remember, six clubs. Use them with 'Contagion' and win. Best of luck from all of us up here!"

"Oh, my God" Munch uttered, looking skyward.

The message was also on the High Def at the Clubhouse where Sink, War, and Snarf began to shout, fist bump, and pound on the bar. "*The Powers That Be*! Whoeeeeee! They are definitely with us!" Snarf shouted.

In his conference room Brawley leaned back and relaxed in his swivel chair. He swung around from the High Def, and saw his Council members staring at him.

"Thinking of taking up golf again, Mr. Chairman?" Big Bill McElfee smiled. Brawley raised both hands and shrugged his shoulders, returning the smile.

Munch tried to clear his head, hearing Pumpkin say, "Ya' gotcha' work cut out for y' Mr. Malone. What's it gonna' be?"

"Three wood," Munch said.

"Nope, ain't doin' it. Same club, three iron," Pumpkin snarled, pushing the club at Munch.

'Gimme' the three wood, Pumpkin, I know what you're up to."

"What the hell are you talking about?" Pumpkin said, chin up, eyes glaring.

"You're not out here to help me win, are you? You're trying to screw me!"

Pumpkin shrugged, "Makes no difference to me, man," he said, unaware that the three wood in the bag was now a legitimate "Dead Man's Club".

"It's your choice, not mine; go ahead, big boy, make a name for yourself," Pumpkin scoffed.

Munch grabbed the three wood, glaring at Pumpkin.

"Definitely something going on," Ryan Andrews thought, watching the bank of monitors in *The Golf Channel* booth showing the action from all sides.

Munch did not hesitate, addressing the ball, swinging beautifully; the projectile left the deck. It soared high above the first bunker, gliding beyond the second, coming to a rest just over bunker three. An astonishing three wood drive that carried 375 yards.

The gallery was silent as the ball flew down the fairway, followed by raucous applause and shouts reminiscent of Masters' play.

Nick Carman's neck snapped around as he watched the searing projectile Munch had hit. "Wow, freakin' unbelievable," he said in a voice filled with awe. Nick grinned and gave Munch a thumb's up. He adroitly ambled up the fairway and slammed his ball a second time. He lay two, 178 yards out.

"Here's the scenario—Malone lays 3 with that out of bounds problem while Nick Carman lies 2. Carman, at 1-up, can be down in 2. Looks like Carman will win the hole—bad trouble for the man with 'Dead Men's Clubs', Munch Malone," Chad Ray said.

War Danson fumed. "*Just let me hit, smartass*," he uttered at the High Def.

Dead Men's Clubs

Munch spent no time with the caddy. He ignored him as he walked the fairway. He pulled the eight iron from his bag, addressed the ball and swung. It left the ground, flying low, sailing across bunkers, plunking down ten feet from the hole.

Munch lay four.

"Awesome shot," Jennifer Allison whispered into her microphone from number Seventeen as the ball hit the green and backed up."

"Incredible," Chad Ray agreed, as the crowd roared approval.

War Danson did a deep bow before the audience that had gathered in the bar.

Carman watched the display and, for the first time, felt uneasy. There might be, he thought, something to this 'Dead Men's Clubs' thing—no 70 year-old guy could possibly play this way. Big Nick shook off his thoughts, addressed the ball and swung. The ball dribbled forward as his mind reviewed Munch's unbelievable shot. Nick lay three.

John Short hustled along the ropes that were blocking the gallery. He tried to get Munch's attention by jumping and waving at intervals. Malone was not looking. His concentration was solidly on his upcoming putt.

Janie and Rooster decided to go to the Eighteenth green at the clubhouse to catch the finale. D.E. Wildoe stepped into a Michelob tent with Rex Reynolds.

"What's the story?" he asked Reynolds as he hailed the bartender and ordered two Ultras.

Reynolds worked the keys on his iPhone and pulled up the latest tracking. "Off the chart, Mr. Wildoe…"

"Call me D.E., Rex," Wildoe interrupted.

"Okay, D.E. The numbers are holding and show an upward trend. I think we can say it's a smash win for Wild-O Golf if

Munch wins. The numbers will probably fall off if he loses, but maybe not that bad," Reynolds said.

"Nope, not putting Wild-O golf, the brand, in jeopardy with a loser. If Munch wins we'll go with a full campaign for used clubs. If not, we'll drop him like a hot balloon," Wildoe said.

"And John Short?" Rex asked.

"Short's back on top. 'The Shit' is out and I'll make absolutely sure every door in the golf world will be closed to that bastard," D.E. said.

Fifty

Nick Carman hit again. His ball landed on the first cut. He lay four, same as Munch.

"Talk about a blowup," Chad Ray said, as a scowl crossed Nick's face.

Big Nick assessed the ripples the ball would have to traverse to make it to the cup and shook his head. "This is gonna' be interesting," he said, his doubt growing. He walked around the hole and looked across the green expanse from the other side of the cup. He shook his head again and walked back to his ball. His putt began with great line, but too much speed. The ball rolled past the hole and beyond Munch's mark. Nick shrugged, and then executed the long putt perfectly, carding a six for the hole.

"Wow, if Munch can sink a ten foot putt, this thing is square," Ray said.

"Easier said than done, Chad," Allison said, "Munch read Nick's line, but this is an intimidating green. A roller coaster."

It was time for Munch to deliver. He assessed the approach to the hole.

Sink closed his eyes and felt the putter in his hands. Damn, it felt good. He judged the distance, took a practice stroke and visualized the line traversing the rolling green. He took the club back and began to execute just as Sheila placed a glass of scotch in front of him. As she did so her hand slipped and a torrent of fine whisky spilled into Sink's lap. Sheila grabbed for Sink's crotch, trying to capture the liquid in her outstretched hands. Sink bolted upright, striking the ball with the hosel of the putter. Still, the ball made it over one ripple and then the second. It slowed, but, incredibly, continued on, over the crest of the fourth mound as it broke for the hole.

The crowd erupted as the ball reached the rim of the cup, teetering; the Scotch cooled Sink's skin.

"Oh, my God, I'm so sorry, Mr. Lair." Sheila said, one hand to her mouth, devastated that she had distracted Sink. Looking at the hand that remained glued to his trousers, Sink smiled and pushed his pelvis forward.

"Some things are really quite better than golf, my dear," he said, adding one more thrust.

The ball fell into the hole.

"He's in!" Chad Ray said in the broadcast booth above the roar.

"Not quite, but working on it," Sink smiled to himself.

The leader board message had said the putter would work. It had. His ball seemed to shimmer on the edge of the cup, and then had dropped in, Munch reflected. "What," he thought, "is going on here?"

"Square. Whatta' match," Ray said as the crowd released a deafening roar.

The Golf Channel went to commercial and Munch calmed himself as he walked to the next and final tee. Looking out toward the Eighteenth green, a 162 yard, par three stretching across Howard's Creek, the fabulous Greenbrier stream known for trout fishing, Munch took a deep breath.

"Get hold of yourself," he thought. "Who would have imagined I would ever experience something like this in my lifetime? I need to remember this moment. Majestic setting, Appalachian mountain range, skies clearing to a crystal blue, warm sunshine on my face, an historic event and help from above." He removed his hat, looked toward the heavens, and thanked the good Lord for this special privilege.

"Very nice, very nice," Brawley said, hearing Munch's thoughts. "Our man appreciates Divine Intervention. Seems only right that we 'Channel' a little more of that his way."

"Well, this will be one for the books," Chad Ray said, painting the scenario for the television audience. "Munch Malone seems meditative, serene, while Nick Carman is no longer the happy, go lucky, guy we've seen the last few days. Two great senior golfers squared at Eighteen—'Minnesota Big' versus 'Dead Men's Clubs'."

"Yes, but it'll be extremely difficult for Malone. He's 70 years of age; Carman's a decade younger. Nevertheless, Munch is a storybook saga that has certainly been a shot in the arm for the senior golfers out there. He's the old man of golf but I wish him the best." Cheryl Ann Roane countered.

"Well, he ain't that old and it ain't over until I say so," the Chairman hummed to himself, shifting in his chair, closing his eyes to better concentrate.

The Wild-O bunch watched the unfolding drama with apprehension. Janie, Rooster and Short Sale were now together, just off the Eighteenth green, known appropriately as *Home*. D.E. and Reynolds joined them as Nick Carman teed up.

Carman drank in the scene. It was a short iron shot that offered an easy birdie. "Just hit the green, Nick," he said to himself.

He drew the club back and hit the ball with a pitching wedge. It screamed hard left and hit the "Horsehoe" ridge that dissected the green, and rolled into a bunker.

Munch knew his dream of winning the Open was possible.

He hesitated and then asked Pumpkin for his eight iron; certainly not his club he would ordinarily use for such a shot, but the closest thing to a wedge among the few 'Dead Men's Clubs' in his bag. Pumpkin was unaware the eight was a true 'Dead Men's Club', having been inserted into the bag by Rooster as Pumpkin was distracted by Janie. Still, he hesitated. Munch seemed so damn certain he could hit the club well. Why take chances?

"Problem, man. You've got no chance with a club that long. Carman hit a pitching wedge. Do you wanna' look silly? Take the pitching wedge.

Munch again felt the urge to take a whack at the bag and then at Pumpkin.

"Take the eight iron," Sink grimaced.

*The Chairman of **The Powers That Be** made a decision. He grunted slightly and let his mind focus fully on Pumpkin Jones. It was time for Munch's caddy to become a changed man.*

Pumpkin reached for the pitching wedge but his hand was somehow directed to the eight iron. He drew it out of the Rodney bag, feeling a strong vibration as he held the club. He had felt that same current when he had first lifted Munch's clubs from the bag in the locker room.

"Was the club actually starting to vibrate? "What have I gotten into here?" Pumpkin thought, holding the eight iron out to Munch. The vibration increased, and Pumpkin saw white lights flashing before him. His ears roared and then suddenly cleared. He felt a heavy weight slide from him as he steadied himself on the Rodney bag, dropping the eight iron.

Munch leaned and picked up the club. "Are you okay?" he asked, "You're white as a sheet."

"Yeah, I'm okay," Pumpkin grunted, regaining his composure. "Just be sure to grip down on this club if you want this to work," he said, shaking his head as he uttered the words, thinking, "What did I just say? Have I lost my mind? Did I just try to help this guy?"

Brawley's closed eyes moved at "Rem" speed.

Pumpkin's ears roared, the white lights returned. The soul-searching resumed. Pumpkin's legs began to shake; he grabbed the Rodney again, steadying himself, wondering what was happening.

'You're kidding me, "Malone is going to use his eight iron? Is that right? Let's go to Cheryl Ann Roane at Eighteen. Is he really using an eight iron, Cheryl Ann?"

"Yep, incredibly so," Cheryl Ann said, "Unbelievable."

Munch and Sink gripped the club.

"Tell him to grip down," the Chairman said, eyes still closed.

"Grip down," Pumpkin said, obeying the Chairman, "you can do this, Munch!"

Munch felt "Contagion" as he gripped down on the shaft.

Sink turned to War and said, "Okay, Congressman, it's Miller time—watch this."

Sink moved the club. Munch's arms and shoulders turned.

Sheila kept her distance.

Sink executed perfect form, right arm stretched toward the hole.

The ball soared skyward, descended low and fast— and headed for the bunker.

Brawley closed his eyes tightly, jerking back slightly in his seat.

The ball seemed to bend as it approached the threatening sand and landed on the green, but thirty feet from the hole.

The crowd roared.

"Look at that 'Bend it like Beckham'," Chad Ray smiled into the microphone. "Great finish. Carman's ball is buried in a bunker and Malone is thirty feet out. We are square, but Carman has the tougher shot."

Fifty One

D.E. Wildoe used his iPhone to call marketing. "Get ready to roll the 'Dead Men's Clubs' campaign, if Munch nails it," he ordered.

The walk to the green at Eighteen was one continuous roar of applause and Munch drank it in, tipping his hat.

"Whadya' think, Mr. Chairman, can we help Munch a bit here and play a little with Carman's head?" Betty Bonanza asked.

"Don't think so, I'm exhausted and I'm not gonna' mess with Carman. I've done all I'm gonna' do," Brawley said.

Nick took little time. He selected a sand wedge to hit out of the bunker. He executed a perfect shot. The ball rolled true and a loud "ping" was heard as it plopped into the hole.

Birdie.

Munch could hardly hear himself think as the gallery reacted.

"Yeah, baby, just when we thought it couldn't get any better. Munch has gotta' make his putt, or it's over," Ray said over the crowd roar.

Brawley assessed the situation. He hummed softly to himself and began to rationalize that an intervention here might indeed be appropriate.

Munch felt perspiration begin to form under his arms.

"How many putts can I pull out of my ass?" he thought, assessing the bend of the grass and the distance to the hole. He stood over the ball. He backed off. He glanced at Pumpkin who was looking skyward, a quizzical look on his face, paying no attention to his golfer.

Munch walked to the ball, made his stroke, and watched, totally terrified.

He had rolled the ball well. It seemed to head directly for the cup and then veered to the right.

Brawley's head jerked left.

The ball changed directions and once again rolled toward the hole. It clanged in.

The Greenbrier seemed to shake as the gallery gave it up for Munch.

"Square! Playoff! Back to Eighteen! We're gonna do this again!" Chad Ray bellowed.

"Not a problem, tee it up, I'm ready!" War shouted, eyes wide, fists clenched, pounding the bar until Sheila pulled him back. Sink watched War's histrionics, sighed and followed the Congressman's lead, trying to mentally prepare himself for the grind of playing again, when it suddenly hit him.

"By golly, that's what this is all about—we're playing again!" He said, turning to War, slapping him on the back, saying, "Relax Congressman! We're playing, man! We're playing again! This is so sweet!"

War stopped, considered the thought, grinned, and reached into his pocket, pulling out the wad of bubble gum he had deposited in its wrapper when he and Sink had last addressed **The Powers That Be.** *He popped the gum in his mouth, laughed out loud, blew a large bubble, and said, "Let's just see if Mr. Carman has a—blow up!" Sheila, at War's direction, popped the big pink bubble.*

Wiping the gum from his lip, War addressed his golfing buddy. "You are so right, Sink. We got what we asked for. I haven't felt this alive in years!" He fist bumped Sink, grabbed Sheila by the waist, bent her back, and placed a large smooch on her lips.

Munch and Nick walked back to the Eighteenth tee. Munch was given the honors. He chose, once again, the eight iron and choked down.

Sink looked intently at the High Def and began to Channel. He envisioned a hole-in-one as he took his back swing and lunged at the ball. It soared skyward and landed ten feet from the cup. Sink was pissed.

"Settle down," War said softly, turning and looking intently at the Scotsman. "You can do this, 'bro," War said. "Just get big Nick out of the way and do your thing." Sink nodded gravely.

Nick Carman strode to the tee box, placed his ball and let fly. Good shot, on the other side of the hole, but inches farther from the cup than where Munch's ball lay.

"Both putts eminently makeable," Jennifer Allison reported.

"So it would seem," Chad Ray responded.

Melinda, pressed tight against the ropes, looked at her husband, shot him a quick smile and gave him a thumbs up. Munch blew her a kiss. Melinda looked skyward and said a little prayer.

She did not know it, but she was 'Channeling' directly to the Chairman of **The Powers That Be.**

Nick lined up his putt. He stroked the ball; it began its unerring way toward the cup.

Brawley watched the High Def and the advancing ball. He had said his mind was made up—he did not wish to interfere, but Melinda's little prayer had touched him. Still, he hesitated. His eyes tightened and the large vein in his neck swelled. He made his decision, and jerked his right hand.

Nick's ball rolled inside the cup, lipped the hole, appeared to fall and, suddenly, reversed order, spitting up and out, landing two feet away.

The crowd moaned loudly.

Brawley leaned back, smiling, humming to himself.

"Wow, major miss by Carman. Malone can win it!" Ray said, not sure he was being heard above the noise.

Munch looked again at Melinda. He felt a surge of strength as the warm summer sun shone from the heavens. "Contagion" was in the air and Sink Lair and Munch were one. "Contagion"—the idea that an object somehow absorbs the qualities of its previous owner—soared through Munch's veins as he came to grips with the fact that he was indeed swinging 'Dead Men's Clubs'.

The stroke of the club was smooth; the result was never questioned as the ball dropped into the cup, ending the playoff and match.

Munch Malone was the USGA Senior Men's Amateur Golf Champion.

The word went forth as Chad Ray roared, "'Dead Men's Clubs'! You've just seen golfing history with 'Dead Men's Clubs'!"

Nick Carman crossed the green and placed a big bear hug on Munch.

D.E. Wildoe shouted into his iPhone, "Roll the campaign! 'Dead Men's Clubs'! TV, magazines, major newspapers, social media, you name it! Make it huge!"

The Golf Channel captured the scene, complete with a group of silver-haired senior citizens on the Greenbrier terrace above the green. The little old grandmother who had money riding on the game was coaching them. The letters they held aloft spelled out "M-U-N-$$$$-H!"

Ryan Andrews and Steve Goldenblue coordinated the coverage at the green.

"Tell Chad to corral Munch and make sure he positions the caddy beside the winner," Andrews said.

Goldenblue relayed the information through his headset and Ray pulled Pumpkin beside Munch and Bruce Tucker, a golf icon of the Seventies, who would present Munch with the USGA Senior Men's Amateur Golf Medal and custody of the Frederick J. Todd Trophy for the ensuing year.

"Munch," Tucker began, his words carried nationwide by television and across the greens and fairways at The Greenbrier by massive speakers located throughout the grounds. "You've been an inspiration to senior golfers all over the world. It's been a real pleasure to have you make history here at The Greenbrier. What you have done with those 'Dead Men's Clubs' has been nothing short of a miracle. With this win, you have a ten-year exemption in this tournament; I assume you'll be back next year."

A roar from the crowd.

"*Got that right,*" *War said.*

Tucker handed the trophy to Munch, who gave it a big kiss.

"Congratulations, Munch, how does it feel?" Chad Ray asked, pulling him next to Pumpkin.

"Well, first I'd like to thank my wonderful wife, Melinda, for putting up with me and all my hundreds of golf clubs over the years. And, second, I'd like to thank the guys 'upstairs' who used to play with these clubs! I could not have done it without 'Contagion' and 'Dead Men's Clubs'!" Munch said with a huge grin, blowing a kiss skyward.

"Go for Pumpkin, probe to see if he'll say anything about a bribe," Andrews said. Goldenblue relayed the message.

Ray swung the microphone to Pumpkin. "And what about the caddy that was by Munch's side all the way, what part did you play in this triumph for 'Dead Men's Clubs', Pumpkin? Any outside forces impact you today?

Fifty Two

Loud speakers blasted the interviews across the golf course, Marcus Appleton stood in The Greenbrier lobby, nervously waiting to check out, cursing Pumpkin under his breath for his failure to stop Munch from winning. Nevertheless, he thought, Pumpkin could still deliver the fatal blow to John Short. Marcus' eyes, as well as those of the other guests who were standing in line to pay their bills, were glued to the large flat screen in the lobby that was broadcasting live the sights and sounds from number Eighteen.

On the green, Pumpkin hesitated when he heard Ray's question as to outside forces. His arm still throbbed from the vibration he had felt when holding the eight iron. He blinked hard.

Brawley again closed his eyes and 'Channeled' directly to Pumpkin, who felt a peaceful sensation sweep over him.

The caddy reached into his pocket and pulled out a wad of cash.

"Yeah, the outside force was a guy who bribed me to make sure Munch didn't win," Pumpkin said, tossing $100 bills in the air.

"Atta' boy, Pumpkin—just say it. 'John Short'," Marcus thought, clinching his teeth into a tight smile, eyes narrowed toward the High Def. "Tell it all!"

"Tight close up!" Steve Goldenblue shouted through his mouthpiece to the cameraman.

The crowd on the green and in the lobby of the hotel went silent as $100 bills filled the screen.

"Say it, say it—'John Short bribed you,'" Marcus muttered to himself.

"You accepted a bribe?" Ray asked.

"Yes, I'm ashamed to say it, but I did. I was paid $30,000 to steal Munch's 'Dead Men's Clubs' and replace them with bogus clubs—making sure he used them instead of his own clubs," Pumpkin said.

"Pumpkin, you're on national TV here, are you incriminating yourself?"

"I don't care about that, I'm not keepin' the money. I'm glad Munch won," Pumpkin said.

"I've gotta' ask the question – can you tell us who bribed you?" Ray probed.

"Say it, say it, asshole," Marcus whispered.

Pumpkin looked directly into the camera and said, "Marcus Appleton. He's National Sales President of Wild-O Golf. Here he is," Pumpkin said, reaching into his back pocket, retrieving the wrinkled Wild-O brochure that prominently featured Marcus' face on the back cover. He held it close to the camera's lens.

Marcus blanched and shook his fist at the flat screen, shouting at the top of his lungs, "You son of a bitch! Dirty double crosser!" startling the lobby crowd.

The little old lady whom Marcus had practically run over in his recent mad dash through the hotel stood in the checkout line not far from Marcus. She carried an umbrella and fussed over her Jack Russell as she bent over to make sure the dog's collar and leash were not too tight for her baby. She looked up as Marcus began to shout. She glanced at the screaming man and then saw his picture on the flat screen. She immediately recognized him as one of the men who had trampled over her and her little dog earlier in the day. Her face contorted into a blistering, high-pitched screech.

"That's him! That's him!" she shouted, pointing a finger at the High Def and then at Marcus, shouting, "See-kur-uh-tee! See-kur-uh-tee!" She began waving her umbrella, pushing forward with her dog in tow, bringing the umbrella crashing down, attacking Marcus from behind. The Jack Russell's ears went straight up and he lunged, grabbing Marcus' pants cuff, growling loudly. The crowd in the lobby looked on, incredulously.

Marcus yelped and backed across the lobby, trying to escape, pulling the dog with him.

"Let go of my baby, you asshole!" Grandma shouted, following Marcus, continuing to pound him with the umbrella

Marcus ripped his pant leg away from the dog, tearing the fabric into a jagged rip from cuff to knee. He ran down The Greenbrier hallway, knocking down unsuspecting shoppers who were entering and exiting the hotel's boutiques and shops. The dog was in hot pursuit but stopped suddenly when Grandma, exhausted, collapsed on one of the benches in the corridor. The Jack Russell ran to comfort her, and Marcus bolted out the door.

Two Security officers raced down the hall, hot on "The Shit's" tail.

Fifty Three

Marcus fled down the winding walk toward the hotel's infinity pool. A security detail in a cruiser pulled into the parking lot in front of the pool, blocking Marcus' flight toward the water and the woods beyond. Marcus broke to the right and down the path toward the pro shop and, before realizing where he was, tore through a crowd of people and onto the Eighteenth green–straight into the middle of the live nationwide television interviews and awards ceremonies.

"That's him! Marcus Appleton! He's the dude that bribed Pumpkin!" Rooster shouted, peering between the legs of a cameraman who had climbed scaffolding on the far side of the green.

"Follow him," The Producer said into his mouthpiece, and the camera panned to show Marcus come to a skidding stop within ten feet of Munch, Pumpkin, Chad Ray, and Jim Justice.

Suddenly, the umbrella-wielding Grandma and the Jack Russell burst through the crowd and into golf history. The dog hit Marcus' legs at the knees, upending him. The little old lady and Rooster jumped on Marcus and pinned him to the ground. The two security cops and a host of Greenbrier County deputy sheriffs pushed their way onto the green, grabbed Marcus and handcuffed him, even as he was being pummeled by Grandma's tight little fists.

"Yowzer!" yelled Snarf, jumping up and down, hugging Sink and then War. "I love this friggin' game!"

Marcus was read his rights as the Jack Russell growled and strained at his leash. A conversational roar covered the green as the gallery and hotel onlookers tried to absorb what was happening. Marcus glared at Pumpkin.

"Double crossing son-of-a-bitch!" he shouted from his prone position as the handcuffs tightened around wrists that were pinned behind his back. Pumpkin simply smiled and spread his arms in a helpless gesture, mouthing, "What's a caddy to do?"

The Golf Channel cameras focused tightly on Marcus' face as he was jerked to his feet while spouting obscenities. The two beefy deputies who dragged him off the green restrained him. The cameras followed the trio as Marcus did the "Perp" walk down a flower-laden path to a waiting police cruiser and a chauffeured ride to the Greenbrier County jail.

Chad Ray concluded his play-by-play of the arrest and then looked at the camera, smiling. He shouted through the continuing tumult, "For those who say golf lacks the excitement of other big league sports—uhhh—I don't think so."

The camera panned back to a smiling Munch Malone, hugging Melinda with one arm and holding his trophy skyward. He was clearly talking to someone above — what was he saying? Hard to tell. The Greenbrier was engulfed in applause, laughter, and a noise index through the roof.

The owners of 'Dead Men's Clubs', however, could hear Munch loud and clear. They smiled appreciatively as Munch made a promise: "Someday, let's hope it's a long time coming, but someday, I want to meet you guys—and play some golf!"

"That's a wrap!" Ryan Andrews said, cueing the commercial.

Fifty Four

The conclusion of events at The Greenbrier forced Munch to forfeit his USGA Senior Men's Open Amateur Championship. USGA rules prohibit use of different clubs during a round of play. Even though Munch was completely innocent of the infraction, the rule was enforced. The USGA certainly sympathized with Munch, but it awarded Nick Carman the Championship and the trophy.

Nick graciously accepted on behalf of Munch Malone, who, Nick insisted, was the man who really deserved to win the prize. The incredible play, and equally sensational events were reviewed time and again by media worldwide. Munch became a storied name in the world of golf, an icon for senior golfers everywhere.

All of Munch Malone's "Dead Men's Clubs" found their way back into his Rodney bag. But they did not stay there for long.

Munch awoke one Saturday morning two months after the tournament and eagerly dressed for a round of golf with Eugene, Dave and John. He trotted off to the kitchen, brewing coffee, downing his first of two cups for the day. He then grabbed the papers from the driveway and ambled off to the hallway bathroom for his morning constitutional and *Island Packet* review.

Morning routine completed and tee time approaching, he quietly stole down the hall from the bathroom to the garage barefoot so as not to disturb Melinda and Amalfi, who were still sleeping. He opened and closed the garage door and reached for his golf shoes on a bench near the SUV.

He sat down on the bench and pulled his shoes on, huffing a bit, face turning red, lacing the FootJoys. Tying the knot in the second shoe, he glanced at his nearby Rodney bag. He did a double take, straightened up, and said, "What the…?"

The Rodney was empty, save for two clubs; his original three wood and seven iron that he had purchased from Wild-O Reconditioned. Attached to the bag was a note:

"*Munch, golf is a game of confidence, as you know, and we 'Dead Men' are totally confident you now have the ability to play the game on your own. The two original clubs you purchased remain in your bag so that you may always enjoy a little 'Contagion' from us. Enjoy your rounds, and be certain to keep these two clubs; you'll need to bring them with you when you eventually become a member of 'Our Club'.*"

The Nineteenth Hole

Marcus Appleton spent two years incarcerated at Club Fed in Ashland, Kentucky. Somehow, miraculously, he seemed to be touched by a Higher Power. He said very little to the authorities about his dealings with Pumpkin Jones, keeping his pledge to minimize damage to the caddy. Upon release, he moved to Jost Van Dyke in the British Virgin Islands. There, he grew a long white ponytail and enjoyed "Painkillers" daily at The Soggy Dollar Bar. He eventually bought a sailboat and hired out as "Wild Man Cruises," sailing the BVI's.

Pumpkin Jones faced misdemeanor charges after The Greenbrier tournament and was given six months of community service, caring for abused animals. He and the Jack Russell he had kicked and cursed during The Greenbrier antics were now inseparable. They lived together and cared for Grandma until she died. Pumpkin bought a home in West Virginia's Canaan Valley, partially paying for it with $100,000 he had somehow accumulated in an offshore account. The Jack Russell, the sole beneficiary of a tidy sum from Grandma, provided the balance of the sales price, with the proviso that he and Pumpkin would equally share the home until one of them passed on.

John Short became CEO of Wild-O Golf when D.E. Wildoe retired. Short immediately expanded the company through most of Europe and Asia. Few dared to refer to him as "Short Sale." That was a shame, for John had come to be rather fond of his nickname. He was recognized as a major force to be reckoned with in the golfing industry, his face gracing the cover of *Fortune* magazine under a headline that read, "Golf, the Short Game." Cheryl Woody, Appleton's former executive assistant, became Vice President of Human Resources at Wild-O Golf.

D.E. Wildoe's award-winning marketing effort following the Senior Championship—"Ragin' Contagion"— was said to be one of the most aggressive and successful since Nike first aired "Just Do It." He met *Golf Channel* broadcaster Cheryl Ann Roane at The Greenbrier Championship and they eventually married. Upon retirement, D.E. slipped quickly away from the grind of business, spending his time in Key West where he and Cheryl Ann bought a home on Sunset Key. He grew a beard and wandered Duval Street, smoking weed and soliciting tourists with a sign that said, "Dirty Jokes, $1."

Rex Reynolds went on to build the largest public opinion research firm in the country, specializing in golf. He remained in Cincinnati, and Rex and his wife delighted in their children and grandchildren for many years. Reynolds became the "go-to-guy" for golf industry research and remained close friends with the Wild-O bunch.

Rooster Rittenhouse and Janie Germaine married soon after the Greenbrier experience. Rooster and Janie established residence in Las Vegas where they founded and grew a thriving business designing and building golf carts for vertically challenged people. Jimmy Frong bankrolled their effort.

Frong himself remained at the Majestic Hotel where he reconciled with Tiffany. They produced three children who eventually became executives at Wild-O Golf.

Eugene Columbus retired to Florida, where he met his alter ego, D.E. Wildoe, in an Ernest Hemingway look-alike contest. Eugene thereafter spent quality time with D.E., partaking of

D.E.'s bottomless stash and writing many of D.E.'s dirty jokes. They remained close friends for the rest of their lives.

Dave Rambo moved to St. Bart's where he found his First Mate, Billy Jean, who had sold her New York City bar in exchange for a place behind the bar at Le Select, home of the world's best cheeseburgers. He then found his calling as captain of the ferryboat transporting vacationers between St. Bart's and St. Martin.

John Henry abandoned medicine, starring in his own show on *The Food Network*. He threw away his scalpel and never looked back. Paula Deen, Bobby Flay and other well-known chefs anxiously awaited invitations to appear on his show.

And Munch Malone? Well, Munch happily used his original "Dead Men's Clubs" for the rest of his life. He never again won a Club Championship and certainly never came close to a Senior Amateur bid. But, he did have enormous confidence in his game and was able to consistently shoot in the nineties, thoroughly enjoying golf, no longer cursing, agonizing or kicking the Rodney, finding a totally new dimension. He was regularly featured in promotional literature for Wild-O Reconditioned Clubs as duffers from all over the world happily bought into "Contagion". His residuals from the advertising in print, radio, television and the Internet made him a wealthy man. To reward Melinda for her many years of patience and tolerance, he purchased her dream vacation home on the Caribbean island of St. John, enjoying regular visits from their children and grandchildren.

At ninety-three years of age, Munch was still playing the game. He ventured forth one late summer afternoon to get in nine holes by himself. He hobbled to the tee and swung the old three wood from an elevated par three on a beautiful fall day and felt a sudden tightness. He fell to the ground as his shot sailed through the air. Prone, he watched his ball dance across the green, pass the cup, back up, and fall in.

"Beautiful," he thought, closing his eyes.

How long he lay there he did not know, but when his eyelids fluttered and he again focused his gaze toward the hole, it was nearing dusk. He thought he saw two figures in the distance, their forms radiating in the late heat of the summer day. They strode toward him, one talking animatedly, the other—what? Was he chewing gum? Blowing a bubble?

The three wood was clutched in Munch's hand. The Rodney bag was in his cart, holding the rest of his clubs and the "Dead Man" seven iron. Munch sensed the approaching pair knew him—and knew his clubs.

"Hello, Munch, great to shake the hand of the winner of the USGA Senior Men's Amateur Championship," the distinguished African American gentleman said, leaning over to help Munch to his feet. Munch lifted the Wild-O as he got up, and the first fellow's companion said, with a brogue, *"Yes, ye need to bring the three wood and that light little seven iron over there in the bag for yet another golfer."*

Munch walked past the cart, lifting the seven iron with the same hand in which he held the three wood. The first gentleman grabbed Munch's bag, turning it upside down, scattering its contents across the fairway. He shouldered the Rodney as though it were a feather.

The trio walked down the fairway as the sun sank into the horizon, seeming to engulf them as they disappeared from sight.

Munch was blinded by a searing white glare. He blinked hard, trying to see what lay beyond. As his vision cleared, he found himself in a long line. His two companions had suddenly disappeared and it slowly dawned on him where he was. He looked up and down a lovely wide, white corridor that burst with color from brilliant flowers of every conceivable hue. Hundreds, if not thousands of people, were milling about, meeting one another, trying to orient themselves as they waited to receive a packet of materials and forms that were to be read and filled out.

He felt a tap on his shoulder.

The dapper, tall, African American said, "Come with me, Munch."

Munch complied, again wondering how the athletic figure knew his name.

He followed along for what seemed to be at least three city blocks, marveling at the incredible architecture he passed. At last, they ventured onto breathtaking grounds surrounding a majestic Country Club.

The two entered the massive structure, walking into a stunning lobby replete with row upon row of trophies and plaques that gave testament to the famous and infamous golfers who had been granted membership to the Club.

Once inside, Congressman Warren Danson led Munch to wide double doors located to the left of a giant bar and the largest High Def television screen Munch had ever seen. It was tuned to the Golf Channel where Chad Ray was commenting on the passing of one of the most unique golfers ever to "win" the USGA Senior Men's Amateur Championship.

The doors opened and Munch found himself standing on a wide balcony, looking out on thousands of golfers who had completed their rounds downstairs. They looked up from white clouds on which they stood — the sky was brilliant behind them. Each of the men and women greeting Munch had a golf club by their side. The thousands waved, and then erupted into thunderous applause. Munch wasn't sure, but he thought he saw, right in the middle of the crowd, a little old lady with a Jack Russell terrier in her arms.

The Powers that Be strode across the marble floor and greeted

Munch, introducing themselves. War Danson followed, identifying himself, his great and good friend Sink Lair, his associate Mr. Snarf Adams, and War's special friend, Sheila, who put a gin and tonic in Munch's hand.

Brawley Rollins moved to the doorway and addressed the crowd.

"To all you golfers out there, 'The Man' has arrived!"

Brawley turned and hoisted Munch's Rodney bag, holding it over his head like a trophy. "This here is 'The Man's' golf bag—it and his fourteen Wild-O Clubs will be on display here in the Clubhouse. At some point in the future, we'll send 'em back down there—they'll need to do their part in continuing to spread 'Ragin' Contagion!' "

The gallery roared its approval.

"Y'all know the story. The Congressman and that old Scot over there"—he pointed to Sink—"came to **The Powers That Be** many years ago with a proposition that would allow, if successful, all of you to again play golf through 'Contagion'—'Channeling' the duffers down there. As you know, it worked like 'Gangbusters', thanks to your fellow golfers Sink Lair and War Danson, with a little help from Mr. Snarf Adams, the Council members here, and, if I may say so, yours truly.

All of you out there are the beneficiaries! You've been on the links since Munch won the Amateur Championship. Here's your chance to thank him!"

A roar of approval filled the heavens.

The End

Afterword

Two years to the day after Munch last swung a "Dead Man's Club", a FedEx package arrived at the New York City penthouse office of Wild-O Golf. An aging and arthritic John Short opened an envelope addressed to him that was attached to the large package. In the envelope were instructions that only he should read the enclosed letter and inspect the contents of the cardboard shipping box.

Short's arthritic hands shook as he adjusted his glasses and tore the envelope open. He felt a strange tingle, run up his arm. His hands filled with energy and seemed once again elastic. He wiggled his fingers and formed a fist with both hands, relaxing them with no pain. Unbelievable. The arthritis seemed to have disappeared.

He glanced at the heading on the page. It instructed, *"For Your Eyes Only."* He read the letter, memories and emotions flooding swiftly through him. Short sighed softly, laid the envelope on his desk, and turned to open the package. He tore the top from the container. At his age it was all he could do to lift the Rodney and its contents. Breathing heavily, he wrestled with the sheer weight of Munch Malone's clubs and golf bag. Finally succeeding in his effort, he set the bag on the lush carpeted floor of his office. With a slight smile, he held back tears and read the letter once more.

"Dear John, thanks for letting Munch Malone use our clubs. We've kept them up here for quite a while, but I think you will agree,

it's time to put them back in play. We would appreciate it if you would inventory these woods and irons of ours in your Reconditioned Clubs Division. One day in the future a Mr. Snarf Adams will request they be sent to a designee to whom we can utilize 'Contagion', just as we did with Munch. Hopefully our clubs will again help a needy duffer provide yet another marketing opportunity for Wild-O Golf—and get one more of our golfers up here back on the course.

"P.S. Please include the Rodney in the inventory. I am certain Mr. Adams' designee will appreciate the fact that, by God, it can take a hit!

"All the best,"

The Honorable Warren Danson, Man O'War
Sink Lair, The Scotsman

Acknowledgements

I want to thank the people who assisted me with review of the detail in this novel. My childhood buddy Jim "Munch" Mahood was the inspiration for the name "Munch." Let me state categorically, however, that the real Munch is a low handicapper who plays the game with tenacity and humor.

My wife, Becky, spent many hours meticulously editing my manuscript and put up with hundreds of hours I spent in my study at my computer writing and researching. My thanks and love to her. Her skills in detail, grammar, consistency of sequence and ability to keep match and stroke play numbers correct were invaluable. She is the light of my life.

Dana Waldo, my great and good friend of many years, was the inspiration for D.E. Wildoe and Wild-O Golf. I call him Mr. Wild-O and he is, as they say in the book, "One helluva' golfer."

Rex Repass, CEO of R.L. Repass and Partners in Cincinnati, Ohio, provided public opinion research expertise and allowed me to name my research guru in the book Rex Reynolds. Rex, a former business partner of mine, is the embodiment of integrity and loyalty, qualities I made sure to instill in the fictional Rex Reynolds.

Harry Peck, my trusted and valued business partner of thirty-two-years, heartfelt friend and confidante, reviewed the novel and gave me select input. Harry's middle name is "Lee", and he is the inspiration for Harry Lee, the "Legendary Marketing

Vice President for the Majestic Hotel." The real "Harry Lee" will always be legendary to me.

Several of my neighbors provided assistance: Dr. Bruce Baumgartner and his wife Cherry gave me encouragement and many hours of manuscript review.

Neighbor Steve Wilson's first hole-in-one occurred on number Four at Harbour Town while he was in the midst of the book. The very day my freind Steve Sherry began reviewing this book; he scored his first hole-in- one at Sea Pines Country Club.

Were the "Steve's" the beneficiaries of " Contagion"?

Golf partner Bruce Haislip gave me assistance with his knowledge of the game and his astute play; he's an excellent golfer and a very funny guy who makes every round of golf memorable.

Thanks also to Barry Fleming, Michael Connally and Rick Barry on Hilton Head Island for their assistance. Barry, owner of *Club Key* and a former PGA tour player, counseled me early on regarding rules governing the USGA Senior Men's Amateur Championship. Any mistakes I have made in that area were entirely mine, not Barry's, or are committed as literary creativity. Obviously, the USGA tournament I have created is completely fictional.

Rick Barry, head teaching professional at the Sea Pines Resort Plantation Club, also was of great assistance to me.

Much of the action in the novel is located on the grounds of The Greenbrier Hotel. The Greenbrier's invaluable assistance came from: Bruce McGinnis, Chief Operating Officer; James (Terry) Miller, Chief Financial Officer and Treasurer; Roger Hunter, Chief Counsel; Robert A. Mickey, Senior Resort Manager; Burton Baine, General Manager of The Golf Club; and Dr. Robert S. Conte; Resident Historian. They were especially kind to review my book regarding detail at one of the truly great hotels of the world.

I realize many descriptions of the hotel, the Bunker and Casino, are inaccurate, but I plead poetic license; all and any misrepresentations are my fault, or I simply needed to invent a few venues for novel flow. I *have* done my very best to convey the world-class service, people and vistas of this historic site.

Liberties taken and mistakes made in Old White course distances, descriptions, etc., are entirely mine for all the aforementioned reasons. The Greenbrier and the Old White Course are to be revered, and I loved placing the fictional USGA Senior Men's Amateur Open there.

About the Author

Charlie Ryan is an entrepreneur who has golfed throughout his business career—entertaining clients for forty years with his high handicap approach to the game. Charlie, his wife Becky and their Maltese Amalfi live on Hilton Head Island, SC.

Charlie founded and sold four marketing firms in West Virginia, Virginia and Washington, D.C. during his thirty-two years practicing public relations and advertising. A graduate of West Virginia University, he was initially a television reporter, anchor, and news director. He has written hundreds of newspaper columns and conducted an equal number of spokesperson workshops across the United States and abroad.

He was the Founding Dean of the University of Charleston in Charleston, West Virginia before moving to Hilton Head Island where he spends his time writing and seeking a lower golfing handicap.

CPSIA information can be obtained at www.ICGtesting.com
Printed in the USA
LVOW062249230113

317022LV00001B/34/P